White Rabbit

Also by Alan Schwartz —
EVENINGS AT THE TANGO PALACE
    XYZ Associates, LLC, 2016
NO COUNTRY FOR OLD MEN
    XYZ Associates, LLC, 2017

White Rabbit

Alan Schwartz

XYZ Associates LLC

WHITE RABBIT
XYZ Associates LLC
Atlanta, Georgia

Printed in the United States of America.

Design: Marian Haley Beil

White Rabbit illustrations based on drawings
by John Tenniel for *Alice in Wonderland*

Revised Second Edition

ISBN-9781098892180

For Joan
for keeps

CAST OF CHARACTERS:

Thad Barnwell – former director of OMEGA

Albert Biggs – employee at the British Embassy in Zimbabwe.

Benson "Brownie" Brown– CIA/London station operative.

Michael (Mike) Buchanan – British, Reuters bureau chief assigned to Zimbabwe.

Nicholas Burns – Director of OMEGA.

Odette des Chavannes – investigative journalist, Nick's former lover.

Arnold Clapworth – the head clerk at LAWS.

Jeremiah Croft – U.S. Secretary of State.

Neliwe Goldstein – Zimbabwean wife of William Goldstein.

William Goldstein – British freelance journalist.

Margaret Groves – secretary to British ambassador in Zimbabwe.

John Hartsdale-Smythe – chief of MI6.

Jeremiah Kananga – Zimbabwe's Minister without Portfolio, and minority leader in Parliament; former Minister of Home Affairs.

Gordon Barret Magombo – Zimbabwe's Ambassador to the U.S.

Gabrielle Martin – UN/NY official, Nick Burns' lover.

Roger Mattingly – U.K. Minister of Foreign Affairs.

Jacqure Monnier – friend of Moran, retired mercenary, a "supplier."

Colonel Jean-Luc Moran – commander of White Rabbit.

Philip Nemberton – CIA station chief in Zimbabwe.

Eric Newman – writer, close friend of Nick Burns

Ralph Perkins – mercenary whose *nom de guerre* is Wesson.

Eliot Randall – OMEGA operative in London

Richard Scalzio – CIA Director of Operations

Frank Smith – mercenary working for Jean-Luc Moran.

(Baronet) Peter Soames – British ambassador to Zimbabwe.

Anthony Trevor-Jones – former prime minister of Zimbabwe during Rhodesian administration.

Matthias Umgawe – President of Zimbabwe.

Joseph Undaka – aide to Jeremiah Kananga.

Van Ness – *nom de guerre* of Oleg Volkov.

Norton Vickers – British charge d'affaires to the U.S.

Oleg Volkov – Russian operative whose *nom de guerre* is Van Ness.

Captain Voortrecker – South African ship's captain, friend of Jean-Luc Moran.

Benjamin Walton – C.I.D. personnel.

Ralph Wesson – *nom de guerre* of Ralph Perkins, mercenary working for Jean-Luc Moran.

Warden Yogun – U.S. Ambassador to Zimbabwe.

Tadzio Zorin – head of LAWS

ACRONYMS AND ORGANIZATIONS

BOSS – South African Bureau of State Security

CIA – Central Intellegence Agency, "the Company."

C.I.D. – Criminal Investigation Department in U.K.

LAWS – London Alliance for World Strategy, a think-tank.

MI5 – British domestic security agency, similar to the FBI.

MI6 – British international security agency, similar to the CIA.

OMEGA – American Oversight Authority for International Clandestine Activities. headquartered in New York.

Reuters – an international news organization.

Special thanks to Marian Haley Beil, whose editorial skill and sensibility made hard work easy.

White Rabbit

PART ONE

1

LONDON
APRIL 1983

BY ELEVEN O'CLOCK in the morning the crowd in front of Buckingham Palace had swelled to nearly three thousand according to the Metropolitan Police estimate. A flawless blue sky, warm sun and the school holiday gorged London with families from all over England and Europe. The casual, expectant crowd, peeling off jackets and orange rinds and candy wrappers, waited for the daily pageant of the Changing of the Guard, cameras ready, small children up on shoulders,

English mothers frowning with annoyance as they were jostled by Asians, Africans and every other imaginable variety of foreigner. Mammoth glass-roofed tour buses lined the outer roadway of the Mall leading to the Victoria Memorial opposite the Palace. The bus drivers, bored and superior, ignored the gapings of their discharged passengers, and lolled, smoked and chatted in the warm April sunshine under the newly-leafed planetrees lining the roadway.

"Fujiyama here?" asked one of the drivers in the group. He was a burly, florid man with a regulation RAF moustache. He looked down the line of parked buses for a glimpse of the Japanese tour operator.

"Oh, you won't be catching him today, Angus," another driver answered. "He's got a load of Nips what needs to take pictures, so he'll drive past the gates at the last minute, blockin' everyone else out while they click away and jabber. Ain't fair like."

"He owes me, Charlie," Angus said, "for the Manchester-Arsenal match, and I can use the fiver."

"Them Arsenal people act like hooligans," Charlie said.

"But they lost anyway," Angus said, rubbing his moustache, "and I'd like me money."

3

"Just make like it's in the bank," Charlie answered with a wink. "Keeps you from spending it too soon."

Angus shrugged and picked at his teeth with the corner of a tour brochure. The sooner he had the five pounds the better. He couldn't trust a man who one-upped the other tours with that cheap trick of the last minute slide past the Palace, but there wasn't much he could do about it now. He'd catch Fujiyama tomorrow. He opened *The Racing News* he had carefully folded into his pocket, and tried for the fourth time that day to decide between Boswell's Cross, favored by the bookmakers, or Royal Jest, whose jockey had said was a sure thing last night in the pub. His fingers tightened on the pencil as he concentrated and the chatter of the other drivers faded from his hearing.

FUJIYAMA WAS SMART. He knew that as long as the police and the other tour drivers continued to "play the game" and "mind the queue" as they said in their silly English, playing with words rather than setting rules, his tour bus would always be packed with Japanese, Chinese, Arabs and Africans who liked to get up front with their cameras. His customers didn't care about "playing the game," only about gawking at closer range than everyone else, and having good pictures to show when they got back home. Then again, the English cold shoulder towards these foreigners made his clients feel better to be together, huddled for protection in his shining silver bus. Soon he'd have a second bus: bought for cash. He didn't like taking loans.

Not bad for a poor student who had started as a translating tour guide ten years ago. Hard work, frugality and clever betting had paid off. Fujiyama was smart.

Always the same trick did it. From the courtyard of Westminster Cathedral, while the other drivers saved fuel by loading their passengers for the short haul to the Mall where they let them walk off into crowd around the Palace gates, Fujiyama took the long way round. He went past Victoria Station, down Buckingham Palace Road to the Chelsea Barracks to give a glimpse of the assembled beaver hats and red tunics falling into step behind the military band as they set out for the Changing, then slid past the Royal Hospital to let his charges gape at the uniformed pensioners. Afterwards he eased up the Kings Road, timing himself to arrive in front of Buckingham Palace just after the change of guard had entered the gates.

Then he rolled past as slowly as he could, while his passengers rushed to the left side of the bus, cameras clicking like woodpeckers. When the guard troop came from the Wellington Barracks, much closer to the Palace, he lingered at the Cathedral after the other tour buses had gone, and managed to arrive for the change at the same time.

He liked the Chelsea route best, because it made him feel more clever. The other drivers didn't like it, with their stupid English principles, but Fujiyama didn't care. He was smart, and besides, unlike them he owned his company. He couldn't afford to "play the game."

Today it was Chelsea, and because the passengers were Japanese, he did the guiding himself, that way he saved the five pounds he would have paid the student who worked for him the money he owed that lummox Angus with his silly moustache.

Fujiyama was smart. Actually, he realized as he eased the huge silver bus into the Victoria Monument roundabout and saw the last ranks of redcoats enter the Palace gates, he was five pounds up.

A tall Caucasian man in a tan suit had slipped him a fiver to sit in the vacant assistant's seat, up front next to Fujiyama. This way, the man said, Fujiyama could answer some of his questions in English as they travelled around . . . he'd had been on this tour once before, but couldn't understand the Japanese guide.

Why not thought Fujiyama — the seat was vacant, and he liked the extra money?

He made a mental note not to bet on football games any more . . . he didn't like to lose to people he knew. Turf accountants were different, and horses paid better.

Fujiyama was thinking about the money, and then realized that the man in the assistant's seat hadn't asked him anything, he just held his red TWA flight bag, stared out the windscreen and kept glancing at a very expensive gold watch.

As Fujiyama was musing about how peculiar some people were, he saw a black Austin taxi coming into the roundabout from the Mall side and heading right towards him. Fujiyama knew the rules — he had the right of way.

What was the fool doing? He muttered under his breath so the guide's microphone he was wearing wouldn't amplify his swearing, and kept moving. The taxi hit the bus just below the driver's seat, metal crunching and glass shattering to the accompaniment of the brass band inside the Palace courtyard.

As he slid from his seat and bounded down the steps to the roadway Fujiyama knew that he was in the right, and that the taxi had to be far worse off than the bus. Horns blared in the traffic behind him, drowning out the brass band. By the time he reached the other side of the bus, a policeman was there, telling both drivers to get their vehicles out of the roundabout, and pointing toward tree-lined Constitution Hill at the left.

"Just ease over there, lads, and I'll join you. Can't obstruct traffic, you know. "

"My bleeding cab won't budge," the irate cockney taxi driver screamed at the cop. "If this 'ere Jap looked where he was going."

"Move it over there," the policeman said less patiently to Fujiyama, "and we'll push him," indicating the red-faced cab driver.

Fujiyama climbed in and dropped into his seat. The bus had stalled. He pressed the ignition switch. Dead. Again . . . nothing. Then he saw the cable hanging down. The harness of wiring that ran under the dashboard had been cleanly severed and hung down almost touching the foot pedals.

He looked across the aisle at the front seat, hoping for some solace, but the man was gone.

The Japanese tourists stayed where they were, unaware, pointing, and chattering, and too busy with their Nikons and Canons. Fujiyama didn't feel so smart.

JEREMIAH KANANGA LEANED his considerable bulk back into the soft leather cushions of the chauffeured Rolls Royce limousine.

Despite his reduced stature in the government, the Zimbabwean embassy was showing him every possible courtesy while he was in London on his state visit. He liked it here, always had, even when he was a young man and had come to study and had dreamed of freeing his homeland from the British. But even then he had liked England . . . the orderliness, the clean streets, the millions of ordinary people going about their business, just working and living their lives without the indifference or despair that plagued his own countrymen.

After the limousine passed through Admiralty Arch, he admired the planetrees alongside the Mall It wasn't so bad being a Minister without Portfolio from Zimbabwe.

Prime Minister Umgawe had effectively stripped Kananga of his power in a cabinet shake up, mostly to shut up critics, but then after that his stupid cousin and his drunken louts killed a white farmer, and *he* had to go. To pacify the faultfinders, Umgawe sent him out into the cold . . . but he'd be back, sooner than that holier-than-thou Umgawe thought.

Meanwhile, he had no ministry to oversee and was just enjoying the role of senior-statesman-paying-calls-on dignitaries, and he was still the minority leader in Parliament — not yet a complete back bencher.

It couldn't hurt for the future he had in mind for himself to be pleasant, to gather information that could help him later, to be seen as still powerful, but ask nothing from his hosts. The old lion wasn't dead yet, just resting and counting his investments . . . waiting. He knew where all the bodies were buried and, politically, that was always useful.

He watched the flags of state flutter on the limo fenders and then droop as the car slowed down in heavy traffic as it approached the roundabout before the Palace. Imagine, Jeremiah Kananga, poor boy from the provinces, freedom fighter, guerrilla chieftain, tribal patriarch, riding down the Mall in a chauffeured Rolls Royce on his way to Buckingham Palace to visit with the Queen!

"Damn," he said, as the car slowed to a crawl and then to a complete standstill. "I can't be late, not for this!" He leaned forward and tapped rapidly on the glass partition. The Zimbabwean driver turned his face towards Kananga, and lifted one hand and his shoulders in a how-could-I-know-and-what can-I-possibly-do-about-it shrug.

Infuriating! Should I get out and walk? After all, it wasn't very far to go. He turned to his aide, Joseph Undaka, who was seated next to him, "We must not keep the Queen waiting — an ordinary minister, perhaps, but not the Queen of England."

"But Excellency," Joseph protested, his head shaking in vehement disapproval, "it is not safe for you to walk through large crowds. People will recognize you . . . and who knows what kind of . . .."

But Kananga was not a man to be told what to do. *Had he waged guerrilla war for so many years so that he should be afraid of walking through the street of one of the sanest countries in the world?* He banged again on the glass partition.

"Stop the car," he said when the chauffeur slid aside the glass divider, "we're going to walk from here."

Without a word of protest, although Kananga was surprised, the driver lowered the side window of the huge car, signaled vigorously with his right hand that he was changing lanes, and then edged the limousine left from the outer lane across three lines of crawling cars towards the sidewalk and halted.

Kananga was out of the car almost instantly, opening the door himself before the chauffeur could reach it. *I am still the man who looks like the chief I should have been, not that spectacle-wearing, mission schoolboy Umgawe who runs the nation now.*

The chauffeur said "Go well, Nkosi," in Zulu to Kananga; and then to the aide, Joseph, who was surely Umgawe's spy, he said in English, "I will wait in the courtyard."

Kananga flashed his teeth in a paternal smile. Joseph merely nodded curtly and followed him.

The traffic crawled on and a few impatient drivers, halted now in the curbside lane because of the flag-carrying limousine, began to toot their horns, hesitatingly at first, being English and deferential to rank's trappings advertised by the large Rolls, and then louder, in a dissonant brassy chorus.

The chauffeur saluted his passengers, then hurried back to the car, and Kananga and Joseph were already thirty yards ahead of the limousine.

"I do not think this is right, Excellency. There were bad signs . . .."

"Rubbish," Kananga cut him off curtly, "then you should have stayed in the car."

"It isn't consistent with my position," protested the aide.

"A foolish consistency is the hobgoblin of little minds,'" the large man said. "That's Emerson, and he was right. Self reliance and all that."

Joseph shook his head uncomprehendingly. "But protocol, sir . . . a minister arriving on foot, it isn't . . .." Horns drowned out his voice.

Joseph was unable to finish his sentence as two men who had been walking towards them, separated as though to allow them pass in between, suddenly grabbed Kananga and his aide and pinned down their arms.

"What is this . . .? HELP!" Joseph shouted.

"One more outburst like that and you're dead," said a gruff British-sounding voice behind them .

Kananga glanced backward to see a tall, white man in a tan suit with a red TWA flight-bag slung over his shoulder behind them. One of his hands was in the bag, and peeping over the top was the short, ugly, perforated barrel of an automatic sten gun.

"Shut up, Joseph, and do as the man says," Kananga ordered.

"Yeh, shut up Joseph," growled the man holding his arm.

"Move it, Big Guy," said the other assailant to Kananga also with a clipped Empire voice, as he steered the big man towards the Mall roadway.

The chauffeur, who had seen his chief and his aide approached and surrounded, leapt from the limousine and ran toward the five men while waving a service revolver.

"Nikosi! Stop . . . Let him go!" he shouted, leveling his weapon.

Then the man with the flight-bag spun around towards the approaching man, and, with no change in his expression, tightened the pressure on his trigger finger.

"Chk-chk-chk-chk-chk-chk-chk"— the gun burped from the flight bag no louder than the revving of a motor scooter, and then the driver pitched forward on his face and rolled and writhed on the ground. His heavy service revolver slid from his hand and clattered across the paving stones towards the tall man, who scooped it up with a quick movement of his free hand, flicked the safety catch back into position and dropped it into the flight bag.

The traffic that had been moving towards the Palace was stopped now by the jam up from the accident and the abandoned Rolls.

The one man twisting with pain on the sidewalk, and five men, four abreast and one behind, crossing in front of the halted cars, were gawked at as though it was a scene from a telly drama.

A black taxi stopped in the outer lane, and swallowed Kananga and Joseph and their escorts. The Africans were shoved to the rear seat, and faced by the two abductors seated on jump seats and pointing snub-nosed weapons.

The taxi swung to the right, pulled a U into the trickle of oncoming traffic easing down from the jam up at the roundabout ahead, and sped off towards Admiralty Arch in the opposite direction, now indistinguishable from any other London taxicab.

The tall man in the tan suit had slipped into the front passenger seat of a grey Opel just behind the taxi, and its driver followed the taxi like a defense player running behind a sprinting quarterback.

ANGUS, BORED WITH *The Racing News*, folded the paper carefully and put it into his pocket. He had decided that he would wait until he collected the fiver from Fujiyama to place another bet.

He needed what was left of his pocket money to avoid going on the cuff at the Green Man tonight. Maybe he'd pick up some change at darts. He was good at that.

Where the hell were the passengers? He had to get on with it, otherwise they'd be late back and there was no overtime paid by his company. He'd have to short one of the sights and that might make a difference in the tips. He walked to the kerbside and looked up the Mall towards the Palace. The faint sounds of the brass band preceding the relieved guards on their way back to the barracks drifted towards him. *What the hell was this traffic tie up?*

"Charlie, what's happening over there?" he shouted over his shoulder to the other driver who was sauntering back from the end of the Mall where he had gone to satisfy his curiosity.

"Your pal Fujiyama's stuck," Charlie said, as he rejoined the knot of drivers near his own bus. "Smash with a taxi. Buggers drive like they own the road!"

Angus turned back to face the Mall, away from the other drivers who were listening to Charlie's elaborate details. He saw the two black men flanked by two whites hopping into an empty taxi. A tall man in the tan suit behind them got into a second car. Nearby, a young man with a bushy head of hair was feverishly taking pictures.

Then the taxi made a quick U turn and as it passed Angus on the opposite curb he saw hand guns aimed at the blacks. *Coppers,* he thought, *they watch too much telly and now they imitate the programs themselves. And the damned cabbies, too. Imagine turns like that on a road like this.* When the Opel did the same thing, and almost crashed into an oncoming car, Angus pulled *The Racing News* from his pocket and with the stub of a pencil wrote down the license plate numbers of both cars. Cops or not, it was the kind of driving that smashed Fujiyama up there, and who knew when Angus would see his five pounds now. He wanted to tell the photographer that he had the plate numbers of both vehicles. *Maybe there'll be a reward.* But bushy-head was off and running after the two cars. *Damn — it'd be a dry sort of night.*

THE TAXI WITH KANANGA, his aide and their captors sped along the Mall towards the Arch, then turned right onto Horse Guards Road, the Opel just behind them. Both cars then merged anonymously with the midday traffic alongside St. James's Park.

Kananga nudged his aide as they passed The Swans. "Aren't they beautiful, Joseph," he said.

"Shut up, Fatty," said one of the kidnappers to him, scowling.

"Not a way to speak to the Chief," Joseph said.

11

"Who asked you?" said the other white man. "You two just do as you're told and nobody'll get hurt."

The taxi continued across Birdcage Walk and crossed into Westminster, the Opel sticking close behind. Past the Abbey and then through the back streets, they headed south,past rows of terrace houses and mews where many an M.P. lived to be close enough to get to Parliament quickly to answer a roll call vote.

Then, like a black beetle scurrying for a hole in the woodwork, the taxi zipped into an alley that opened into a nondescript mews not far from the Tate Gallery, and bustled into a garage the doors of which opened when the driver drew up in front.

A minute later a bright-red Royal Mail van pulled out of an adjacent garage, and stopped once it had cleared the entrance to allow the grey Opel, that had been idling at the alley entrance, to roll into the open garage.

A few minutes later, the tall man, carrying a canvas mail sack, and the Opel driver emerged wearing the uniforms of the mail service. They then closed the doors of the garage, and climbed into the Royal Mail van, which immediately pulled away from the garage and sped down the street.

After working his way into the traffic on Vauxhall Bridge Road, the driver of the mail van kept pace with the flow, turned left after a few minutes into the district called Pimlico, and then right again onto Belgrave Road. Once across Eccleston Bridge, that spans the tracks of Victoria Station, the driver eased the van to the right into Chester Square behind an anonymous block of grey commercial buildings. As he backed the van against a loading bay of one of the buildings between windowless brick walls, two other vehicles slipped into place on either side, a dirty brown delivery van and a gray Ford Escort. Their drivers left the engines running and walked in opposite directions towards the opposite ends of the small street.

Kananga and Joseph were ushered out of the mail van and into the rear doors of the brown van and locked in. The two assailants, now wearing green coveralls, got into the cab of the van, which quickly pulled out of the loading bay.

Seconds later the two men who had earlier donned the mail service uniform, descended from the Royal Mail van wearing heavy sweaters in place of the uniform jackets, got into the gray Ford, and began to follow the brown van.

The two men at the opposite ends of the small street, their jobs done, waved to each other across the distance and walked away in different directions.

As the Ford followed the delivery van out to Belgrave, the driver looked over at the lanky man and asked, "Satisfied, Van Ness?"

The man — no longer in the tan suit — smiled and said nothing. *The operation had gone smoothly*, he thought. No hitches. All as planned, and all within a mile of the snatch site. He was an expert planner and he knew it. He hadn't anticipated Kananga's driver would enter the fray, but he felt no remorse. "*C'est la guerre*," he said to himself with a slight shrug of the shoulders.

His driver allowed two cars to slip between them and the van to diminish the appearance of tandem driving. After they had swung around past Speaker's Corner and Marble Arch onto the Edgeware Road, he let a few more cars get in behind the van. At Hendon, the northbound traffic thinned out and he allowed the distance between them to increase even further, until past Bushey, he could see that the van was a mile ahead.

When he slowed down to pass through Radlett, the van was out of sight, but then, far ahead at the top of a rise, he saw it turn right onto the side road that crossed Colney Heath. Ten minutes later, skirting the monotony of Welwyn Garden City, they turned into a tertiary road heading north. The van was not in sight. Anonymous as the car that followed it through the quiet lanes of Hertfordshire, it had disappeared with its living cargo into the quiet greenery of the mild April countryside.

It had gone well. Well worth a king's ransom.

2

NEW YORK

"HAPPY BIRTHDAY TO YOU. Happy birthday to you. Happy birthday, dear Director . . ." sang the five OMEGA staff members who had just then filed through the office door. The beginning of the end of a week, and the TGIF mood added zest to the singing.

Nick was surprised they knew and, more so, chose to commemorate the event. But then, in an intelligence organization there was little you could keep secret, especially vital statistics.

Milly, his secretary, was the speaker for the delegation; Doris, her assistant, carried the cake with a single candle; Peter, Nick's assistant, carried a tray with coffee; Carlos, the general muscle of the office, carried some wrapped presents; and Elizabeth from Codes brought her broad smile.

"Nicholas Burns," Milly said, "we, your staff, take pleasure in wishing you a very, very happy day with many returns, and want to use this occasion to express our warmest appreciation for you, the best boss ever." Embarrassed by the formality of her speech, she blushed slightly, walked over to where Nick stood and placing her hands on his shoulders, kissed him on the cheek. Doris and Elizabeth did the same.

Peter and Carlos shook hands with Nick — the latter with a bone crushing grip.

For their pleasure, Nick faked a wish before blowing out the candle, but a muddle of thoughts were running through his mind. *What do I really wish for my birthright?* For years he thought he knew. And now he seemed to have it, but there was something missing, a hollow space, a sort of negative area in his middle, a spatial black hole of small size but enormous density that randomly asserted its substantial magnetic field in the midst of what should have been unalloyed pleasure, and sent the molecules flying in unexpected directions.

"There . . . I've wished," he lied behind closed eyes, and then blew out the candle.

"The presents now," Milly ordered, after they had all tasted the chocolate cake she had baked and were sipping the coffee.

From the shape of the first box, he knew it was a pipe, and groaned inwardly. To an untrained eye, a gift pipe was a trap for the unwary, and he dreaded finding some varnished, ornamented contraption that he would have to — out of obligation — smoke around the office. But the Dunhill box underneath the paper assuaged his fear somewhat, and the pipe itself laid the anxiety to rest. It was a tan, sandblasted briar in a classic billiard shape. A surefooted, reliable choice; he would need to make no excuses. He was both pleased and relieved.

A single malt whiskey in a stone jug from an obscure Highland distillery, a record album of Jean-Pierre Rampal playing Bolling's *Suite for Flute and Jazz Piano*, and a large, illustrated *Connoisseurs Guide to Collectibles* were the other presents.

Nick was sure someone had looked at his personnel file for de-tails and clues about what he liked — that, or sought the advice of Gabrielle, his companion, who worked at the U.N..

"I'm really pleased and grateful that you remembered," he said to the five well-wishers, "but you shouldn't have gone to such ex-pense . . .."

"Nonsense," Milly interrupted, and cut through the Gordian knot of disclaimers with her usual sharp stroke.

"And I'm really surprised. Thanks all. You're like a family to me. I mean that."

He was suddenly moved emotionally. They were, in fact, just like a family. Over the years, especially since he had been Director, his life and work had become so inseparable that he could hardly distinguish between them. No way around that, even though to at least one person it was a constant cause of complaint.

WHEN THE "FAMILY" HAD GONE back to work, Nick put his gifts in a Zabar's shopping bag he'd found in the coat closet, and was walking out of his office door when the special telex behind his desk started clicking madly. Mechanically he walked to the clattering printer and watched the coded message appear on the white paper in its peculiarly ugly square type. Nick ripped the sheet off as soon as the machine stopped, and sent for help from Codes.

"Can you help with this, Liz?"

"Anytime, Mr. Burns."

"Will you run this through for me right away, it's a short one."

Seeing the seriousness of his look, she turned and walked swiftly back down the corridor to her office with the paper in hand.

OMEGA automatically received all top priority messages that went to the various government intelligence services that it monitored and kept in line. Burns' job was to prevent as much duplication as he could and, when possible, to head off the counter-productive internecine battles for prestige and control that lamed the warriors before they got to the real enemy, whoever that was.

Within five minutes, the young woman was back. "There," she said, handing him the original and the decoded copy, "I logged it, too. Anything else?" she asked.

"No. Thanks for the quick service," he said, and turned back into his office.

```
KANANGA KIDNAPPED LONDON STOP
TERRORISTS STOP
IMPLICATIONS USA RE LAWS STOP
MEETING SAT NOON #9 APRIL STATE STOP
WILL CONFIRM STOP
AVAIL ESSENT STOP
HAYES
```

"Damn," he said when he finished reading. Always the weekend, and always that "availability essential" tag. On his birthday, no less, and he had promised Gabrielle he would be free. On a stack of bibles, he had said. Well, she never believed him anyway. The more he swore to it, the less she believed. It was already an old joke between them.

ONE WORD IN THE TELEX caused Nick more concern than the rest of the message, and because of it he picked up the telephone receiver from its multi buttoned console box, pressed the button marked "S," and waited for the switchboard to get on the line.

"Get me Randall, London, shielded," he said when the operator finally responded. He had ordered the highest priority scrambled and bug-proof line.

"Eliot, give me the five W's and the how," Nick said when Eliot Randall, OMEGA's London resident operative picked up the priority line.

RANDALL, WHOSE COVER as Assistant Press Attaché at the American Embassy — a "flak" in reporters' jargon — was Nick's own man, recruited by him nine years earlier when Nick, in the early days of his directorship and freshly recycled back to New York and a desk job, felt caged. He had offered to teach a course on "Foreign Correspondents and Government Policy" at the Graduate School of Journalism at Columbia University and Randall was one of his students. The dean, a friend, welcomed the free boost, and Nick, restless after years of less confining assignments around the world, liked to get out of the office twice a week and to face the bright young men and women in his seminar.

Randall was the brightest student in his class, and Nick had decided to recruit him. The same thing that had happened to Nick himself. The irony wasn't lost on him, nor the double irony that he was across the street from where his good friend Eric had taught until Nick involved him in the Chile business. Now Eric was in Paris — which Nick greatly missed, having been pulled away by his promotion to the directorship. And on top of that Eric was living with Odette, the only woman Nick had ever loved and intentionally lost. He had been very lonely until Gabrielle transferred to New York . . ..

18

ONCE ELIOT HAD completed his run-down of the details of the snatch, Nick said, "What bothers me is that the State Department has already breathed on me about the London Alliance for World Strategy contract. How the hell did that happen?"

"Beats me, sir," Randall answered.

Nick sensed some trepidation in the young man's voice.

"But it wasn't five minutes after the news went on the air about the kidnapping that Tadios Zorin called me . . . on an open line! As head of LAWS, I'd say the man is a fool, I tell you . . . to announce in a panic that he has to protect the reputation of LAWS, and that just because it worked out some strategic hypotheses for us he can't have it bruited about that they had a hand in all this. The man was, frankly, hysterical."

"That still doesn't explain how State got onto me so soon," Nick said, annoyed. He glanced at his watch. It was almost noon. Damn. The afternoon would be busy and Gabrielle would be waiting again.

"Five minutes later," Randall continued in a breathless rush, "John Hartsdale-Smythe at MI6 rang me to say that Zorin had called him, too, essentially with the same bit, and that we had to prevent the story from surfacing. What the hell am I going to do, though, if Zorin goes around crying aloud. Someone's going to pick it up for broadcast, and then the proverbial will hit the fan."

Hartsdale-Smythe, the pudgy, sarcastic head of MI6, was a man Nick respected for his professionalism, but didn't particularly like. He had probably spoken to the American Ambassador, and that was all Nick needed . . . everyone in Whitehall running about taking pot shots at the Americans to avoid their own responsibility for protecting visiting dignitaries. The British were notoriously lax about that. What they wouldn't do in public themselves they thought nobody else would do. Myths die hard.

"There's something else I think you should know, Director," Randall said, hesitating for a split second.

"Is this the coup de grâce?" Nick asked.

"In a way, yes," Randall said. "Bill Goldstein, who is a free-lance journalist in Africa, some-time tourist guide, and one of our operatives, happens to be in London now, and he was waiting at Buckingham Palace for Kananga to arrive, when he spotted a top man from the neo-colonialist terrorist group White Rabbit getting off the disabled bus that had caused the traffic jam. Goldstein then followed him down the Mall and saw the snatch."

"That's not news, Eliot," Nick snapped. "You already knew that. You told me they left a calling card."

"Right," Randall said, "but Goldstein met the guy in Zimbabwe a few months back, and found out that he — his *nom de guerre* is Van Ness — is one of ours. And they are underwriting White Rabbit!"

"You're telling me that we are backing this terrorist group? Evidence?" Nick asked.

"Nothing but the man's say so. Goldstein had filed a report, but I decided it was rumor mongering and not valid. Philip Nemberton, CIA head of station in Zimbabwe, said it was ridiculous, so I let the whole thing go. I hope I didn't goof, sir."

Nick thought for a moment. "No, Eliot," he said finally, "you were probably right."

Randall, with evident relief, said: "Goldstein is too impetuous anyway. A while ago he burst in here, against all procedure, to insist on an 'I told you so' routine."

"Well, you are a press attaché, Eliot. There's nothing wrong with a journalist coming to see you openly."

"He's a hot head," Randall said, "and I tend to worry about guys like that."

"So what did you tell him today?"

"To get lost in the woodwork, but where we can find him. He'll register at the Russell Square Hotel and hang around for a few days before returning to Africa. He has a number of stories to file for African papers that should keep him off the streets."

"Good," Nick said, and to reassure his protégé he added: "You've done right, Eliot, and I trust your judgment, so just keep a close eye on this and stay in touch if anything breaks. You have my home phone?"

MUCH LATER THAT AFTERNOON Nick walked out of his office door, his gifts dangling from his fingertips in the shopping bag.

A furious study of files and tapes and a flurry of phone calls had kept him at his desk . . . even for a gulped lunch. Now he was hurrying before the telephone or telex could catch him again. The elevator at the back of the Washington Square townhouse took him down to the garage level where his driver was waiting. He said good-night to the security man as he passed the shopping bag through the X-ray machine.

His driver, Carlos, drove a black sedan out of the garage as soon as the guard opened the electrically activated doors, and eased down Washington Mews onto University Place, then worked his way westward to Sixth Avenue and into the late rush hour traffic for the trip uptown.

Nick sat in front, mentally running through the tapes of all he had just heard, and replied to the driver's attempts to make desultory conversation with mono syllables.

Just what I needed to queer the week-end, he thought. He had survived blown covers, plans that backfired, one defector and three Secretaries of State. But he couldn't tolerate a failure that involved OMEGA wholesale, because he was too close to it.

Like his predecessor and mentor, Thad Barnwell, Nick had become OMEGA. He had written, edited, and published the book. "He who touches me touches a man," and if OMEGA fails, so does Nick Burns. He couldn't stand that.

"Curiouser and curiouser," he mumbled, remembering his former chief's favorite saying — "It fits here, but where the hell is Wonderland?"

"What did you say?" Carlos asked, glancing over at his boss.

"Nothing," Nick answered, "just thinking aloud."

The big man shrugged, and later, as Nick exited the car across the street from his apartment house on Central Park West, Carlos said, "Happy birthday, Chief, once again."

Nick thanked the driver with a hearty clap on the shoulder, then walked across the street and into his building.

GABRIELLE HAD ALREADY let herself into his apartment, and he could hear the clinking of silverware and glasses. She was setting the dinner table, humming tunelessly an old French popular melody that inevitably surfaced as she worked around food.

"Oh! Oh! Cheri," she said, startled as he walked into the dining room. "I didn't hear you come in."

She put down the china-ladened tray and stepped closer to him, and put her arms around his neck. He could smell her perfume, her favorite, L'Heure Bleue. He kept her well supplied from the duty-free shops in the international airports he passed through around the world. Whenever she complained because he had to go abroad yet again, he told her he had to get her perfume. It also reminded him of Paris, and a time of innocence that had passed almost before he knew it was there.

"You are late," she said, hugging him. "What's her name?" She laughed, stepped back a pace and mocked a stern jealousy.

"Oh, there were three others," Nick retorted, "and two men just to round it out. My office staff made me a surprise party, and I couldn't escape on time." It was only half a lie, and white at that, so it didn't bother him. He tried to keep things straight with Gabrielle, as much as security made possible. Life was less complicated that way, and what he wanted with her, above all, was simple refuge.

"You went shopping?" she asked, noticing for the first time the shopping bag that still dangled from his fingers. "But I brought everything we need except wine!" she said.

"These are my presents, from my staff."

"Very likely," she teased. "You mean your alibis. You bought them yourself. But let's see anyway."

Looking at the pipe, she said, "Another one?" About the whiskey, "Cough medicine?" The record, "I love this music!" And the large book — she took it in her hands, and walked several paces away, turned her back to him and began leafing through it as if looking for something particular in its pages.

He was amused by Gabrielle. She had always accepted him as he was, even though she occasionally teased him about his love of collecting things or complained about the trips made too often with no advance notice. "Am I part of your collections, too?" she would ask, "and do you expect to find me on the shelf when you return?" And he would answer that she was the prize in his collection.

She was by no definition beautiful, but rather what people referred to as handsome. Short, dark blond hair, simply combed and parted so that the larger part fell forwards towards her forehead and overhung one side of her face. Her eyes were pale green, her features regular, and she had a full, womanly body with pronounced breasts and hips. What Nick liked so much in Gabrielle was her amiability. She was a friend as well as a lover, and never crowded him.

"*Alors*, you are hungry?" she asked, "because we should start to make dinner now or it will be midnight before we eat."

"I like midnight."

"I have other plans for then," she said, taking his hand. "Come. You help me in the kitchen . . . you drink your cough remedy and give me a glass of wine and we talk in zere."

In the kitchen she set him to peeling some small onions, chopping parsley and fresh thyme and pulling apart some lettuce, while she floured and braised chicken pieces. Baby carrots were set to steam and some zucchini sautéed while the chicken cooked.

He sensed that Gabrielle was a bit distracted, and noticed several times as they were chopping and chatting that she became lost in her own thoughts and seemed only vaguely there. But she could have moods, he knew, and tended to be sentimental about dates of remembrance, which he wasn't, so he didn't comment and pretended he noticed nothing.

"It has been quiet in your work lately?" she half-asked, half-stated when they were eating the salad — after the main course, she always insisted that eating salad first was an American barbarism she wouldn't tolerate, and the years Nick had spent in France accustomed him to such niceties.

"More routine than not," he said, pouring them both more of the dry red wine he had opened for the cooking and which they now continued to drink, "Do you like the wine?"

23

"Very nice. What is it?" She turned the bottle so she could read the label.

"Côte-du-Rhône . . . from California?"

"From the West *Cote*," he quipped, drawing the short laughter he expected. "The fellow at the wine shop recommended it and it's quite nice," he continued. "I think I'll order a case."

"Mmmn," she muttered, half-listening, and began to clear the table. "Stay where you are," she ordered.

He heard the electric beater buzzing in the kitchen, and a few minutes later Gabrielle emerged with his favorite dessert, a sinfully rich black chocolate cake, fudge moist, covered with the fresh cream she had just whipped. It was topped with a single candle, and he feigned astonishment.

"You just made that?"

"No, you silly man, only the cream. The tart I baked last night at home."

"More?" she asked when he had finished.

He hesitated, and she took the pause for uncertainty and loaded his plate with a second slice. "You just enjoy it, because it is your celebration, while I go and make *ze* coffee."

He heard the grinder going, the water poured into the espresso pot, and then Gabrielle said, "Please go into the sitting room; I'll bring the coffee."

A MOMENT LATER Gabrielle joined him on the couch with the pot and cups on a brass tray that also held a small, wrapped box.

"This is your birthday present. May whatever you wish for the coming year be true."

"Has your wish come true?" Nick asked. "What's the track record of birthday wishes among us?"

"We're still together," she said, "and I managed to get transferred to New York when you were sent back, so that's not bad. Other things, no, but I shouldn't be greedy . . .."

"What other things?" he asked, his fingers absently plucking at the red ribbon. "Why are you being so mysterious, talking in riddles?"

24

"Open your present. "

Under the glossy paper, a polished wooden case, and inside on wine-red velvet lay a gold medallion. Nick picked it up and examined it. "Ferdinand I," he read under the engraved head, and turning it over, "*Fiat Justitia, Pereat Mundus.*"

"This is beautiful," he said, thanking Gabrielle and drawing her to him with his free hand. "What is it?"

"A coin of the realm of Emperor Ferdinand of the Holy Roman Empire who ruled from 1556 to 1564. I just checked it in that reference book you got from your staff. It's there. Very rare, like you, Nick." She kissed his cheek.

He struggled with his rusty Latin. "Help me," he pleaded.

"Justice must be done, though the world perish,'" she read with certainty.

"I'm impressed."

"By the gift or the translation?"

"Both. "

"I cheated on the translation. I looked it up."

"Still! And the coin is beautiful."

"I thought it applied very well."

"An emperor?"

"No, the motto."

"Is that how you see me?"

Did he impress her as an unrelenting idealist who would rather see things destroyed than compromise his principles? After all these years more or less together? He had made all the accommodations he could to Gabrielle, except for living with her. Nick had always felt that they were better off each in his or her own apartment, even though they might spend four nights a week together, sometimes the whole seven. But he had become accustomed to being alone, to placing things where he wanted them, to making the minutest choices of decor, or of objects on view just as he liked them. And so had she. But the caring, the love . . . he hesitated at the thought because it felt like a sentimental trap, its jaws lubricated by the wine and meal and mellowness in the aftermath. Yet he did "love" her. And possession? No more of that. He stuck to objects of art, paintings, books, pipes . . . his sudden ending couldn't hurt them.

"I see you as a man with a passion," she answered, bringing him back into the room as his mind drifted away, "and the passion is for your work."

"You don't think I love you?"

"I know you do, *mon cher*, but it is in the way of caring, of comfortableness — there is such a word in English? — it is a luxury limbo."

"How could it be different?" he asked.

"What will you get me for my birthday?" she asked. "Or will you forget?"

"Why are you trying to start a fight with me?" Nick asked. "How could I possibly forget your birthday? . . . We met. . . ."

"I don't know, Nicholas, I don't know. I feel very tense and I'm sorry. I don't want to spoil our celebration."

"What is it that is bothering you?" he asked, embracing her where they sat and holding her tightly to him. He could smell the cleanness of her hair, the perfume of her skin, her soft round body pressed to him.

Gabrielle shrugged her shoulders without answering and buried her face in his neck, kissing him gently. "I'm sorry," she murmured, "please forget it."

HOW COULD HE FORGET her birthday?

Over ten years ago at a party for the Press Corps, Nick was using the cover of press attaché — and actually doing the job very well, he had been told — and presiding over the embassy's annual lubrication and servicing of the Fourth Estate, a traditional PR event. Very posh. Evening clothes. Of course, he knew Odette would be there, and he both wanted to see her and dreaded it.

He made conversation, chatted with people, especially the ones he hadn't seen for a while, a few of whom were editorial writers who had been particularly unpleasant towards American involvement in Asia in their columns. Nick didn't like it either, but he had a job to

26

do. The writers with the sharpest tongues were the most pleasant this evening, and he was bored already.

Then he saw Odette. He even knew her from the back. She was talking to another man and woman he didn't know when Nick slipped in next to her. Apprehension tempered delight. Her expression was warm and welcoming. The chance meeting they had both dreaded for so long had happened and they survived it. A kiss on the cheek, a squeeze of the arm, the fear was past.

"Let me introduce you to your host," Odette said to her companions.

"The Ambassador is over there," Nick said.

Laughing . . . Odette's ringing laugh gave him pain, got in under the scar tissue of years and salted memory . . . she said: "He is not bright enough to host this ritual. I know it is your doing."

"Don't print that," Nick warned, and the other two smiled.

"Antoine Borgeret of MATCH, and Gabrielle Martin who is with UNESCO, Nicholas Burns, *un vieux amour*," she said, and the double-entendré stung.

They continued with polite conversation, uncompromising pleasantries, a few questions about his print collecting, then Odette, taking Antoine's arm, said: "We have some business to discuss, so will you please excuse us, and you, *mon ami* Nick," she pronounced his name 'Neek,' "can buy Gabrielle a drink; it's her birthday." She edged away with the other journalist and was gone from his life again. Over and out.

"She is not too subtle, our mutual friend, eh?" Gabrielle said, smiling at him.

HE LOOKED AT GABRIELLE closely for the first time. Not his type, really. Good looking enough, fleshier than he liked, but she looked warm and friendly. There was no flamboyance.

During the recommended drink she told him about her work at UNESCO . . . translations.

"Comfortable but dull," she said, "like me . . . .." Soft were her words, as she looked vulnerable behind the eyes.

A leading statement that he was meant to deny, and did, because he found her very nice indeed. He knew that he had to circulate among the guests, a ready escape. This was business after all. A whim filtered through: "Is this really your birthday?" he asked.

She said yes, and only her mother and brother had remembered, but it was all right.

"Will you let me take you to dinner after this?" he asked. "We can make it a birthday party for two . . . mine was a few weeks ago, and no one remembered it either," he lied.

Agreement reached, he left her and made the rounds, smiling and nodding at the guests until the ranks began to thin.

GABRIELLE HAD KNOWN Odette at school. "And I know about the two of you . . . so no lies to save my feelings," she said. The wounded-doe look in her eyes saddened him.

"You've been hurt too?" he asked, wondering what it was about Gabrielle that made him feel so safe in asking personal questions when he knew her so short a time. He had decided not to analyze too much; it would get in the way.

She smiled sadly. Shrugged. "And now," she said as they finished their cognac, "you will ask me to see your prints?"

He laughed. "You are very cynical for one so young."

"Older today," she reminded him, "and if you don't invite me to see your prints, I'll ask you to look at my African masks!"

He had shown her the prints, and made some more coffee, and hesitatingly kissed her as she was looking at a prized Durer. Her response was immediate and unhesitating. She was warm and delicious in bed, and very responsive, coaxing him to find pleasure beyond the usual satisfying of lust. And in her quiet softness he felt safe and comfortable, but most of all, not bored and wanting to run when it was over . . . as he had been with almost every woman since Odette.

The night turned into a week-end of lovemaking and shopping and dining out and more lovemaking.

Ten years had passed since they had been introduced by Odette at a Press Corps party, and he and Gabrielle had settled into that loving comfort with no questions asked and no poison of possession. Usually she didn't ask about the necessity of his frequent trips, had transferred to New York when he was moved from the field into the directorship, and though she probably knew better, never mentioned that she knew that his real work was not what it said on his business card. For her, he was simply 'the Director of the Center for International Exchange of Scholars,' and that was that. It was good, he thought, and there were no hostages to fortune. He couldn't have them.

"FOR YOUR BIRTHDAY," Nick said, "the surprise is so secret that I can't remember it, even if I wanted to tell you . . . and don't. What do you want?"

"You silly man," she said. "Don't ask or I'll tell you."

Self-interest made him obedient, and saying no more, he put his arms around her and kissed her, long and lovingly.

On the way to the bedroom, he placed the new record on the turntable and set the machine for repeated plays.

After their love-making, Gabrielle lay with her eyes open, staring at the play of reflected light from the passing traffic below. Central Park West was still noisy because it was Friday night and the revellers from all over the city were attracted to the West Side.

Gabrielle's place on East End Avenue, across town, was quieter and frankly she didn't know why Nick liked it over here so much. For a man of his natural elegance and taste, it couldn't have been the ideal place, but he actually enjoyed its raffishness. He said that it reminded him of Paris and, in a way, it was similar. At least some of the apartment houses had a European quality, but she found the hurly-burly of the streets too distracting. Her quarter of Paris was a more staid place, more uniform, freer of the endless tourists. Most of the people she knew here in New York from her work at the U.N. lived on the East Side, too — it was easier to get to work.

Oh, what was the difference where one lived? She was just piddling about over this, which she knew was a mask for something else. Under his veneer of complaisance and orderliness she felt that

Nick was unpredictable. He lived the life of the haute bourgeoisie, the upper-echelon civil servant, and without anyone to support but himself he always had plenty of money to spend. She thought that sometimes he must give money to his sister, because he seemed to like her very much . . . too much for Gabrielle's pleasure . . . and Nick had once dropped a hint that he was paying the college tuition for her older child, the girl, because his sister, since her divorce, was not having an easy time of it financially.

Oh well, it didn't affect Gabrielle, at least not financially.

She heard loud voices in the street, an argument, and the sound of horns. The claxon of the American cars was so loud, so bellowing, and here in New York City they blew horns all the time, for hardly any reason and without any consideration of a person's right to some sleep.

SHE LOOKED OVER at Nick, who lay face down, breathing deeply, undisturbed by the sounds in the street. Funny, he told her that when he was alone or travelling he slept lightly, unevenly, but whenever she was with him, cannons going off would hardly make him stir. Maybe he felt more comfortable with her in the house. She certainly did with him around.

Many nights when they didn't make love, both tired after long days, or after Nick had to suddenly fly off to Washington or somewhere else, he would come over to her place, or she would be here, and they just sat, and read, or talked. Nick would fiddle about with some new drawing he had bought, occasionally framing it himself, or would look through a book on one of the things he enjoyed collecting — he even had books on those silly pipes.

They both felt more comfortable together than apart.

Yet underneath all of the owning of things, the pride of possession, the obvious enjoyment of sharing domestic time, she felt that Nick could walk away from it all on a moment's notice and never look back. At his core there was something indifferent to it all, or at least a part of him that only regarded all of this as temporary. If his superiors said go to New Zealand and stay in a cave for five years and live on berries, she felt that he would do it. And worse, something in him almost relished the idea. International Exchange of Scholars indeed! She had looked in their registry and had seen his name listed as director all right, and there was little question that he went to an office every day, but she was certain that it was only a ruse.

She was certain that he worked in some secret capacity for the American government, she had seen an identification card with his picture: Office for Management and Evaluation of Government Agencies. And what did they do? Send scholars abroad? Academics with guns? Nick had no weapons in the house, she knew that. He didn't like them, he had told her.

There were mysteries, but she couldn't solve them, wasn't meant to. She knew she was a woman of limited capacities, and what's more, she didn't care. She made no pretense to understanding world affairs, and sometimes couldn't understand what Nick enjoyed in all those ponderous journals he subscribed to, those political science and economic and foreign policy quarterlies that lined the shelves of his library-study. To her, they were incomprehensible — especially the French and German ones. She understood all the words, of course; that was her job as a translator. But the sentences didn't make sense, or if they made sense, she didn't see why the same thing couldn't have been said more simply.

Much ado about nothing, she thought.

She liked that English phrase. But she was French, after all, had gone to the Lycee and the University for language study, and she had a built-in respect for the intellect. Would she have cared much if Nick read those silly things or piddled with his collections if she knew he was always there? She thought not. If they had been married, she could also know what it was he really did for the government. Would that have made a difference, to know? Hadn't they made an agreement when she wanted to follow him back to New York that there wouldn't be a marriage, that there would be no questions, just a good feeling between them, time spent together and no regrets? She knew about his first marriage, and the death of his wife and the business with Odette afterward. Nick said that he didn't want that

31

kind of pain again, and she respected that — she had at the time, and she still did. But she felt more and more as if she was living in limbo.

She had been hurt before she met him, and this loose relationship with no contracts and the room they gave each other had made her comfortable. Even after she had been seeing Nick for a while in France there had been an occasional date with someone else, a week-end in the country with a former lover, who like most of them had married someone else and she was sure that Nick hadn't been one-hundred percent faithful either. But it didn't matter then. It was what they both had wanted, they told themselves. Although they never discussed the others, both knew.

But since coming here, it had been different. She found most other people boring: they didn't have the right keys, and she tired of their company, only wishing to spend time with Nick. She thought it was the same for him. As if they were married, in fact, the separate households notwithstanding. But what was it Freud had said? She had read it in a newspaper: "Biology is destiny." It was true, even though the writer who quoted it was screaming shrilly about the great psychologist's sexism. How hysterical these American feminists were sometimes.

THERE WAS another commotion in the street.

Gabrielle slid out of the bed quietly and went into the sitting room to peek out of the blinds. Someone on the street below was arguing with a cab driver in a very loud voice. A police cruiser had pulled up with its lights flashing, and she saw the two policemen, one was talking to the cabbie, and the other, trying to calm an irate man. Nearby a lady in a fur coat stood in the headlights waving her hands about.

The park lay dead, dark and silent beyond them. She watched the lights for a few minutes across the park on Fifth Avenue, and then turned back into the room, almost knocking over a large potted plant. *Merde*, she hated its ugly leaves. Ugh, she wished she could make him throw away all of them. The room needed flowers. She brushed away a bit of loose soil that had spilled.

The gold coin she had given him was still on the coffee table in its plush case. She picked it up, and in the dim reflected light thought of the motto again — "Justice must be done, though the world perish." How apt it was, and Nicholas hadn't missed the irony either.

Well, her world was perishing. She wasn't that much younger than he, and she wanted . . . she knew that she had to admit it to herself or she would get no peace at all this night . . . she wanted to be married, she wanted the child that she hadn't told him was inside her. And she also knew that it wouldn't happen, that she'd get rid of it as she had done a few years ago, also without telling him. But this time? She didn't know.

Gabrielle, she said to herself, *stop this. You're acting like a baby yourself.* She would have the child, she'd keep it . . . and if Nick ran as a result, she'd hate that, and him, but she'd live. Maybe she'd take it back to France and go back to . . . to live with her mother? A pleasant change, an old fantasy she had run through many times. Was that what she wanted, really? She knew it wasn't; she knew that she would call her doctor on Monday, and that would be that. At least she had this week-end with Nick, and maybe, just maybe, she could introduce the question. Maybe his feelings had changed; birthdays did mellow you a bit. That, Gabrielle was sure, was a fact. If not for her own birthday, the day they met . . . well, that was all the past, and unlike Proust, she found it boring. What was now, was. Nothing else. Maybe the future would work out after all, one way or the other.

"Gabrielle, where are you?" she heard Nick's sleepy voice murmur from the bedroom down the corridor.

He slept like the dead as long as she was in the room, but if she got out of bed he was up in a few minutes. She had some use, after all, if only as an anodyne.

She answered him, and made sure that her eyes were dry before she slipped back into the warm bed and felt his arm encircle her waist.

3

NEW YORK

A BELL STARTED TO RING. It must be the fire drill Nick had read about. They were going to do that today.

It kept ringing.

Then, with a groan he reached out a hand from under the covers and answered the phone next to their bed.

"Yes," he said, and then noticed that Gabrielle was wide awake. Next to him. "Why didn't you get it?" he asked.

"It's got to be bad news this early," she said. "I was afraid."

The echo on the line told him it was a transatlantic call. "Hold on, please," he said to Randall in London, when he recognized the voice.

He padded out of the bedroom, wrapping his robe around his bare body as he walked. In the study, he picked up the extension and then called into the bedroom for Gabrielle to hang up.

"Where are you?" he asked Randall.

"The office."

"Hold on. I want to put this on S and S, but I haven't used it here before. Installed last week. New equipment." He needed to talk before listening to get his brain working.

Only half of him was awake as he stared sleepily at the scramble and shield console.

"If we disconnect, I'll call you back," he said, and then pressed the buttons in his desk drawer in the combination that Technical Services had said was maximum security for this type of installation. It worked, or at least the pilot light was indicating that, and Randall was still there, somewhere in the grey London morning.

"What is it?"

"Sorry to get you up so early," Randall apologized, "but you wanted to be kept informed, and we just got some news."

"They found Kananga?"

"No. They found Bill Goldstein, the 'travel guide' I told you about, who made the fuss up here yesterday. He's been killed!"

A wave of nausea swept through Nick.

"How?"

"It was a very professional job. Twenty-two. Must have been silenced. In his hotel room. No struggle. Possibly he knew the hit man. Clean job. One in the heart, coup de grâce. That's it."

In his mind, Nick heard the pfft-pfft sound of a silenced twenty-two caliber pistol, the professional assassin's favorite. The high velocity round was devastating at close range and hardly made more noise than pulling a cork out of a bottle.

"You have any idea why?"

"Because the asshole disobeyed orders, that's why." Randall was clearly upset, agitated.

Nick waited in silence for the man to go on.

"I told him," Randall said, "to get lost and write his stories, but he decided to play James Bond and went to LAWS to pressure Zorin about the de-stab scenario."

"How do you know that?"

"Zorin tried to reach me here last night after I had left; called three times. Switchboard found me. I called him back a few minutes ago and was on the phone listening to him bitch about being harassed by our people when the call came in on the other line from Whitehall."

"Does Zorin know?"

"Not yet . . . unless he is wired to the police or White Rabbit."

"And you think there's a connection?"

"With Zorin . . . no, he's just protecting his business. But between the kidnap and the murder there's got to be. Late yesterday the papers and TV here were told that White Rabbit made the snatch. And a White Rabbit marker was left near Goldstein's body. Voila! They're cool, I tell you, audacious."

"Sounds like you admire the bastards!" Nick said.

"They are *very* professional."

"Bastards anyway," Nick said.

After speaking with Randall yesterday, he had skimmed reports written over the past few months on what the recently-formed terrorist group was doing in Zimbabwe, and he didn't like the patterns. Neo-colonialist thugs who turn to terror when the tides of change surround their lily-white paradise.

"It's MI6's baby, Eliot. Stay as clear as you can."

"But Hartsdale-Smythe thinks it's our responsibility."

"Why?"

"As I mentioned yesterday, Goldstein told me that White Rabbit is a Company outfit — and he's not alone with that opinion. Apparently a lot of people out there in the field have that impression, too."

"You checked London station?"

"Yup! Benson "Brownie" Brown says it's not theirs."

"Did you believe him?" Nick asked.

"He usually levels with me because we rub elbows too much. Our wives are friends and the kids are in the same school, and all that. He's a good guy."

"And he emphatically denies?" Nick pushed, probing for a weak spot in the summing up. But Randall was certain.

"Now, it could be that it's an op beyond him and, in fact, he's lacking information, but I gave him a chance to double-check and he got back to me with a second 'no.' If they're in it, why should he lie?"

"I don't know," said Nick. "If it's Company and some fancy footwork has danced the funds in from elsewhere, I should have known about it, yet I don't recall seeing anything come through New York at all. I'll have to go downtown and check it later. So who is this White Rabbit group supposed to be?"

"They act like the usual collection of pro-apartheid trouble-makers, but they're very well trained and disciplined. Only been operating three months or so, and no casualties at all in a few skirmishes with Special Forces and RA patrols, except for the patrols. They blew up a government arms depot and wasted some jets, too. Also the usual

— burning villages and driving off cattle, but no civilian deaths . . . yet, except one local headman who went after one of their guys with a *panga,* like a big heavy machete. Goldstein went out to see them and did a story for one of the London papers. He implied that they weren't local crazies, but real mercenaries, professionals."

"Mad Mike Hoare variety?" Nick asked.

"Apparently. And the one Goldstein interviewed was an American, he said. California, I think. Uses the handle Van Ness. That's who Goldstein saw at the snatch site — it's what brought him in here hopping up and down."

"Van Ness in charge?"

"Apparently not. He's number two. White Rabbit is the boss. Supposed to be a very experienced professional. . . the rest is blank."

Nick drew a sharp breath. "Okay, Eliot," he said, "I'll find out what I can and get back to you. Thanks."

"Sir?"

"Yes?"

"I'm not sure I can handle Hartsdale-Smythe, the Ambassador and all the other brass here. Wouldn't you think it wise for you to come over for a day or two?"

"Eliot, if I didn't think you could handle it, I wouldn't have you there in the first place. You'll just have to cope."

Randall acquiesced, but Nick knew that he wasn't too happy. "By the way," he said as an afterthought, "what is the kidnapper's message? What are their demands?"

"None yet," Randall said. "A very carefully worded press release arrived at all the London papers, the BBC and ITV, at the same time in the late afternoon. It just said that they had Kananga and that their demands would be forthcoming."

Nick whistled through his teeth. "They sound as though they really have their act together, don't they?"

"I told you that they're pros. I think we're in for a hard one."

"Comes with the territory," Nick said.

"What?"

"Never mind. I'll get back to you. Leave a forwarding."

NICK PUT THE PHONE DOWN on its cradle and re-set the buttons in the desk drawer, selected a small, well-used briar from the pipe rack on the bookshelf, crumbled a slice of matured Virginia plug in the palm of his hand, and filled the pipe. Then he walked into the kitchen and put some coffee and water into the coffeemaker, and waited.

The ritual first sip taken, he lit his pipe and carried the mug of coffee into the living room. A blood-red band of light stretched across the sky to the east, pushing the black up as though someone were slowly raising a window shade. "Red sky in the morning, sailors take warning," he remembered, and wondered if the old folklore was reliable. Would it rain before evening?

The woody fumes of the pipe and the richness of the fresh-ly-brewed coffee hung in the air. They were an intense pleasure he treasured in the mornings — the first cup, the first pipe, before the world began to intrude.

Poor sod, Goldstein. Playing hardball with the big boys when he wasn't ready, didn't realize he could get hurt. There was something nagging at Nick. Something that didn't fit yet, but he didn't know what it was.

It had vaguely to do with White Rabbit . . . and why they should want to push the button on some schnook of a reporter who, after all, was going to give them the publicity they wanted anyway. Some-thing was not right. Curiouser indeed.

"Are you up for good?" Gabrielle asked, from behind him. Nick hadn't heard her come into the room. "You look like you're getting ready to start the day," she commented, noticing the coffee mug and the smoldering pipe.

"No, just thinking."

"Some international scholar got a footnote wrong?" she asked sarcastically . . . waiting.

She's looking for an argument, he thought; they'd been here before, and he didn't want a repetition, not now. "Something like that," he responded.

"And you have to fly off and correct his bibliography, n'est-ce pas?"

39

"Not for an hour or two."

"You promised!" she said angrily. Don't you deserve it? Don't I? The whole week-end."

"We do," he assured her. "I only have to go to Washington for a couple of hours . . . later. So now do with me what you will," he teased.

And she did.

WHEN THE TELEPHONE RANG at eight o'clock, they were still in bed. Nick was ready for another night's sleep. The universal male fantasy was for a faithful woman with an insatiable appetite for sex, but he had to admit that it knocked him out. *Age catches up to you just when you just begin to realize your power.*

The call was from State confirming today's meeting.

Priority, the Deputy Under Secretary said. They had brought the ambassador home and representatives from all the security services, too. Nick knew he'd better tell Gabrielle he might be back late. *She'll see it . . .,*

She didn't though . . . wouldn't.

"It isn't that I don't understand that your work is important, Nick," she said, sitting up in bed, "and I even know that when you have to go away to correct a 'footnote.'" She stuck to their old joke. "The work must be done. It's just that lately I worry more. I think that someday you'll go off somewhere and I'll never see you again."

Tears were running down her cheeks, and she looked like a distraught child. Helpless, vulnerable and hurt.

Nick wanted to take her in his arms and comfort her, promise that this would be the last time, that he'd find another job, ask her to move in with him; anything that would give her comfort, stop the tears. But he couldn't. He would be nothing if it weren't for his work. Just another guy who lived and accumulated. A bag of bones and a heap of junk. *"Fragments I have shored up against my ruins." Where was that from?*

"I love you, Nick," she said, her eyes still streaming, face moist, "and I'm afraid."

So was he. Afraid that what Gabrielle was asking was impossible and that their relationship would, therefore, be over soon because he couldn't do what she wanted. After Phyllis had died along with their child, he had sworn never again. No hostages to fortune.

Then Odette. And his love for her drove him mad. And she, with her globe-trotting aspirations was even ready to accept the demands of his work; all she wanted was Nick, no strings, just a wedding band.

But he couldn't take the responsibility. He used to imagine himself lying dead in some alley or desert and Odette waiting, tortured by anxiety. He had wanted her more than any other woman, including, he admitted to himself years later, his own dead wife. But he had said no. Had broken it off. He remembered the evening in Paris he had told her . . . and after that, whenever love began to blossom, it was cut off, either by him, or by outside events. That was the way it was meant to be. He had little doubt about it.

So ironic, too, that with Gabrielle he had stuck it out, because in a way she was like Odette. She had wanted strings less than he, always the separate apartments, separate lives, catch as catch can. What the hell had come over her?

"What the hell has come over you?" he asked. He undid his robe, and put the artifacts of his morning ritual on the dresser. He had to get going soon.

"I know what you're thinking," Gabrielle said angrily. "'She's just like all the rest of them, possessive. Like a sommelier she wants to keep me in a dark bin somewhere, under lock and key, for exclusive use.'"

"Bullshit!" he yelled. "I'm no rare vintage and don't want to be. I'm just a guy with a job that I happen to love, and you, Gabrielle, are setting up a phony rivalry between the job and you. I resent that!"

"And I resent never knowing whether you'll keep a date or interrupt a long-anticipated stretch of time together because of some stupid business that someone else can handle. You aren't much of an administrator if you can't delegate responsibility!"

"Why don't you stick to the issue and stop attacking me personally?"

41

"Because it is you, personally, you stupid, redundant man, whom I want. And I don't care if you sweep streets for a living."

"Well, I do. There's no further point in this discussion. I have to get dressed and go."

She dropped back onto the pillow. "Can't it wait?"

"No, and the sooner I take care of what I have to, the sooner I can get back to see you."

"Promises, promises."

"I'll be back for dinner. We'll go to Lutece, how's that?"

He was trying to negotiate, even though he knew it was futile. The issue was far deeper than the minor attention he could offer, but now wasn't the time to settle it. Not that he knew when the time would be — perhaps never. If she couldn't stick to the pact they had made, then they couldn't continue together. He knew that, but couldn't bring himself to say it. Not now.

"Someday you're going to go off on one of your missions and I'll never see you again," she said from the bed.

It was the first time she had used the word "mission." There was a tacit understanding that she accepted the myth of his cover and never pulled it away.

He stopped, one foot inside the bathroom, and half-turned, "I'm only going to Washington for a board meeting. Hardly a dangerous expedition!" He laughed aloud, trying to coax a smile from her.

Gabrielle raised her short round arms from under the covers. "Come here, you stupid man," she said, a smile pushing through the tears.

He was glad the tension had broken and walked towards her.

AND THE COST . . . he was late, and had to rushed on to the 11:00 shuttle to D.C. just as they began to pull the boarding steps away.

4

LONDON

HABIT MEANT COMFORT to Tadzio Zorin — pencils always sharp in the cup on his desk, bills paid before the tenth of the month, lunch in the same pub down the road from his office every day, and on Sunday, the train to his sister's in St. Alban's.

He felt that the life of the mind was more vibrant when there were no impediments in its path. When he was a young professor in Hungary, and afterward in exile at Cambridge, his beloved dead Evsha looked after him. Now the housekeeper left his evening meal warm in the oven. A book was his companion at the dining table in Bayswater.

ZORIN ALWAYS ENJOYED working on Saturday mornings in the LAWS office on Smith Square. If the weather was fine, he would leave the front window open and catch the random strain of music from the orchestra rehearsing at St. John's across the road. The refurbished 18th century church and the scaled-down townhouses reminded him of the University, especially when the trees were greening and the moist smells of spring drifted through.

But the professor had no taste for music this morning. He didn't bother to open the window for the innocuous pleasures of sounds and smells. Ever since yesterday afternoon his worst nightmares seemed to be coming true.

First, that silly African gets himself kidnapped and then that nuisance Goldstein, imagine, his own former student from the University, who shows up out of the blue — or rather the black of Africa — where he is running around playing foreign correspondent instead of turning his fine mind to the scholarly work he trained for, to pester him about the Zimbabwe study and threaten to expose LAWS' connection with the CIA. Preposterous, annoying man, that one.

Not that Tadzio Zorin was worried about compromising any secrets. He knew what the study was. He had tried to measure the effect of various input to the political situation in Zimbabwe and speculate on the effects of these variables upon the stability of the country. Purely a set of "ifs."

But he knew also what the press would make of it. He had sent Goldstein away empty-handed and the fool had the nerve to say that he'd get proper authorization, implying that he was some sort of secret agent. *Oh, why did the academic world breed these boy-men who won't grow up?*

Refusing to be soothed by the sound of the choir rehearsing the Bach Magnificat in D that he would be going to hear at the lunch hour concert next Tuesday, Zorin threw himself into his paperwork with fury — first the bills and then the correspondence.

Brookings Institute wanted his opinion on a study they were undertaking. He answered them with some suggestions. There might be a commission for LAWS in that.

The American Enterprise crowd wanted him to come and talk about the European perception of the effect of the sanctions the president had authorized against the Soviets. He thought that he'd like to go to Washington and renew some contacts anyway, so he told them he would come in June.

But Zorin's mind was elsewhere — it was in the conversation he would be having with that flunky Eliot Randall at the American Embassy.

ZORIN HAD JUST worked out what he was going to say when the phone rang. He'd let it ring a while, but then he remembered that Americans are impatient and hang up quickly, so he picked it up on the fourth ring.

Randall told him that Goldstein had nothing to do with the Embassy and had acted of his own volition.

Randall just wasn't understanding.

"I don't run this institute like a supermarket," Zorin said, "our goods are not wrapped up in plastic for anyone to examine who comes shopping. LAWS is discreet. Our clients know that. I must protect our reputation. And while we value your patronage, I feel that I have to insist that you alone take must responsibility for letting others view any study that you have commissioned. You may show copies to whomever you please, but kindly don't ask me to do so. This isn't the first . . .."

He had the feeling that Randall was not listening, and then he heard voices and another telephone ringing at Randall's end.

"Excuse me," Randall said, "I didn't catch that last bit. I have another call waiting. Can I get back to you, Mr. Zorin?"

"Indeed you can, and must, Mr. Randall," Zorin said, trying to sound authoritative. "I am concerned that LAWS not be in any way identified with this kidnapping . . . only speculation . . . ruin the reputation so carefully built . . . years." Then he heard the silence that meant a hand was covering the mouthpiece at the other end.

"I'll get back to you, Mr. Zorin," a voice at the other end said, and before Zorin could answer, the telephone was dead.

Zorin muttered some choice Hungarian epithets at the useless piece of black plastic and slammed it onto its cradle. There were no more manners left in the world, no foundations left. What could anyone expect?

Methodically, he began to go through the other papers that demanded his attention.

AT MIDDAY ZORIN stopped work. Time for his meal at The Marquis of Granby just the other side of St. John's.

Saturday lunch at the pub was no different in form from the other days of the week except there were more of the local people sipping their late morning pints, and fewer of the office workers and executives from the neighborhood.

On Saturdays Tadzio Zorin relaxed at lunch, allowed himself a second half pint of Old Peculier after the game pie — the "special" of the day — and read the morning's newspapers with his lunch. He had been consistent in this habit for the past twelve years. Actually eleven years and seven month . . . since Evsha died. It made the day special, and as the *Standard*, which he usually read on the way home wasn't published on weekends, Zorin was able to take his dosage of information in a huge, yet leisurely, gulp with lunch.

But relaxation was not on Tadzio Zorin's menu today. *The Times*, *Daily Telegraph* and *The Guardian* were filled with stories about the kidnapping, and featured sidebars on the political history of the troubled African state, speculations on the White Rabbit terrorists, and suggestions about their origin and who was supporting them — which ranged from South Africa to Israel to Cuba and Syria.

Only *The Guardian* had what Zorin was looking for though — there was a hint buried in the penultimate paragraph of its background story that the American and British intelligence agencies had jointly authorized the development of a plan for the destabilization of Zimbabwe that included the abduction of a key official.

When he read this, Zorin coughed some of the brown ale into the newspaper and his necktie, choking on his own fury. The bastards, they would destroy him yet . . . and all because some damned reporter was paying his own bills by crippling the livelihood, the life itself of other people.

Zorin went to the bar for a refill. The crowd had thinned somewhat as the convivial morning drinkers meandered homeward or to football matches.

As Zorin waited for the tapman to come over with his beer he eyed the telly in the corner. At first the details of the report he was seeing seemed like the usual gore: the body covered with a sheet, the genteely shabby hotel room, the reporter in a macintosh standing in the corridor, the front of the hideous Victorian hotel in Russell Square. Murder was relatively rare in England and the media would always make a do of it . . . and the police say that "they have several leads at the moment in the grisly execution of William Goldstein, a twenty-eight year old free-lance reporter who had been recently filing reports for both *The Guardian* and the *Standard* from Zimbabwe. Goldstein, a British subject who grew up in Rhodesia, attended the local grammar school and then Trinity College, Cambridge, was apparently killed by a professional assassin. A source in Scotland Yard had indicated that there may be some connection between this murder and the abduction yesterday of the prominent African diplomat, and that the same terrorists may be responsible."

"Your Old Peculier, sir," the barman said, putting down the glass in front of Zorin.

"You'd better bring me a double whiskey," the elderly émigré said.

"Not your usual," the barman said matter-of-factly.

"It's not my usual Saturday," sighed Zorin as he gulped down the scotch. It didn't help, but it felt good.

Zorin left the ale standing on the bar, put a pound on the counter and left.

The barman, who never expected a tip from the old foreign gentleman except on Boxing Day, pocketed the change, made a mental note of remembering to remind Mr. Zorin that he had a half pint and twenty pence coming to him, and sipped the ale himself.

"THE EDITOR IS NOT in today," said the young man on the phone at *The Guardian* who Zorin spoke to, "but you can reach him on Monday."

"That may be too late," Zorin said.

"Well, perhaps I can help you."

Zorin hesitated, asked the assistant to hold the wire, cupped his hand over the mouthpiece, though there was no one else in the LAWS office, cleared his throat and then spoke in an agitated voice. "The report on the death of that reporter, Goldstein, suggests that there is a link between the unfortunate man and my organization, the London Alliance for World Strategy, and I want to disclaim any association."

"Excuse me, sir, but there must be some confusion. Our paper hasn't reported on that case . . . perhaps you saw the report on the television."

"Ah, yes, of course, Mr. . . .?"

"Hughes."

47

"Mr. Hughes then. But there was a suggestion in your report on the abduction of Dr. Kananga concerning the role of my agency in developing a plan used by the abductors."

"Wait a second," said Hughes, "I want to find the reference you're talking about."

Zorin heard a rattling of paper at the other end of the line.

"It's in the next to the last paragraph on page four."

"Oh, yes, indeed . . . thank you."

There was a silence at the other end which made Zorin uncomfortable. He cleared his throat unnecessarily.

"Tell me . . ., Mr. Zorin, why do you make the connection between the death of this Goldstein and the work of your institution?"

"I don't," Zorin said with annoyance. He was overly warm and his tongue felt slightly fuzzy from the whiskey he had gulped.

"I mean . . . if Goldstein was killed by the same people who abducted Kananga, then there could be. . .," Hughes stopped. "What are you saying? What could the connection be?"

Zorin didn't answer. He didn't know what there could be, but there was surely something.

"What, Mr. Zorin?"

Zorin didn't know what to say.

"There is . . . I can't . . . LAWS is only a 'think tank' not . . . I can't allow . . . I have spent half a lifetime building up this organization from nothing. It . . . .."

"Can I call you back? Mr Zorin? I have an urgent call waiting."

He knew that Hughes was lying, but gave him his telephone number, and said he'd wait for the call.

ZORIN WENT TO THE WINDOW and stared out at St. John's Church across the way. He had wanted of his own life to have the same kind of symmetry that the building exhibited — balance, the golden mean. When he had first seen the small house across the street from the church that was to become LAWS headquarters he knew that he would lease it. There was a sense of just proportion in the house on Smith Square.

Zorin's work imitated that as well. It was balanced, judicious, and took into account all sides of any issue under study.

He tried to make his personal life the same. His marriage had been calm and rational, effective without passion. His life as a widower was equally collected. No extremes. Saturday evenings were usually spent with Mrs. Cribb, a widow who worked for Inland Revenue . . . and that took care of his sex life. More was hardly necessary.

He stared at the dome of St. John's. The musicians and choir were leaving their rehearsal. Young people mostly, calling to each other and joking in the hazy April sunlight. Then it was quiet, as the last of the cars left. A man walked a corgi under Zorin's window. Another man in a macintosh was lighting his pipe on the steps of the church. Why did he need a mac on such a lovely day? Three teenagers in blue jeans and leather jackets and shaved heads marched past with angry steps, clacking boot heels on the pavement.

Zorin was reminded of the Nazis.

THE TELEPHONE rang.

"Mr. Zorin?" the voice of Hughes asked, "Why do you think there is a connection between the work of your agency and the kidnapping of Dr. Kananga, as well as the death of Mr. Goldstein?"

Zorin was perspiring. He used his free hand to unfold the handkerchief that had been neatly triangulated in his jacket breast pocket, wiped his forehead, and then he refolded it.

"Are we being taped?"

"No sir we are not. . . and if there is anything you want to be off the record, just say so, because I am taking notes."

Zorin felt a wave of nausea and tasted game pie and ale gurgling up from his stomach.

"I don't want you to write a story about this!"

"Then why did you call me?"

"To set the record straight."

"But there's nothing to straighten yet."

"To make it clear that any allusions to a plan for kidnapping the African are false — that is, any such plan developed by LAWS."

49

"Well, all I have to go on is your say-so, Mr. Zorin."

Zorin didn't care for this journalist. The man was being disagreeable.

"We are a consulting agency, Mr. Hughes. All we do is try to solve problems that our clients present to us, and write unbiased reports based on the consensus of experts drawn from the academic, private and public sectors."

"What then does the word 'Strategy' mean in your title?" Hughes interrupted.

"Method for approaching a given problem," Zorin shot back.

"Such as how to get rid of a member of the disruptive opposition in Zimbabwe?"

Zorin's head began to pound, a migraine was returning after years of banishment.

"I don't understand, Mr. Hughes, why you are being provocative," Zorin said as calmly as he could, feeling as though an actor were speaking from underneath a mask of pain. His temples throbbed as though the thin skin would burst."

The young man at the other end was nonplussed. "I'm only doing my job, sir!"

"And where have I heard that before?"

"I'm . . .."

"What I mean is that you should put yourself in my place. Can you put yourself in mine?" Zorin interrupted. "I develop a perfectly legitimate consulting organization for geo-political and economic development projects, and I spend almost twenty years doing this for innumerable clients from the English government to Brazilian mining companies, and now a hint of collusion in some terrorist plot made irresponsibly by a newspaper, ruins my business and my reputation? Can you understand that!?" When he raised his voice at the end of speaking his head hurt even more.

"I appreciate your concern, sir," said Mr. Hughes, "but I don't think you know what you're asking of me."

"NOT TO PRINT LIES!" Zorin shouted. Sledgehammers beat in his skull.

"Please . . . I can hear you very well, you do not need to shout," said Hughes. "You are asking of me that I print *your* version of the truth. . .."

"You can attribute it to me . . . I do have a reputation, after all."

"I think we would need objective verification, sir," Hughes said.

The man was sly, certainly, under the blandness.

Zorin could play cat and mouse, too.

"To say that Dr. Theodor Zorin, the Executive Director of LAWS emphatically denies any connection between his organization and the heinous deeds is surely sufficient."

"You are not on trial, sir."

"But you can ruin a man with unsubstantiated allegations!"

"We try to substantiate everything."

"I am giving you fair warning that I'll take this up with my solicitor immediately. There are libel and slander laws in this country, you know."

Hughes laughed slightly.

Zorin didn't like the patronizing tone.

"Mr. . . . Dr. Zorin, I am fully aware of the law, and we always try to act within it. Of course, if you wish to speak to your solicitor, I can't prevent you, but there is another solution."

"What?"

"If you let us see the documents in question and they are as you say innocuous . . .."

"I didn't say they were innocuous," Zorin snapped back.

"I merely said that there were no strategies for abducting Dr. Kananga, and that when Mr. Goldstein came to this office yesterday asking for the same . . .." He stopped abruptly, realizing that he had just torn a hole in his own screen.

Hughes showed no sign of noting the slip. "You realize that the unfortunate Mr. Goldstein was not a member of our staff and was acting on his own?"

"Not on your staff?"

"Strictly speaking, no. He was what's called a 'stringer.' He filed stories with our bureau in Salisbury or supplied information for the

AP bureau chief, and occasionally wrote a feature that we bought directly. He received a small monthly stipend and was paid for each story we accepted. But he also did the same for other papers, the *Standard* for example, and for the wire services. As far as I know, he was acting on his own, hoping to scoop everyone. We can't therefore take responsibility. Besides, his beat was Southern Africa not London. We'd never give him an assignment here, because we're more than adequately covered."

Zorin was crestfallen, and his head beat a tattoo, regular, incessant, savage drumming.

"What do you suggest, Mr. Hughes?"

"If you'll let one of our staff see the documents for the study in question, and he can ascertain that it is as you say . . .we'll be happy to print your side of the story should the necessity arise."

"But that's a breach of confidence. These are not public documents. The people who pay us would never . . .'"

"Then we have nothing to discuss, do we, Mr. Zorin? Thank you for calling . . .."

"Wait!" Zorin shouted. "Let me think."

"Yes, you do that, sir, and meanwhile I'll speak to the editor. We will have someone call you tomorrow or Monday. Can we reach you at home?"

Zorin reluctantly gave Hughes his phone number.

I wouldn't, I couldn't do it. Such a breach would be worse than an erroneous report. No one would trust LAWS anymore.

"I'll sleep on it," he said and rang off.

He found the pills in his desk drawer and quickly swallowed two, washing them down with cold tea left in his cup from the morning. Saturdays he had to wash the cup himself and usually left that for last. He knew that the headache was too far along to be helped by the medication now, but to try was better than to give up.

What to do? What to do?

He tried Randall at the American Embassy. One of those damned recorded messages told him that the offices were closed and that any urgent matters were to be referred to the Consular Section. There a bored-sounding clerk told him that Mr. Randall was not from that section, and that he would make note of the call, although there was no way he could reach Mr. Randall. He should call back on Monday.

Zorin asked then for the Central Intelligence Agency and was told that he'd have to call the Embassy. He tried the Foreign Office. Maybe Hartsdale-Smythe . . ., but there was no answer at all. On the verge of dialing the Metropolitan Police at Scotland Yard, Tadzio Zorin, Ph.D., LL.D. slammed down the telephone and buried his throbbing head in his hands atop the desk. His shoulders heaved as he sobbed.

The ringing of the telephone cut into Zorin's private lamentation. His temples were thumping like a tympani and he felt flushed and hot. He raised his head, ostrich-like from the desk, lifted the receiver and heard Eliot Randall's carefully modulated tone, "I understand you've been trying to reach me."

"Wait a second, Randall, please," said Zorin, and laying the telephone on his desk he went to the window and pushed up the sash. Cool April air with a haze smelling of the smoky London spring pushed in, parting the gauzy curtains like an intruder. Zorin's glance traced the church across the way habitually. And then he knew what they were about. He rushed to the telephone.

"Randall! They're going to kill me, too," he screamed into the mouthpiece, "and it'll be on your head. I need police protection, a bodyguard . . . something, anything . . .."

"Who is going to kill you, Mr. Zorin?" Randall asked.

"The same ones who got Goldstein. They want my report. Everyone wants to see it, and I won't show even the editor at *The Guardian* . . . you'd think he'd believe . . . after all, I'm not exactly a nobody."

"What makes you say that they — whoever 'they' are — want to kill you?"

"The man in the macintosh . . . across the street by St. John's . . . he's watching the office. I know he is. He's been there too long now. And why is he wearing a mac on a day like this?"

"Perhaps he's a tourist who doesn't trust the weather, maybe he's overcautious, or his wife insisted."

"You can be facetious, Randall, but it's me they're after, and I want you to send someone over."

"Who did you speak to at *The Guardian*?"

"A Mr. Hughes, the assistant editor . . . but what does that have to do with it.?"

"Maybe the man is a reporter they sent over."

"He was there before I spoke to Hughes!"

"It could be coincidence."

"It could be," Zorin interrupted, "but it isn't! I'm not going to die because of some cock-up by your people. I should have known something was afoot when you sent that man."

"What man . . . the macintosh? . . . You think he's from the Embassy?"

"No, not him . . . last month . . . wait a minute." Zorin put down the telephone and went to the window.

He didn't part the sheer curtains, but stood to the side watching the entrance of St. John's. The man was there, sitting on the steps, leafing through the pages of a book. Next to him a shoulder bag, the kind photographers use for cameras and equipment, drooped on the stone steps.

Returning to the phone Zorin said, "He's not an American, I can tell by his clothes, but he could be one of those hit men you read about. He's got a bag that looks like a camera bag, but God knows what he could have in there."

Randall laughed.

Again someone is laughing at me. The second time within the hour. For almost sixty years scholars and businessmen, whole government departments had taken me seriously, and now, two upstarts who thought they were somebodies were snickering in their sleeves at an old man with delusions . . . paranoid. His head throbbed like a tom-tom.

"IT ISN'T FUNNY!" Zorin screamed into the phone, and then took a long deep breath as the pain in his head reached down the side of his face and neck into his chest, clawing at him, a ravening beast. His gasp came out as a sob.

"I wasn't laughing at you, Mr. Zorin," Randall explained quickly, sounding alarmed at Zorin's agonized gasp.

Zorin thought he had gotten past the bureaucrat to the man.

"It's just that I don't think that professional hit men sit around with camera bags, gawking at old churches."

"Maybe he's got guns in the bag. Should my life be risked because you don't think that assassins carry camera bags and dress like tourists?"

How dare that young man be so presumptuous and reassuring without any hard evidence?

"I want you to send over people to protect me, Randall. I demand it."

"Mr. Zorin . . . I don't have a police force at my disposal . . .."

"Oh, stop the sham, Randall. I know what you are. I'm sure that one phone call on your part could protect me until this all blows over."

"I can't, Mr. Zorin. You don't seem to understand," Randall pleaded.

"Well, then I'll call the police."

"What will you tell them? That there's a man dressed like a tourist across the way who wants to kill you? They'll think you're just another looney."

Rather that than dead, Zorin thought. And then he realized why Randall didn't want him to call the police. The assassin was from the Americans. What a fool he'd been not to see that before!

"I'm onto you, Randall," he cried, his head splitting and the pain grabbing at his shoulder now. "I know what you're trying to do here. No evidence! I'll show you," he shouted and slammed the receiver down hard.

It wouldn't do, no, not at all. If the Americans were going to be devious, and for all he knew the man across the street was from MI5, with or without American sanction. In fact that was more likely, because an English agent could operate easily while an American would be too obvious . . . and the audacity of that Randall, pretending he didn't know anything and laughing at him as though he were a fool. Well, Tadzio Zorin was nobody's fool and would show them a thing or two. If they were going to treat him as though he were just disposable goods, then to the devil with discretion. Dr. Zorin would have the last laugh over those fools. He wasn't preeminent in his field for nothing. They had approached him, asked him to do the study, and now that the project was proving an embarrassment, they would get rid of it . . . and him. Zorin wondered if he should warn Pomeranz and Rossiter, his academic colleagues who had contributed the economic and political sections of the Zimbabwe paper. Maybe hit men were after them, too? Maybe not. Still. He'd show the bastards what Tadzio Zorin could do.

He stepped to the window and peered through the curtains. The man in the mac was gone and the steps of St. John's Church were empty. Or was he hiding somewhere, behind one of the columns in a doorway perhaps, waiting for his victim to step out of No. 9 Smith Square so he could mow him down in a hail of bullets. Zorin regretted watching all those police dramas on the telly. They gave him these horrible ideas. He thought them silly, but now it was coming true for him.

Hold on to yourself, Zorin, he thought. *Your imagination is running away with you. Steady on, old boy. This is London after all, not Chicago or New York.*

The square and the church steps were empty. Zorin cautiously parted the curtains and raised the sash of the window to peer out. Mild, hazy April rushed into the room again, and he breathed the air of the deserted square with relief. He leaned out to look around, inhaling deeply. The pain in his temples would go soon now, but the sudden dosage of fresh air made him a bit dizzy. Still, it was wise to take precautions.

He began to pull back into the office when he saw the man. Sighting through the oblong telescopic lens of an expensive camera, the man in the mac inched a step or two forward out of Lord North Street towards St. John's. He had been out of Zorin's line of vision, obscured by the corner of the small street which ran into the square on the right of the LAWS office. The man didn't see Zorin — or pretended not to — as though absorbed with his photography. Maybe he was an amateur camera buff after all, and had been waiting to take some pictures until the square was deserted? Zorin rejected the thought as wishful thinking.

The man moved closer — just across the street, and Zorin could see the his clothing even better now. A suit of good, if very baggy, tweed covered by the long tan macintosh, and a checked, cloth cap. Gum soled shoes. A large, furled umbrella dangled from the strap of the camera bag. Zorin knew the look. A Yorkshireman on London holiday. Cautious about the weather . . . but what if it was a clever disguise — a deception for the unwary?

Then Zorin heard the click of the shutter on the still Saturday street, and as the man noticed Zorin looking at him, the camera was lowered.

"Fine day," he said, removing his cap and wiping a pink forehead with a pudgy hand.

Zorin nodded and pulled back quickly, slamming the window down. He watched through the curtains as the man put the camera into the shoulder bag and fished into its depths for something. His gun? Now that he had identified the victim he was going to get the job over with.

Zorin shuddered, and his headache had returned with greater intensity. But what came from the camera bag was a packet of cigarettes. The man put one in his lips and then patted his pockets for a match. He couldn't seem to find any and put the cigarette back into its box.

A ruse, Zorin thought. *Stalling for time. Trying to win my confidence, so that he can get close without my raising an alarm.*

Zorin peered through the curtains expecting to see the man walk towards the LAWS doorway. He didn't, and headed instead towards the church steps.

Now Zorin knew he was a phony. What could anyone want there? Who would spend so much time nosing around St. John's? No, the man was after him, Zorin was sure. He wouldn't delay any longer. He had to protect his reputation, if not himself.

The telephone rang.

Zorin stared at it. Should he pick it up? Would they try to scare him with threats? His head hurt increasingly. The phone wouldn't stop. He grabbed at it.

"Dr. Zorin? You're still there. I'm glad," Randall said.

"Are you really? Wouldn't it be more convenient if I wasn't here — or anywhere any longer?"

"I don't know what you're talking about, sir, but you do sound upset."

"How would you feel if someone was trying to kill you?"

"Not very pleased, I'm sure, but . . . "

'But nothing, Randall. You know very well what I'm talking about."

"Look," Randall said, "I'm sure you're worried but let me reassure you . . . ."

"I don't want reassurance, Randall, I want protection."

"I can't do anything about that."

"Please don't, Randall. I'd rather have Scotland Yard. I trust them more than anyone you might send to do your dirty work."

"Why don't you stay put," Randall said, "and I'll come over right away."

"DON'T!" Zorin shouted. "I don't want you to come near me. Do the job yourself, eh? I rue the day I first agreed to work for you bastards."

"I'll be right over."

"Nol!" Zorin said and put down the receiver quickly.

He had to work fast now. It would take Randall at least fifteen or twenty minutes to get to Smith Square from Belgravia. Zorin rushed to the locked file where the typed reports were kept. No time now for the big computer, too complex. He quickly found the fifty-page Zimbabwe study and removed the clasp binder. Thank goodness for the copying machine he'd allowed the IBM salesman to talk him into. He had been cautious about spending so much and hesitated for a long time before buying the elaborate copier/collator . . . but had allowed the salesman's 'cheaper-in-the-long-run' argument to convince him.

Now it would prove cheaper in the long run, perhaps. Zorin placed the Zimbabwe study face-down on the automatic feed platform, set the machine for three collated copies and pressed the "Copy" button. The electronic noises hummed quietly as the copier began its task and the ch-ch-ch-chunk of the collator told him that the copies were being sorted.

Zorin took three heavy manila envelopes from the supply cabinet, and thumbed through his card file until he found the addresses he wanted, copied them onto the envelopes. Hurriedly he scribbled three notes on his own LAWS letterhead, and inserted them with the by-now photocopied and collated copies of the report into the envelopes. The original went back into his file. Zorin knew that they could get it easily if they wished to, but then again, they already had one. Why should they want the original? To destroy evidence? He didn't worry about that any longer. Three insurance policies were in his hands ready to be put into effect.

The telephone began to ring as he was closing the office door behind him, but Zorin didn't go back to answer it. Probably Randall checking up on him, wanting to make sure that he was still there before sealing off the escape routes. Zorin smiled as he thought of the look on Randall's handsome vapid, American face. This fox wasn't so old and feeble that he'd be caught napping.

He opened the street door cautiously and peered out, just in case the macintosh man was there. But he was nowhere to be seen. Maybe it was a ruse. Zorin could be watched from any window on the square. The man might be peering out from the church portico. Or maybe there was no one after all, and he was just overreacting. Well, whatever the case might be, Zorin wanted to be sure. His head still hurt, but a little bit less. He had put the extra pills in his waistcoat pocket, but hoped he wouldn't need them.

Slipping into Lord North Street, Zorin hurried to the next corner, turned right, and walked as fast as he could to Millbank. There, on the roadway along the riverside, he knew there would be a number of people . . . tourists mostly who had wandered away from Westminster Abbey and the Houses of Parliament. He'd be safer in a crowd. Maybe he'd just take a taxi . . . but when the first and then the second passed without stopping he knew that he could walk a few streets to the Westminster tube station. Why not? He always went home that way, and habit fit him like a comfortable old shoe.

Zorin walked fast and the afternoon was warm. He dodged the groups of tourists who clustered with guides or guidebooks looking at the Abbey or craning their necks while the guides pointed to some ornamentation high up on the delicate stonework of Parliament.

Big Ben struck the half hour and Zorin looked at his watch mechanically. By the time he reached the entrance to the tube station he was perspiring with the effort of his rapid walk and his head was pounding rhythmically once again.

A tatty looking pub near the station entrance reminded him that he was thirsty, and he stepped into its beery smell gratefully and asked the barman for a half of their best bitter.

With his briefcase tightly clutched under his arm he used his free hand to fish the pills from his waistcoat pocket and washed them down with the tepid amber brew. The doctor had said no more than two every four hours and it had been less than half that time since the last dose . . ., and certainly the alcohol was a constrictor, the opposite of what his migraine needed, but it was too late. He should have thought of that before. He knew that the pills wouldn't work anyway. Zorin's collar felt tight and he was perspiring profusely.

He left some coins on the bar, rushed into the street, flashed his season pass at the ticket collector at the tube station, and stepped onto the escalator. He looked around. No one behind him, and in front a group of Swedish girls, buxom blondes with birch-white skin, jabbered excitedly.

He wasn't used to so much alcohol in such a short time and felt woozy. He smiled to himself pleased to be a crafty fox after all and had been able to give the hounds the slip. He felt brave and cunningly courageous.

The Central Line train whooshed into the station just as he reached the platform, and Zorin made for the closest door. He plopped into a seat breathing relief. Maybe it was all wrong, he thought by the time the train had stopped at three stations. He should go home and forget the whole thing. Randall was just being obtuse, and no one was out to get Tadzio Zorin. Who would want to. And that pompous ass at *The Guardian* was only doing his job, overdoing it no doubt, but he wanted evidence just as Zorin did when he wrote a report. Well, the evidence was in Zorin's briefcase, but maybe he would just hold off. Go home, bathe, eat his dinner, spend the evening with Bertha Cribb, see his sister Ruth and family tomorrow as usual — another deathly boring afternoon in the suburbs: lunch, a walk, tea, some telly, George complaining about inflation and the effect on the import/export trade, some supper and home on the 8:12. That was the ticket. He felt very weary, and had had as much excitement as he could stand for one day.

At Notting Hill Gate Zorin rose from his seat and stepped onto the platform. It was here that he always had to make a decision. On fair Saturdays he walked to his flat on Orme Lane. If the day was wet or too cold, he took the Central Line one stop to Queensway, which left him closer.

He always rode to Queensway during the week, but the walk, like the ale at lunch and Mrs. Cribb at night, made Saturday a little different for Zorin, and he relished the variety.

The question was, did his headache and the pain in his neck and shoulder and the wooziness he felt disqualify the day as fair? He had to decide by the time the escalator reached the top, whether to exit or transfer to the other train. Given all the factors involved, it wasn't easy.

Mulling over the problem as the escalator rose, Zorin stood to the right as was customary, so that those who wanted to pass could do so. Several boisterous youths brushed past, shoving and jostling each other, and then Zorin felt a sharp jab against his leg as a man pushed past, poking Zorin with an umbrella.

"Pardon me," said a man with a smile and continued climbing with no hesitation.

Zorin gasped and drew his breath sharply. It was the man in the macintosh who had poked him! So Zorin wasn't as crafty a fox as he had imagined. They had been on to him all along. Professionals, they were. And he had thought that he could trick them.

What a fool. He began to sweat again and the migraine banged so hard that he thought his head would split.

By the time the escalator reached the top the man in the mac had disappeared. No doubt, Zorin thought, because he knew just where Zorin lived and would get there first, let himself in and be ready with a deadly surprise.

What could he do? What could he do? He suddenly felt old and tired and helpless. He couldn't fight them. They were more powerful than he, and good at their work. If they wanted him dead, he would be, and there was little he could do. Should he go to the police? They wouldn't believe him. Randall had said so . . . and *he* knew.

Maybe Randall was in league with the police. After all, MI5 was in on the deal. They had worked it all out together. Zorin was an embarrassment, get him out of the way, he was dispensable after all. Just an old man, a fussy old refugee. Who needed him? There was nothing to be told out of school, there would be no survivors . . . and no tales.

Get him they might in the end, but he wasn't going to help do it. Zorin would make it hard, and maybe he'd even have a chance, or at least more time.

When the escalator reached the top he turned without hesitation and stepped onto the down escalator. Gripping the briefcase tightly under his arm he ran down the moving stairs as fast as he could returning to the platform he had just left. He watched the platform tensely, grimly, for the man in the mac or some other like him to come into view, and listened intently for an approaching train.

His heart pounded so loud he thought that everyone around him could hear it, and his headache thumped like a tom-tom. Each bang of the drum sent a message of pain through his neck and shoulder and into the side against which he clutched the leather case with white knuckles. Only a Jamaican couple in bright pastels and two old charwomen entered the platform after him. He thought of his dinner warming in the oven in his flat. The housekeeper would be leaving by now. He'd take care of what he had to do, and call Bertha, maybe eat in a restaurant, or ask her to meet him someplace. She'd like that. They hardly ever went out.

But the assassins probably knew his haunts and they'd follow Mrs. Cribb. Why put her in danger, too?

Ruth! He could call his sister, and take the train there now. But what would that do. Give him another day's time? Would they come for him in St. Albans on Sunday if they didn't get him on Saturday? He could borrow George's car and drive away somewhere. Out to the country, stay in an inn, maybe go to Cambridge. Rossiter would look after him. He had a country place, too. Maybe Zorin could use it for a couple of days.

His mind was growing muddled and the perspiration dripping inside his shirt made him feel cold and clammy. He had to remember to call Rossiter and Pomeranz. To warn them. Maybe they'·d think he was crazy, too?

The train flooded the station with its clacking. Zorin stepped aboard. What could he tell them, he reasoned, or tried to, as he took a seat in the almost empty car?

A man in a mac who was taking pictures, had followed him home and poked him with . . . Oh God, now he knew he was done for. That's how they had killed that Bulgarian defector last year. Poked him with an umbrella and poisoned him with some toxin. Undetectable. And the man had thought nothing of it until he had a heart attack shortly thereafter and died in hospital. Zorin felt the blood drain from his face. He was shivering, and the pain burst in his head and side.

If he could get to a hospital and tell them that he had been injected with the same toxin in the same way, maybe they had an antidote by now. Maybe they could operate on his leg immediately and remove the micro-dart before it festered properly. He reached his free hand to touch the place where he had been poked and caught himself before touching the spot. Could be that rubbing spread the poison. Oh God, oh God, what could he do? Zorin wasn't a religious man, but for the first time in over forty years he prayed.

63

He got off at Paddington station and ran up the escalator and onto the street. The warm air hit him in the face like an insult. How could such horrors happen to him on a day like this? It was not a day for death. He rushed through the crowds of commuters and day trippers, shoppers with parcels and little children in tow, bumping blindly into people until he reached the Post Office on London Street opposite the lumbering monstrosity of the Great Western Royal Hotel.

Wasn't it there that they had killed Goldstein? Or was the hotel in Russell Square? Zorin was sorry he had been so abrupt to his former student. Poor fellow. They had gotten to him quickly enough, and all because he knew or surmised something about the LAWS report. Zorin regretted his rudeness the day before. What a waste. And how stupid, all because of an innocuous report.

He ran up to the registry window, and waited impatiently while an elderly Scottish lady dickered with the clerk over the cost of a package she was sending to her son in Aberdeen.

When she had stepped aside grumbling, Zorin cautiously withdrew the three manila envelopes from his briefcase and shoved them through the opening beneath the polished brass bars.

"Will they arrive Monday morning?" he asked the bored-looking clerk.

"Registered first class mail gets priority, sir," the man said, "so these probably will be there on Monday, seeing as they are all going within London . . . that is two are.

"Thank you," Zorin said, taking his receipts. "You will try to get them there by Monday, won't you?"

The clerk smiled thinly, "We will surely try, sir."

Zorin thanked him and left, first putting the receipts into another envelope and mailing them to himself at the LAWS office, just in case . . . as evidence.

Back in the warm sunshine he felt a wave of nausea overwhelm him, and he staggered with the dizziness and pain. He stumbled towards a pair of constables who were ambling down the street chatting. Oh to be young and dumb and without a care in the world.

"Please constable," he cried, rushing up- to them. "I think I I've been poisoned!" Blue and green and yellow lights were spinning before his eyes, and he felt himself go down.

The policemen were holding his arms, holding him up and he was sitting on the ground. Several people stopped to watch.

The fools think I'm drunk, Zorin thought.

"I'm not drunk officers . . . I'm sick . . .they're trying . . .."

Zorin didn't finish the sentence, and the next thing he knew was the policemen were lifting him, holding him up.

"Can you walk, sir?"

Zorin nodded.

"St. Mary's Hospital's just down the street.

"Emergency Room" was the last thing he remembered. The lights were flashing in his head, and the skin on his temples felt thinned to bursting from the pounding. He couldn't breathe. It was as though his chest were pressed in a vise, while a clawing beast tore at him from within.

He was on a table watching the lights pass him overhead.

Wheeling along down a pale green corridor. The lights were very, very bright when they stopped, and then it was dark.

5

WASHINGTON

"ACCOUNTABILITY," said the Secretary of State Jeremiah Croft. "We must consider that first."

Apt for a Sabbath meeting in the hushed abandoned church of the empty State Department, thought Nick. Theology up front, like guilt to the Jews, shame to the Catholics. And no one lost any time in pointing fingers at the others.

The story of the kidnapping was big news in all the papers and on TV this morning, and Gordon Barret Magombo, ambassador from Zimbabwe to the U.S. had already received the ransom demands forwarded to him from Salisbury.

"It is uncanny," the Ambassador said, wiping his profusely perspiring forehead, "because at practically the same time as Dr. Kananga was abducted, *we* received the demands of those hoodlums."

He was a tall, thin, professorial-looking man with small, round, gold wire glasses perched at the end of his nose. The gold contrasted strongly with the dark color of his skin.

"Well organized," the Secretary said.

"More than that," the Zimbabwean retorted. "They have penetrated our security set-up. The demands were delivered to the man who would become the minority leader if something were to happen to Dr. Kananga."

"I don't find that peculiar at all," the Secretary said. "It simply shows that we're dealing with a very professional outfit. Not the Red Brigade sort of lunatics."

"I don't think you understand, your excellency," the Ambassador said. "No one outside of the cabinet knew who the successor would be. Not even the man himself. I didn't know until the cable

67

came through from our Foreign Secretary. It is Zimbabwe's way of avoiding internal strife due to ambition."

"That narrows your investigation of suspects, doesn't it?" Secretary Croft asked the Zimbabwe Intelligence Service representative who sat next to his ambassador.

The short, rotund man was evidently uncomfortable with the question. "Of course there'll be a security check, Mr. Secretary, but that would take ages, and our priority at the moment will be to assure the safe return of Dr. Kananga." Though polite, the response had the hint of surliness.

Nick thought the Secretary of State had a distorted view of intelligence procedure if the plugging of leaks was foremost in his mind. That was a politician speaking, not a foreign service professional.

"Our Ambassador to Zimbabwe told me that President Umgawe received the terrorist's terms directly," said the Secretary.

"It sounds to me, then," Hartsdale-Smythe, from MI6, spoke up from the depths of his double chin that hung over a not-too clean white collar and the food-stained lapels of a dark grey suit, "that the double notice had two purposes."

A dozen pairs of eyes stared at him, waiting, suspiciously.·

"The first is to let everyone know that White Rabbit is a knowledgeable outfit and they have sources inside the government," he continued, "and the second is to say that they do not trust President Umgawe to make the terms known."

The mild-looking Zimbabwean Ambassador was greatly annoyed and showed it by speaking harshly, "I find that comment gratuitous and offensive, sir, to imply that President Umgawe is not a man of honor."

"I'm sorry, Mr. Ambassador," said the Englishman, "but I didn't think that we gathered for this unusual and inconvenient meeting to observe political niceties." He emphasized the word with disdain. "It is very much in the interest of President Umgawe to have Dr. Kananga out of the way. He is a thorn in the president's side."

"Outrageous!" the Zimbabwean blurted, his eyeglasses clouding with the heat of his emotion.

"Perhaps," said Hartsdale-Smythe," but I am not making any accusations, sir, simply observing what seems to be a fact. What I mean to say is that by notifying both governments and their executives and the media simultaneously, the captors are making a public statement, nothing subtle. Namely, that they do not trust either branch of government, and want the public, or at least the knowledgeable public made up of the world diplomatic and press corps to recognize that, and perhaps even to accept the implied smear as truth."

Nick liked the man for speaking his mind with no deference to the pecking order of rank. You could rely on a man like that to conduct an investigation without bowing to "expediency," the ultimate consideration of politicians, which they euphemistically labeled "diplomacy." Hartsdale Smythe was no diplomat. He was a cop who wouldn't get promoted unless "they" couldn't avoid it. Nick grudgingly gave the Englishman extra points.

Warden Yogun, the American envoy to Zimbabwe had kept silent, doodling on the yellow pad in front of him with a slim, gold pencil.

"I think, Mr. Smythe . . .."

"Hartsdale-Smythe," the Englishman corrected him.

"Hartsdale-Smythe, then," Yogun smirked gratuitously, "I think that interpreting the subtleties of the announcements had best be left to Zimbabweans, for whom this is an internal affair, or for those of us engaged in diplomacy who have to deal with such matters. The question before us is how to deal with a kidnapping that occurred on British soil, in plain sight of the palace, no less, and how to assure that Dr. Kananga is returned unharmed."

"You miss my point, sir," the Englishman said.

"No, I do not," retorted Yogun. "I think your reaction is just what the terrorists want. According to my information," said with a glance acknowledging the CIA and Defense Intelligence Agency representatives who were sitting opposite, "the White Rabbit group is a white supremacist organization whose purpose is to wreck the fragile peace that has come to Rhodesia . . . pardon . . . I mean Zimbabwe, after fifteen years of bloody turmoil. They will lose no opportunity to discredit any black government and to destabilize the power structure. Moreover, there have already been suggestions in the Salisbury papers that the former white rulers and Trevor-Jones are linked to the terrorists . . .."

"Then it's a shotgun," Nick interrupted.

Yogun glared at him, "I don't know what you mean," he said.

Nick continued, seemingly oblivious to the enmity of the interrupted diplomat, and feeling justified in protecting his colleague Hartsdale-Smythe from the patronizing and hectoring of this political lightweight who was seeking a ready-made whipping boy, "I mean that White Rabbit has seen to it that no one gets by unscathed. The President of Zimbabwe looks bad, the security system seems infiltrated, the white minority group looks guilty, the British appear lax, and the Americans . . . ."

"The Americans want to do whatever they can to release Dr. Kananga," Secretary Croft cut in. "Let's leave all the bullshit for the pundits of the press and get on with the purpose of this meeting. We can analyze the hell out of the situation now and it won't do a damned thing to get Kananga back . . . and I assume, in good faith, that that's what we all want."

"Well put, Mr. Secretary," said Ambassador Magombo, adjusting his gold rims higher on his nose," but the demands are not reasonable!"

He reached into his briefcase and produced several typed sheets, which he passed to the others.

The ambassador continued, "This is what they want," and read aloud, ". . . five million dollars in American currency or Deutsch-marks in used, non-sequential bills . . . the release of twenty-three prisoners from Zimbabwean jails," he read the entire list of names, "with safe conduct guaranteed out of the country, and all this by the fifteenth of the month. It isn't possible!"

Richard Scalzio, the CIA director of operations, said, "It is possible, Mr. Ambassador, depending upon how much you want him back."

"Of course we want him back," snapped the Zimbabwean, "but we are a poor country to begin with, and if that wasn't bad enough, these thugs are asking us to release convicted felons!"

"This document calls them 'political prisoners,'" Scalzio said.

"Must we indulge in more hair splitting?" the Secretary of State asked. "The question is, can you do it?"

"We might be able to raise the money," Zimbabwe's ambassador said, "but President Umgawe would never agree to releasing the prisoners . . .."

"Here I happen to agree with the Ambassador," said Hartsdale-Smythe . . ..".

"An unexpected ally," said the diplomat.

"Strange bedfellows and all that," quipped the Englishman, "but Her Majesty's government policy is not to capitulate to terrorists. It just gives the next lot ideas."

"Then you'll have a dead Kananga," Yogun said. "Are you willing to add that to your responsibilities?"

The Englishman let the barb pass by and said, "I think that White Rabbit's demands should not be answered immediately. We should have the opportunity to try to discover where they are hiding Dr. Kananga, and rescue him. That's the only way to put an end to this business for good."

"It might put an end to Kananga for good," said Yogun.

"We would not attempt any rescue if we thought that we would jeopardize his life," Hartsdale-Smythe responded.

"But you wouldn't mourn his passing especially either," Yogun said.

"I don't make policy, Ambassador Yogun, I just implement it," Hartsdale-Smythe replied. "However, for a sovereign government to lose face to some common criminals who wave an ideological banner is not something Whitehall wants to encourage."

"Well, as Kananga was abducted because of your country's poor security, I think it isn't becoming of your government to play tough now."

"Public officials in the UK are not subject to the same kinds of violent aggression as they are in this country, however," the Zimbabwean ambassador said coming to the Englishman's defense unbidden. His dislike for Yogun's irascibility was clear. "And it is completely normal for a visiting dignitary to arrive on a State visit without being surrounded by a phalanx of police and security forces ."

"Gentlemen, gentlemen," the Secretary of State pleaded, his irritation showing. "What are we to do?"

"We want some time to find White Rabbit, and flush them out properly," Hartsdale-Smythe answered.

"Pay the money and release the prisoners," Warden Yogun said, "or you make it clear to the world that you don't give a damn about Kananga."

"My government will not capitulate to terrorism, ever," the Zimbabwean ambassador said.

A man from his security force, who was seated nearby, nodded in agreement then spoke, "There has been some talk that the CIA is unhappy with President Umgawe and is trying to foment a coup by Kananga's people."

"That's a lie," objected Scalzio "We have no interest . . .."

"That may be," said the Zimbabwean security chief, "but you must understand that our President will not take any step that lets the world regard him as weak. Paying money is one thing, but releasing enemies of the state? A different horse color."

"Aren't they politicians?" Scalzio asked.

"They are criminals," the Zimbabwean answered. "Army deserters turned robbers and murderers, and mercenaries from South Africa who were caught attempting to blow up our main rail line. That's not what we call political prisoners. Those *are* criminals, and I doubt whether your government would capitulate in such a case either. You are thereby admitting to the tacit injustice of your courts, and it is to us, unthinkable."

"You have a point," admitted Scalzio.

"That's the shotgun effect," once again," Nick said. "No matter what you do, someone, everyone, gets hit."

"White Rabbit did some very clever planning," Yogun said.

"You sound as though you admire them," Secretary Croft snapped.

Yogun answered, "I don't, but. . .," and then decided to swallow the rest of what he was going to say.

The Secretary ignored him, and said, "What do you want to do, Mr. Ambassador?" addressing the Zimbabwean.

The man removed his gold-rimmed glasses, and began to polish them. Speaking without looking up, he said, "We might find the money for Dr. Kananga's release, but we will never release criminals from our jails."

"I want to catch those sods," said Hartsdale-Smythe.

"Lots of luck," said Yogun.

Nick wondered whether the Englishman had the hang of that sarcasm.

"You are going to have to satisfy our president that your government is not behind this abduction," said the Zimbabwean ambassador to the Secretary of State.

He had placed his glasses back on his nose and stood up. His security chief also got up.

"I'm surprised to hear you say that," the Secretary said, sounding miffed. "And how can we do that?"

"As for the first part of your question," said Ambassador Magombo, peering down at the men seated around the conference table as though he was addressing closing remarks to a graduate seminar. "I am speaking under the instruction of my government," reciting the ancient formula, "and as for the second part," he continued, "I believe that only the assurances of your chief executive to ours will suffice. In your nation's eyes we may be insignificant, poor and black, but our pride and honor cannot be dismissed cavalierly. To us, we are important, and you cannot push us around. The next move is yours."

With that he nodded curtly and left the room with his security chief.

THE MOOD RELAXED once the Africans had departed. The drop in tension was almost tangible.

"How do ya' like them apples?" asked Scalzio, addressing Nick. "Ambassador Magombo wants the president's assurance that the CIA isn't behind this."

"Are you?" Nick asked.

"No!" Scalzio was adamant.

"Because if you are, and we don't know," he spoke quietly directly to the CIA Director, and then glanced around the room as if to underscore that 'we' meant the Americans *and* the Englishman, "then we are chasing our tails . . . if we catch them, it's going to hurt."

"I promise you, Nick, the answer is 'no.' We are clean in this."

"Then I see no harm in getting President Dalton to assure Umgawe . . . if that will make the whole thing easier."

"I suppose not," Scalzio said grudgingly. "I just don't like the 'black is beautiful' bit . . . especially up on a high horse . . . ."

Ambassador Yogun, sitting directly across the table from the two intelligence officers glared at Scalzio.

"I would resent that remark under any circumstances," he said, "but it's particularly offensive in this context, especially since I'm certain that you know my own background."

With one black grandparent, Warden Yogun was actually lighter than the dark-skinned Scalzio, whose Neapolitan forebears lingered in every movement of his hands or head, but Yogun took pains to 'pass' in reverse and make much of his racial roots, while his smoldering temper and outspoken manner had earned him a reputation for his own version of candor, and he was popular with both establishment blacks and the white liberal left. That same outspokenness, however, had also led him to espouse publicly the politics of the PLO, an ideology the administration disavowed immediately, and which resulted in Yogun being banished to Zimbabwe, and his additional tenure as a diplomat was made conditional on him keeping his opinions private except for officially sanctioned utterances. The Secretary of State had told Yogun that his job was to implement policy, not make it with his mouth.

Scalzio, a tough, street-smart former New York cop who had joined the CIA in the early sixties and had made it to the top by hard work, was the antithesis to Yogun. Scalzio, who could handle most situations, but had the New York native's antennae that fed back immediate antipathy towards pretension and a disdain for phonies, was about to respond when Nick put his hand on his arm.

"Ambassador," Nick said, "I'm sure that Director Scalzio intended no slur against your people, it just seems contradictory that the envoy from Zimbabwe comes here ostensibly to ask our assistance . . . and we know who's going to pick up the tab in this case . . . and then demands gold braid and oak leaf cluster protocol before they'll consent to let us do what they can't."

"Nevertheless," Yogun said, "Mr. Scalzio finds it appropriate to find fault with pretentious behavior in racist terms."

"I'm sorry for that," Scalzio said, "but I was speaking to Director Burns, not making a public statement."

Nick winced internally. Richard Scalzio couldn't resist the little needling to offset the apology.

"Shall we get on with it, gentlemen?" asked the Secretary, who meanwhile had been busy talking to Hartsdale-Smythe and musing over some papers, and if he had heard the exchange among his subordinates, pretended not to.

The Englishman then took a seat next to Nick and murmured to him, "The LAWS business, me boy, who's going to drop that bomb?"

"Is it essential now?" Nick asked.

"The Secretary knows about it, so we'd better not play games. He just asked me about it and I hedged, but it's your field in here."

Of course the Secretary knew.

"Let's cut through the baloney here now that our guests have gone," said Secretary Croft, a former general known for both his bluntness and his short fuse. Behind the disarming smile on his square, bland face lay an arsenal of destruction ready to go off.

"Hartsdale-Smythe informs me," he continued, "that a tactical game plan worked out by the London Alliance for World Strategy seems to be in play by White Rabbit and that it's bruited about that they are your boys, Scalzio, running in your game. And then Zimbabwe comes in here asking for an executive guarantee that it isn't, and I'm left standing in front of the fan with the shit flying. I don't like it, Mr. Scalzio, not one bit!"

Nick, Yogun and Scalzio began to talk all at once.

"What about my credibility.?" Yogun objected.

"We had absolutely nothing to do with either LAWS or the snatch," Scalzio denied.

"Nothing is confirmed," Nick said.

"Then where the hell does the rumor come from . . . the sky?" asked the Secretary.

"One of our ops who covers as a journalist got it from the White Rabbit number two man," Nick said.

"Got what?" demanded Yogun.

"The information that the terrorists were underwritten by the Company . . .?

"A fucking lie," Scalzio shouted. "Excuse my French!"

"I didn't say it was true," Nick responded, "but that's what our man learned."

"I've heard that, too," Yogun said, "and I asked the station chief in Salisbury to check it out and he came up negative."

"As he should have," Scalzio said hotly.

"Yours! And why would he lie to you?"

"These terrorists are not underwritten by the Company."

"It's happened before," Yogun retorted. "What about Chile?"

"It seems pointless to flog a dead horse," said Hartsdale Smythe, lighting a crumpled Player's, and putting it in a holder. "The point, it seems to me," he went on, "is that the agent was terminated yesterday . . . after he visited the LAWS group. Perhaps he discovered something he shouldn't have."

Nick felt all the eyes in the room boring into him. "The visit was not only unauthorized," he said, "but there is no way that the operative could have known that LAWS had the scenario, unless our British colleagues dropped that morsel on his plate." His own credibility was at stake here, and like the Englishman, he knew that he had to cover himself at anyone's expense. He couldn't let OMEGA take a bum rap.

"I should like to come back to the point with which the Secretary opened this meeting," said Yogun. "Namely, accountability. Who is responsible for the leak and how can we plug it?"

"It's plugged," Nick said. "The agent was terminated."

"You really meant 'terminated?'" Yogun asked, shocked.

Nick nodded, "I didn't mean fired. He was killed, and not by us. Someone thought he knew too much."

He looked around the room. Scalzio? Hartsdale-Smythe? The MI5 chief just gone? The State Department Security spook who sat silent on the Secretary's left? Even Randall undercutting his boss? It could have been any of these, but he didn't know who yet. It pointed most readily to Scalzio, since the information put the Company in a bad light. But how would he have known that Goldstein reported to Randall?

"It's in the English press today," said Hartsdale Smythe, pushing the *Daily Telegraph* across the table to Ambassador Yogun.

"There's no connection made between the kidnapping and the reporter's death? GOLDSTEIN!? That little pushy Jewish bastard," Yogun exclaimed, forgetting that he disdained ethnic slurs.

"*De mortuis n'il nisi bonum*," cautioned the Englishman, pushing his cigarette out of the holder and carefully placing the holder in the Player's box.

"Thank you for the Sunday School lesson," Yogun retorted. "I didn't know that Goldstein was working for the CIA,"

"He wasn't," Scalzio said.

"He was OMEGA," Nick said, "and very low level, mostly extra ears in a sparse post."

Yogun put in, "That guy was always snooping around the embassy trying to find a story, and he printed a few that were total fabrications, detrimental to me personally."

"Well you needn't worry about him anymore," said Nick.

"How come there isn't any connection established between Goldstein and the Kananga business? They haven't put two and two together, yet?" asked Yogun.

"Not yet," answered Hartsdale-Smythe, "because we subtracted one of the numbers."

Everyone looked at him, puzzled. He then reached into his vest pocket and pulled out what looked like a playing card and tossed it onto the polished mahogany conference table. It was a playing card — a jack of diamonds — illustrated with a large white rabbit in a checkered coat staring at a pocket watch.

Nick picked it up. "John Tenniel," he said.

"Who's that?" asked Scalzio.

"Illustrator of *Alice in Wonderland* and other late nineteenth century English books . . .."

"Thanks for the lesson," Yogun said, "but what's the point?

"Rather trite," said Hartsdale-Smythe, "it's what you Americans would call 'corny,' but I'm afraid in this context it's rather sinister. The terrorists have adopted this illustration as their emblem, and manage to leave one of these cards at the site of each escapade. Unfortunately, the whimsy of the illustration is a sad counterpoint to the ruthlessness of their acts."

"Like the ace of spades as the death notice, out of some old movie?" asked the Secretary.

"I'm afraid that that's the contradiction we're faced with," Hartsdale-Smythe went on. "White Rabbit is encouraging attention with this kind of signature; it would be cute, if they weren't so deadly earnest."

Yogun looked puzzled. "So why hasn't Goldstein's death been connected with them if they left this at the scene?"

"Well, I'm not sure whether they sent it to him first, left it afterward or whether he had it all along. In any case, as I said before, I 'subtracted' it from the equation before the press could add it up. This, by the way, is a duplicate. The original is at our laboratory for analysis."

"This is all very interesting," said the Secretary, "but we're getting off the point. How much did Goldstein know about the LAWS scenario, and who else knows? If it's the press, can we keep a lid on it?"

"We have an Official Secrets Act," the Englishman said, "but the information could surface before we can get to invoke it,"

"And there is nothing to hold the reins on the American press if they get hold of it," said Scalzio, drumming his fingers on the table.

"And what a story! That a secret plan for the abduction of a leading African diplomat was worked out by a British think tank!"

Yogun said. "If your security is so lax," he continued, addressing Hartsdale-Smythe, "it's too bad. You'll have to take the flak."

"I'm afraid, Ambassador," said Nick, "that MI6 had a partner in this. It was a joint project with OMEGA."

The Ambassador steamed with righteous indignation. "WHAT? Why in God's name didn't CIA do this study instead of giving it to some ticky-tacky think tank? At least there would have been a tight security around the project."

Scalzio, supported for once, nodded in agreement.

"Well, you see," Nick explained, trying to avoid sounding defensive, "it was, ironically, to avoid just this sort of situation. We didn't want to run a study from the perspective of vested interest."

"That's a gratuitous slur," Scalzio said.

"Unintended," Nick apologized. "I mean that what we wanted was not a plan, but rather an objective look at what would happen in Rhodesia — I mean Zimbabwe — if . . . and that's a big IF . . . any of a number of situations were to occur. This was just one of them. And the London Alliance for World Strategy seemed the ideal outfit for such a study."

"Why not Brookings, at least?" asked Yogun.

"We felt," said the Englishman, "that the British experience in Africa has been more extensive to date, and less influenced by the classic *bête noire* of creeping communism under the bed, so to speak, which seems to haunt every one of your strategic studies."

The Secretary laughed, "It's not an unfair assumption, but I think that a legitimate concern has been raised. Namely, why was there so little security about this study, that an ordinary reporter or a terrorist group could access it?"

"It was never considered a strategic study, sir," Nick answered. "In fact, it meant to be an academic exercise to examine all the contingencies involved, the various possibilities by which opposition could destabilize the new government of Zimbabwe. In no way was it a plan for action."

"Even if a group of Oxford and Cambridge dons sat around spinning hypotheses? objected Yogun.

"That is, in fact, all it was," interrupted the Englishman, "no more than a high level seminar on international relations."

"Then I don't know why I wasn't apprised of the results," Yogun went on. "I might have found it interesting in my position."

"But you were," said Nick. "Both you and the British Ambassador were notified that there was such a study available. And State has it, too."

The Secretary shrugged. "I haven't seen it."

"I haven't even heard of it," Yogun said, pensively, but nevertheless . . .."

It seemed to Nick that Yogun was turning up his public outrage once again. He attacked when he couldn't defend.

". . . there should have been security measures taken to assure that the study didn't fall into the wrong hands."

"There were," Hartsdale-Smythe said. "You know, it's not as though LAWS is a public library. Not just anyone can walk in and get a piece of work they've done. They're contract thinkers, you might say, and the results they come up with are for the eyes of the clients."

"Nevertheless . . .," the Ambassador started to say.

"Nevertheless . . .," the Secretary interrupted, "it is absolutely clear that the information was accessed."

Nick wondered what the language watchers in the Sunday *Times* would say about the Secretary's jargon.

"The information," Nick said, "was not *information*. It was informed, expert opinion about a 'what if' situation, or rather several of them. No secrets were contained, no strategic plans. In fact, you might say that the LAWS study was a series of scenarios, speculating on the effects of certain input to the Zimbabwean situation. Nothing more. And all of the information contained would be equally available to anyone who read a few foreign affairs journals or some of the world press."

Yogun was not to be pacified, however. "The 'input' you mention becomes more like 'outtake' now. An important statesman is abducted and it looks like we planned it and did it, or at least abetted the process. Whether or not the LAWS work was just an academic pipe dream or whether it was a nefarious plot hatched by evil-doers is completely unimportant. If the news gets out that there was a model for this kidnapping developed by the United States and its major ally, we will seem responsible, and appear to be the perpetrators of the deed, however much we protest, and notwithstanding denials by even President Dalton."

"I'm afraid that I have to agree with the ambassador," Scalzio said, looking at Nick.

Political bastard, Nick thought. *Wants to come up smelling clean. Couldn't blame him too much. Protect your own rear was the first rule of the game.*

"What's to be done, then?" asked the Secretary.

Hartsdale-Smythe, lighting another Player's placed it in the holder, breathed out a cloud of smoke and said, "Well, I suppose we have to make sure that the press doesn't hear of the LAWS business. Over the pond, you know, we can restrain them from publishing it."

"But if this damned Goldstein knew of it, and he is, was, only small fry, the question is, who else knows and may rush to print before a restraining order is issued?" asked the Secretary.

"We don't know that, yet," Nick answered.

"Well, hadn't you better find out, damned quick?" sneered Yogun.

"Soon enough," Nick answered. He didn't like this man, but then again, it wasn't his job to like or dislike, or at least to act officially on any emotional basis. Sometimes he regretted that limitation. Like right now, when it would have given him great pleasure to insult the ambassador.

"In any event, Goldstein freelanced," Scalzio said, "and he may have filed for other papers. If they get hold of it over here, it's going to be our headache. OMEGA doesn't exist officially, remember?"

Nick did remember. Technically, he was CIA, too, of the same rank as Richard Scalzio, and on loan to OMEGA only. Any word fudging would make the LAWS document a CIA-authorized plan. The exposure on the whole business was too great for everyone.

"Then in terms of accountability," the Secretary of State said, "I think we have come to the conclusion by consensus that the permutations worked out by LAWS at the behest of OMEGA and MI6 will make it appear that the United States and the United Kingdom have a stake in the current situation . . . that we are somehow behind the kidnapping of Dr. Kananga."

"Yes, but . . .," Nick objected.

"But," the Secretary continued, "should the LAWS document come to public attention, the Department will disavow any connection with it!"

"So the Agency will look like the perpetrator of yet another scheme to overthrow a government abroad?" Scalzio asked, irritably. "Why should we take that rap . . . it isn't our responsiblity . . .. If you want to talk about accountability, Mr. Secretary, it seems that OMEGA and MI6 should take the heat."

"You said yourself, Mr. Scalzio, that OMEGA doesn't exist officially. How can we allow, therefore, the public to be apprised of the fact that a government agency that doesn't exist, authorized a study that does?"

"Well, you could let it be known that the thing is a piece of disinformation foisted on everyone by the opposition," said Hartsdale-Smythe.

"That won't work,' Scalzio said.

"Why not?" asked Yogun.

"Because,"Nick answered, "the opposition will deny it, and then retaliate by hanging something on us that we find even more of an albatross. We try not to play cheap shots like that with them, because, frankly, they are better at the disinformation game than we are."

"So where are we?" the Ambassador asked.

"I think," Nick said, "that we have taken this accountability concern a bit too far, with due respect to the Secretary . . . as we don't really know whether or not the information will surface at all."

"That all depends on how much Mr. Goldstein knew, and just what he wrote and where he filed stories . . .," the Englishman said.

"That shouldn't be too hard to run down," Nick said. "And, if need be, we can retrieve the study from LAWS, destroy all records of it, and make sure that it isn't heard of again."

"That would be wise in any case," said the Secretary.

"It should not have been done to begin with," Yogun said petulantly.

"Mr. Ambassador," Nick said, turning to face him, "we run OMEGA as chartered, and decide our own policies within the framework of our mandate. This current situation is a compounding of mishaps, but not a breach of security. This great embarrassing study that LAWS worked up is about as secret and strategic as the discussion in a foreign policy seminar at a university. You can magnify the embarrassment way out of proportion, if you wish, and try to make everyone culpable, but, 'frankly, my dear, I don't give a damn.'"

Everyone laughed and for a moment, the tension was broken. Even the obstreperous ambassador was forced to smile.

"All that aside, for the moment," Hartsdale-Smythe said, "we have a much larger problem in front of us. Namely, what are we going to do about getting Dr. Kananga back?"

The talk stopped. The Englishman had just splashed cold water on the heated bickering over 'accountability,' and who would be embarrassed.

"I think," he went on, "that we had better decide just what our concerted action will be, and then go ahead and do it."

"Yes, of course that's so," said the Secretary, embarrassedly, "but I felt that we had better clear up that other matter first."

That the Secretary had been forced into a defensive posture was bad because Nick knew that it would cost them all in the long run. Top administrators don't like to be made defensive before their subordinates, but Nick was glad at least that the Englishman had been the one to open his mouth and speak to the real issue, because Hartsdale-Smythe didn't have any direct subordination to the Secretary of State, only by deference.

"We should 'lend' Zimbabwe the money on the condition that they release the 'politicals,' and be done with it," Ambassador Yogun said immediately, as though he had been waiting for the moment the discussion would turn to the real issue, and had rehearsed his position statement.

Norton Vickers, the British charge d'affaires, who had been silent all this time, leaned over and whispered to Hartsdale-Smythe, "Are they in fact, 'politicals,' as the Secretary stated, "or was the Ambassador from Zimbabwe correct in saying that they were criminals?"

"It's really a question of whose ox is gored," said Yogun. "From my understanding, they are mostly political prisoners, but of course I'd have to check my files in Salisbury and consult with my staff to give you a more considered answer."

"Her Majesty's government will not accede readily to the blackmail of terrorists," said Vickers, "because it sets a precedent that has great ramifications elsewhere."

"We'd rather try to locate the captors and Kananga, and try to rescue him," Hartsdale-Smythe said.

"To compensate for your laxity in protecting him to begin with?" Ambassador Yogun said.

"No," the charge d'affaires retorted immediately, "to show that we will not be terrorized, and will not allow such violations to go unpunished."

"Yes, but it's not exactly a group of Iranians who have taken over an Embassy in London," the Secretary objected.

"The situation is different, but the method and the purpose is the same. That's how we see it," said the British diplomat.

Hartsdale-Smythe nodded agreement.

"I'm inclined to say let's at least have a go at retrieval before we say, 'okay, here's your money and go away,'" Scalzio said.

"You have to locate them first," Yogun said.

"We can try," said Scalzio.

"How long do we have?" Nick asked.

"Two weeks," the Secretary said.

"I would like to suggest an alternative approach," Nick said. "We should go all out to locate Kananga and his captors, but at the same time make plans to meet to their demands and secure the financing in the event that we are unsuccessful. I shouldn't like to challenge White Rabbit because I have a hunch that they'll do as they say and kill the man."

"I don't think so," Scalzio said. "What value would that have to them? No release of prisoners, retaliations on those identified as sympathetic to White Rabbit. It doesn't wash."

"We can't take the chance," said the Secretary, "and throw Zimbabwe into civil war again. We can't have that."

"You're right, Mr. Secretary "Nick said. "It's just what the LAWS study suggested . . .."

"Haven't we heard enough about that for today," the former general snapped at Nick.

"Zimbabwe won't agree to the ransom and prisoner release," Ambassador Yogun said.

"That's your job,"the Secretary said. "To convince them."

"It won't be very easy," Vickers said. "Don't forget that they were trained by us, and are more likely to view it our way. No concessions to terrorists."

"Let's let them decide," the Secretary said.

Nick looked around the room at the different men, each powerful, opinionated, effective in his own way. Strength conflicting with itself and becoming ineffective. *Empires declined because of meetings like this.*

"I'd like to propose that OMEGA coordinate the entire operation to offset our 'accountability."

The stress in Nick's wording had intended sarcasm, but no one seemed piqued. Disappointing. He was throwing a bone to Yogun and wanted to keep Scalzio and his dirty tricks boys at arm's length.

"Will that be acceptable to our British colleagues?" the Secretary asked.

The two Englishmen agreed without delay. Scalzio grumbled something about being superseded in the Agency's proper theatre, and Ambassador Yogun sourly said "yes," too, looking at Nick with great annoyance. It was out of the diplomat's hands now.

The meeting was over, and with a shuffling of papers, and a snapping of locks on attaché cases the men began to leave the room.

"Mr. Burns," the Secretary of State said, just as Nick, the last one leaving, reached the door. He turned and faced the former general who had risen from his chair. Nick was surprised to see how short the ex-army man was.

"I'm not pleased with this damnable internecine bickering," he said, across the room, and then approaching closer, "but I'm afraid that it's par for the course."

Nick didn't answer.

"If you made the suggestion that OMEGA run this 'recovery' for the reasons I think you did, then you're a helluva sharp cookie, even putting aside your smart-ass corner shot at me with that accountability crack."

Nick wondered whether any English instructor at West Point had ever told the one-time plebe anything about metaphor.

"It didn't seem to make anyone too happy except for the English."

"Well," the Secretary smiled as sheepishly as though he was revealing a secret, "if you hadn't said it, I would've. I don't like the whole damned thing. Something smells and I can't finger it. Everybody's too edgy, and there are too many stakes involved. Besides, I don't believe Scalzio. The Agency hasn't been happy with the whole Zimbabwe thing since Trevor-Jones bowed out but . . . they're not running this show. I am. Get it?"

"And I report to you."

"Right! Smart man."

As Nick started to leave, the Secretary called, "One minute, Mr. Burns. Whatever those *prima donnas* want to claw at each other about, when the shit hits the fan it'll be all over all of us. Don't forget that. You must get Kananga back safely by any means. And if you find dirt under someone's, anyone's, fingernails, I want to be the first to know. Use money or blood or whatever, but get him back. Clear?" He then turned and left the office.

Hartsdale-Smythe, who was standing in the anteroom, said "Burns . . . I'd like a word with you in private if you don't mind."

Nick looked at his watch. He had hoped to catch the three o'clock shuttle to New York.

"It won't take long," said the Englishman, ""Let me buy you a drink."

86

"In this part of town, on Saturday?" Nick asked. "Besides, I have to get back."

"Perhaps I'll hop out to the airport with you, and we can talk there," Hartsdale-Smythe suggested, accommodatingly. Nick liked that. He might make the plane after all . . . and he had told Gabrielle that he'd see her in the late afternoon. What he didn't need now was another hassle from her. It was getting on his nerves.

At the bar at National Airport, the Englishman curled himself around a lager while Nick sipped a whiskey.

"Thought they'd never get to the issue back there," Hartsdale-Smythe said. "More concern over the public relations than the fact that these blokes are likely to do away with the big man. And your people and the Rhodesians . . . pardon, I mean the Zimbabweans, don't even know the full picture LAWS hypothesized."

"They don't read reports . . . except after the fact." Nick said, "Good thing you didn't bring it up. I was counting on you."

"Likewise," Hartsdale-Smythe said, fishing in his pocket and coming up with his cigarettes, that he began to toy with.

Nick took out his new Dunhill pipe and filled it halfway, very carefully tamping in the rubbed-out flake tobacco. It gave him time to think before talking. He knew that the Englishman had come to the logical conclusion: if the terrorists were operating to optimize the effect of what they had done in abducting the black leader, and the air was already thick with rumors of collusion by the Americans and the English, then Kananga would not be returned alive — money or not. Chaos for Zimbabwe with one stroke.

"Nice pipe," said Hartsdale-Smythe, staring at it in the dim light." Must have set you back a few pence."

"Birthday gift," Nick answered, carefully lighting and tamping down the burning tobacco. "Got to be careful breaking it in."

"Oh, I know all about that," said the Englishman. "Used to be inseparable from my briar. Gotten too lazy recently."

Nick puffed in silence.

The pipe draws wisdom from the mouth of the philosopher, and shuts the mouth of the fool. "I came across that bit from William

Makepeace Thackeray somewhere," Hartsdale-Smythe quoted into his beer.

"Guess I'm somewhere in between," Nick said.

"Well, then, you should tell your people to hold on to their money. It's wasted, as far as I can see."

"They feel they have to make the gesture to affirm their innocence," Nick said.

"Better to back a manhunt, if they mean business. That's the only hope of seeing Kananga again."

"I think the Secretary knows it," Nick said. "Perhaps the others do, too."

"Yogun?"

"He protests too much."

"Scalzio? How did he know that Goldstein freelanced?" Hartsdale-Smythe asked, finally lighting the cigarette he had been examining so closely.

He was more attentive than Nick had realized. "You're suggesting . . .?"

"That there is some CIA involvement that goes beyond what your State Department knows, and it comes from higher authority . . . President Dalton perhaps?"

"Action creates policy, you mean?" Nick let his pipe go out.

"Something of that sort."

"What is it you want from me?" he asked.

"Help. I want to find Kananga and give those bastards a run for their money, or rather without their money. I think you want the same . . . and since we're going to be held responsible for whatever outcome, especially the worst, I'd like you working with me in the field, rather than sitting behind your desk in New York. Come to London tomorrow."

"I can't," Nick said, "I've got too much."

"You might have more if you don't," Hartsdale-Smythe said, "Think about it, Burns."

"I'm not a fieldman any longer, John. There are younger legs than mine available."

"This is too important for delegating, Burns."

"I'll think it over."

"I'll nag you from London," the Englishman said, putting some money on the polished dark almost empty bar.

"Is that it?"

"For now, yes."

"Then I think I'll make the three o'clock," Nick said.

"Ta." Hartsdale-Smythe answered, and slipped off the stool. He didn't look back.

Nick hurried to the boarding area and made it to his seat just in time for take-off.

He was beginning to like the bedraggled Englishman, but someone was being set up for a fall, he thought, as the jet banked and turned above the Washington Monument onto its northerly heading, and he wasn't sure who by whom. In this business you stopped trusting even your friends and became wary of anyone who tried to tell you something "for your own good." They were all suspect. The Company wasn't happy about State's policy of accepting Umgawe's leftist regime. And Kananga's alternative wasn't exactly their dream either. But if he died, Umgawe wouldn't be able to hold the country together. Two birds with one stone. But who was tossing the stone?

Back at LaGuardia, he re-lit his pipe to burn off the dottle in the bottom of the bowl.

One couldn't be too careful about matters of importance.

6

ENGLAND

"SO YOU THINK THEY'LL PAY without complications?" the stocky, sunburned man had asked, squeezing Oleg Volkov's extended hand. He might have been any businessman who arrived in London from Paris on the morning airbus.

His bespoke grey suit, neatly-layered dark hair that was graying at the temples, and soft black slip-on shoes were but a slight variation on the uniform worn by other members of the international business community who shuttled around the Common Market with regularity.

But the comparison stopped there. Jean Luc Moran carried himself like an athlete, his compact form was muscle not flab, and his square, hard hands gripped Volkov's so hard that he winced. Moran spoke flawless English with a slight French accent, the result of his public school days in England and his university training as an engineer in France. With a French mother and English father who divorced when he was young, he had grown up ping-ponging between the two countries, and held passports in each.

Moran thought like a soldier, not like a diplomat. Drafted when he completed university, he was trained for the crack French airborne division sent to pacify Algeria, and found that he liked soldiering more than engineering. He remained in North Africa after Algerian independence — De Gaulle's treason, he called it — and joined the outlawed right-wing Organisation Armée Secrète for spite.

From there Moran went on to work as a mercenary in the Sudan, Ethiopia, Angola . . .anywhere that the pay was good and the enemy was Red . . . preferably the black variety. For almost twenty-five years he soldiered through Africa killing — a job that he did with efficiency. Demobilized at the cease fire in Rhodesia, he returned to a comfortable life in Europe, investing carefully and dealing legitimately in armaments with the men and governments who had learned to trust him throughout his career.

A FEW MONTHS AGO Volkov approached Moran at Auteuil as he watched his horse lose one afternoon.

He had a job for Moran and the pay would take care of his needs for life. He could handpick his men, have his own banner. It would to be the stuff of history.

Moran told Volkov that he was interested in getting back to Africa in fatigues, not a suit and tie, and he didn't much like the job, but after an hour's talk in the race track bar, he had accepted the offer.

VOLKOV THOUGHT he had grown accustomed to Moran's frontal assaults on every problem, yet the man took him by surprise at the airport. He made neither a vestige of a greeting nor a reference to the success of the first stage of the mission — the kidnapping. It was as though it was expected, and nothing less, then move on to the next phase — the exchange — without looking back . . . losses were cut, gains were taken for granted and incorporated into the future plans.

"I think they'll pay," Volkov replied tersely as he ushered Moran through the maze of Heathrow's multi storied car-park to a large, dark-blue, executive model Ford Granada on the third level.

Moran threw his hand-luggage into the back seat, took off his suit jacket, folded it neatly and placed it on his case. He then climbed into the front passenger seat of the car, and fastened his seat belt as Volkov started the engine.

"You don't trust my driving?"

"I don't take chances if I don't have to. When will they pay?"

"In two weeks, as we told them in the communiqué this morning."

"And where?"

"We haven't told them yet. Remember? We agreed on that." Volkov let out a long breath, snorting as his nostrils flared, the only sign of his pique.

Moran smiled, pursing his lips slightly and narrowing his eyes to a slit. When they first met, he and Volkov had disagreed about both the method and delivery of the ransom. Moran wanted the money paid in his own warren of southern Africa.

Volkov said that he favored a European drop. "It's much easier to disappear."

Moran didn't think so. If the people Volkov worked for had some tricks to play let them try on his territory, not their own. He had accepted a job as number one and would not take orders. As long as Volkov delivered . . . and he had so far, but he was number two, and that was that.

"You have any trouble with the African?" Moran asked.

Volkov was watching the rear view mirror very intently.

"No," he answered, ". . . just a second . . . ." Then without signaling, he crossed three lanes of the almost empty motorway, zipped up an exit ramp, crossed over a viaduct and entered the same motorway going in the opposite direction. "Wanted to be sure, I thought that I saw the same car behind us back at the airport."

Moran shrugged. "It's not likely. There was no one on me coming across . . . unless they'd picked *you* up earlier."

"No way."

"Then why are you so worried?"

Volkov smiled, "Something like your safety belt perhaps." Then he repeated the same driving maneuver at the next exit and once again they were heading in the original direction. "I didn't see a car heading back towards us so it must have been my imagination."

"As to the big man," he resumed the conversation, "he played along just fine. Joseph was really surprised, and your boys, the inseparable Frank Smith and Ralph Wesson, didn't know of our . . . .." He paused and looked over at Moran who shook his head, no. "Well, they laid it on real thick."

"I want to know about Kananga," Moran said.

"He's fine. Having a good time."

Moran seemed satisfied with the answer and sat watching the green countryside flash by.

Volkov made no other attempts at conversation during the two-and-a-half hour drive until they reached the house near Bramfield.

Smith and Wesson were lounging on the front step of the stately home and rose when the car door opened.

"Good to see you, . . .," Smith started.

"Trade names only," Moran said curtly.

". . . Colonel, sir," Wesson continued.

"Mr. Van Ness told me that everything went as planned."

Smith glanced quickly at Wesson, and Moran caught the look in midair. "It didn't?" he asked.

"Very smooth," Smith said.

"Neat job," Wesson said.

Moran shrugged his shoulders, and entered the house.

"I think they're bothered by a follow-up I was forced to do," Volkov said. Then he handed Moran a copy of one of the London Sunday papers.

JOURNALIST MURDERED BY TERRORISTS

William Goldstein, a free lance writer who covered events in Southern and Eastern Africa for several newspapers was found shot to death in his hotel room last night. Sources at Scotland Yard have now indicated that the White Rabbit terrorists who successfully kidnapped a visiting African dignitary Friday may be responsible for the reporter's death . . . .

Moran had read enough. He dropped the paper onto the table and stared at Volkov, "Tell me why."

Moran walked to the window and peered through the curtains to see where Smith and Wesson were. They were now sitting on lawn chairs twenty yards away playing cards.

"Goldstein was too smart for his own good, and he was on to something. He had come to London from Harare on the plane with Kananga, and the fat man dropped a hint."

"How do you know?"

"Kananga told me."

"And?"

"I put a tag on Goldstein. He went to the American Embassy and then to LAWS, a think tank they use."

"So you pressed a button."

"I had to."

"Without *my* clearance."

"You weren't here."

"It could have waited a day!"

"Then you would have read a different story in today's papers." As he spoke, Volkov took a sheaf of papers from the inside pocket of his jacket. "This is the story Goldstein was working on when he was terminated. "Kananga abduction a sham: the victim was willing," he read aloud.

"That's no reason!" Moran said stonily.

"Do you want rain on your parade?" asked Volkov.

"I don't."

"I acted in our best interests."

"I don't like it," the mercenary said, "we are soldiers, we are not assassins."

"I didn't act alone. I conferred first," Volkov said.

"With whom?"

"*My* superiors."

"I'm your superior," Moran said. "No one else. This is my command, and I don't share it with anyone."

"They are the people who are paying for this assignment."

"They got what they paid for already. What White Rabbit has done in Zimbabwe for the past few months is more than their money's worth. You knew that was all a prelude," Moran responded, "and I went along with it because the money was so good. But I tell you, Volkov . . .."

"Trade names!"

"Okay, Van Ness," Moran continued angrily, "I don't like assassinations. I feel as though I've stumbled into the wrong side of this business."

"Well, you're in it now, Colonel!"

"I can see that. Just don't forget who's in charge here from now on. No more spook stuff. We get Kananga back to Zimbabwe . . . and we are soldiers. Understand?"

Volkov nodded his head in agreement.

Moran paced back and forth in the room, his eyes ranging around the dark polished furniture and floral print wallpaper. *Volkov was brassy and unyielding.* Moran wanted to quit . . . and he said so.

"Then do it," Volkov sneered. "You're the boss. I'll finish the job and keep your share of the ransom."

The mercenary said nothing for a moment. He stared at a woodcut of a hunting scene hung above the fireplace mantle.

"What makes the police think that we're connected with Goldstein's death?" Moran asked.

Volkov grinned. "I left a calling card," he said, then handed one to Moran.

Moran's eyes glinted hatred. "You arrogant asshole," he said, rocking slowly on the balls of his feet as he moved them apart and dropped his hands low.

Volkov's face registered fear for a second as he backed away a few paces, and then relief as Moran suddenly strode past him as though Volkov was furniture, and left the room.

LIVING UNDER MINORITY RULE in Rhodesia, Jeremiah Kananga and Matthias Umgawe had both been in and out of prison, serving long sentences for minor political offenses. Finding that all peaceful actions were proscribed, they had agreed upon fomenting an armed insurrection, and after fifteen years the whites were worn out by the guerrilla warfare.

By the time a truce was signed, Umgawe had developed a grander vision for himself. He was no longer content with the role assigned him by Kananga — junior to Kananga and with no real power in a Parliamentary system, so instead of supporting his commanding officer in his run for the post of Prime Minister, Umgawe opposed him in the first democratic election in the country . . . an election both men had jointly struggled to bring about for so many years.

Umgawe won.

Kananga's loss relegated him to a back seat in the new government, and with that, he sank into a deep depression.

IT WAS THEN THAT VOLKOV had approached Kananga. He introduced himself as a member of the CIA, and said that his name was Van Ness. He told Kananga that he wanted to help him return to his rightful position as leader of the people of Zimbabwe.

Kananga listened to Volkov as he described a plan to stage a kidnapping of Kananga for a sizable ransom in a city of international importance. That exploit would then be followed by a triumphant return of the "kidnap victim" to the limelight, thus providing an opportunity for the people of Zimbabwe to see that Umgawe had been an inept and uncertain head of state when a major crisis confronted him.

To make the plan even more appealing, Volkov promised to split the ransom with Kananga.

Volkov had been so sure of his plan that he had already had an associate deposit a million and a quarter American dollars — half of Kananga's promised share — in a Swiss bank account.

Kananga was convinced after hearing that, and told Volkov to go ahead with his plan. *It was brilliant. The CIA was a fierce enemy, but a good ally,* Kananga thought.

Volkov then explained to him how the operation would be conducted. A group of mercenaries would be brought together under the command of White Rabbit, the group that had spearheaded the white Rhodesian forces and kept the guerrillas on the run all those years. These soldiers-for-hire had a reputation to be reckoned with— a trail of carnage-filled victories all over Africa. The mercenaries would act as terrorists, as a group of white dissidents, and wreak havoc in actions against Umgawe's security forces, making a name for themselves as anti-black-rule, pro-apartheid terrorists, who would hit and run, and make it appear as though they came out of South Africa. Volkov had thought it all out. Once the terrorists had established credibility, Volkov and a small team would stage the abduction for the world to see, collect and divide the ransom, and disappear forever with their tribute.

Umgawe would be made to seem to be such a fool and blunderer as he dealt with the crisis that would unfold, and a rumor campaign would make him seem to be a conspirator in the kidnapping. Parliament would voice a vote of no confidence in him, and Kananga would return as a hero, shortly to be made Prime Minister, as he deserved.

The plan was seductive, and Kananga, no virgin to intrigue, became a willing kidnap victim. His recent public appearances exposed his depression and the futility that he felt following his defeat at the polls. To everyone it seemed as if the grand old man of Zimbabwe had finally accepted his role as patriarch emeritus, and was ready to serve the nation in any way he could, but he was not.

IN ANOTHER PART OF THE HOUSE Jeremiah Kananga leaned forward and switched off the television set, then let his considerable bulk flop backward on the sofa. His ham-wide arm reached over to hug the woman's shoulder.

"They are worried half to death, half to death," he said to the air, and a wide grin spread across his face.

The woman smiled and murmured inaudibly.

"What's that?" Kananga asked. "My hearing isn't so fine anymore."

"I'm worried, too," his aide Joseph Undaka said. "If I had known that you were going to do something like this here in England, I would have advised against it very strongly indeed."

"What's wrong with England?" asked the woman.

"Nothing," Joseph retorted, removing his glasses and staring at the woman with watery, bloodshot eyes. "Nothing. But we are dealing with a sophisticated country, with all the modern methods of detection at their disposal."

"What do you think should have been done, smarty?" asked the woman. "Jeremiah be abducted from his office or the farm?"

She looked at him from under a mass of blond hair, and toyed impatiently with a bracelet, twisting it round and round her wrist.

Joseph watched her for a moment, opened his mouth to speak and then said nothing.

"If I had disappeared in Zimbabwe," Kananga said kindly, there would be little attention paid, and the government would choose not to act . . . or gamble with my life. Here, the action commands world attention, and President Umgawe cannot be complaisant. He must show good faith to the eyes of the world."

"Yet I am concerned, your excellency, that the English police will locate us, or prevent our escape, and the entire plan will come to naught."

"You need not worry, my loyal friend," Kananga said. "You will not see any such thing happen."

Changing the subject, he said to the woman "And you, my dear, this is where you spent your childhood?"

"The whole time," she answered. "Isn't it a bore?"

"No not at all. I only wish I had had the opportunity to grow up in such a place. The greenness of it, those wonderful fields," he gestured towards the open window of the study. "Look at the hedgerows, and the daffodils. I wish I could walk openly through those fields and smell the cut grass and the flowers."

"You mustn't, excellency," Joseph interjected. "It would be most dangerous and unwise."

"My good friend and helper," said Kananga, "you are too concerned about being discovered."

"No," Joseph said. "I am concerned about what these men will do. They are hard and dangerous men. They act without emotion, no love, no hatred, just like automatons. I think that if their plans were foiled they would kill us all without a second thought. Like flies in a bottle."

"You are a bleeding coward, Joseph," the woman said. "No one is discovering anything. Who would think to look for Jeremiah in a place like this? Frankly, I think he could go for a walk if he wants, there's no one to see."

"Now there, my dear, I think that Joseph is correct in urging caution," Kananga said. "Any neighbor who sees a large, black man strolling on the public footpaths or across a field in Bramfield will surely make note of it. When I was a student at Cambridge, I don't mind telling you, all I had to do was take a walk in the country and someone would call the local constable. Fear of the black man is very deep here, indeed. No, I'll go out after sunset, if need be. I'm harder to see then." He laughed at his own joke, his chins and girth shaking like a jostled pudding.

Kananga stroked the woman's shoulders and ran his fingers through her shoulder-length hair.

"Send him away," she whispered.

"Joseph, go tell Mr. Van Ness that I'd like to see him in half an hour, and then go amuse yourself elsewhere."

Joseph stood, looked expressionlessly at the woman who gave him a smug little smile, and locked the door after himself.

"ONLY A FEW PEOPLE know the truth that I am living on the anticipation of my just deserts . . . of them," Kananga confided to Volkov, "Joseph might be a problem . . . he melts too quickly when the water gets hot".

Volkov exhaled the smoke from his cigarette, and said that the problem of Joseph was compounded by other factors. "He works for Umgawe, too," he said bluntly.

"I don't believe that, Mr. Van Ness!" Kananga shook his leonine head slowly. "Joseph has been with me for many years; he's like my right hand. He couldn't be a spy."

"Well, he is," said Volkov. "I just found him trying to get away."

The big man looked at Volkov incredulously.

"Joseph went out into the garden, and when he thought my men weren't looking, he jumped the fence and ran across the field to the road. We picked him up as he slipped through the hedgerow."

"And after our conversation about being seen?"

"What's that?"

"It's not important," Kananga said. There was a tone of sadness in his voice. "But this is surely not proof of his betrayal, perhaps only an error in judgment."

"I wish it was, but what about *this*?" Volkov said as he placed a miniature transmitter receiver on the table.

"I didn't know he had this with him here," Kananga said with a smile, "but I have seen it back home. Many of my men have them . . .. You know, in Zimbabwe we don't have telephones everywhere. This doesn't prove . . .."

"I thought you'd say that," Volkov interrupted. "Why would he have it here?"

"Habit?"

"And what about this?" Volkov took a short-barreled revolver from his pocket and handed it to the big man. Kananga looked at it with a frown on his face. It was standard issue for the secret police in his country.

"Anyone can obtain this," Kananga said.

"It's an unlikely choice if you have to choose a weapon, unless it's issued to you."

"This is still not proof," the big man said, raising himself from the sofa and facing Volkov. He sounded less certain in his denial of the evidence.

"How much does Joseph know about what we're doing?" Volkov asked.

"He knew nothing until it happened."

"You're sure of that?"

"I had speculated in his presence about what would happen if I were abducted, but said only that I thought President Umgawe might make such a move to get rid of me for good."

"That's all?"

"That's all!"

"I wonder why he didn't try to use his weapon when we grabbed you in London?"

"Perhaps he thought it unwise . . . or he thought that . . .," Kananga hesitated.

Volkov finished the sentence, ". . . that we were acting for Umgawe? He didn't know that we were White Rabbit at that time, did he?"

"No."

"Then maybe this will convince you."

Volkov handed Kananga a thin business-card case that was embossed with a stone bird, the state insignia of Zimbabwe.

Kananga opened the folded case slowly. In it there was a photo of his trusted aid, grimly staring out at him from a pink card identifying the bearer as an officer of the Zimbabwe Intelligence Service. Looking crestfallen, Kananga glanced at the card and gave the case back to Volkov. He then turned his back to him, and briefly passed his hand across his eyes.

"Is there no one in this world one can trust?" he asked.

"Start with number one, and if you're lucky enough, you can stop there," Volkov said.

Jeremiah Kananga turned to face him, drawing up his slumping shoulders to his full height, for a moment he was the powerful chief of a warrior nation once again. "I have seen what there is to see . . . you may act accordingly." Majestic anger had replaced the hurt in his eyes.

Volkov pocketed the evidence without a word, and turned to leave.

"Oh, Van Ness," the big man called as the other reached the door. Volkov turned.

"Painlessly, please," Kananga said.

Volkov smiled deferentially and kept walking.

THE BLOND WOMAN WAS waiting for Volkov in a room above the garage that had been servants' quarters.

Joseph lay bound and gagged on a narrow bed in the corner, asleep from a heavy dose of a sedative. From the window she could see the driveway and Smith and Wesson, the two tough-looking South Africans, sitting on the lawn chairs playing cards.

Volkov seemed to have everything figured out, but she had told him that he was going too far with this one. Jeremiah was not going to believe that his aide was an agent for President Umgawe. Never. His mind, though subtle indeed, was monolithic on the subject of loyalty, and Joseph was a distant member of Kananga's clan so that

Jeremiah would find it very hard to take steps against him, even it Volkov produced irrefutable evidence.

Yet when Volkov had told her that Joseph was Umgawe's man, she was worried. How much did he know already, and was her work in Zimbabwe already in the past tense? She might have to go back to Moscow for good if she was blown. Orders had to be obeyed. She was told that this was a joint operation that would be officially denied. She didn't like it, but finally accepted whatever she had to do with the rationale of the greater good of the country. Hers not to reason why, and so on. She rose from the rocking chair when she heard Volkov's soft tread on the stairs.

"I told Kananga," he said. "No problems."

"And he went along?"

"The way I presented it, he had no choice. He's a political animal. He wants power again and he'll do anything to get it."

"And Smith and Wesson?" she asked.

"They knew nothing. Just as you said. When Joseph got to the hedgerow where you told him to meet Kananga, they were waiting . . . the end."

She walked to the window and looked out at the bright sunshine, the bushes coming alive with flowers. So Jeremiah had passed the sentence. She hadn't seen him in the same light as Volkov, and she was a bit surprised that he had gotten his way. Oh, it was true enough that Jeremiah could be ruthless and cunning, but there was that paternal part of him, the soft human underbelly. Had he been a harder man, his protegé Umgawe would never have seized the reins. Jeremiah thought that nothing rumbled under his embrace but his own heart. *What would he do if he found out about her?*

"What exactly did you tell him?" she asked.

"The less you know about it, the better," he answered stonily.

"But the story has to be consistent," she said.

Volkov seemed to relent a bit. "I said that he was working for Umgawe."

"And he believed that?"

"I documented it," he said flatly. "Anyway, it's true."

103

"Look," he continued, "that's enough. Now leave me. I've got work to do."

The woman closed the door behind her as Volkov unrolled a kit he had taken from his jacket pocket containing a hypodermic syringe and several vials of clear liquid marked with numbers.

7

LONDON

BY THE TIME NICK BURNS ARRIVED in London, Tadzio Zorin was dead.

"Missed him by an hour," said Hartsdale-Smythe, when Randall ushered Nick into the room. "He lapsed into a coma after a second heart attack last night," the bedraggled Englishman continued.

"How did you find him here?" Nick asked, looking around at the greenish walls and the dim lights hanging from the ceiling.

The hospital was right out of Dickens, with its long wards of white metal beds almost touching each other, and the starchily pinafored, stiff nursing sisters. The stern one who had led them through the interminable corridors to the tiny private room where Zorin had concluded his life acted as though they were interlopers, trespassers on the grounds of some ancient manor of which she was a bound vassal.

"He was a regular type, our man here," Hartsdale-Smythe answered. "When he didn't show up at his sister's for the usual Sunday family lunch, she rang his flat. No answer, so she called the woman who keeps house for him, and she went over to find that he hadn't been home, dinner still in the oven, bed not slept in. She called a Mrs. Cribb, a widow he always saw on Saturday nights, because she thought that he might have stayed over there as he sometimes did, but he hadn't shown there either. Then the sister called the police. Some constables had brought him here after he collapsed on the street. Common enough. It's in the record.

"I decided to contact the old man immediately when I got back from Washington on Sunday, rang up his sister and was told he was here. Then my man at *The Guardian* called me this morning. Zorin had sent them everything — *The Telegraph* and *The Standard* also received the whole lot."

Nick exploded. "Shit . . . can't you . . .?"

"Easy old man." Hartsdale-Smythe laid a calming hand on Nick's arm. "We did . . . for the nonce."

Zorin's corpse was an ashen color, the thin lips set in a faint smile, two white lines on a mask.

"He thought he'd been hit, Randall told me," Nick said.

"Was absolutely convinced," Hartsdale-Smythe said, "and he said that it was the same way they got rid of that Bulgarian a couple of years ago. . . invisible dart in an umbrella . . . producing a 'heart attack.' Doctors say it's rubbish. But we'll know after the post mortem. He was convinced that we did it to him to keep him quiet."

"Did you?"

"No!" the Englishman said emphatically. "Besides, it's not our M.O. No, I think it was sheer terror. Frightened little man this. Survivor psychology. Saw bogey men everywhere, and the ticker couldn't take it."

"The damage is done," Nick said. "Where to now?"

"I've put a watch on the LAWS staff."

"After the horse . . .?"

"Look here, Burns, who would have thought? "

"Zorin called and asked me for protection," Randall said. "I brushed him off."

Nick walked away from the two of them and stood between the corpse and the grimy window overlooking a dark air shaft. *It wasn't their fault. In the same situation I probably would have treated Zorin as a crank or as delusional.*

"I did try to do something afterward," Randall said after a moment of silence. "I went over to LAWS to see him, but he was gone by the time I got there. He thought that I was after him, too . . . and then I drove to his house, but he wasn't there. What else could I have done?"

"You could have found him!" Nick shouted at Randall. "Before this!"

"Burns, I'd like to speak to you privately," Hartsdale-Smythe said, "Randall, will you excuse us?"

The younger man didn't look too pleased as he closed the door to the corridor.

"Young Randall's not to blame for this, Burns, and I'm sure that you know it . . . .."

"By the corpse of an innocent man," Nick answered, "and we say 'sorry about that, it couldn't be helped?' I don't buy it."

"I'm not selling it," the rumpled man retorted. "Simply this. Zorin may or may not have been murdered. If he was, then we are being finessed by some very clever types. If he wasn't, then we're witnessing some version of higher coincidence, or the combination of a bum ticker and some fear of exposure."

"To what?"

"You saw the covering letter he sent to the papers?"

"I only glanced at it in the car from Heathrow."

"Look at it." Hartsdale-Srnythe pulled a folded copy from the inside pocket of his smudged tan raincoat.

Nick let his eye run down the page . . .

In submitting these documents to the press I realize that
I am betraying a trust placed on me by agencies of the
governments of both the United Kingdom and the United
States of America . . . But honor compels . . . and there
is a fundamental duty to protect myself and the research
institution I have built so painstakingly over the years . . .
But having served . . . inconvenience . . . threaten my life
. . . suggestions of complicity must be absolved.
    Speculations based on examinations of data are not
recommendations . . .'

What he gleaned from Zorin's letter confirmed the image in Nick's mind of a man who was trying to reverse a tide by an act of will, for the tone betrayed the writer's desperation, his anxiety that his life's work should be turned into something so banal as the plan for abducting a diplomat, as though LAWS was an institution that helped thugs with government license carry out a reign of terror.

"Where's the report?" he asked, wanting to see the pages he would surely find in the *New York Times* or *Washington Post* when the whole thing was reprinted verbatim. "They'll print this letter, your papers?"

"They know better than that," Hartsdale-Smythe replied. "The editors could be prosecuted under the Official Secrets Act, so they checked with Whitehall first, and we said no, of course."

"Handy gadget," Nick said.

"Freedom without limits is anarchy," said the Englishman.

"Philosophical today, aren't we?" Nick chided.

"It's rubbish, naturally . . . but one does need justification now and then."

"Oh, does one? Why?"

"See here, Burns, you're the one with some sort of crisis of conscience, not me," said Hartsdale-Smythe. "I just have a job to do, but you seem to need some grand overview. I don't. Pick up the pieces and get on with it. Full stop. And the 'accountability' nonsense your Secretary of State tried to rub our snouts in . . .. I don't care much for that either. No guilt in this game, just winners and losers. That one," he motioned towards the corpse with his head, "simply wasn't up to it. He lost."

Nick fought against accepting the Englishman's premise. It had to be more than a game, otherwise one might just as well sell used cars or manufacture sausages.

"He didn't think he was in the game," Nick said. "Perhaps he saw himself as something more . . . as a scientist in a way."

"That, my friend, is a fantasy born in the halls of academe, where our lamented Dr. Zorin spent his youth. But it's not the world I have to deal with daily, nor yours. When you commission a study, those who accept it are on your side. Don't give me that 'value free social science' rubbish. I've had enough of it."

Nick looked at Hartsdale-Smythe with a puzzled expression. The Englishman noticed and said, "I read Sociology and History at university, and tried a lectureship at Sussex for a few years, back at the year dot, but got out. Couldn't take the thin air."

There was a knock at the door.

Randall poked his head in, "The orderlies from Pathology are here."

"Just a moment, Randall," said the Englishman. He then shut the door and turned to Nick. "Young Randall's a good lad, Burns. Don't let this blasted pique of yours lose him for you." He opened the door without waiting for Nick's reply.

"ELEVENSES, GENTLEMEN?" asked Hartsdale-Smythe as the driver turned into Smith Square. "There's nothing at the LAWS office that can't wait a few minutes."

Nick's biological clock was already so confused by his fitful dozing on the overnight flight, that he thought a drink couldn't make him feel worse. He looked at his watch, still set to New York time. It was 6:00 A.M. for him. Nothing like a tepid pint of bitter to start the day.

Hartsdale-Smythe directed the driver to the Marquis of Granby on a quiet street behind the old church. "Came here with Zorin a few times," he said, "so it's appropriate for the obsequy."

"Aah, gallows humor . . . it's too early for me," Nick protested.

"That would be an exequy," Hartsdale-Smythe said. "We English excel at that. Why, look at Raleigh, and various seventeenth century worthies who went to the scaffold and made speeches to the crowd that had come for the event. Entertainment it was. A grand spectacle."

"Sorely missed," Randall said.

Once settled at the pub, the Englishman fetched three pints from the bar for the group to a table in the corner. Other than a few office workers who had drifted in, the three intelligence men had the place to themselves.

HARTSDALE-SMYTHE SIPPED HIS ALE, smacked his lips in clear appreciation, fitted a cigarette into his holder, and began to explain his government's position.

"Zimbabwe had been Rhodesia, a British territory since 1890, one of the areas Cecil Rhodes had laid claim to. The "white man's burden" had been shouldered, rebellious tribes defeated and pushed onto reservations of the poorest land, and the Crown, along with its emissaries, had prospered. Indeed, all of British South East Africa had been a godsend to the eminent Victorians whose pockets became so heavy that they put down the burden from their shoulders.

"More recently, from Kenya to South Africa, the winds began blowing change, some violent as with the Mau Mau, some peaceful and political. In Rhodesia, however, the white minority couldn't countenance the majority rule that the Commonwealth was trying to bring about, and like their American Confederate cousins a century before, seceded — a rebel nation in jealous guard over a way of life too comfortable and profitable to lose.

"But England didn't send troops, they simply shrugged in despair and disgust at the racist policies of Trevor Jones, Rhodesia's Prime Minister, outlawed trade with the rebel nation, prevailed upon British allies not to do any business with the government in Salisbury, and continued to work behind the scenes for a peaceful settlement of the impasse.

"In the alphabet soup of political parties, mostly outlawed as soon as they were established, the majority rebel leader most visible was Jeremiah Kananga. He had combined the contradictory figures of tribal chief and liberal social democrat. Trained at Cambridge, he stood between both worlds. Philosophically a Marxist, he nonetheless believed in self determination and freedom in the Western sense. Admiring Soviet ideology and English pragmatism and American technological prowess spurred by capitalism, his beliefs were a creed of confusion.

"The intransigence of the Salisbury government and the impossibility of achieving the aims of national majority rule from a jail cell took Kananga out of the country into exile in neighboring Zambia where he formed a government in exile and declared war against Trevor Jones's white minority. The war of attrition that ensued lasted for more than ten years of guerrilla skirmishes, fifth column activities and too random bloodshed on the part of both blacks infected with hatred and whites reacting with the fire of fear.

"Over the years Kananga's control of the Zimbabwe African National Integrated Front, ZANIF, weakened as factionalism developed. Matthias Umgawe, a man ten years his junior, who started as his personal aide, began to acquire more power as Kananga left many decisions to the younger man. Umgawe's promotion to Divisional Commander was a kick upstairs, mostly because of Kananga's need to quell the factionalism that most outsiders saw as having its origins in tribal rivalry. Umgawe was a member of the Shona ethnic group, which constituted roughly a two-thirds majority of Zimbabwe's blacks. Kananga was from the Matabele, the other third, and he reportedly felt that his young lieutenant would provide the tribal link to the Shona guerrilla fighters in the eastern sector of Zimbabwe."

"But they wince if you say tribalism," Randall interjected.

Nick was glad for the interruption because it gave him a chance to order another round from the bar and find the men's room while the tapman refilled their glasses.

"I was telling young Randall here," Hartsdale-Smythe said when Nick returned, "that the Africans are sensitive to the tribal question because they know — that is the more educated leaders do — that to the European or American ear, 'tribal' suggests half naked savages running about with spears and loincloths and eviscerating each other.

"But the ethnic ties remain as a political force even when you no longer have real tribes any longer. It's a political fact.

"While Umgawe's ascent helped Kananga to win the war, it cost him the P.M.'s hat when the transition to majority rule eventually became a reality three years ago. Umgawe formed his own party and polled two-thirds of the vote, and it's not too difficult to see where his mandate came from."

"And he is a Marxist," said Nick.

"Yes, and not such a philosophical muddle-head as Kananga. Much more orthodox in his attitude, and not so trusting of piecemeal reform as Kananga is."

"What does this tell us about Kananga's abduction?" Nick asked.

He appreciated the background information, but began to see the Englishman warm to his subject like a university lecturer, and was afraid that the talk would continue longer than he felt he could stand. He wanted to get on with the visit to LAWS. Besides, the tiredness he felt was increasing, aided by the surprisingly potent brown ale.

"It tells us," Hartsdale-Smythe said, with a slight hint of annoyance in his voice, "that Umgawe is pushing towards a one-party state, and with his most potent rival out of the way, he can do it. Umgawe already set the groundwork for discrediting Kananga when his people dug up arms caches on a farm Kananga owns not far from his home and power center in Bulawayo."

"That was only a few months ago," Nick said. "I read a report from the station chief in Harare who reported the arms dump was common knowledge until Umgawe decided to use it as a political weapon, thus giving him an excuse to strip Kananga of his ministry — Home Secretary, sort of a national chief of police — and send him abroad as a good will ambassador."

"Another political mistake?" Randall asked.

"Maybe not," the Englishman said, lighting yet another cigarette in the chain that mostly-burned unpuffed as he talked. "If Kananga is out of sight, he can't attract too much attention. It doesn't really matter what he says while abroad, because the papers in Zimbabwe only report what Umgawe wants them to, and in the meantime he can consolidate while the old boy is off playing visiting dignitary abroad."

"Then if Kananga is kidnapped and killed it serves Umgawe's purpose, doesn't it," Nick said.

"In a way, yes, in another, no."

"Pray tell," Nick said, taking out his pipe and starting the filling ritual.

"Yes, it gives Umgawe a clear field, for his power play."

"And Kananga, who knows where all the bodies are buried could make it difficult if he's in the country or if he returns," Nick continued.

"I don't think he'd have much of a chance if he came back to a *fait accompli*. He doesn't have the manpower and he's sincerely tired of the political fighting. No, he's been feathering his own nest lately, making big investments — hotels, golf courses, a private game park. He just wants to wax fat and prosper."

"Then why the abduction?"

"Well, this White Rabbit group has been stirring up a lot of trouble there lately, and it could be that they really are going for the big money with this caper to finance their activities further."

"You don't sound convinced."

"I'm a professional skeptic."

"What, then?"

"If Kananga is hurt, there'll be a bloodbath in Zimbabwe," said the Englishman.

"You mean tribal warfare again?" asked Randall.

"Possibly, but not likely," Hartsdale-Smythe said. "More than likely it'll be racial. The remaining whites will be massacred or flee the country in fear of such. All that the tinder needs is a spark, because there are unconfirmed reports floating through the air in Zimbabwe that White Rabbit is the arm of the white minority, former soldiers turned terrorist to keep the blacks in fear. We learned that their leader is the mercenary who led the government forces prior to the truce."

"Moran?" Nick asked, surprised.

"The same."

"You didn't let on the other day," Nick said with a grimace."

"I didn't know then," Hartsdale-Smythe said.

"Moran is one tough son of a bitch," Nick said, "but he's not a terrorist. A soldier, yes. But if this campaign has been one of hit and run nonsense, farm burnings, cattle slaughter, it doesn't sound like his style. He seems to go for big stuff, and in this case the kidnapping is substantial."

"And if Kananga is hurt," Randall said, "that's also quite substantial."

"Yes, then everybody loses. They can't run Zimbabwe without the whites, and Umgawe knows it. The whites produce eighty percent of the manufacturing and agriculture. The country would sink like a stone. Umgawe doesn't want that," said Hartsdale-Smythe.

Nick sat back and lit his pipe again carefully, breathed the smoke in and out several times, his brows knit together, his eyes fastened on the Englishman's face in a penetrating stare. *The slovenly man's analysis is too neat . . . something doesn't fit.*

"If Kananga dies," continued the Englishman bluntly, "whites are washed up in Zimbabwe for good. And that means almost a hundred years of British stewardship is down the drain with the pulling of one plug. Only a viable white minority can help keep a British trade and strategic hegemony in the area. And that means the Americans, too.

"We all know that South Africa is just about over for both of us . . . or will be soon. If we don't stay in the picture in Zimbabwe, my guess is that the focus will be on Russia, through their Cuban friends a hop, skip and jump away in Angola and Namibia."

"The old domino theory again?" Randall said. "I thought that was discredited."

"Only in foreign policy seminars at universities," Nick said. What he had learned about containment, domino reactions and hegemony during his own college years was still the basis of operation of the professionalized branches of foreign service and intelligence corps. The terminology coming out of the White House and the Secretary of State's office changed with the temperature shifts in the political climate, but the groundwork remained the same.

"That's why I got out of the rarefied air of the sacred groves," said Hartsdale-Smythe. "We've got to get Kananga back for reasons of expediency. There's no moral issue in this."

"Who ever said there was?" asked Nick, standing and pocketing his pipe. "Let's see what LAWS can tell us."

8

LONDON

TWO DETECTIVES FROM SPECIAL BRANCH were poking through the contents of Zorin's desk, while Arnold Clapworth, the head clerk of LAWS fussed about, putting back in order what they had examined.

"Is this all necessary?" Hartsdale-Smythe asked the small man.

"If you ask me, no," Clapworth said, clucking over a file of letters that had been looked at and not rearranged to suit him.

"It is, sir, I'm sorry to say," said the senior detective, "because there's a question of foul play instead of natural causes."

Nick thought he was seeing one of those late-night television Scotland Yard procedural movies played out before his eyes. The old fashioned furniture in the somewhat dowdy office, the two detectives in dark brown suits, the nervous assistant who might be a suspect, the professorial Hartsdale-Smythe as a superior authority commanding respect but without jurisdiction . . . he checked himself. His mind was playing tricks, probably because he was feeling groggy from the beer and lack of sleep.

Hartsdale-Smythe introduced Nick and Randall to Clapworth as American colleagues, and asked to see the LAWS file on Zimbabwe.

Randall remained in the outer office with the men from Scotland Yard while Clapworth led Nick and Hartsdale-Smythe through the inner office and a conference room to a surprisingly modern, air-conditioned, windowless room that housed a large IBM computer.

Clapworth seemed very proud of "Bertha," and with a rapid punching of the access code upon the keyboard he had the large machine humming. He checked a file card, and then fed Bertha another set of numbers.

"If you'll sit here," Clapworth said, indicating the video display terminal and pushing two chairs over to the screen, "you can read the display . . . unless you'd prefer a copy, which Bertha can print in a short time."

"No," Nick said, "Hartsdale-Smythe has a copy, I think."

The Englishman nodded yes.

Nick had a copy of the report in New York, too, and had glanced through it only a few days before. It seemed so routine and boring that he hadn't paid too much attention to the details. He was more curious at the moment to look at the LAWS operation and the file along with Hartsdale-Smythe to see whether there was anything he had missed, any reason there should be a fuss over this in the corridors of power . . . or were the chiefs just looking for fall guys to take the brunt of the shock waves of guilt and blame with which public opinion would flood their governments.

"Other than the unique lettering of the VDT, I don't see any difference between this and what's in my file . . .. " He broke off in mid sentence as the screen flashed . . .

ADDENDUM ADDENDUM: TERRORIST ACTIVITY
CONCLUSION SEMINAR DISCUSSIONS PROFESSORS
MILLERTON, THIGPEN, ZORIN.
NO ATTEMPT WILL BE MADE ON PART OF LEFT ELEMENTS
TO DISRUPT THE NORMAL PROGRESS OF GOVERNMENT AS
THE PRESENT ADMINISTRATION INCLUDES ALL PREVIOUSLY
DISSIDENT ELEMENTS. POSSIBILITY EXISTS FOR INTENSE
POLITICAL RIVALRY AND PARLIAMENTARY MANEUVERS TO
CAUSE STALEMATE OVER KEY DEVELOPMENT ISSUES. KANANGA
DISSIDENTS IN ARMY A POSSIBLE PROBLEM IN FUTURE.
ANTICIPATE DANGER WILL COME FROM THE RIGHT. LARGELY
WHITE. DISPLAYS GREAT DISSATISFACTION WITH BLACK
RULE. APPROX. 1500 EMIGRATING PER MONTH, MOST TO S.
AFRICA, REMAINDER TO ENGLAND. HARD CORE ANTI BLACK
ELEMENTS DEEMED RESPONSIBLE FOR BOMBING OF PUBLIC
BUILDING IN SALISBURY. FARMER KILLED BY RAIDING

PARTY OF BLACKS WAS KNOWN TO BE MILITANT. FORMER
PRIME MINISTER TREVOR JONES PUBLICLY DISAVOWS ANY
CONNECTION BUT SUGGESTIONS THAT S. AFRICAN BOSS
FINANCIAL SUPPORT AVAILABLE.
PANEL'S OPINION IS THAT MAXIMUM DESTABILIZATION WILL
DEVELOP FROM CAMPAIGN OF TERRORISM ACCOMPANIED BY
ASSASSINATION OF KEY POLITICAL LEADER. DEATH OF JONES,
UMGAWE, KANANGA, WOULD FOMENT RENEWED CIVIL WAR.
CLEAREST OPTION FOR TERRORISTS IS ABDUCTION AND
ASSASSINATION OF KANANGA. WOULD CAUSE REPRISALS
AGAINST WHITES, REBELLION OF MATABELE AGAINST
SHONA, EXODUS OF REMAINING WHITES AND IMPOSITION
OF MARTIAL LAW BY PRESIDENT UMGAWE, RESULTING
IN INSTITUTIONALIZING AUTHORITARIAN GOVERNMENT,
AS UMGAWE UNLIKELY TO RELINQUISH CONTROL ONCE
ESTABLISHED. KANANGA'S DEATH KEY ELEMENT. EFFECT
WOULD BE TOTAL OUSTING OF WHITES, DETERIORATION OF
LIBERAL MODES, ESTABLISHMENT OF ONE PARTY STATE,
EROSION OF USA-GB INFLUENCE, OPENING TO USSR IN
TRADE RELATION
SUBMITTED RESPECTFULLY 15 MAY 1982
AT REQUEST OF USCIA CONTACT AGENT VAN NESS

"You know about this addendum, John, don't you?" Nick fumed
when he read the last line. He got up and paced back and forth in
the small room as Bertha hummed and closed herself down after
the transmission. Suddenly it was silent.

"I asked if you know about this, John?" he repeated. "Not until
early this morning," Hartsdale-Smythe said.

"I was here when Arnold Clapworth opened the message, and
I learned about it then."

"You're sure?"

The Englishman's expression darkened. "It's I who should be up
in arms, Burns, not you. Your CIA chum Scalzio was having you on.
They knew, and they used LAWS, stuck their finger in the same pie."

"That's hard to believe. Scalzio's a mean SOB, but he wouldn't try to fake something like this. I'd have his ass in a sling."

"Who, then, is Van Ness?"

"Call that assistant . . . what's his name?"

"Clapworth. Arnold Clapworth."

"I REMEMBER HIM very well, indeed, sir," Clapworth answered. His voice trembled and beads of perspiration popped up on his prematurely balding scalp. His pasty indoor pallor turned even grayer with Hartsdale-Smythe's questions.

"Was he American?" Nick asked.

"As apple pie, as they say," Clapworth chortled nervously, his thin fingers fluttering.

"What did he look like?"

"Tall, stylish blond hair, blue eyes, handsome in a rugged way, wore a light colored suit both times I saw him and very expensive Italian slip-on shoes."

"You're very observant," Nick said.

Clapworth's pallor grew red suddenly as he blushed and laughed nervously.

"Could you identify him from a picture?"

"Immediately!" Clapworth said. "He had met with Doctor Zorin about half a year ago and had paid him one thousand pounds for additional work to be done. Then I heard Zorin summarizing the information for him on the telephone a month or six weeks later. About a month ago Van Ness appeared at the office, demanded a printout of the LAWS report, paid Zorin twenty-five pounds for it, and was gone."

"One unusual thing, though," Clapworth continued, "both times he paid in cash. Usually we have to bill our clients and then wait. Dr. Zorin always complained about that."

"Oh, and Arnold . . .," Hartsdale-Smythe said after he told the slightly trembling man that he could go, "nothing about this to anyone, do you understand?"

He nodded acquiescence.

"You're sure that the man who came here is not the man who is waiting for me in the outer office?" Nick asked Clapworth.

"Absolutely. I never saw him before."

When the little man had closed the door. Nick said, "How did he remember Van Ness in such detail? You have to train people to be able do that."

"Not his kind," said Hartsdale-Smythe . . . one eye winking slowly. "If a man is handsome and well groomed enough, the Clapworths of the world remember," said the rumpled head of Ml6. "You'd better watch out, Burns."

"Are you trying to tell me something, John?" Nick asked, smiling.

"Me?" Hartsdale-Smythe laughed hard. "This your version of comic relief? I'm a happily divorced man."

HARTSDALE-SMYTHE EXCUSED himself and left Nick to consider the new information.

If the agency really was pulling a fast one and the LAWS report got out, they were up the proverbial creek, not only without a paddle, but without a boat as well. The addendum was damaging because it suggested clearly that if any one wanted to truly throw Zimbabwe into chaos, then they should follow the report as though it was a game plan . . .and guess who would be clearly seen as the planners? It would be truly an "international incident" because the British would blame the Americans for a unilateral undertaking because the CIA had authorized the additional study.

A few minutes later Nick left the computer room, and he and Randall departed the LAWS office.

"There's something we're missing here, Eliot," Nick said as the younger man opened the door to the street, "and I can't see what it is . . . something that doesn't fit."

Randall didn't know about the material that had been added to the LAWS report . . . Nick told him.

"They wouldn't do that," Randall said. "If the Company wanted something like that they would run it themselves, and keep it under very tight wraps. Even you wouldn't get to see it unless they wanted to go operational with it, and then only if Defense was also about to pull a rabbit out of their hat."

"Unfortunate choice of metaphor."

"But that is it, isn't it?"

"Out of the hat . . . the White Rabbit?"

"Yeah, I mean, if you look at the whole picture in a pattern, the terrorists seem like an ad hoc group, almost designed from this LAWS plan rather than leading up to it."

"I'm not sure what you mean, Eliot."

They crossed the street stood talking in front of the steps leading up to St. Johns.

"It's as if the rabbit was pulled out of a hat, a sleight of hand with the purpose of making everyone look bad."

"You mean that the terrorists don't have any political aim?

"Certainly not like the Red Brigade . . . they have no program, no manifestos," Randall came back."

"How do you read their demands?"

"Money . . . and the release of prisoners."

"Nothing else?"

"No."

"And conditions being met, Kananga is set free?" Nick asked.

"If they're for real, and are trying to milk and embarrass the government in Harare, yes . . . if not, they act out the LAWS speculation as though it was a strategy because the ransom and prisoner release is just a ruse . . . it kind of legitimizes their actions."

"Legitimizes?" Nick asked.

They both stopped talking for a moment as some tourists came down the church steps.

Across the street in front of the LAWS headquarters, Hartsdale-Smythe was getting into his car. He waved from the back seat as the driver rounded the corner, as though they were casual business acquaintances. Just another business meeting, more money to be spent. Oh, and a couple of odd deaths thrown in for good measure.

"That's what terrorists do, sir, I don't have to tell you " Randall continued as Hartsdale-Smythe's Rover sped away. "They bring governments to their knees, show their power, take the money and run . . . or whatever else they demand."

"Only when the demands are met," Nick said, "that's the kicker, isn't it?"

"Explain, sir."

"If the money's paid, the prisoners are let go, and Kananga is free."

"Right. But, what if it all doesn't matter. If all of this . . . even the incidents of action in Zimbabwe, are only a ruse, a smokescreen?"

"They don't want the money?" Nick was beginning to feel light-headed. *Why should he be asking Randall this, and not the reverse?* He couldn't quite follow Randall's reasoning, although it sounded clever . . . perhaps too much so.

"The money is a red herring."

"Red herrings, white rabbits . . . this is getting to be a regular zoo."

Randall forced a laugh, "Listen, just for another sec."

"That's your limit."

"Okay. My case is that Kananga is going to be done in, no matter what. Because, the plot works backwards, like an Agatha Christie mystery."

"But we're not in a novel," Nick objected. "This is real."

"But you do see how it fits?" Eliot asked.

Nick nodded his head.

"This scenario puts everyone at everyone else's throat and creates chaos."

"So who stands to benefit from that?" Nick questioned. "Not Trevor Jones, not Umgawe, not Kananga's people."

"Maybe the last. They have a martyr, and then someone up and coming in their group moves into position. They've created another Lumumba incident. We look like the villains, and they come up as the persecuted minority."

"It would be a great catapult in the Third World. You've got to look at who is on the make in Kananga's camp," Nick suggested. "But at this point it seems to be too much like a Procrustean bed . . . you're chopping the facts short or stretching them to fit your framework. Maybe we just don't know enough."

"Like what?" Randall challenged.

"Like why Goldstein was killed, or what the Company connection is, or who is paying White Rabbit."

"Well, it was a good reach for the brass ring," Randall sounded disappointed.

"I'm not throwing out what you said, Eliot. Just saying that there aren't yet all the ingredients in the mix. Keep stirring though."

"There's something else," Randall said. "This hot shot mercenary . . . why would he get mixed into this batter. That's the biggest lump."

Nick looked at the church behind them. "Enough," he said. "My brain's addled for the moment. Let's go see what's going on inside here . . . and Eliot?"

Randall looked at him quizzically.

"Don't talk for a while. I've got a headache."

THE RENOVATED CHURCH was a jewel of English Baroque style, a miniature St. Paul's and what Nick liked about it was that it was still being used, albeit not for religious purposes, but as though it was merely part of everyone's daily life. There was no special fuss made over either St. John's antiquity, or that the illustrious Thomas Archer had built it.

While Nick and Eliot had been talking just outside, a chamber orchestra and chorus could be heard rehearsing Bach's Magnificat in D, accompanied by the bellowing of the conductor who abused his musicians as though they were total incompetents. He had something to shout over the ongoing music at every other measure. It had sounded fine to Nick.

"I wonder when they're giving the performance," he said in an undertone to Randall, who looked at him as though he were mad. What could have been running through the young man's mind about his chief who in the midst of a serious mission, stopped to listen to an orchestra rehearse and to admire a beautiful building. And to think of going to a concert no less. Nick wondered if he was slipping.

Time was when his life was work, work and more work. He had perfected his own craft by shutting out the world. There wasn't enough time, except for the job, and some sex, and a little friendship, although lately, he had combined the last two. Since he had been booted upstairs from the Paris post to New York, and then his good friend Eric had gone to Paris with Odette, he had only seen them seven or eight times. He had no other friends.

Now that he had no need of an official cover, he didn't even attend public functions behind a mask, and he often felt the world was closing in. Music was one opening in the densely woven fabric of his life, his random collecting of art and artifacts another.

"ALL RIGHT, ENOUGH ALREADY!" the conductor shouted very un-English-like with a broad New York accent. "Let's break for lunch. Be back at three o'clock sharp."

Nick glanced at his watch. He relented and set it five hours ahead. It was just after one o'clock. "Sounds like a good idea to me," he said to Randall. "How about a walk along the Embankment towards the Tate? I need some air and exercise. We'll talk on the way."

Randall, no doubt thinking that his master spy boss was entirely out of his tree, had a question in his eyes, but followed.

The plane trees in Victoria Tower Gardens and along Millbank created a deep green shade over the strollers who ventured away from the tour buses parked near Westminster Abbey to photograph the "natives" on lawn chairs or benches in the little park. Cameras were as plentiful as the tulips and daffodils. A group of Japanese stood listening to their tour guide, nodding their heads and smiling intently, while one man taped the lecture on a large SONY.

"Ever want to be just a tourist, Eliot?"

"You mean walk around with a camera and plaid shorts taking pictures of everything? No thanks!"

"I don't mean that, obviously," Nick said. "Just to have the sense that there's nothing to be done but to enjoy what you see, amuse yourself, delight the eyes and ears with new things to look at . . . to be ordinary?"

"Not too much," answered the younger man. "I get my fill of the ordinary from my family." He reached into his jacket pocket and fished out an envelope with writing on the back. "How's that for ordinary?" He showed Nick the writing. It was a shopping list headed, 'at Commissary:

Uncle Ben's Rice
Marlboro's
Scotch
Pampers 6 boxes
Beech Nut Infant Apple Sauce, sugarless
1 case Pepto-Bismol

Nick stopped reading and handed the list back to Randall. "I get lists, too . . ."

"You could drown in it," said the younger man.

"You could also swim," Nick answered.

He looked at Randall as they walked along. The younger man's tall, lanky frame, his dark hair, not yet beginning to go grey as Nick's was, and mostly his intensity, the need to get the job done right and shine in his own eyes and his superior's — all reminded Nick of himself fifteen years ago . . . or more. What would have happened to his own career if Phyllis, the soft-spoken Connecticut country girl he had married after college, hadn't died along with the baby son he had wanted so badly? He reminded himself to send an Easter card to her parents, the once a year touching of the scar tissue of the past. Would he have been like Randall, carrying around shopping lists of things to buy in the bargain-ladened commissary? Would he have felt the same sense of engulfment? And would he have gotten to the position he was in now if he had a family tagging along, hostages to fortune to worry about? He had entered the arena unencumbered, in circumstances that made him weep, but he had gained from them his absolute mobility. And here he was riding free, fulfilled by a successful career at its height, . . . or was he? Lately, he was moody and depressing thoughts were bothering him.

"I guess there's always a pension to look forward to," Randall said.

This was the ultimate rationale of government service gone sour?

"You looking forward to your retirement or mine?" Nick asked.

124

"Um . . . uh. Well," the younger man stammered, embarrassed and flushing red. "Mine. I meant that there's some future security for a man with a family if he sticks it out to the end."

Security? Was that the end of the road for a man with a family to worry over? "I thought you joined us for the adventure and intrigue, Eliot? Foreign parts, mysterious women in cloche hats. Men in trench coats boarding the Orient Express?"

"Some of that hangs over from adolescence, I suppose," Randall said, "but the black and white and the vivid colors have all become a general grey. It has its moments though!"

"Like now?"

Randall nodded, looking a bit sheepish.

They crossed the road to walk nearer the Thames. An apple-green barge loaded with bricks floated by. Lunch-hour lovers strolled arm-in-arm.

Nick felt that there was always the potential for a sudden shift in the wind . . . a chance encounter. Could he have responded to those occasions during the Paris years if he hadn't been free of any responsibilities other than his work?

Randall probably did feel stuck. Nick felt sorry for him with his lists, but envied him at the same time. At least the young man had something to work for, a goal, other lives he was responsible for. Nick had only a better job, a nice woman who gave him enough space, and a collection of valuable art and artifacts. *Pension indeed!*

They had reached the steps of the Tate Gallery. "Lunch?" Nick asked. "I remember a relatively decent cafeteria downstairs."

Again Randall looked at him as though he was mad, and he was about to say something when a beeper made some noises from the depths of his coat.

"The office," he said. "Think there's a telephone inside?"

TOAD IN THE HOLE and two cups of tea — it wasn't much of a lunch, but it took care of Nick's sudden craving for institutional food, the taste of English sausage, and the unique background smells of lard and pine disinfectant only found in cafeterias.

He didn't bother to explain to Randall, who probably had enough to think about just with his boss's other peculiarities without adding another jot.

Something else was preoccupying him anyway, "Why didn't Goldstein say he had pictures?"

"Maybe he thought that he'd score *un grand coup* and convince all of us what a master spy he was," Nick said.

"What for?"

"A promotion . . . a full time job carrying out deeds of romantic derring do . . . all that trench coat, Orient Express stuff we talked about a while ago."

"He was a damned fool," Randall said.

"If only our dreams and fantasies about our lives could always be in Technicolor on a big screen with background music playing . . . but if they aren't . . . or hardly ever. Unfortunately Goldstein was the kind of guy who wanted it that way. I'd never hire a guy like that for more than leg work, because he's too unstable. Romantics like that need illusions of power and importance, and have half-assed Promethean illusions that they are saviors, but they are just one peck of the eagle away from failure. We can't use romantics in this business, Eliot. Remember that if you hire someone."

And that, Nick thought, *is why Randall was stuck with a shopping list and I have a steady mistress and the paraphernalia of an amateur collector.*

"Save romance for the boudoir." he added.

"Cynical," Randall said

"Cynicism is the last refuge of the idealist," Nick quoted from somewhere. "Who said that?"

Randall didn't know.

The beeper that had earlier taken Randall to the telephone had brought a message from John Hartsdale-Smythe. The MI6 chief wanted Nick to meet him in a small mews only a few blocks from the Tate.

They had some time to kill, and Nick joked, "Come on Eliot, let's get some culture," as he led Randall upstairs to the galleries.

There were the Constables and the Monets, without which no visit to London was complete.

Half an hour later as they were looking at Lewis Carroll's original manuscript for the Alice story, a picture the author had drawn of the White Rabbit brought Nick back to the workaday world. "By the way, don't say anything to Hartsdale-Smythe about the photos, not until we have a chance review them."

Randall looked surprised.

"Does Macy's tell Gimbel's?" Nick asked.

"But I didn't think we were in competition with . . .."

Nick smiled. There was a lot Eliot had to learn.

"I DID THINK IT rather peculiar," the short, gray-haired woman was saying to Hartsdale-Smythe, when Nick and Eliot arrived at Ponsonby Mews on foot. The Englishman introduced them as American colleagues.

"Please, Mrs. Smigley, tell these gentlemen what you told me."

Mrs. Smigley wiped her hands on her long white apron, adjusted her eyeglasses that had slipped down her nose and said: "Like I said, these two gentlemen came to me two months ago in response to an advert I put in the newspaper about renting the garage and they paid me two months in advance. I never saw them again, even though they said they'd be back to pay me for April. So this morning, what with it already being the fourth of the month and all, I went to check if they was still using the place and I saw two cars in here that shouldn't be here. So I went back to the house to get a pencil and paper to leave them a note about paying the rent and taking one of the cars out. When I came back to put the note on the windscreen I saw that gun on the seat of the gray car. Then I called the police."

"Did it strike you as unusual, Mrs. Smigley," Nick asked, "that one of the cars was a taxi?"

"Not at all, sir. A lot of the taxi men what owns their own vehicles and lives in the suburbs keep their taxis here in London and drive in in their regular cars and change vehicles. My sister rents her garage to a man who does . . .."

"Yes, we understand that, Mrs. Smigley," Hartsdale Smythe cut her off in mid-sentence, "Is there anything else you remember?"

"Well, no sir, not exactly. You see there's no entrance to the house from the garage, you have to walk around the back here, so I don't get back here too often."

"But you did sometimes? "

"Oh my . . . well . . . yes from time to time, just like to see what was doing. I would open the garage door and take a peep." She seemed embarrassed by her admission of nosiness, reddened slightly and patted her tightly-pinned grey hair as though checking for errant strands.

"And . . .?" asked Hartsdale-Smythe sounding peremptory. He then placed a cigarette in his holder, but didn't light it.

"The other day . . . last Thursday, or maybe it was Wednesday . . . I took a peek in here and saw a mail van instead of the taxi."

"Wasn't that strange?" the Englishman demanded, "and shouldn't you have notified the police then?"

"The thought did pass my mind, sir, but then again it wasn't my affair . . . maybe Mr. Smith . . . that was the gentleman who rented the garage, maybe he bought it at an auction . . . they do sell used ones you know, and people turn them into camping caravans, and so on. My brother Ralph, in fact . . . .."

"Thank you, Mrs. Smigley," Hartsdale-Smythe interrupted her again before she could launch the tale. He lit his cigarette, and then said, "Do you realize that the mail van, the taxi, and the Opel were stolen vehicles, and that you could be held as an accessory to the crime . . . a very serious charge?"

Mrs. Smigley paled sharply, and she began to cry, "Oh no sir . . . I swear, I knew nothing about that. Oh please don't, I'll lose my job if that happens. You mustn't!"

"Don't you own this house?" Randall asked.

"Oh no," Mrs. Smigley answered, wiping her eyes with the bottom of her apron. "No sir, I'm only the housekeeper."

"And the owner?"

"Mr. Burke, Jonathan Burke. He's away just now."

"And you rent the garage?"

"Oh, he don't mind, sir, seeing as it doesn't connect to the house, and now that the children is grown and finished with school. Mrs. Burke went back home and they have no car in London, so I pick up some extra shillings, you see, to add to me own money. That's all."

"It's common with absent landlords to allow that," Hartsdale-Smythe said.

Mrs. Smigley nodded, "My sister Rose . . . ."

"Where are the Burkes now?" Nick asked, cutting off the coming tale.

"Oh he's a government official over in Africa, you see. Rhodesia. They've got a new name for it, but I still call it Rhodesia."

Nick, Hartsdale-Smythe and Randall all looked at each other.

"Is Mr. Burke a black man?" asked Hartsdale-Smythe.

"I daresay no!" answered Mrs. Smigley, "no, he's as white as my apron. A real Englishman. And my family has worked for his family for two generations. My mother before me. . . ."

"What does he do over in Zimbabwe?" Nick asked.

Mrs. Smigley drew herself up: "He's the Minister of Finance, just as he was when that Mr. Jones ran the government. I was there once you know. Mrs. Burke paid for me to spend my holiday . . . ."

"Thank you, Mrs. Smigley." Hartsdale-Smythe prevented her from going on. "Just stay where we can reach you."

"Oh, I've no place to go," she said, "I'll be right here. And . . . you won't tell the Burkes about this, will you, Inspector?"

"I may have to," Hartsdale-Smythe said, "but if, as you say, that you have done nothing wrong . . . then you have nothing to fear."

"But stolen cars, sir . . . they'll think me a hazard to have about!"

"I doubt that, Mrs. Smigley, I doubt that," Hartsdale Smythe said. "That will be all for now," he added, dismissing her. "When my men finish here, they'll remove the vehicles and lock up. Call me immediately if the renters contact you."

She grasped the business card he held out to her, and patting her hair and wiping her eyes, she walked towards the end of the mews and disappeared around the corner of the last house.

HARTSDALE-SMYTHE'S OFFICE, in an anonymous looking corridor in Whitehall, bore a resemblance to its inhabitant. The floors, tables and chairs and desk were littered with papers, reports, books, computer printouts and the various other paraphernalia of bureaucracy.

The Englishman cleared two chairs of reports marked "Top Secret" by piling all the papers on the floor in the corner, and waited to flop into the chair behind a metal desk until Nick and Randall were seated.

"Would you say that I am cooperating with you in this investigation?" he asked.

"Of course," Nick answered.

"I brought you to that mews garage just as soon as we knew of it. . .."

"What's the point?" Nick cut in.

"I think you're not playing cricket with me," the rumpled Englishman said, and without waiting for the look of surprise that crossed Nick's face to disappear, he continued, "because, you see, I know about the photographs."

"What photographs?" Randall said.

Hartsdale-Smythe took a cigarette from his box and placed it in the holder, and tossed the match into an ashtray full of similar matches and butts.

"I'll pretend I didn't hear that, Randall, so we won't start off-side."

"How do you know about photos?" Nick asked.

"One of the tour bus drivers who was at the scene came forward this morning or rather the information got to me this morning. He had noted the license plates of the taxi and the Opel and reported them to the police the other day . . . but when he saw Goldstein's picture in Sunday's papers he recognized him as the man he had seen taking photographs at the time of the kidnapping. I've just put two numbers together gentlemen, and assume that you have the photos."

"Or the killers took them!" Nick offered.

Hartsdale-Smythe smiled wanly, shaking his head. "No," he said, "I'd hazard that Goldstein brought them to a laboratory before anything else — he wanted to create a sensation — and then he probably went to your boys at the embassy."

Nick's mind churned with possibilities — *was the rumpled Englishman telling the truth, that he guessed skillfully, or did he have a contact in Technical Services over at the American Consulate? Goldstein had apparently used his agent status to get a quick job of developing the photos from the lab, and Randall, presumably, wouldn't even have known about them, if the dead man had retrieved the pictures himself. Was the Englishman playing poker?* Nick decided not to bluff.

"We haven't even seen the pictures yet, John. In fact, we didn't know about them at all until just before we got your message to meet at the mews."

"Certainly there's no desire to not cooperate," Randall said.

"I'm not saying that there was," Hartsdale-Smythe said, "but I do feel that if we're in the soup together, we sink or swim together, otherwise we're going to be working against each other."

"Agreed," Nick said. "Let's go look at pictures."

MONDAY'S *EVENING STANDARD* had been delivered by the time the three intelligence men arrived at Randall's office. "Terrorist Kidnappers Kill Two More," read the banner headline. The story told about Tadzio Zorin's death from a suspiciously convenient heart attack, and the murder of Goldstein who was reported to have visited Zorin prior to their deaths.

Nick read aloud, ". . . and LAWS, according to the note received from Mr. Zorin, had developed a scenario for the kidnapping of Mr. Kananga at the behest of American and British intelligence. The actual plan, sent to this newspaper by the late Mr. Zorin just prior to his untimely decease, is not, in fact, a detailed plan for a kidnapping, but rather a somewhat academic speculation on the effect of Mr. Kananga's disappearance on his country."

"Well at least they made that clear," Randall said.

"After the damage has been done," Hartsdale-Smythe growled. "Rotters — all they want to do is embarrass the government — Laborite rag!"

131

"Do you think anyone will read that far into the article, or even care?" Randall asked.

Hartsdale-Smythe took the tabloid out of Nick's hands. "Look . . . that bit is in the next to the last paragraph."

"Buried, I'd say," Nick said.

"And so are we," said the Englishman, "if we don't act . . . and soon!"

"What about that 'Official Secrets Act,'" Nick asked.

"We'll get them on the carpet," the Englishman said, "don't you doubt that, but meanwhile the damage has been done."

"Let's look at those photos now, Randall," Hartsdale-Smythe said abruptly.

Randall opened a brown envelope and spread the glossy blowups on the desk. The three men bent over and peered at photographs of Kananga and his aide being escorted into the waiting taxi by the abductors, the tall man in the light suit getting into the grey Opel, and the two cars turning to speed off in the opposite direction.

Goldstein had used a 300 millimeter telescopic lens and the pictures were remarkably clear and close.

"Got a marker?" Nick asked Randall. He took the red felt pen Randall handed him and circled the picture of the tall man walking behind the kidnap victims. "That's curious," he said. "I can't place the face, but it's familiar."

"What?" Randall asked.

"This guy. Do you recognize him?" Nick pointed to the figure sporting aviator-style sunglasses under a smart hat and a large bushy mustache.

Randall shook his head no.

Hartsdale Smythe asked for a magnifying glass, studied the picture then pursed his lips to let out a low, tuneless whistle. He walked to the window and stared out at Belgrave Square.

"One second . . . let's see this other picture," Nick said.

In the photo he held up, the tall man, now seated in the Opel that had turned in the road to head in the opposite direction, was staring directly at the camera that was just a few yards away.

"It doesn't make sense," Hartsdale-Smythe growled from near the window.

"Eliot," Nick said, "get another print of this and take one of the other two white men and go show them to Zorin's assistant at LAWS. Ask him if one of them is the man who came to him from the Company."

Randall seemed unhappy about his marching orders, but said nothing, took the pictures and left.

Hartsdale-Smythe crossed the room from the window, picked up one of the photographs and stared at it through the magnifier once again. "Who are they?"

"I don't really know," Nick said.

"Did Goldstein know?" Hartsdale-Smythe asked.

"I'm sure he didn't," Nick said, "but they must have known he had a connection with OMEGA, and that we'd see the photos he'd taken. That's why the sap got his. If he hadn't gone running with his camera, he'd be alive. Was any film found in the room?"

"Not that I recall," Hartsdale-Srnythe said.

"Photographic equipment?"

"It had all been dumped on the bed," Hartsdale Smythe said, "but Goldstein could have done that himself. It didn't seem unusual."

"It is unusual for a professional level photographer to have no film whatsoever among his equipment, isn't it?"

The Englishman agreed.

Nick put the photographs back into the brown envelope and handed the packet to Hartsdale-Smythe, who removed the negatives and gave them back to Nick, "Here, have your file boys run a check on these characters."

Nick slipped them into his jacket pocket. *Washington would know.*

"Why did you freeze out Randall?" the Englishman asked.

Nick looked gloomily at Hartsdale-Smythe, took out his pipe, and began to fill it slowly from a leather pouch before he answered. He stared, then finally said, "Because we either have the whole thing on backwards, or we've been diddled incredibly."

"And you suspect Randall?" Hartsdale-Smythe asked.

Nick hesitated, then lit the pipe, and from behind the haze he said slowly: "Everybody, John, until I know who. If Goldstein's killers surmise that we have the photos they'll have to adjust, won't they change plans, that is, if they care about positive identification. Let's see if the info surfaces."

"Perhaps they don't care," Hartsdale-Smythe said, coughing.

"Then why'd they eliminate the link to OMEGA if not for the pictures?" Nick asked.

"Poor sod, he served well after all. Carried the flag to glory," the Englishman said sardonically, cleared his throat, dropped into a chair, and lit a cigarette, forgetting to place it in his holder. He went on bitterly, "You know, justice at all costs . . . honor. Sending Tommy off to die for a hunk of rock in the South Atlantic and all that."

Nick remembered the rare coin Gabrielle had given him. "Fiat justitia," he muttered.

"What's that?" the Englishman asked.

"Something about justice "

"Surely you don't belong to that camp?"

"It would be nice to think so," Nick answered.

"Don't try," Hartsdale-Smythe answered, with a snort. "Where's the loo?"

While he was gone Nick put through a call to Gabrielle, reaching her at her apartment. She was tense and irritable, especially after he told her that he couldn't say precisely when he'd be back in New York. Saying that he loved her and missed her made her crankier. He was sorry he had called. So much for generous impulses.

PART TWO

9

HARARE, ZIMBABWE

WHATEVER NIGHTLIFE Harare boasted of took place in the bars, restaurants and cabarets of the major hotels. The most popular of those with the black government crowd was the Meikles with its cavernous lobby and multiple watering spots. It had also been popular with their white predecessors when the city was called Salisbury. Perhaps it was the need to prove majority rule was an idea whose time had come that continued the old hotel's favored status.

Opposite Cecil Square in the center of the city, the Meikles seemed like a magnet to everyone; it was *the* place to be before, after or during the evening. For Max Lumbola, a local legman and general "op" who worked for the Americans, the Meikles bar off the lobby had been promising when he was there earlier, and he hoped it would be even more so later.

At the moment, he was sitting in his car parked behind the rear entrance to the British Embassy, not too far away, the portable transmitter receiver next to him on the front seat crackling with static and an occasional word from Vernon, his counterpart on stake out, who was watching the front entrance.

There had been hardly a passerby to relieve his boredom since ten o'clock as no one lived in this area of office blocks. It was half past eleven now and Max watched the luminous dial of his Japanese watch with impatience. At midnight he'd be relieved and could get to the Meikles in five minutes without traffic.

The woman had said she'd wait for him, and before he had reluctantly left the bar, where the former freedom fighters like himself drank their Lion lager and boasted of their days in the bush, Max had called his wife to say that he was on an all night assignment.

Well, that was one way of looking at it! It wasn't exactly a lie — Nemberton had handed him the first assignment, and Max had given himself the second one.

He looked at the glow on his wrist again. Twenty-five to . . . the relief man should be coming on soon. Max closed his eyes for a second, knowing he shouldn't, but he was unable to resist the weight of his lids. The woman was wearing a soft black dress that evening that made the orange-beige of her small, high breasts stand up like two luscious fruits . . .her round rump stuck out the way he liked. . ..

"Max . . . MAX!" Vernon's voice crackled on the transmitter next to him. It jarred him from his sexy doze.

"Check!" he said into the transceiver, lifting the instrument to his mouth, fully awake now.

"Car cruising here, coming around your side. Light blue Cortina. Two men, white."

"Got it," he answered just as the dim headlights swung around the corner. He slouched lower in the seat and watched the car pass. Because of the way he was sitting he could only see the top of the driver's head.

When the car braked for a left turn that would bring it past the embassy once again, Max called Vernon and told him. "The whole thing is a stupid waste of time. Probably the Brits' own security making a midnight check."

"Never mind," Vernon's hoarse whisper came back, "better than watching the leaves grow."

Max waited, hoping to hear Vernon say the car had continued down the boulevard. *The relief man should be here any minute and the woman with the big rump waited.*

"Turning again," the box crackled.

"Check," Max answered, and slunk down lower in his seat so the headlights wouldn't outline the back of his head above the rear window.

Again the Cortina slowed and turned at the corner to come round the Embassy. *Where the hell were the guards who were supposed to watch this place to begin with? Asleep in their booths, probably.*

Since the bush war ended, Max knew nothing much happened in Harare, except for random attempts to attack Umgawe's residence by hooligans the government called "dissidents." How convenient those guys made it for the government. They set themselves up as disgruntled Kananga supporters and then robbed innocent people in the name of political protest. Max had known those guys in the bush. They were bums then, and were now. He had fought for the fat man himself. But then it was over, and he needed a job. How about the Americans? They paid well. Max didn't care much about politics . . . as long as it wasn't that Marx-Lenin rubbish . . . those guys made him sick, they were so earnest.

The Cortina slid past, slower now, and Max heard the dry hum of the engine as the driver seemed to come inches close to his parked car. He closed his eyes and scrunched lower in the seat, hoping that if they looked in they'd think him just another car dweller, not unusual in Harare, where any number of young working men drawn in from the country by factory jobs owned cars and nothing else.

Cautiously he moved his hand to the glovebox, opened it and closed his fingers around his automatic. He flicked the safety off and lay absolutely still, listening for the slam of a car door or the creak of one opening.

But instead, the sound of the engine passed and as he raised his head to peek over the dashboard he saw the Cortina turn the corner once more towards the front of the British Embassy. *Must be their security boys. Who else?*

He reached for the transceiver. "Vernon," he whispered, unnecessarily.

"Check."

"Coming round again, over."

There was no answer on the walkie talkie and then Vernon, whose post was at the window of a darkened office in a building across from the embassy, whispered urgently: "One of them is getting out . . . package in hand . . . placing it on the steps below the guard booth. Where's the fucking . . .?" Vernon stopped talking and Max heard only the static of the walkie talkie.

Vernon then said, "They're coming round again . . . your tail, Max. I'll call the bomb squad."

"You okay Vern?"

"Yeah. Relief crew should be here in a second. Go!"

Shit, double shit, Max thought as he started the engine. It kicked over and hummed softly. He didn't think the men in the car would hear it. Max didn't turn his lights on, but lay low as before while the Cortina, moving faster this time, buzzed past him. *The woman in the black dress . . . she said her name was Franey . . . funny name . . . maybe she'll wait a while if I don't show. If these guys don't go far I can be back to the Meikles in a half hour, maybe. Harare isn't that big.*

When the taillights of the Cortina disappeared around the corner, Max switched on his dims and shot forward. He wanted some distance, hoped when they got onto a larger road there'd be some other cars he could let get between. Out on Mt. Pleasant Avenue the Cortina headed east through the better suburbs where the whites used to live and out towards the University. A taxi shot across an intersection in front of him, and he hit the brakes hard. Then another car, a Fiat pulled out from a side street and was between him and the Cortina. Max slowed a little and doused his lights. He could still see well enough with the occasional street lamp. He had dropped back a quarter of a mile or so now and could still pick out the Cortina's tail lights up ahead of the Fiat when the road went into a long curve round a wooded tract.

Max pressed hard on the accelerator as the road began to climb, but the small, four-cylinder engine didn't respond too well. *Damn it*, he muttered, as he watched the speedometer drop from eighty kilometers to seventy-five, then seventy. Still dropping. He shifted down to third gear, but could only just barely keep the car climbing at sixty.

Then the road straightened and flattened at the same time. He could see the squarish tail lights of the Fiat a quarter of a mile ahead, but the broad band of the Cortina's lights were nowhere to be seen. With the accelerator to the floor, now that he was on flat ground, the car sped up, and he passed the Fiat quickly. A black man drove with one hand, the other draped over a woman's shoulder.

Max thought of Franey and her round rump. *Is she still waiting for him at the Meikles? Shit on this kind of stuff. I needed an office job . . . that's too much like work.*

He shot ahead of the Fiat and scanned the road ahead. No tail lights . . . and in the clear moonlight on the open plain dotted with dark farmhouses and barns, he could see nothing, no one ahead on the road. *I might have an office job quicker than I think if I flub this assignment.* He'd been warned on the last one he'd blown.

He slowed the car down slightly onto the gravelled verge, turned the steering wheel quickly and spun around across the road to return in the direction he'd come from.

The Cortina could be in any one of these side lanes leading up to the farmhouses, but Max hadn't seen it after they had crested the hill onto the flat high plain. He remembered that there was one road into the wooded tract just before the road flattened. He headed for that, two miles back, his foot holding the accelerator to the floor, pushing the Mini to 100ks — its top speed. The little car rattled and sounded like a coffee grinder.

The turn off was ahead on the left and Max was sweating despite the chilly air coming through the open window. He felt for the automatic, double checked the safety, and then flicked on the headlamps as he turned off the moonlit highway into the wooded lane.

The Cortina was parked at the roadside not more than two hundred yards onto the dirt road, its rear reflectors glinting in the Mini's headlights.

Max pulled up two car lengths behind the car, switched off the engine and then the lights, and after thirty seconds to allow his eyes to grow accustomed to the dark, he eased himself out of the door of his car, the heavy automatic in one hand, electric torch unlit in the other. His crepe-soled ankle boots made hardly a sound on the pebble strewn dirt, but to Max's ears each step sounded like a drum roll.

He could smell the sweat of his body . . . like the war again . . . on night patrol. He had survived by caution. No unnecessary chances. *I do not like this assignment.* He felt for the safety catch with his thumb again. It was off and ready.

No one was in the Cortina. Max looked around before he switched on his electric torch and peered into the car's interior. He opened the front door and was startled when the dome light came on, and was just closing the door when he heard a shuffling sound on the gravel behind him, then there was a sound like a cork being pulled from a wine bottle and then simultaneously . . . he heard the deafening explosion of his automatic and felt a searing pain in he back of his head.

Max's round had gone into the Cortina's upholstery, and a soft-nose .22 bullet cratered his brain as his body jerked convulsively backward onto the dirt road.

"I'll have his piece," said a gruff voice.

"Take him over to his car," another softer voice ordered, then as Max was being dragged, face up, towards the Mini, bent over and pried the .45 from the dead man's sweaty hand.

When the gruff voice returned from Max's car, Van Ness holstered his own weapon underneath his arm, and handed the other man the automatic . . . safety firmly locked, the cartridge clip removed.

FRANEY LOOKED at her watch. Half past twelve already. She guessed that Max had decided to stand her up, so she slid off the bar stool where she had been perched and said to the thin guy who'd been buying her drinks all night, "Let's go . . . my date's canceled."

The thin man had already booked a room upstairs at the Meikles . . . just in case.

U.S. AMBASSADOR WARDEN YOGUN usually liked the Harare posting. He was comfortable with the verbal context because the slogans reminded him of the 1960s "movement." The unity of Black Africa, downtrodden by years of white colonialism and economic oppression, and the themes of the formerly banned African National Congress had now surfaced as legitimate clarion calls in Zimbabwe since the official independence two years ago, and Yogun felt com-

142

fortable with the social sloganeering. President Dalton's appointment of Yogun to Zimbabwe had been astute, and, after Yogun's mouthing off at the United Nations once too often in favor of the PLO, necessary. True, the Israelis had objected to the appointment, but they had no diplomatic accord with Zimbabwe anyway, and Dalton was deaf to their complaint.

Yogun used his nominal skin color to advantage in the post, and liked the way all good things flowed from being identified with the ruling pigment. Even with white women . . . not that he had ever had any difficulty acquiring lovers of all shades before . . . at home, he "wasn't like the rest of them." Here he was, except that one look told you that he wasn't . . . Choate, Yale, Harvard Law, and Brooks Brothers were clearly what had determined his parameters. This was unlike the politician he had just been summoned to visit so early in the morning.

The new nation's president, Matthias Umgawe, had learned his three Rs in a mission school, his philosophy on bivouac in guerrilla camps, and his law in a correspondence course from the jail cell he occupied for ten years.

The American flags on the front fenders of the chauffeured limousine went limp as the car stopped at the gate of the Presidential mansion, fluttered briefly as the driver was waved through the gates by the guards, and collapsed once more as the car stopped at the doorstep.

Yogun's unique sense of his own importance also collapsed when he saw British Ambassador Peter Soames' car parked a short distance past the house in the chauffeured waiting area. Yogun had thought the summons to be exclusive; now he felt vaguely one-upped, by both the anticipated presence of the "Baronet" and by his gleaming black Bentley. Warden Yogun would have dearly loved to have the latter and be the former.

If Sir Peter had similar feelings towards Warden Yogun he didn't show them. His impeccable background — Eton, Oxford, service to crown and country, followed in the line of father, grandfather, and great grandfathers tracing a lineage back to Chaucer's day. Devotion to public life was noblesse oblige: his salary he gave to charity, as his West Country estates brought sufficient income for all his needs.

The lanky, silver haired aristocrat rose from his chair as Ambassador Yogun was shown into the Prime Minister's study, and he waited, as he knew was proper, until Umgawe had greeted his second guest, to extend cool fingers in a perfunctory handshake with his American counterpart.

"You are perhaps aware of the reasons for which I asked you to come here at such an early hour," said the Prime Minister, removing his wide eyeglasses and polishing the lenses with a tissue as he stared myopically at the American.

Yogun was. He had called his *chargé d'affaires* as soon as he received the Prime Minister's 6:00 A.M. summons, and learned that there had been a suspected bomb placed on the steps of the British Legation in the small hours of the morning, and that an agency surveillance team had tried to intercept both the package and the droppers. The pursuing agent had not yet reported while the other had been prevented from retrieving the parcel by the British security men who cordoned off the area and called in the bomb squad.

"I am aware that a suspicious package was left at the British Legation last night," he said. It wasn't yet clear where the question was heading and something counseled caution to Yogun.

Umgawe placed his glasses on his dark face. "Yes, that is true," he said touching his long fingers together in front of his face.

He was scholarly looking, intellectual, despite his long years as a guerrilla fighter and blood-drenched revolutionary, thought the American. The man looked small and harmless behind his tortoise frames and huge desk.

"One would have thought it was an explosive device," Umgawe continued, looking over at Sir Peter, with a suggestion of collusion — some shared significance from which the American was excluded.

"Was it?" Yogun asked, keeping his voice level, his tone innocently curious.

"In a way, yes," Umgawe answered, "but see here, and judge for yourself." He leaned over to press a button on a console near his desk.

144

A large television screen across from the ornate mahogany desk lit up and the round face of Jeremiah Kananga grew larger until it filled the screen as a shakily held video camera moved in for a close up. The camera panned across a blank wall to Kananga's right to focus on a television set and a woman's hand reached across the set to turn up the volume, the first sound heard. An electronic fanfare of trumpeting beeps was followed by a carefully modulated voice announcing, "This is the BBC evening news, April 1982. Your newsreader tonight is St. John Whitcomb."

A face came into view, saying, "The whereabouts of the kidnapped diplomat from Zimbabwe . . ."and then the woman's hand reached across and lowered the volume of the television as the hand held camera panned across once more to the face of Jeremiah Kananga speaking —

"People of my country, peace loving democratic peoples everywhere: as you can see I am not harmed and am being treated respectfully by my captors. However, I can assure you without hesitation that they do mean what they say and will not balk at carrying out their intentions if their demands are not met. They are highly disciplined soldiers, if my experience as a former commander of our own freedom fighters does not deceive me, and they will carry out their objectives without remorse.

"Now, while my own existence is worth no more and no less than any other man in the eyes of God on the day of divine judgment, I do sincerely believe that it is in no small part through my own efforts and personal sacrifice that our nation has achieved its long sought and even longer deserved freedom and independence. I feel that I must be allowed to serve my country until God chooses that I do so no longer, not until a group of men whose power is arbitrary and reinforced by weaponry chooses.

"The men who captured me are not concerned about rebuilding our long suffering country so that it takes its

145

rightful place as a leader among African nations. Their motives and actions are mercenary — for gain. They cannot be considered traitors because they have no allegiance to any cause but their own.

"On the other hand, there are those in our great country who are daily betraying the revolution for which we all sacrificed in blood. They will sell us as slaves to the highest bidder if people like myself, who have no greater goal than to preserve our nation's freedom, are not around to halt the perfidious masquerade. Traitors must be dealt with severely.

"I appeal to you, therefore, freedom loving people of Zimbabwe and everywhere, to do what is necessary to set me free from captivity, so that I may return to my beloved homeland and my rightful place among those who guard it from betrayal from within."

The camera backed away from Kananga's face that had filled the screen and now showed his aide, Joseph, sitting next to the kidnapped leader, a glum expression on his face.

Then the screen flickered and went dark.

Prime Minister Umgawe reached over and pressed a button on the console, and turned to the two diplomats across the desk from him, "Did you find that edifying?"

"Extraordinary," said Sir Peter.

Sir Peter removed a gold cigarette case from his pocket, caught a warning look in Yogun's eye, and slipped the case back into his jacket. President Umgawe, a large part of whose country's revenue came from the sale of tobacco, disapproved of smoking. Yogun was amazed at the panache with which the British diplomat didn't even let the near blunder register on his smooth facade — even the man's steel blue eyes showed nothing.

"Kananga doesn't lose a moment of campaigning, even when his life is on the line," Yogun said, rushing into the breach.

"Do you think his life is on the line?" asked Sir Peter. "He seemed remarkably diffident, even opportunistic. Always the politician."

"Yes," said Umgawe, removing his glasses once again to polish them needlessly.

Yogun wasn't sure what the P. M. was saying "yes" to — his own observation or Sir Peter's. It was just like the aristocratic to-the-man-or-born type to allude to politics as though it was something soiled, and Yogun, who had not exactly struggled to his present position but had nevertheless used the route of party politics to achieve status, resented the remark, and thought it blithely insensitive, more so because Umgawe was ever the politician, and had overcome far more than Yogun to get where he was.

Yogun's father, a chauffeur for an old-line Atlanta family named Jordan, had married their cook whose grandparents had once been slaves on the Jordan plantation. Fortunately, Mr. Jordan, the descendant of those slave holders, had taken a liking to young Warden, paid for his education in the best northern private school, seen to it that the boy was accepted to Yale, his own Alma Mater, and had paid for his law school tuition. Mr. Jordan had said it was the least he could do to expiate for the sins of his fathers. But the boy didn't care too much. He shut his eyes to causes and opened them to results.

"Nevertheless," said the P. M. polishing his eye glasses yet again and staring at the diplomats absentmindedly, "I do not see how we have a way out of this, unless Mr. Kananga is rescued alive in short order, because I am afraid that the captors mean what they say . . . and I — we — cannot afford to take that risk."

"If he is harmed . . .." Yogun started to say.

"I think we should call their bluff," Sir Peter interrupted.

"I can't chance that," Umgawe said. "The country will be in turmoil if it perceives that I didn't do what was necessary to save him. There'll be more of what happened over the weekend!"

A former brigade leader of Kananga's guerrilla army had led a group of armed men to the cattle ranch of one of the white minority leaders because he was convinced that White Rabbit used the place as a base, and had gone in with guns blazing. He had no proof but his own suspicions, no cause but his own hatred, and had killed the farmer and seriously wounded several of the ranch hands. Umgawe had imprisoned the perpetrators, but it wasn't a move calculated to add to his own popularity.

"As a gesture of friendship and sympathy," Yogun said, "my government is willing to arrange quietly for the money to be paid . . .."

"And we oppose that capitulation to terrorism," Sir Peter said. "You never know where that leads. Take a stand against them."

"Like the Charge of the Light Brigade?" asked Yogun.

"There is something to be said, Ambassador Yogun, to standing up for principle," said Sir Peter.

Yogun seethed at the put-down from the high and mighty colonialist snob with his built-in obsolete values. But he was interrupted by an aide entering the room with a wheeled cart of coffee, tea and pastries.

"Some breakfast gentlemen? I realize how early it is," said Umgawe.

The aide filled the cups, passed freshly baked pastries, and left silently after Umgawe had whispered something to him.

Yogun was still holding his half-emptied second cup of coffee when the aide returned with a corrugated carton.

"I think you should be aware," the Prime Minister said to his guests, "that I am not basing my concern on air . . . White Rabbit *will* do as it says."

He then motioned to the tunic-clad servant who approached the two seated diplomats with the cardboard box, having opened the fold over top.

"This is the box with the 'bomb,' about which you have been informed, that was left on the steps of the British Embassy last night. Look at its contents.

Both diplomats leaned forward to peer into the carton.

Sir Peter turned aside quickly, his well-controlled features suddenly distorted.

For a moment Warden Yogun just stared, and then he felt the coffee he had just drunk rising from his stomach faster than he could control it. The cup in his hands tottered and fell onto his trousers, but he hardly noticed as he grabbed for his pocket handkerchief and held it to his mouth to catch the explosion of vomit.

Nesting on a heap of crumpled newspaper, tightly sealed in a large plastic bag, a face leered at them, its eyes wide open, its teeth showing in a bloody grin. The severed head of Joseph, Kananga's aide and bodyguard, gave the lie to both speculation and diplomatic skill.

A smile without amusement crossed Umgawe's face as he removed his eyeglasses, and standing, turned his back toward his guests to stare out the window at the carpet-like lawn beyond the broad French doors.

"Fucking savages," Yogun muttered, as the image of the severed head came flashing before his eyes and a another wave of nausea flooded his chest.

"They come in every shape, size and color," Sir Peter replied. He inhaled deeply on his cigarette, feeling the nicotine rush with pleasure, after his hour of deprivation in the Prime Minister's company. "You don't think it's an African exclusive, do you," he asked the American diplomat.

Yogun looked puzzled by Sir Peter's question, then shook his head.

They were riding in Sir Peter's Bentley, following the wide tree-lined avenue along the park.

Sir Peter had offered Yogun a lift. . . a chance to chat informally," he said, and the Ambassador had accepted. The American's Cadillac followed at a discreet distance.

Yogun glanced at the chauffeur in front of the glass partition and then back at Sir Peter.

"Don't worry," said the Englishman, "it's completely sound proof and we're not wired either if you are concerned."

The American still didn't answer, but put his hand to his mouth, more afraid of the substance that might emerge instead of words.

Sir Peter got the message. "You need a drink," he half ordered, half asked, and without waiting for Yogun's response pressed a lever in front of him and pulled a concealed bar from the paneled wood compartment that housed it.

"Bourbon, if I remember correctly," he said and half filled a tumbler with Jack Daniels, and handed it to the American. He then poured some scotch for himself. "A bit early for both of us," Sir. Peter said affably, "but I think we deserve it."

Yogun downed his whiskey in a single gulp.

Sir Peter sipped. He was enjoying Yogun's vulnerability, a characteristic the man covered very well with that chip on his shoulder, always on the offensive as though by seeking out any threat, he could brow beat it into submission. But underneath all the bravado the Englishman suspected there was a big baby who prided himself on being 'streetwise' as the Americans said, but had in reality, a very limited range of experience. In thirty years in the diplomatic service, Sir Peter had seen the type before. He was sure that Yogun had hardly ever seen a dead body . . . perhaps as a gussied up corpse at a funeral, but not the stinking, torn flesh of battlefields, of terrorist bombings and auto crashes.

"Umgawe," he said, "understands the messages in that box better than we do."

"Meaning what?" Yogun asked. The whiskey had seared aggressively down his gullet, met the nausea halfway and beat it back . . . he was beginning to feel better. "Meaning what?" Yogun sounded cocky once more. The chip had returned to his shoulder.

Sir Peter regretted seeing the human side so quickly suppressed.

"Meaning that decapitation was reserved for traitors, spies, enemy agents . . . and Kananga's Matabele warrior forebearers practiced it, not Umgawe's pastoral Shona cattle-raising traders.

Yogun cocked his head at the Englishman, eyebrows raised, "Anthropologically very interesting. What does it have to do with the present?" he asked.

They were cruising slowly past large houses with well tended gardens. Nannies pushed infants in prams along the carefully swept sidewalks. An open truck loaded with fruits and vegetables was parked at a corner; housewives and cooks were buying produce from a wizened little black man with a wisp of beard who rushed around filling string shopping bags, weighing purchases, and collecting money.

Then a traffic light ahead changed and the Bentley rolled on, the American's car directly behind.

As far as Yogun was concerned, this was a civilized country, and the savagery he had referred to was the work of those damned bloody terrorists — the white trash of White Rabbit. He then realized that he had given Sir Peter the impression that he thought the blacks were savages.

Sir Peter went on, "The killing suggests,that the aide, Joseph, was employed by Umgawe to keep tabs on Kananga and was found out."

"Found out by whom . . . Kananga?, asked Yogun. "How could a man who is a prisoner himself even have the capability of such a thing. No, no, no. It's those terrorist bastards showing that they mean business and saying that this is what they'll do to Kananga if the money isn't paid."

Yogun wondered why the Englishman was being so obtuse . . . over subtle, as though he didn't see the forest for the trees.

"Why should the kidnappers care where Joseph's loyalties lay, or whether he was a double agent for Umgawe or not?" Sir Peter asked. He finished the scotch in his glass and put it down on the bar.

"Perhaps Joseph was working for them and they wanted to be rid of the evidence, so they eliminated him and made it look like a tribal vendetta . . . to really throw the fat in the fire," Yogun answered.

"I hadn't thought of that," Sir Peter said softly, looking away from the American at the green suburb sliding by. Not too subtle this Yogun, he had missed the point, the hint of collusion between Kananga and White Rabbit. "Umgawe didn't show you the note?" the Englishman said without turning.

Yogun was puzzled. "What note?"

"It was in the box. A crudely printed thing that said if the English hadn't abdicated responsibility by turning Rhodesia over to a bunch of bloody savages, then White Rabbit wouldn't be necessary. I'm rather concerned about that in Umgawe's hands."

Yogun replied, "I think that he has his hands full at the moment so that you needn't worry about the inflammatory garbage from racist thugs . . . it's cheap enough, and plentiful . . .."

"In South Africa," Sir Peter interrupted, "and it used to be here, before the big white exodus. But not now."

"A reversion to type," Yogun said.

"Nevertheless," Sir Peter trailed off. *Why is the American so obtuse . . . almost by design ? What besides political preferment got you to the ambassadorial level in America? Not that all of his own countrymen in the service were such outstanding examples of diplomatic sagacity, but at least, those who weren't usually had the sense to keep their mouths shut. Yogun wears his ignorance and crassness as though it was a badge of honor.*

The American was waiting for him to go on.

"Nevertheless," Sir Peter said again, "think of the uses Umgawe can put that note to if he wants. It could become the justification for a bloody retaliation against whites . . . Kenya, the Mau Mau . . . all over."

"But that was different," Yogun said. "That was before the blacks in Kenya had any power. Here . . . .."

"Here it could spark general revenge, and get rid of the rest of the whites in a hurry. A few dozen dead and the rest will go. What an opportunity!"

Yogun glared at Sir Peter angrily. "You seem to have very little faith in the kind of self determination your government has preached."

"I have very little faith in opportunistic politicians," Sir Peter said, "and the entire episode, from the kidnapping to this latest death, seems custom tailored for Umgawe."

"You think he's behind this?" Yogun was incredulous. He hoped his voice and the expression on his face conveyed his disdain for Sir Peter's insinuations. He wasn't going to discuss this any further with the god-damned snooty racist.

"It suits his purposes, doesn't it?

"Offing his rivals?"

"If you insist on putting it that way, it's not unheard of."

"Next thing you'll remind me of is Patrice Lumumba . . . and then what we did to Allende."

"The list could be elaborated at will," Sir Peter said, "and without necessarily keeping it an exclusively American pastime. We English have had our own little *peccadilloes*."

"That diminutive helps tide you over, does it?" Yogun asked angrily. "Just a mishap, an unfortunate circumstance. Well, I'm afraid, Sir Peter, that I can't treat the life and death of anyone, let alone a leader of his people, as a petty disturbance, a pesty buzzing fly to be slapped down."

Sir Peter believed that there was no room in diplomacy for the moral outrage of any diplomat. That was a private affair. Even in the disguise of privacy, such as this little *tête-à-tête*, there was no room for the personal. But confrontation was not the style of either Sir Peter's generation or his nation. His American colleague had been reared on it, it seemed, from what he knew of Ambassador Yogun's rise to public prominence. In the black power movement of the 1960s he starred with his talent for finding an issue he could defend while bringing notoriety to himself.

"That's all beside the point, Ambassador Yogun. The point is that Umgawe benefits from Kananga's disappearance so long as Kananga doesn't become a martyr. And if he should . . . it would be much better if Kananga was murdered by white racists rather than by anyone else. Don't think that Umgawe doesn't know that my government backed Kananga. He can make an awful lot of mileage from this situation if he's clever enough."

"And you don't think that Kananga's life is important, either in political or real terms?" Yogun asked, simmering with anger.

"I'm not dealing with the moral issue."

"Perhaps you ought to."

"That's not what I'm paid for, to be a philosopher or a judge."

"What *are* you dealing with then?" asked the American.

Sir Peter removed his half-lens eyeglasses from his nose and polished them with a silk handkerchief that had been carelessly stuck in his jacket breast pocket, and said "As someone described your own Stokely Carmichael some years ago, he is a man with a following of fifty blacks and five thousand reporters. That, *mutatis mutandis,* is the way I feel about Joshua Kananga."

The Bentley arrived at the American Embassy and the Marine guard, recognizing the car and seeing Ambassador Yogun's driver directly behind, waved them through. The Bentley drove up the circular driveway and stopped at the broad limestone steps leading up to the main entrance.

"Thanks for the drink," Yogun said to Sir Peter.

"By the way," said the Englishman as Yogun exited the car, "what were your shadows doing around the British Embassy last night anyway?"

The American registered surprise, then shrugged his shoulders and held his hands out from his sides as though to say "Beats me!" He then stepped away from the Bentley and, without turning to face Sir Peter again, bounded up the stairs. He was seething with rage at the Englishman's lordly arrogance, and knew that he had lost his cool, and as a result his response hadn't come off as well as he might have hoped . . . that made him even angrier.

Protocol be damned, he thought when he stopped at the door of the CIA Station Chief's office, knocked once and walked in without waiting for a reply.

Philip Nemberton was sitting at his desk going through some mail and cables that had been waiting for him when he arrived ten minutes earlier.

"Nemberton, who authorized surveillance on the British Legation?"

"Langley," said the intelligence officer, who quickly stood, surprised by both the sudden entrance of the Ambassador and his question. He was in his mid-forties, wore clear plastic-rimmed eyeglasses and had thinning, sandy colored hair. Beads of sweat stood out like pimples on his pink scalp.

"Why wasn't I informed?" the Ambassador asked, infuriated. "Do you know what sort of embarrassment you people create for me? Why only just now . . .."

"You were informed, sir!"

" I was with the British ambassador," Yogun yelled at Nemberton, ignoring the reply, "and he asked me point blank about that surveillance . . . what the hell was I supposed to answer him?"

"The report was on your desk two days ago," said Nemberton.

"I saw no such thing," shouted the Ambassador.

"We sent it," Nemberton responded, mopping his brow with a red bandana.

"Well, then my secretary never showed it to me," Yogun said. Turning to the door, he gripped the knob, and twisted it hard . . . it was stuck.

"Why don't you get this damned thing fixed?" he asked.

"Yes, sir," said Nemberton.

"There's going to be hell to pay around here," Yogun muttered as he finally succeeded in throwing the door open.

"Hell to pay," he said again as he stomped down the corridor towards his own office. He brushed past the secretary, slammed the door to the inner sanctum behind him, and reached for his private phone to call Maggie Groves, Sir Peter's private secretary.

Yogun thought of her as the best lay in town, and he needed something more than food for lunch. Besides, he could pick her brain about what her boss, "the Baronet," was really up to with his la-di-da accent and all that bullshit.

Halfway through dialing, Yogun remembered that Maggie was away on vacation, and slammed the phone into its cradle. He thought of her creamy white, soft thighs and the pink nipples of her heavy breasts. *Pity.* His very beautiful, but very brown, wife would have to do. She expected him for lunch anyway. Play that one by ear. Then he remembered the stewardess from the British Airways flight the other day. She said she'd be at the Meikles for a few days. He reached for the telephone, already grinning with anticipation.

10

HARARE, ZIMBABWE

ON THE HIGHVELDT — the flat upland southern African plateau surrounding Harare — the dawn was spectacular. The entire eastern horizon began to glow while a deep amber band of light pushed up against the clear black of the night sky. Overhead, the constellations Nick hadn't seen in years sparkled clear and unfamiliar, and across the tarmac towards the terminal, beyond the ugly, fluorescent-blue lights of the boxy concrete 1950s-style building, the shapes of camel thorn, jacaranda and eucalyptus trees were silhouetted against the brightening eastern sky. A spectrum of color was spreading from the orange disk of the rising sun to the retreating indigo of the night.

Nick hesitated for a moment, and took several deep breaths to clear his head of the flat, filtered air of the plane. His tongue was fuzzy from too much tobacco, and he had a slight hangover from the brandy the first class steward had poured like water. Eleven hours on the British Airways 747 from London had given his clothes, his hair, his skin the inevitable stale ozone smell, and he wanted to shower and change clothes.

"Purpose of visit?" asked the immigration officer, thumbing through Nick's diplomatic passport, examining all the stamped and visaed pages one by one while a long line of people waited. There were just two inspectors for a planeload of close to four hundred. "Welcome to Zimbabwe" read a big sign where the passengers entered the immigration area. Next to it a large picture of Matthias Umgawe smiled benevolently down on the arrivers.

"Official business at my embassy," Nick said, smiling professionally. He knew that entering and leaving African countries was inevitably difficult, as it was in Latin America . . . an opportunity for petty officialdom to swagger and exercise its authority. A family of Indians, the women in saris and the men in rumpled business suits, was having a particularly difficult time with the immigration officer at the adjacent window. Traditionally the shopkeepers of Africa with their dark, pungent and high-priced general stores or *dukas* in the remotest villages, the Indians were hated and envied, for their clannishness, their foreignness, and their miserly thrift.

"How long will you be in Zimbabwe?"

"No more than a week."

"You are certain?" the immigration officer asked sternly.

"Pretty sure."

"I'll put you down for two," he said, "just in case. This way you won't have to go through the trouble of an extension if you need it."

"Thank you," Nick said, surprised. "You are very kind."

"I like your country," the man said. "Some don't . . . but I do. Perhaps one day I will travel there."

Nick said he hoped the man would do so, picked up his two-suit carry-on and walked towards the customs and currency control.

"You can't enter the country without a paid return ticket," Nick heard the immigration officer at the next window say loudly to the Indian woman. She looked confused, tired and ready to cry.

Nick walked on to customs where the inspector insisted that he open his fold-over bag, and then proceeded to look at and finger every handkerchief and doubled-up pair of socks probing for contraband. Satisfied that Nick's shaving brush contained no diamonds and asking for the fourth time whether Nick was sure he had nothing to declare, the inspector stamped the form and waved him on.

When he declared the seven hundred American dollars he had in his wallet at currency control, a young woman with closely-cropped, densely-curled hair, who looked as if she had just been awakened to come on duty, said that he should be sure to save all receipts for expenditures and currency exchanges.

He was finally cleared and welcomed to Zimbabwe. The procedures had taken more than an hour, and Nick was one of the lucky ones who had carried his baggage aboard the flight. Most of the others who had passed through the wringer ahead of him were still waiting for their luggage to arrive so that they could begin to clear customs.

"Wonderful incentive for tourists," he complained to Phil Nemberton, who was waiting for him in the lobby, and approached as Nick crossed towards the taxi rank. He had never met Nemberton, but the CIA Station chief had walked towards Nick with certainty.

Nemberton drove rapidly along the two-lane, macadam highway leading into town, without saying very much.

Nick watched the dry, flat landscape flit past. Early commuters were waiting on street corners for the buses into town and work, and children in school uniforms were walking in groups of twos and threes.

Nemberton broke the silence, "Day starts early here."

The white stucco houses with corrugated tin roofs, and the palm trees in the gardens reminded Nick of South America except that there the roofs were clay tile but the scale seemed the same. He hadn't really done much travelling in the past ten years, since being kicked upstairs into the Director's slot, and he missed it — missed the sense of anticipation on a mission to an unfamiliar place, missed the anonymity he preferred to cloak himself in rather than the visiting fireman treatment.

"Colonial heritage, I suppose," the CIA man continued, "start early, get the most out of your men before the heat gets too intense."

"Does it get so hot here?"

"Only in Spring . . . October especially . . . they call it the 'suicide' month. Humidity builds up until you can't stand it."

Nick wound down the window of the embassy motor-pool Ford several inches and let the cool, dry air blow into his face. The slight acrid odor of woodsmoke carried into the car along with a fresh tint of the aromatic weeds that grew year round on the Highveldt. The sun, stronger now, was no longer subtle in the sky, and blazed into their eyes. The landscape was dry brown-green, with scrubby growth, parched earth.

"Not enough rain this year," said Nemberton, "hard on the farmers and ranchers. Crops failing, cattle dying, all that. Bad times for the government." Nemberton put on dark sun-glasses for the glare. "The ambassador is driving me nuts, sir, over this situation," he said quickly, turning his head quickly to gauge Nick's reaction, and then back to the road.

"How so?"

"Came screaming into my office yesterday about the tags we put on the Brits, saying he hadn't been informed, which he was but didn't read. Then, later in the day, when we got the news that one of our tags bought it when he had attached himself to the package droppers, Ambassador Yogun was furious because he said I was going to cause a scandal for him. He told me to cease all surveillance."

"He can't do that," Nick said.

They were approaching the central business district of Harare. Nemberton slowed for a traffic light, stopped. There were no other cars at the intersection. A policeman on a motorcycle pulled up alongside them, looked into the car, saluted, and then gunned his machine through the red light, indicating to Nemberton that he should do likewise.

"You just keep everything in place, and in fact, I want to know more about Mr. Yogun's movements as well . . .."

"Doctor Yogun," Nemberton corrected. "He was given an honorary degree by the university here, and now he insists on being called . . .."

Nick smiled. "Whatever . . . and I want an ear on his phones as well."

"He'll have my ass in a sling," Nemberton said.

"I'm in charge of this operation," Nick answered firmly. He wanted to know just what that clown was up to, and wasn't ready to have him queer any deal by undue interference.

"All chiefs and no Indians," Nemberton muttered.

"It's too important," Nick said. "We can't have amateurs messing up our work with their hysteria, whatever their own intentions might be."

The CIA man nodded.

He pulled up in front of the Meikles Hotel.

As the doorman opened the car door and called a porter, Nick told Nemberton he wanted to take a quick shower and change. He suggested Nemberton have some breakfast and wait.

Twenty minutes later he rejoined the station chief who was sitting in the coffee shop working his way through a pile of newspapers.

"They do a great English breakfast . . . kidneys, the works," Nemberton said.

"Not today," Nick answered. He took some fruit from the buffet, poured some yogurt over it, and asked the waiter for coffee. Even the acidic taste of the African beans was better than the swill on the flight. English coffee could drive you to tea. Anyway the whole purpose of breakfast was his first pipe of the day, which he filled and lit while the waiter cleared the dishes and poured a second cup of the pungent brew.

"We managed to keep the package drop on the Brits and the death of our man out of the papers. But Umgawe has all the data," Nemberton said.

Nick nodded approval. He liked this guy. Seemed a bit timid at first, but was really quite business like and professional underneath the blandness.

Nemberton went on to tell Nick about the tape, the head, the note, and the White Rabbit marker dropped onto his agent's body.

"Does Umgawe know about the last?"

"Has to, his police found it."

"How did you find out?"

"I have my assets."

"Do you have any with White Rabbit?" Nick asked.

Nemberton looked surprised. "You think we're running them?" he asked.

"It had occurred to me."

"Absolutely not . . . why should we?"

"Destabilize a pro-Marxist government . . . you know, the Allende bit all over again."

"Not us," Nemberton protested, "we're really clean on this one.

"Anybody in-house," Nick continued, "DIA or the Brits maybe?"

"Not that I know or heard of."

He sounded sincere, but Nick wanted more.

"Can you make contact with White Rabbit?"

Nemberton looked surprised. "Why?"

Nick didn't answer. He fished a pipe cleaner from his pocket and ran it through the stem of the smoldering briar to pick up some moisture.

"Can you?"

"We're not really that well wired here now. When Anthony Trevor-Jones was running the show, a couple of years back, we had it all locked up. But since independence . . .the network's been closed down. We're just getting started all over again."

"I want to have a parley . . . without the Yoguns and Soames."

Nemberton thought for a minute. "There's the Reuters guy, Michael Buchanan; he knows everyone. He set up a contact for that poor slob Goldstein . . .maybe . . . ."

"I want to see him."

"I'll arrange it."

Nick called for the check, signed his room number, and stood. "Now I can face 'Doctor' Yogun."

"DO YOU REALIZE what's happening here, Burns?" Ambassador Yogun asked as soon as Nick was seated opposite him across the big mahogany desk.

Nick noticed that he hadn't been asked to sit in the "conference" area, with its two soft sofas facing each other across a glass coffee table. Instead the Ambassador was using his desk as a barrier, his seat at the control center, a reminder of his rank and status. *Pecking order is very important to the insecure.* Nick refused coffee.

"This is an 'escalating crisis situation,'" the Ambassador continued, as if the jargon conferred status. "I just learned that a group of armed Kananga partisans shot up a white ranch the other day and killed the rancher because they thought that White Rabbit was using the place as a staging point, or a base. Don't you see where this could lead?"

162

Nick was about to answer that he could, but the Ambassador went on: "It could lead to a war of attrition against the remaining whites; there's every excuse for the hotheads . . . or even for the cooler ones like the Prime Minister, to make gestures but do nothing."

Yogun looked tired, harried, Nick thought.

"No calls!" he screamed at his secretary when the intercom buzzed, and then said, "Okay, put it through," more calmly. "Excuse me," he said to Nick, and smiled as he picked up his private line. "I just thought . . .," he was smooth, almost unctuous, ". . . yes for lunch . . . I had today in mind. Did you have other plans? . . . Good. I'll pick you up. One o'clock okay? . . . See you then. I'm looking forward to it."

He smiled and put down the telephone, "Just one second more," he said to Nick. "Helen," he said into the intercom, "call my wife and tell her I won't be home for lunch . . . that's a sweetheart."

He turned back to Nick, clasped his hands to stop a slight trembling, and his smile vanished as he said "If we don't get Kananga back, Umgawe will have every excuse he needs to really hassle the whites and that's gonna hurt everyone in the long run."

"I can't imagine that you don't think they deserve hassling," Nick said. He wanted to needle this irritating, pompous pain in the ass.

"I don't think that's clever, Mr. Burns, and in any case, I'm not concerned about the hassling, as much as I am about the long range effect on our government's policy. If Umgawe makes this kidnapping into the kind of issue that winds up fanning the flames of resentment into violence, then public opinion around the world will turn against him, in the States especially, and that's gonna make this government seem just as bad as many another in Africa. Hell of a short shrift for an independent black majority established by treaty and a democratic procedure. Those bastards in South Africa will be chortling with pleasure, and their smug I-told-you-so's will justify their holding on to their obscene apartheid more strongly."

Nick stared at a sculpture in polished green serpentine on a credenza behind the Ambassador's desk. It was fabulous beast that shared shoulders with a human head. It had the clarity of a newly discovered mythology, a solid, squat stylizing not unlike the elongated Nigerian tourist art.

"Your perspective seems more global than the State Department's, Dr. Yogun," he said, trying to make sense of the distance between the sculpture's sureness and its owner's shrillness.

"I'm not sure I appreciate the ironic tenor of your remark, Mr. Burns."

"No tenor, no irony, none were intended . . . just an observation."

"Do you find it peculiar that a black man such as me should have a stake in seeing a democratic black republic establish itself as a model for the rest of Africa?"

"Dr. Yogun, I don't find it peculiar at all. If anything, admirable. But I'm not here to judge your attitude, only to move along a single issue . . . namely, how do we get Kananga back here unharmed. We are ready to pay. The British don't want to . . . or not yet. How do you read Umgawe?"

Nick found Yogun tiresome, because he used any opportunity to get up on his soapbox and bray a bit. A split in the man between the person sensitive to fine art and the blowhard, maybe not.

"I don't really care about him, per se; he's just another politician, perhaps more enlightened than most, and, I suspect, less corrupt than Kananga. Don't you see, man . . . it's the chance this government has to make it that I care about, the chance to prove that you don't have to be a little dipshit dependent client state just because you're black Africa, and that the friggin' colonialists and *kaffir* haters south of us are wrong. If the shit hits the fan here they'll have the last laugh and reinforce their Neanderthal practices. But if Umgawe can make this country work, it's a spit in their eye."

"Thank you, Ambassador," Nick said, getting up to leave. He hated being a captive audience for Yogun's speech-making. *This isn't a 'movement' rally in the 1960s; I have a job to do that this yo-yo . . ..* He smiled to himself at the appropriateness of the put down nickname that jumped into his mind.

"You find what I'm trying to tell you amusing, Mr. Burns?" Yogun asked, a tone of sudden suspicion in his voice, the clarity of his political theology clouded by what he thought was a slight on Nick's part.

"No, not at all," Nick answered. "I was thinking of something else. Thank you for your time, but I have a lot to do."

"I hope that you're not going to go into one of those cloak and dagger routines that leave me here with a lot of embarrassing things to explain to the Zimbabweans . . . like these spooks following people about and various dirty tricks?"

Yogun came around to Nick's side of the desk and held out his hand in a sort of conciliatory manner, a slight, wary smile on his lips.

Nick gripped Yogun's hand. *In another context, I might have liked him. Too late.* "I will do no more than I have to do to move this situation along satisfactorily. How, by the way," he continued, "do you read the British ambassador on all this?"

They walked to the massive oak doorway leading out of the Ambassador's office to the secretary's antechamber. There was a vigorous primitive painting on the wall behind Yogun, unsubtle as its owner. He put his hand on the doorknob and held it there.

"I think he's in cahoots with Umgawe to make noise but do nothing. Then if Kananga dies at the terrorists' hands, Umgawe has an excuse to impose martial law, get the army into a mop up action . . . and we know what that means . . . a one-sided civil war, and he'll consolidate his one party state . . . you know he wants to do that, don't you? That's good for the English . . . they think Umgawe's their man." He snorted ". . . but they're wrong, he's . . . well, I'm not sure!"

Nick nodded, saying nothing. *Under the hot headed and ideology spouting exterior there was a good brain in Yogun, but chaotic and too quick off the mark. At least he admitted not knowing something . . . that was a plus.*

"Frankly," continued the Ambassador, "I think that Umgawe cooked up a deal together with Trevor-Jones, and that White Rabbit is nothing more than a ruse for getting Kananga out of the way. How he could have lured Trevor-Jones and the British into such a deal is beyond me, but that's what I think anyway. The whites and the British must think they can work the game better with Umgawe on a clear path sans the obstacle of Kananga. But they'll find out better. Umgawe's just another Stalin. He'll gobble up anyone in his way, after he gets them to do his dirty work."

"Thank you again," Nick said, "I'll keep you posted. Your interpretation of all this is very interesting. I'll have to think about it."

Ambassador Yogun opened the door and beamed a smile for everyone in the outer office to see.

It was an interesting perspective, Nick thought as he walked down the corridor towards Nemberton's office, but more for what it told him about the Ambassador Yogun . . . Dr. Yogun . . . he corrected himself, than for its insight into the situation. To Nick the Ambassador sounded cracked. The wild swings in one direction then another, the conspiratorial perception of everything around him. Nick thought that the Ambassador needed help, if you could do anything about paranoia. And yet, some of what he said was plausible. The real question was what was Yogun's role in all this. His announced suspicions were based on something omitted. Something missing Hell, the man was just crazy . . . then again, he remembered Kissinger once saying that even paranoids had their enemies.

Nemberton was engrossed in some paperwork when Nick knocked on his door and then entered the room without waiting for a response.

"I spoke to Buchanan, the Reuters guy, and he said he'd get back to me by this afternoon. I asked if he could set up a meeting with someone from White Rabbit for tomorrow. Would that be okay?" the station chief asked.

"No problem . . . my dance card is empty," Nick said.

Nemberton returned half a smile. "I received a copy of the Kananga tape," he said.

"Let's see."

Both men turned to the video cassette player.

As the screen went bright, Nick felt the residue of weariness creep up on him. When he was at the command post in New York, he longed for the field, the good old days. And when, rarely, as now, he took on a situation as a personal responsibility, he felt that the world was running away and his own age was catching up with him, slowing him down. Maybe he was just tired from the long flight, the tension of having to deal with that prickly pain Yogun, and feeling it all. Situational. Or was he weary? The difference? He pushed the feelings back into a corner and concentrated on the black face on the flickering screen.

AS THEY RODE OUT to a Harare suburb of modest bungalows, the taxi driver asked Nick, "You know that it is an Indian neighborhood?"

Nick said he didn't.

"Yes. Now that Prime Minister Umgawe has made it illegal for them to send money out of the country, they are buying homes here, not living in the backs of their dirty stores, like mice in the wall. Before, they used to live like paupers and send all of their money home to India. Get rich here, you know, and then take it all away."

"And Umgawe made it different?" Nick asked. "The Indians want to be Zimbabweans now?"

The taxi driver grinned broadly in the rear view mirror, showing a broad fence of large white teeth. "Oh no sah, we don't say that. The Indians cannot be Zimbabweans except maybe the children what is born right here. Only Africans can be Zimbabweans."

"And the whites?"

"Some here long time, sah . . . they another tribe."

So much for liberal ideas of national liberation. The Shona feared the Matabele, the Matabele distrusted the Shona, they both disliked the whites, the whites looked down on the blacks, and they all hated the Indians.

Satisfied that his explanation was complete, the driver said no more until he stopped in front of the address Nick had given him.

Nick walked to the front door and knocked. Soon Neliwe Goldstein opened the front door with a baby in her arms. He was startled to see her beautiful, grieved, black face and hoped he hadn't betrayed his surprise. During their telephone conversation to arrange this meeting, he had assumed that she was white. Her English pronunciation was clipped and British sounding and had none of the singing variations in pitch that came through the speech of her countrymen. Also Nick had thought that perhaps the name Neliwe was Israeli, especially since it was coupled with her husband's last name of Goldstein. Now he chided himself for the clichés of his own thoughts. Racism? Stereotypes? He had thought himself past all that, and it surprised him when he encountered those prejudices in himself.

"I CAN'T GET OVER THE FEELING that somehow the whole thing is my fault," Neliwe said, her face looking drawn and sad. She was young, perhaps twenty-five; her hair was cropped very close to her head; she was small framed. She continued to nurse her baby without any self consciousness, as though Nick wasn't there, or she was talking to another woman.

"William would be alive today if it wasn't for my relationship to Kananga," she said. Behind oversized, tortoise-shell eyeglass frames with lenses tinted in the French style, her eyes looked wet, but she didn't cry.

"I don't think you should blame yourself," Nick said to the young widow of the "travel guide" who had gotten himself in over his head in London and drowned.

"Billy wanted so much to be a success at what he set out to do, don't you know, to vindicate himself to his parents. They didn't forgive him for marrying me, wouldn't come to see the baby .We met as students in England, and then we returned as a married couple." Two tears rolled down from the corners of her eyes. "Now I don't know what I'll do."

Nick thought there was some death benefit due her, but he couldn't say anything. He had told her that he represented Associated Press . . . he had established the cover with their head office years ago, and he knew that the company automatically covered free-lancers who worked for them, and Goldstein was working for the wire service in London. He'd make sure Neliwe received a lump sum from OMEGA . . . paid through AP. She was a hostage to fortune, desperation and grief.

"You said you were related to Kananga?"

"Same clan, a distant relation on my father's side, a third cousin, I think. And when I was younger, in the year I finished school and before I went away to study in England, we were intimate."

The beefy bulk of the old chief and the slight delicate form of this young woman made an odd pairing to Nick as he tried to visualize them.

She looked at his face, it was noncommittal, but she took his lack of response as judgmental.

"It's not all that unusual, you know. It is an honor among our people to have a child chosen especially by the chief. And I was so impressionable then. I joined the ANC . . . probably only because it was banned. I thought I was rejecting the white world. . .and then of course the acceptance and scholarship to Cambridge arrived, and I went there and married William. Here in Zimbabwe, we never would have met . . . there, we fell in love. I suppose I'm a hypocrite after all."

Nick shifted in his chair, uncomfortable with her confidences, not quite knowing how to respond.

"I don't see . . .," he started.

"I'm sorry to burden you," she said. "It's not your concern."

He protested his interest . . . he didn't want her to stop before she completed the story about Kananga, hesitating between avidity and nonchalance. *Why is she pouring this out to me?* Of course, he realized . . . *here was another modern African caught between two worlds and accepted by neither.*

Her husband dead seven thousand miles away, she detached from her family, and with a mixed-race baby who would carry the symbol of indeterminate origins forever, and would be rebuked by black and white alike. Neliwe Goldstein was alone, alienated, with no one to talk to. Nick the "employer" was the only one to bear witness. *Bad job, the whole thing.*

"I am interested," he said.

"You knew him?" she asked.

"Not personally," Nick said. "I knew his work."

169

"His work killed him," she said, "and the only reason he went to London was because he had been such a damned opportunist. He played on my old connection to Jeremiah to ingratiate himself and get 'exclusives,' and when Jeremiah suggested that Billy go to London and promised him exclusive stories to file, Billy thought it was a great opportunity. Besides, his parents are there now, they left here after Independence and I think he wanted to try to make it up with them. He said he'd send for me if it was all right."

The baby had fallen asleep at her breast, and now she stood and carried it towards the door.

"I'll just put him down, Mr. Burns, and return straightaway. Can I get you some coffee or tea?"

He said no, then changed his mind. Rejecting an offer of hospitality was perhaps insulting.

While she was in the kitchen, Nick looked around . . . the room told him nothing important. There were magazines and an old Zenith world band shortwave radio on a small table; unpainted bookshelves were filled with paperbacks — mostly sociology. Posters were tacked to the walls. All advanced graduate student style.

Neliwe returned in a few minutes with a tray and coffee . . . it must have been readied earlier. She found Nick sitting where she had left him. She poured coffee for each of them.

"You see this bracelet?" she asked as she shook a large, silver bracelet carved with what looked like a serpent and an eagle. It was set with colored stones and intricately wrought. "When I went to Jeremiah the first time, he gave me this. It's like a badge of office among us Matabele . . . the symbol of the royal concubine."

Nick nodded befittingly.

"I think it's just so much rubbish," she went on, her expression full of disdain.

"The bracelet itself? That's beautiful," Nick said appreciatively. The collector in him appraised the artifact, the need to possess. A gluttony. The eagle and serpent were stylized, elongated, and pressed together in a symbolic embrace, one of the eagle's wings spread on the serpent's back, the snake coiled loosely over the bird. No threat in it. Rather a mutual union of strength in freedom. Nick knew he had seen something like it before, but couldn't remember where.

"Of course I don't mean the thing itself," Neliwe said. "I mean the idea. You know that Jeremiah thinks he's the rightful heir of the great chiefs. He claims that he's descended from Lobengula himself, and that he has the right to use such royal emblems personally. He's a great man, but he's also a pretender. Just a politician with grand delusions."

Nick took a sip of coffee. It was instant, and not very good.

"Why do you think your connection with Kananga led to William's death?" he pressed, sensing that the moment allowed the question.

"You're very persistent on that," she said, her eyes flashing a moment of anger.

"Just curious," Nick said. "After all, you introduced the idea, not me, Mrs. Goldstein."

He started to get out of his chair, "I'm sorry I bothered you. . .."

"No don't go," she said, reaching out her hand to touch his arm, to prevent him from leaving.

He sat again, not so far back on the seat.

"Jeremiah used Billy, just as he used me, just as he uses everyone," she spat out bitterly. "If I had the courage I would take off this ridiculous totem and throw it away. Except that I must be practical now. I might have to sell it. Such a reminder, but that was another time, and the world was fresher for me, and I was filled with hope. Now there's just this poky little house and no more William; the great hope for black majority rule in my country is being destroyed by the revolution eating its children . . . oh, nothing, Mr. Burns. Nothing." She dropped her eyes to the bare wooden floor.

"How did Kananga use William?"

Nick didn't like sympathetic interrogations; they were harder than the hostile ones. When you allowed feelings for the person to come between you and your purpose, the dynamics changed. You had to relent, miss a point, drop an opportunity to drive home for the truth. Or was he just getting too soft . . . aging and sentimental.

"He told him," she said, head still lowered, practically hissing between her teeth, "that there would be a great story, a super scoop for him if he tagged along. Jeremiah claimed that he'd devised a way of regaining power. And William was such a fool, so greedy for success, that he went. One large ambitious old fool leading a younger, smaller one."

"I see," said Nick, rising from his chair, unimpeded this time.

"Quite a scoop," she said as they began to walk to the front door. "Except Billy didn't get it, he *was* it." A bitter laugh escaped from her lips.

Nick held out his hand, and she grabbed it with both of her hands and held tightly.

"Why are you here, Mr. Burns, really," she asked, her sad eyes boring into his.

"As I told you earlier on the telephone, Mrs. Goldstein, I'm looking into certain circumstances concerning the death of your husband . . . ."

Cutting him off angrily, her voice close to breaking, she asked, "You're from the American government . . . aren't you? And Billy was a spy, wasn't he?"

"Definitely no to both questions," Nick said. "He was a journalist working on a story.. . . and I . . . ."

"Then why in God's name should your government be interested in him?" She sounded as if she were on the verge of hysteria. "Are they?"

"U.S. Ambassador Yogun contacted me, and asked if I would come to see him . . . just to see the whole picture, perhaps," Nick said. *What was Yogun up to?*

"Billy *was* a spy, wasn't he?"

"He was probably a source of information, just as journalists have sources for their work, governments have sources for theirs. That is not spying."

"Then why should anyone want to kill him?"

"That's what we're trying to find out." Nick slipped with the "we," hoped she missed it, and didn't draw attention to it by making a correction. "Did Billy ever tell you what sort of scoop Kananga promised him?"

"No!"

She was emphatic, but Nick sensed she was holding back.

By then, they had walked to the corridor, just inside the front door. Nick looked around at the bare walls, the uncarpeted stairs leading to the second floor, the adjacent dining room with a minimum of unmatched furniture. The emptiness of it all was a condemning sentence. Suddenly, everything seemed pointless. He turned to open the door.

"He called me from London," she said abruptly, hurriedly, as if she wanted to detain him, like a hostess who remembers that she forgot to serve dessert.

"To say what?"

"He sounded so happy, said he was in his hotel working on a great story in which he made all the connections. The men he saw taking Jeremiah away were the same ones he had seen here," Neliwe said breathlessly, her eyes far away, twinkling as she recalled her husband's enthusiasm.

Nick looked puzzled.

She hesitated, then grabbed his hand, "You know that he did an interview with the White Rabbit, don't you?"

"No," Nick said to encourage the rush of words.

"He did . . . but the government controlled newspaper wouldn't print it. They said they didn't want to give terrorists publicity."

"But everyone knows that White Rabbit was responsible for Kananga's kidnapping . . . the terrorists announced it themselves," Nick said.

"I know, but not that White Rabbit is led by an American from the CIA! That was Billy's exclusive. The leader is really the American he interviewed here. Van Ness from the Central Intelligence Agency.

Nick freed his hand, "I've got to go."

"You're from CIA too, aren't you? Just covering up, checking out if I know too much." She was shouting now. "Well, do I? Do you have to kill me too? Why don't you, you assassin?"

"I'm not!"

She looked at him disbelievingly, then lowered her voice. "I thought you had come here to shoot me too." A little nervous laugh.

"What for? You've got the wrong TV show," Nick said.

She was terrified. The world he inhabited didn't touch too many ordinary lives directly, but when it did, the mark was indelible.

"Well, what are you then?"

"I told you — I'm from Associated Press. I'm sort of an insurance investigator," he answered, and stepped into the street.

As he walked toward the corner in search of a taxi, aware of Neliwe Goldstein's angry, hurt, pretty face on the doorstep behind him, he wished that he was.

"THE GOOD NEWS," said Nemberton, when Nick walked into his office, "is that Mike Buchanan has worked it out for you to talk to White Rabbit tomorrow."

"Himself?"

"Buchanan did it . . . yeah . . . no help."

"No that's not what I mean. Do I get to see the chief bunny?"

"I don't really know, sir," Nemberton answered. "I doubt it, because he shuns publicity. Probably you'll see his factotum who uses the trade name Van Ness. Goldstein said he's supposed to be an American."

"What's your line on him."

"Very little. That's the bad news. I told you, we're piss poor in assets since independence. Just beginning to develop some in the government and the police now . . . .."

"You're not leveling with me, Nemberton."

The other man looked pale. He removed his glasses and blinked.

"You're right. We have no lines on White Rabbit." He put on his glasses again, and stared at Nick with watery, tired eyes.

Nick lit his pipe, making a cloud of smoke, to give himself some time, and let Nemberton's tension build up.

"Van Ness is yours, not just an asset, but Company, or so I hear," Nick said, nonchalantly taking the pipe out of his mouth and examining it. *Ah the Dunhill was beginning to darken to a very nice rich brown.*

"WHAT?" Nemberton shouted, jumping up. "Who the hell told you that, Goldstein's café Marxist wife?"

"She's a sad woman, Nemberton."

"Let's leave that aspect out, please, sir. I feel for her, I do, young woman left on her own with a small baby and all that. But that story about White Rabbit being Company is bullshit, malarkey, intentional disinformation fed into the press. We don't know the guy. Only that when Goldstein went to have a secret meeting, this "Van Ness" let it drop, and Goldstein thought that he had the story of the century . . . imagined himself another Woodward and Bernstein all in one. Even Buchanan, a hound for good copy, wouldn't print it . . . and nobody else would either."

"Did you lean on them?"

"Who?"

"Editors. Publishers."

"No way. Some of them got to me for verification, and of course I denied it."

"Well you'd do that even if it was true."

Nemberton smiled and sat down. "Sure I would, but this time it was not true. Look, this is a supposedly Marxist government, as the Prime Minister never tires of telling everyone. They'd love to cut our balls off with a sensation like that. But even *they* didn't. It was an out and out lie, and that bastard Van Ness was putting Goldstein on, and the little putz didn't even know it. He came running in to me, and I told him it was a lie, but he thought that if it was true it would make his career as a journalist. So he went ahead and wrote it. Served him right that no one would publish it. I even checked it out with Langley, asked if they were running something out of jurisdiction. They denied."

"It wouldn't be the first time," Nick said. "Desk officers pull stunts like that from time to time . . . and then there are all the other agencies . . . .."

"Including OMEGA?"

Nemberton paused. "Yes," he said finally. "Like Goldstein for example, and it makes life difficult for me. Left hand not knowing and all that. Sorry."

Nick smiled. "Not at all," he said, "that's what OMEGA is supposed to monitor, and I appreciate your difficulties . . . ."

"I'm sure you do, but I had no authority over Goldstein, so I couldn't even order him to drop it. I think it was actually Mike Buchanan who crushed him. Told him it was irresponsible journalism and that he'd land in the soup."

"What's Buchanan's interest?"

"Just an old Africa hand. Been around long enough to have the shit detector highly tuned."

Nemberton stopped, poked around in his drawer and came up with two hard candies. He offered one to Nick who waved it off.

"Since I quit smoking," Nemberton explained. "And I know," he continued, "that Buchanan has an MI6 connection, high grade."

Silence.

Nemberton rolled the candy around in his mouth, clicking it on his teeth.

Nick puffed and relit his pipe. *Was it likely that Goldstein was terminated by Langley or Whitehall because he knew too much? A pawn who stuck his nose into the general's tent. Everyone in this game lies to everyone else and you either accept it as fact or became paranoid. Goldstein was too young, too naive. He probably was caught by the lure, hooked, and then somehow landed. Question was, by which fisherman?*

"He shouldn't have been in," Nemberton said. "A mistake."

"Fine epitaph," Nick said. "'His life was a mistake.'"

Nemberton didn't answer.

"What time do I go with Buchanan tomorrow?"

"He picks you up at the hotel at nine in the morning."

"And what if I verify what Goldstein learned?"

Nemberton grinned. "Nobody'll print it," he said.

Nick decided that he liked Nemberton. "Can I get an overseas call through?"

Nemberton picked up the telephone, asked the switchboard for a priority line and shoved the phone across the desk at Nick.

"Business?"

"Personal . . . don't worry."

"Thanks. I'll go have a cuppa at the canteen."

Nemberton left the room and Nick gave the operator Gabrielle's number in New York.

11

ZIMBABWE
EAST OF HARARE

THE NEXT MORNING Mike Buchanan phoned from the hotel lobby as Nick was breakfasting in his room to say that he was ready to go.

Buchanan's sources had told him that Nick Burns was a big intelligence honcho who ran OMEGA — the super-spook supervisor, so to speak — and he hadn't been comfortable when Phil Nemberton called to ask him for a contact with White Rabbit on Burns' behalf. He owed Nemberton, and wanted to keep him as a quiet asset, but this was a big one and he had about used up his vouchers.

Buchanan was a short, stocky man with wavy grey hair, a mop of it combed back. His eyes twinkled gray-blue mischief. When they shook hands Nick felt the strength of his grip — the stockiness was all muscle, not fat. He was in better physical shape than most of the journalists Nick knew.

"THE OLD BUS RUNS WELL ENOUGH," Buchanan said as he adjusted the sun visor to keep the light out of his eyes. They would be heading east, directly into the sun that was shining brilliantly in a cloudless sky, towards the Mozambique border. "It's the last of the good Peugots — the 504," he continued, "before they went in for the fancy stuff to grab the American market."

Nick opened the car window to let in some of the sweet fresh air to dilute the smell of the particularly foul cigar Buchanan had lit.

About an hour outside of Harare, Nick began to feel the vastness of the highveldt he had only sensed when he first arrived. Large farms went on and on, fields spreading out on both sides of the road from a central compound of a farmhouse, barns and outbuildings.

Some of the compounds were surrounded by high cyclone fences with venomous coiled barbed wire extensions leaning outward at the top. Others had sentry boxes at the gates, huge floodlights with bulletproof plastic deflectors, or sandbagged machine gun pits . . . all to assure security for some, while others seemed to have no defensive aspect whatever.

Small African villages — called *kraals* — dotted the landscape. He spotted women and children moving about doing their morning chores. Two young women, balancing large bundles of cut reeds on their heads, waved with shy smiles on their faces as the car passed.

Mike told Nick that he was planning to go back to England shortly "for some R and R — whiskey that isn't imported, and to get laid in earnest."

"No sex out here?"

"Plenty," Buchanan said laughing aloud in the easy camaraderie they had established within minutes after they met, "but it's mostly bored wives from the diplomatic corps, or from the old Rhodesian business crowd. Had a couple of wonderful black girlfriends when I first came out about four years ago, but after the sex and the good times there wasn't much left. Y'know, there's always the cultural thing. It's inevitable. And I decided that I'm too old to spend my time proving anything. No, I'm going to try my hand at the head office . . . see if sitting on my fanny and calling shots from London will do, find a nice English girl with a warm heart and a big bum, and settle down next to her. Go to the office in the morning, come home to snuggle and grow tomatoes. Give everything a try, I say."

He tossed a soggy dark-brown stogie butt out of the window and reached for a fresh one in the box he kept next to the driver's seat.

"I'll miss these," he said, "cheap as dirt here, local stuff."

"You can ship the car though," Nick said.

"I'll sure hate to give it up, but I'm not that sentimental," Buchanan answered, lighting a fresh cigar. "And I can get a lot of money for the old girl here."

The road flicked by as they drove along in silence, as each man pulled back into himself for the moment after an hour of non-stop talk. Buchanan was a man who instinctively seemed to understand the rhythm of things.

NICK ALREADY HAD what Buchanan wanted. Gabrielle fit the bill — big heart and everything else, comforting, forgiving. Yesterday, on the crackling overseas telephone, she was terribly apologetic for her snappishness when he had called from London. He heard her soft accented voice from ten thousand miles away. Pregnant. Tests. Upset because she had always wanted a baby. Knew it was impossible and that he would say no, so she had an appointment for an abortion. Long conversations with her shrink. Wanted to tell Nick first, she decided.

"Don't worry, it'll be all right by the time you get back," Gabrielle said during the phone call.

Business as usual.

"This is all wrong for us."

She couldn't be selfish.

And Nick had stood there in Nemberton's office feeling hemmed in, pressed, staring out the window at the row of jacarandas swaying in the wind on the street below, the fat leaves of the flowering aloes, the marine guard inside the front gate of the embassy grounds chatting with the two black policemen outside, and he felt his eyes get wet. *Big, tough guy.* Glad he was alone in the station chief's office and knowing that the conversation was probably being recorded. He hadn't cared . . .

"You don't do anything yet, love, until I get back," he heard himself saying.

"Why not, Cheri? It's happened before."

He hadn't known.

"Well this time is different . . . maybe," he'd said.

"Not if it hurts *us*!"

"It's different . . .you wait for me," he shouted into the phone. "I'll be back next week."

"I love you, Nick," Gabrielle said.

The crackling was getting worse; he could hardly hear her.

181

He promised to call her in two days, and she promised to cancel her appointment at the abortion clinic. He put the telephone down, wiped his face with a tissue from the box on Nemberton's desk and went to join the station chief in the canteen. He needed both the coffee and the briefing, but barely tasted the former and hardly heard the latter.

NICK STARED AT THE ROAD, a single lane of new macadam with wide dirt shoulders. When two vehicles approached each other they both had to ease their outer wheels onto the shoulders to pass. Double lanes existed only at curves, and parts where there was no room for the dirt shoulder there was a lay-by with a sign that said "Give Way" at either end of the single lane. Right of way went to whichever vehicle was in the passage at the time.

". . . think I'll miss Africa," Buchanan was saying, "because I've spent the last seventeen years out here, in one place or another."

"You like it." It was a statement, not a question.

"I love the room, the expansiveness. You can be what you want to be out here, but you pay the price. 'The worm in a turnip thinks the world is a turnip' my old Irish grandmother used to say, and I'm beginning to feel very wormy . . . claustrophobic."

"In all this space?"

"Funny, isn't it?"

"And two-up two-down in a garden suburb with a broad-beamed *hausfrau* and pet tomatoes running amuck, the 8:14 and the 5:19 every day won't be confining?"

Crazy world, and all its people too. Buchanan wanted to be like Randall; Goldstein had wanted to be like Buchanan; Burns wanted to be . . . he didn't know any more . . . *everything all at once and together.*

"Perhaps," Buchanan said, glancing over at Nick and giving his cigar an appreciative chomp as he rolled it from one side of his mouth to the other. "But," he continued, "I'm going to try to leave my work at the office, and lead a normal life. Out here I'm on duty all the time. LOOK!"

Buchanan slowed the car and pointed ahead. A herd of some fifty kudu — small, light-brown antelope — were ambling across the road up ahead. Buchanan edged the Peugot closer, inching along in second gear. Then one of the kudu spotted them approaching, peered nearsightedly at the two men in the grey metal box and leapt across the road with a single bound. In a flurry of springing legs and bobbing white tails held aloft, the rest followed the leader and were hidden by the tall savannah grass in an instant.

"That I'll miss," Buchanan said, as he accelerated and they drove on, "but I'm at the stage in my professional life where I need some regularity. I want to have the time to write the obligatory book on African politics . . . you know, regulation form for foreign correspondents . . . witness to history and all that. And it'll never get done chasing tail around here. Either the female human or antelope variety."

His hearty laugh at his own joke brought a smile to Nick's face as well.

"You find globetrotting to your liking?" Buchanan asked, swerving the car to avoid three vultures pecking at a small dog's carcass on the road's edge. The vultures hardly noticed.

"Oh, I traded that off some years ago for the kind of job you want now . . . office, regular hours, an occasional hot situation to keep the interest up," Nick answered.

"Like it?"

"Not when I think about it for too long."

MIKE BUCHANAN HAD thought about it for too long. The well-established cover as first a correspondent then a bureau chief for the news agency in various parts of east central and southern Africa had served him, and his superiors well, and years back he had even won some coveted journalism awards for his reporting on the mercenaries in the Congo and later, on the Mau Mau situation in Kenya. But all that was the froth on the beer.

The reports he wrote that were read by the fewest people were what Buchanan was really about. His drive to uncover, discover and report critical stories had lost its momentum over the last few years, and he was bone weary grinding out the dull snippets of meaningless information he pulled together on a daily basis and wired to London, so that commuters could glance at their papers in the morning and evening and read of the events they cared little about halfway around the world.

He'd fallen into the whole thing years back when he was a university student and had come out to Kenya during a long holiday to visit with his roommate, the son of a British Army officer stationed there.

Africa captured his interest, especially as he watched the Mau Mau terror take hold among the colonials. Encouraged by his host's father, he wrote a story on the mood among the British officers and sent it, naively, to *The Times*. To his great surprise, their man in Nairobi called him within the week, told him that the paper had taken the story, and if Buchanan would come down to the office, he'd have a check ready.

Buchanan remembered the bureau chief's annoyance at being superseded, but then he offered to take stuff from the young student through the regular channels. So Buchanan became a stringer for *The Times,* and during the month he stayed in Kenya, managed to get two more stories into print, the last with a byline.

What started as a whim blossomed into a career. Buchanan returned after graduation to work as correspondent for *The Guardian*, then *The Times*, and finally as Reuter's bureau chief.

He had covered some of the most important events in Africa — the 1961 assassination of Patrice Lumumba, the Congo crisis during the early 1960s, when the ruling whites declared Rhodesia independent of England in 1965 and then battled insurgents and the world's sanctions for a dozen years before reluctantly giving way to black majority rule in Zimbabwe in 1980, Idi Amin's rise to power in 1971, the Soweto uprising in 1976.

Once he had thought he discerned a pattern in what was happening in the continent, he'd wanted to help; and when approaches were made to him, he'd accepted. Changes were inevitable, but they needed to be directed toward the right goals. Looking back it all seemed chaotic . . . just so much anarchy masquerading as some liberating ism, and the only thing liberated in the longer run was the leadership of the winning side. After a few years of governing, the new leaders always managed to liberate enough wealth from the national coffers and allow it to emigrate to a Swiss bank, so that when their government's power was threatened, as it always was, by those who were waiting their greedy turn at liberation, the former could fall with enough profit to have made the risks worthwhile.

Buchanan was heartily sick of it all; he needed some distance to regain perspective, some time to read and think and perhaps discern a pattern in the carpet once again. He had to get away from Africa, in any event, because some hot stuff was being mishandled and might explode in his face.

"I'VE GOT what's probably a terminal case of Africa-in-the-blood," Buchanan said, slowing down for a stretch of broken pavement, "but I need some distance from it for a while. Maybe I'll miss it, maybe I won't be able to stay away.

"It's a no-win situation," Nick said. "Confining inside, missing something outside."

"Maybe from the outside I can regain the long view, from a distance see the forces at play . . . you know, kind of similar to watching rugby or American football on the tube. You can see the moves, watch the strategy . . .."

"Or at least imagine that you're seeing it," Nick interjected.

"Yeah," Buchanan answered with a sly grin. "But from the scrum line, you'd think that nobody knows what he's doing, except to try to batter the other team's peckers and run off with the pigskin bacon."

NICK KNEW THE VIEW from inside the office windows very well, and sometimes a nameless melancholy would drape its black veil over him as he stood there looking out — like Alexander weeping because there were no more worlds to conquer. All good careers lead to the top . . . if you are good enough as an outside man they take you inside to manage and direct the less able outside men . . .

185

the nature of bureaucracy. Now it was almost ten years since Thad Barnwell retired as director of OMEGA and named Nick his successor. Could he have said no at the time?

He could have but wouldn't. And what if the same thing were offered again? Behind the rationalizations of the man seated next to him were the same questions Nick had asked himself. Except that Buchanan was making that decision at a more advanced age, and probably was really tired of being in the field. Nick had been plucked from the tree before he was really ripe enough.

As he stared out the car window, the landscape of farms having given way to reddish-brown, hilly scrub-land, his mind kept going back to Gabrielle's pregnancy. Had she really wanted to get rid of the baby she was carrying without telling him? *Bullshit*, he told himself. Had I really wanted to remain in the field I would have said so.

Was it parallel? *No!* He knew his reasoning was false. She wanted a family, a baby to nurture, a husband to love, a home to care for. Perfectly normal . . . and he had wanted all that once too . . . before he gave himself the opportunity to think about it all. He had married Phyllis when he was on his first posting in Buenos Aires because it felt right . . . brashly. And then she died along with the baby, something happened inside him, too. The hurt was still there, the tissue under the scar still throbbed with pain when the wind was right.

And then came the grandest reason of all for denial — he couldn't be free to work at a career he coveted with the sword of Damocles hanging over his head. Those hostages to fortune who might be left behind should he come to an untimely end. And he knew, sitting here next to the cigar-chewing Buchanan who guided the old Peugot along the empty flat ribbon of macadam, he knew for the first time that his excuse was transparent. He had said no to Odette, whom he had wanted more than anyone in his life, including even the dead Phyllis — though he felt shame in admitting it. He knew now that he wasn't protecting them at all; he was protecting himself, making himself invulnerable to pain, to loss, to responsibility, to being human. So here he was, an *Übermensch* of his own design — he turned what he had devised to guard him into a soulless suit of armor. Gabrielle was offering him the chance to become human again. Could he take it, was he brave enough? Swords into plowshares.

BUCHANAN SLOWED THE CAR at an intersection and turned onto a side road. At a bus stop by the corner, a man wearing dark trousers and a wrinkled white shirt under a mismatched suit jacket was seated on a bench.

After they had passed the bus stop, Nick noticed that Buchanan was intently watching in the rear view mirror, so he turned to look back just in time to see the man lift a small walkie talkie from under his coat and speak into it.

"We've been announced," Buchanan said.

"You anticipate any difficulty?" Nick asked, drawn out of his reverie.

"Don't see why," Buchanan answered. "Anyway, you and Van Ness speak the same language."

Nick looked at him hard, unsmiling. "Not clear," he said.

"Van Ness is one of yours . . . he should greet you like a long lost relative."

"One of mine?"

"He's an American spook."

"No way."

"Then the left hand doesn't know what the right is doing," Buchanan said, tossing his soggy cigar butt out the window.

"You think that White Rabbit is a *sub rosa* American action?" Nick asked.

"That's what Goldstein picked up, and that's probably why he died," Buchanan answered, slowing the car slightly.

Half a mile ahead on the flat road the forested area thinned out to savannah and Nick could see a large, flat building surrounded by an enormous parking lot. A wire mesh fence separated the whole thing from the road.

"Why would Nemberton or I need you then?" Nick asked. "If we were running White Rabbit, we could have made our own contact."

"For objective verification in the press?" the journalist said.

"Look here, Burns," Buchanan continued, slowing the car to a crawl, "I really don't care who's running these characters. I'm past all that. It's a free for all in the forest out here, and I don't give a shit anymore who wins. There's no principle involved. Sometimes I think that the black Africans were better off before. At least they could focus their resentment on the privileged whites and could put a direction to their hatred. Now they run around popping off each other and nobody's better off, mostly worse. Maybe Trevor Jones was right, maybe the South Africans have it right. I'm not here to judge. I just write my stories, leave out what I can't prove, and avoid trouble if I can."

"I appreciate the favor Buchanan," Nick said, "but if you're so pissed off about the situation, and so convinced that my government is behind all this business, why the hell did you bring me out here?"

He was sure that his voice carried the anger he felt. Buchanan could do or say as he wished, but the cat and mouse stuff irritated Nick and added to the tension unnecessarily.

Buchanan grinned and reached for another cigar in the box next to him. He lit it, blew a cloud of foul reek out the open window and said, "Okay, Burns, I'm sorry for the mouthing off. I suppose I think that Kananga is or was the best hope of this place, and the idea that the Yanks might be offing him in a roundabout way ticks me off. Anyone who can get your ambassador Yogun where he lives is okay by me . . . hats off to Kananga I say."

"Get him about what?"

"About a woman . . . one cocksman outdone by another."

The Peugot was edging along in second gear along the perimeter of the steel fence.

"Ya know what, Burns?" Buchanan asked, "I brought you out here today because I thought that maybe there was a story in it, that I could see that the Yanks were running this show, and even if I didn't print it, I'd know. Just for curiosity like."

"Sorry to disappoint you. What is this place?"

"Hospital that they started to build a year or so before independence, and stopped when the government changed, and was never picked up again. It's needed here, too, to serve the entire area, but it wouldn't do for the advanced thinkers of Umgawe's administration to complete something started by the 'racist-imperialists.' So there's no medical facility within a hundred miles, but ideology triumphs."

They rolled slowly along the steel fence. The grass was very high and weeds had begun to climb the mesh that was torn in a few places wide enough for a man to slip through. At one spot a whole section was cut open and tire tracks had flattened the grass and worn grooves. Somebody had rolled the cut steel halfway back across the opening.

"Locals come and take what they can carry away since the site was abandoned," Buchanan explained.

"Beds went first, then all the plumbing and electric fixtures."

The one story building was built of poured concrete, stuccoed and whitewashed in a style which reminded Nick of 1950's functional American architecture. Nothing soft, nothing to catch the eye. Just a sort of oblong egg carton or cracker box. The concrete was already beginning to show cracks, and whole sections of window including the frame were missing . . . not just the panes, which were curiously unbroken, unlike abandoned buildings in most other places. He supposed that the glass was so valuable to the locals that that particular form of vandalism didn't occur to them. In fact the hospital wasn't vandalized; it was cannibalized. He thought of thatched huts in nearby kraals with casement windows set into their walls. *I wonder what they use the drains and rain gutters for?*

They had reached the front gate of the hospital. It stood open. At the far end of the parking area was a small car. A man lounged against the front fender looking in their direction.

"That your man?"

"Can't tell at this distance," Buchanan said, "got to get closer."

"No don't," Nick said. Something felt wrong to him. "Stop here, please."

The Peugot was about halfway between the gate and the corner of the lot where the small car waited with its lounger.

Nick could see the head of another person inside the car. "Do you mind walking from here?" he asked.

Buchanan shrugged. "All the same to me."

"In that case, would you leave me here, and walk over to them? When you come back alone and tell me it's all clear, we'll drive over."

"Why all the maneuvers?"

"Keeps options open," Nick said.

"You armed?" Buchanan asked.

"Never."

The journalist smiled. "Yeah, you don't have to live in Africa," he said. "There's a Magnum in the compartment under here," he pointed to the tray where the box of cigars lay and sprang the catch to show how the lid opened, "and an Uzi under the seat you're in. Know how they're used?"

"I used to."

"Wish me luck."

"Break a leg," Nick said as Buchanan stepped out of the car.

The newsman turned and looked at him, puzzled for a second, then realized what Nick had said, laughed, and walked toward the other car with a nonchalant swagger.

When Buchanan was halfway across the several hundred yards that separated the two cars, Nick reached under the dashboard to the convenience shelf that held an assortment of junk and pulled out a pair of binoculars. He raised them to his eyes and focused on the other car. Buchanan's back was directly in the line of vision blocking out the man who leaned on the car, but Nick could clearly see the driver inside. Blond, bearded Scandinavian looking. Not the Frenchman he wanted to talk to.

He slid over to the driver's seat for a better view.

It was getting hot in the car, the bright sun reflecting off the concrete surface of the parking lot. He wound open the sun roof so the air flowed freer and the car cooled.

Now he could clearly see the man leaning on the small car without Buchanan's back in the way. Nick raised the binoculars. The man stood erect, moved a few steps towards Buchanan, took off his sunglasses and extended his hand in greeting. Nick felt the muscles in his neck tighten and the tingling sensation run across his jaw — the recognition slammed home before he could put a name to it. Then the name called up from the past flashed across his mind — Volkov . . . Oleg Volkov.

IT WAS A RAINY, COLD, WINTER NIGHT in the American sector of Berlin. On Friedrichstrasse with The Wall just visible behind them, two prisoners stepped out of a similar black sedans that were parked facing each other in the middle of the midnight street. Both walked toward the other car, and as they passed they walked through the beams of the cars' headlights.

Their recognition was confirmed by the awaiting officials.

The young KGB officer stood next to one of the cars, facing his young CIA counterpart across the wet blacktop. He was blond, hatless — he had no mustache then — and sported a fashionable western haircut. He raised his hand to his forehead in a casual salute to the CIA operative. There was arrogance in his gesture, because the Americans had gotten this deal on their own terms . . . this time. "Next time on the other side of The Wall, Nicholas Burns," the man had said, with a slight smirk as he stepped back into his car.

Nick had been stunned for a moment, not by the words, but because they were spoken in English, not the academic German he had expected to hear, and it was flat, unaccented, and with a twang of the Midwest.

Nick learned later that Oleg Volkov had spent three years taking a degree in economics at the University of Chicago before returning to Moscow, and showing up as a junior political officer with the Soviet Mission to the UN, a position with clear affiliation.

East Berlin was his second assignment, and by that time he was up a grade and thought to be trained for political assassination.

Nick had never forgotten that face, and the name had surfaced any number of times over the past twenty years, and almost always in a situation where the Americans were vying with the Soviets for influence . . . and when Oleg Volkov was involved someone always died. He specialized in "wet-operations" or "wet-ops." Blood.

191

NICK WATCHED THE FACE through the binoculars — it was the same arrogant smile, same loose-handed American gesture, the reach for the handshake coming from the shoulder rather than the elbow. *He's a good actor . . . he has become the role.*

Volkov was too smart not to know that Burns recognized him.

Nick's mouth went dry as he realized that he had fallen right into a trap he had created himself! Volkov wasn't going to let him get away. He was too valuable to the opposition. They'd drain every drop of information out of him and then trade him in for some opposite number who had been taken, or maybe some Angolans or Cubans. *This is "the other side of The Wall."* He guessed that he'd be held in Mozambique while interrogated. It was close enough to get to without major problems for them. And with drugs . . . he'd tell them everything, no one could resist. Then he'd wait . . . weeks, months perhaps . . . while a trade was made. Speak of early retirement. He'd be finished in OMEGA, they'd put him out to pasture. Maybe finally Gabrielle would be happy. Gabrielle waiting, the life growing inside her. *Shit!* If only for that he couldn't let them take him.

Buchanan had turned and was walking rapidly back towards Nick smiling, looking for all to see like a man with good news.

Suddenly there was a loud roar of an engine as a double-trailer truck labored up the slight hill fronting the abandoned hospital, its flatbeds loaded with large, precast concrete that looked like foundation supports for a bridge. The truck changed gears as it hove into sight, the huge diesel belching heavy, black smoke, the supercharger whining with labor as the truck headed in the same direction Nick and Buchanan had come from earlier. "Henchard Brothers, Reinforced Concrete Castings, Umtali," Nick could read on the door of the cab.

Using the noise from the truck as cover, Nick started the engine of the Peugot, released the emergency brake, depressed the clutch and ran through the gear positions once. Shifting with his left hand on the right-drive, English market car wasn't going to be easy. No choice. He reached into the glove compartment for the Magnum, quickly checked the clip, slipped off the safety and put it on his lap under his folded jacket.

"White Rabbit couldn't make it," Buchanan said as he reached the door, "but his second, Van Ness, will talk with . . .."

"Get in . . . quickly," Nick shouted over the din.

"You want to drive?" Buchanan asked, looking puzzled. "I told them to meet us in the middle, on foot," he continued while sliding into the passenger seat.

Nick slammed the Peugot into reverse as soon as Buchanan touched down and spun the car in a reverse semi-circle.

"What the hell!" Buchanan yelled.

Nick saw Volkov standing in the shade at the end of the parking lot. He must have realized what his trapped quarry was doing.

The Russian leaped into his car and he and his driver were rolling towards the Peugot as Nick straightened the wheels and accelerated towards the gate.

"Where the fuck are you going, Burns," Buchanan shouted, "are you loony? I thought you wanted to meet these guys . . .."

"Explain later!" Nick yelled over the engine roar as he goosed it up into second then third gear.

"My credibility . . .!" Buchanan said.

"If you want your sweet fanny back in England next week, shut up and make sure the Uzi works," Nick snarled at him. "Look!!!"

Two men wearing bush camouflage had appeared out of nowhere and were closing the gate.

Nick's stomach slid with the car as he cut a sharp right, put the back wheels into a rally-skid turn, braked hard on a sandy patch and double clutched the transmission, pushing the gear lever on the steering column into second.

Buchanan was thrown against the left hand door and almost out of the car as the door swung open. He quickly slammed it closed when Nick straightened out the wheel and began heading back towards Volkov's car coming directly at them.

"Press down the fucking lock," Nick shouted, "and get the goddamned Uzi ready."

Buchanan's face looked drained as he poked under the seat for the weapon.

Over to their right there was a two-foot high concrete barrier that separated the parking area from what was probably to be an ambulance lane running to the back of the hospital. Nick swerved hard to the right again and saw the other car do the same before the driver realized that he couldn't cut the Peugot off and would only hit the concrete ridge straight on if he kept going. It would cost him some time.

Nick grinned. He felt the adrenalin pumping, his reflexes sharpening.

"THE UZI . . ." he yelled at Buchanan, "GET THE UZI!"

"I don't want to shoot anyone!" Buchanan shouted.

"You won't have to," Nick growled, "just get it out and ready."

Buchanan finally pulled the stockless submachine gun from under the seat, and Nick, driving with his left hand, slipped his right hand under the folded jacket on his lap and gripped the Magnum. If Buchanan turned the Uzi on Nick he'd have to kill him. He knew they wanted his ass in one piece and wouldn't do anything except try to disable him, but he still wasn't sure of Buchanan. The set up was too cozy.

In the rearview mirror he saw the other car round the barrier at the end of the lot and straighten out in a line with him.

The edge of the building loomed up.

Nick's finger was on the trigger, the Magnum under the jacket aimed at Buchanan's chest as the journalist slipped the catch on the Uzi, pumped the first round into the chamber and then laid the weapon on his lap facing away from Nick, who swallowed with relief, but kept the pistol where it was.

"What's in back?" Nick asked as they got to the side of the building. He had to decide whether to go behind the structure or hang another right and try to double on the small car and side swipe it.

"Emergency room bay . . . ramp goes out the other side," Buchanan shouted over the whine of gears as Nick slammed the shift down into second and made a sharp left behind the building. At first the sudden dark shadow of the building after the brilliant sunlight out on the open lot obscured everything. Then Nick saw a sand-camouflage-colored troop truck backed up to the bay and two men in berets, boots, and battle fatigues running towards the cab. He floored the accelerator and the Peugot screamed in protest, but moved out quickly, and faster yet as he pressed the lever up to third, jack rabbiting violently as the gears grabbed each other out of sync. He passed the front of the truck before the men reached it, and were screaming towards the other end of the building when Nick glanced at the rearview mirror and saw the little car spin into the driveway behind them, teetering on two wheels.

Buchanan turned his head to look behind. "That fucker's shooting at us . . . I'll kill him." He fired a blast from the Uzi through his window harmlessly chipping the concrete wall racing past.

"Stow it," Nick shouted and he turned his head for a second to see one of the mercenaries aiming a fat-barreled weapon at them.

"TEAR GAS!" he yelled, cranking up his window. "CLOSE YOUR WINDOW AND YOUR EYES AND MOUTH. DON'T BREATHE!!"

He grabbed the sunroof handle and wound it closed just as he heard two clunks of metal on metal as a cannister bounced off the trunk and roof of the Peugot and puffed a belch of the searing gas harmlessly behind them. *Aimed too low.* He saw another puff explode in front of them slightly to the side. He swerved quickly and just avoided the cloud.

Volkov and his driver weren't so lucky; they got the full effect of the three cannisters their comrades had fired, and Nick, turning his head for a split second, saw the little car slow down as it passed the truck, then heard a screech of brakes. But it kept coming on, losing ground rapidly.

Then they were at the corner of the building and the Peugot zipped out of the shadows into the brilliant sunshine of the parking lot.

Nick turned left and stopped the car fifty feet from the driveway along the side of the building. There were no windows above him, just a blank wall. He hoped nobody was on the roof.

"Give me that," he said to the puzzled Buchanan, and grabbed the Uzi, shoved the Magnum into his belt, safety on, and pushed himself up so that he was standing on the seat, head and shoulders through the now wide-open sun roof. He rested the machine gun, aiming low.

As he had expected, the small car nosed out of the ambulance driveway a few seconds later, but going slowly, the two men coughing and rubbing their eyes. Before it had completely cleared the exit ramp Nick opened fire with the Uzi purposely aiming at the concrete. Both heads went down as the burping of the weapon echoed amplified off the side of the building, and Nick whooped gleefully as he saw the tire nearest him flattened like a pancake and the car's engine begin to smoke as a line of holes punctured the hood. Water sprayed through the openings. He dropped into his seat and dropped the gun into the door compartment — *Buchanan didn't know how to use it anyway* — he put the Peugot in gear and started forward.

The unmistakable crunching sound of metal and glass was the next thing they heard.

"Truck rammed the car!" Buchanan said laughing like a kid, and Nick glanced around to see the car pushed farther out of the driveway, its rear end totaled by the heavy steel bumper of the four-ton troop truck, Volkov stumbling out of the ruined car waving his arms wildly and screaming at the men in the truck.

Nick laughed as the Peugot reached the short end of the abandoned hospital. He turned the car, this time without screeching tires, into the wide open parking lot and headed for the gate. His heart pounded wildly.

Other than the fact that he was being hunted like a wild beast wanted for laboratory experiments, he hadn't had so much fun in years.

"Glad you keep your car in good shape," he said to Buchanan as they sped toward the exit across the empty lot.

"No longer," Buchanan shouted.

"It's fine . . . long as it holds up."

"Not the way you drive it, Burns."

"Want to fish or cut bait?" Nick shouted back.

"Don't understand American," Buchanan said.

Nick turned to avoid the concrete barrier he had used for protection a few minutes earlier and was approaching the exit gate when the two guards in fatigues came running towards the speeding car. He aimed directly at them. Neither had a chance to raise his weapon before they had to dive to either side to avoid being hit by the madman behind the wheel. Most drivers, even in crisis, will stop if a body raises itself in front of a vehicle. But not Nick. "Everything's a weapon if used as such," he heard himself repeating from the training manuals he hadn't looked at in twenty years . . . and kept the car moving as the men dove. He then hit the brakes hard, hoisting the Magnum at the same time. If they were going to take him, they probably had orders not to fire. Nick banked on it.

But Buchanan was out of the car first, the Uzi aimed at the men on the ground thirty feet away. His face was red and the veins bulged at his temples and jaws.

Nick stepped out on the driver's side. "Don't shoot," he shouted at Buchanan, "don't shoot." He leveled the heavy pistol at the men on the ground. "DROP WEAPONS AND MOVE!"

They hesitated.

"DO IT!" Nick screamed at them.

The two mercenaries, one African, the other Cuban or Portuguese, left their weapons where they had fallen, sprang to their feet and began backing away.

"Run, RUN you sodden shits," Buchanan yelled, his face distorted with anger.

"Get their weapons, Mike, and hurry," Nick said.

Buchanan ran back to where the automatic rifles lay, grabbed them and hurried back to the car, threw them into the back seat.

Back in the car, Nick steered the Peugot toward the gate. It had been closed with a chain and huge padlock.

"Better I should have killed them," said Buchanan, "at least we'd have the fucking key."

Nick took the Magnum from the door compartment and fired at the lock from a yard's distance. The heavy slug dented the huge brass case and ricocheted away.

"It'll never do it. Shit!" Nick swore.

He had to get moving before Volkov backed the truck out of the driveway and came after them.

"Get in," he said to Buchanan.

"What are you going to do, ram it?"

"If I thought we'd make it, I would," Nick said, reversing the Peugot to a distance of twenty feet from the gate, "but I think we'll just total the car . . . and then we'll be fucked good and proper. Just sit and wait for them to take us."

"What do they want us for?" Buchanan asked, "they had me back there and let me walk!"

"Nothing with you, chum," Nick said. "It's me they want, alive. That's why they're not shooting. But once they get me, they'll probably kill you before you know it."

Buchanan's face blanched. He had been used by those clever bastards.

"Then what the fuck are we sitting around for, find a way, Burns you got us into this by being such a treasure . . . .."

Nick laughed. "Nobody ever called me a treasure before."

"Nobody?"

"You're the first, darling," Nick said.

"Up yours," Buchanan said, unable to stop himself from grinning.

"Promises, promises," Nick said as he saw the tan Army truck coming out from the entrance to the Ambulance ramp. "Shit. They must have reversed and backed down to the emergency bay where they could turn around."

The truck slowed down to pick up the two soldiers who were trotting towards the building and then accelerated towards the Peugot.

"Let's fucking get out of here," Buchanan said, as Nick revved the engine and slipped the Peugot forward.

They were picking up speed across the parking lot going towards the scrubby woods at the end.

"Even if we have to leave the car, Burns . . . I'd rather run through the woods . . . .. We've got their guns. Ambush and kill the bastards if we have to."

"They're better at that than we are, Mike, that's their business!"

Nick remembered something. He swerved the car to the right along the edge of the parking area, next to the grassy perimeter. Then there is was, the gaping section cut out of the fence by the locals when they brought their trucks in to pilfer the fixtures.

"*Man, oh man* . . . the hand of God!" said Buchanan. "I'll push it aside."

"No, stay in the car," Nick ordered sternly.

The tan truck wasn't more than two hundred yards behind them.

"I'm going to crash it through."

"Oh my poor beauty . . . the paint job."

"Stop bellyaching and cover your face with your arms in case of glass," Nick said, as he turned in a wide circle.

The truck was even closer, maybe a hundred twenty yards away.

Nick could see its driver and passenger in the cab and half a dozen men hanging onto the railing above. He had an impulse to stop the car and use all the firepower he had now with the captured automatic rifles and the Uzi to put an end to the truck and at least that bastard Volkov who was probably in the front with the driver, but he knew it was foolish . . . John Wayne heroics were out because that wasn't what this was all about. He HAD to get away safely now, negotiate for the prisoner another time, not get caught himself, a double ransom, for the pleasure of killing a few of those pricks. Too bad, he was pissed off enough and would have enjoyed it. But instead he dug into the accelerator, keeping the Peugot in second as they screamed up the grassy verge cracking hard on the curb and flying upward a second, but landing with wheels spinning. He popped the clutch for an instant so he wouldn't spin the wheels like power saws into a hole they dug in the ground; let the clutch back in as soon as they hit the ground and were rolling and stayed in second against the protests of the whining engine and shuddering gearbox and Buchanan's alternating shouts of "Oh God!" and "Oh shit!"

The Peugot hit the cyclone fence in the full torque of its powerful second gear and knocked the heavy section of the already cut chain links to the side, but not before there was a ripping sound of metal and the crashing of glass echoed through the car as the left fender went ripping to the side, stuck up in the air like the jagged open end of a sardine tin.

"Oh super!" Buchanan shouted, and they bounced down the embankment on the other side of the fence flying over the ruts.

 Nick prayed that no axle would break or tire give.

Buchanan screamed one or the other of his "God!" "Shit!" or "Super!" alternatives as his head hit the roof hard, but the car and the two of them held, and soon they were rolling fast along the very welcome macadam ribbon of road, back in the direction they had come from only a short time ago.

The engine still felt strong and fine as Nick dropped the car into fourth gear for the first time since he had slipped into the driver's seat when Buchanan had walked across the no man's land.

Buchanan kept his eye on the road behind them. "They're still coming on," he said. "Hand it to the bastards, they don't give up. Come on, Burns. Move this former beauty the hell out of here."

Nick looked in the rear view mirror to see the troop truck lumbering down the embankment the Peugot had just bounced and flown over. Then it turned onto the road behind them.

"No problem now, Mike," Nick said, "as long as this wreck of yours holds up, we have the speed and the distance."

"It wasn't a wreck before you got hold of it."

"But you're alive . . . and I'll pay you for the fucking car, okay? Now shut up about it."

"That's not the point," Buchanan said. He stared ahead, mouth agape, following Nick's stare. Out in front of them, less than a mile down the narrow, straight road was the reason Nick didn't answer him, and Buchanan stopped quibbling.

12

ZIMBABWE

EAST OF HARARE

LIKE THE GIANT, GREY NEOLITHIC MONSTERS that had once roamed these very plains, the double-trailer truck with the concrete castings was lumbering along the road ahead of them, its bulk taking up the entire width of the macadam surface.

Nick saw that the truck was dropping back as the Peugot zipped along the road. They were gaining on it rapidly on an incline; the truck was losing ground.

"Van Ness is too smart, Mike. If his car can't catch up, they must have a fall-back to stop us up ahead should we pass the truck."

He floored the accelerator and watched the speedometer needle climb to 120 km/h, then 130. At 140, the car developed a vibration that shook the transmission and wobbled the steering wheel in Nick's hands.

The Peugot was only a hundred meters behind the truck . . . then two car lengths. A "No Passing Zone 500 Meters" sign flashed by as Nick pulled to the right and began to pass the truck. Pebbles drummed like shots on the under-body as the whirling tires threw them up. A cloud of dust rose in the hot, dry air and obscured the giant tractor-trailer as they rattled noisily past it.

Nick heard the valves clattering in protest over the hammering of the flying gravel. They were still on an incline that had grown steeper and he felt the Peugot slow somewhat as the surface traction lessened on the dirt road. The huge grey truck towered over them, its mammoth tires higher than the roof of the car. The needle dropped to one hundred and ten, then one hundred as Nick eased a bit on the gas because he needed the directional stability only a slower speed could give him on the dirt road.

Two-thirds of the way along the length of the truck he could see ahead where the road narrowed into a single lane between a cut through a rock formation two hundred meters ahead.

Suddenly an old farm wagon pulled by a team of horses and loaded with hay slipped from the bottle neck into the passing lane. The Peugot was closing fast!

Nick leaned on the horn certain that it couldn't be heard over the high-pitched roar of the car engine and certainly not over the thundering drone of the heavily laboring deisel truck.

A hundred meters now. They were alongside the rear of the diesel cab and the horses were dead ahead with no place to maneuver or turn. The Peugot wasn't going to make it!

If only he could get a bit more speed! He floored it, felt a passing gear engage and the car spurted forward fishtailing from side to side, bouncing on the rutted dirt strip.

"YOU CRAZY BASTARD! YOU'LL KILL EVERYBODY!" screamed Buchanan. "STOP THE FUCKING CAR!"

"NO CHOICE," Nick yelled. "IT'S TOO LATE! HOLD ON."

The truck driver must have heard the car's horn, or seen the cloud of dust or the wild manic gestures of the farmer on the hay wagon because he hit the air brakes and a loud explosive *hiss* escaped from the heavy brake pistons.

The Peugot shot past the front of the truck cab and Nick wrenched the shuddering steering wheel to the left, and the car leapt onto the macadam road, clearing the horse team by no more than twenty feet.

He saw the face of the farmer embalmed with fear and rage for a split second before a massive cloud of dust the car had raised covered the hay wagon and obscured the front of the tractor-trailer from view.

The truck's driver let off several angry bellows on his horn that sounded like the foghorn of an ocean liner.

"Never thought we'd make that," Buchanan shouted, laughing with relief.

"Me neither," Nick answered.

Then they were driving along on a narrow, single-lane passage, that ran down hill like a groove cut in the rock face. There was only the ribbon of macadam road with two feet of dirt shoulder on either side.

Nick slowed a bit on the decline, and dropped the shift lever into neutral to allow the gear box to cool. The hill fell in front of them without a curve for almost two miles.

Behind him, coming out of the dust, he could see the tractor-trailer completely filling the roadway, and saw that it was slowing as the driver eased down his gears to hold back the heavy load on the steep decline.

Good. Volkov and his crew can't pass that rig now. He felt a momentary relaxation come over him.

"Think we're clear now?"

"I'd like to, Mike, but I doubt it . . . not until we hit the main road. How far is that?"

"About two and a half miles. This single lane ends at the bottom of the slope a mile ahead. Then it's flat with a passing verge the rest of the way."

They'd be somewhere along that last mile or so, Nick thought. Then he recalled the man with the walkie talkie at the bus stop White Rabbit wouldn't risk something out on the main road . . . no . . . it would have to be soon, somewhere between the T-junction with the road to Harare and the end of this single lane cut.

Still on the downward grade, Nick kept the car in neutral, and pumped the brake slowly, bringing their speed down to fifty kilometers, and then forty.

He wanted to keep the tractor trailer as far behind as he could to serve as a buffer. Another look in the mirror told him that the big truck was easing down the hill very, very slowly. Even at the Peugot's present speed, the truck was being left in the distance. *Better.*

"Take the wheel," he said to Buchanan.

The other man looked at him with his mouth agape. "What?"

"You heard, Mike, take the wheel!"

"While we're moving? Are you mad?"

"Are you alive?"

Buchanan nodded.

"Take the wheel, then."

Buchanan leaned over and placed one hand on the steering wheel.

"Now just keep it steady, straight on."

Nick pressed down on the brake pedal softly and slowed the car to thirty km's, then pulled the handbrake until he felt it grab slightly. Next he pushed himself up to a standing position, then put each of his feet on the driver's seat . . . his head and shoulders were poking up through the sun roof.

"Slide over, Mike, slide . . . *Now*, you slowpoke come on."

Nick was standing crouching on the raised housing of the drive shaft tunnel between the two front seats, his legs out of Buchanan's way, and the journalist heaved his weight across from the passenger's to the driver's side of the car, finally taking control of his own pampered car, much abused since he had driven it last.

Buchanan dropped the car into fourth gear, clucking his tongue at the damage to the front fender, which he could only see as a jagged tin edge sticking out. He hated to think what it would look like when he finally was able to get out to survey the damage. But what the hell, nothing went as planned. Besides, Burns said he'd pay for the damage, or at least Uncle Sam would, so Buchanan wouldn't have to throw more cock and bull with his boss's secretary, Maggie, to whom he'd promised to sell the car. She'd be back from vacation by now, he thought, with nice crisp pounds . . . cash for him to take back to England and buy another. Damn! If he wasn't so lazy he'd have rented a car for the day, protected his baby. He'd have to explain that it was damaged in an accident, arrange for it to be fixed and then have it delivered to her after he'd gone.

"What are you doing back there, Burns?"

Nick was in the rear seat, checking the action on the rifles they had retrieved from the guards at the hospital gate. Czechoslovakian made. Pykgorney SG 427s. The Czech version of the Kalishnikov, but known in the international weapons trade as the best. Their high powered slugs and massive bore could stop an elephant, and they were fully automatic. He checked the magazine on each, readied them both and laid them again on the rear seat.

"Just keep rolling the way you are," he said to the journalist instead of answering him, "slow and steady."

The front passenger seat was a complete recliner so he twisted the knob on the side between the seat and the door until the ratchet wheel released from its gears and bent the seat back forward so that it lay flat on the seat bottom. Then he reached forward, found the catch to release the sliding tracks under the seat, and holding the lever to one side pushed the entire seat forward under the dashboard. It clanked off the tracks onto the front floor well.

"Not enough that you wreck the friggin car, you have to dismantle it as well," Buchanan remarked.

"Drive!" Nick said. "We'll put it back later. You know, Buchanan, if that girl with the big bum you're looking for in England finds out what a nag and worry wart you are, you're never going to get your hands as full as you want."

Buchanan laughed, "I will if you won't tell her! What are you doing?"

"Getting ready."

"For what?"

"For what's next, I think," Nick answered tersely.

He stood upright so that his head, arms and shoulders were sticking up through the open sunroof. One of his legs he planted firmly where the passenger seat had been, the other was straddling the drive shaft and resting in the rear compartment behind the driver's seat. He slipped one of the Czech rifles upward through the sun roof and steadied it, and adjusted the sight. The new road had been hardly used and was very smooth, consequently he found that with a slight lift of the wrist he could still the vibration. Nick quickly adjusted the sight altitude for 500 meters, then leaned in and fixed the other rifle for half that.

They were reaching the bottom of the long hill, rolling at about forty kilometers. He looked back. The large tractor-trailer was almost a mile behind them, easing its enormous load slowly down the smooth road. With rigs like that, good truck drivers didn't take any chances on the downhill, too much weight and momentum to trust to brakes. They geared down and let the transmission hold the weight back.

Nick could make out the tan troop carrier behind the tractor, and he knew that they were stuck there. Until the big momma reached the bottom, they couldn't pass. By that time the Peugot should be out on the main road and home free . . . so to speak . . . depending on what happened next.

"Mike," he said, leaning into the car, "listen carefully. I want you to drive this as steadily as you can, in a straight line, at no more than fifty-five, no matter what. Don't swerve or change speed until the last minute."

"Last minute for what?" Buchanan looked at him, puzzled by the instructions. It was clear enough that Burns had set himself up as a gun turret.

"Just before you hit anything . . . then gear down to third and hit the gas as hard as you can. Just warn me so I can drop down. Have you got it?"

"Got it," Buchanan replied, not too happily.

When they reached the flat stretch where the roadbed emerged from the cut into the rising shale escarpment and widened to allow a full dirt shoulder on either side, Buchanan increased the speed to a steady fifty, and Nick readjusted his position above the roof of the car, leveling the Pykgorney 427 into the wind and settling the heavy polished stock against his shoulder.

They rolled onward for a minute. Nothing to be seen, just an empty road heading west like an arrow. Maybe he had been wrong, there was no back up. It was all over, all they had to do was get back to Harare.

Then he saw them. A vehicle pulled off the verge about three quarters of a mile down the road and headed straight for them. He sighted through the rifle scope for magnification. It was a desert tan jeep and two men were in it. He saw the black berets sticking up over the windshield.

" Close both windows, Mike," he yelled down into the car "and keep her steady as a rock."

He felt Buchanan's arm push past his leg and roll up the passenger window. Nick knew that glass could be a greater hazard, but at least they wouldn't be able to toss gas pellets into the car, except through the roof that his body now blocked.

He waited as the distance closed between them and the jeep. His eye was focused through the telescopic sight, his hands struggled to keep the rifle from jumping too much.

God hope they're not regular army or police on patrol he thought in a flash.

Then the next movement of the men in the jeep confirmed that they weren't. Through the dancing scope he saw the driver talking into a handset. At a nod from the driver, the other man lowered the windshield flat to the hood of the jeep and moved into the back seat where a heavy gauge machine gun was mounted on a fixed tripod. They were out to stop the Peugot. That was certain . . . one way or the other. Taking his eye away from the scope for a second, Nick realized how minute the two figures still looked to the naked eye. Luckily Buchanan couldn't yet realize what was happening in front of them.

"You okay, Mike?" Nick yelled into the car below him.

"Steady as you go, chief," Buchanan said jokingly, adding, "Who's that ahead?"

"Just drive . . . and remember what I told you!"

Nick pulled his head back into position, squinted into the scope and when the horizontal line across the scope told him that the jeep was 500 meters distant, he squeezed the trigger and held it. He kept the pressure up for ten seconds, watching the trajectory of the daytime tracers as they smoked like rockets to the target.

Even with Buchanan's steady driving, the rounds were flying high and wide from the vibration.

The machine gun on the jeep opened fire . . . though Nick couldn't hear it he could see the smoke as the man fired and hear the slugs whistling past. One scored the roof of the Peugot a foot away from him, and he heard a splat of glass and a scream from Buchanan at the same time.

The Peugot swerved wildly from one side of the road to the other, onto the right then the left shoulder.

"YOU OKAY, MIKE?" he shouted down into the car. He was almost afraid to look.

"Just bloody," Buchanan yelled back.

Nick glanced down. Blood was dropping down the journalist's face from a wide gash on his forehead.

"Just some glass I think," Buchanan said, as he steadied the car on the macadam again.

Nick hardly heard him. Assured that Buchanan was still driving, he squinted through the rifle scope again at the jeep and aiming low this time to compensate for the shorter distance, he squeezed the trigger and held it for the entire magazine to empty.

The tracers pounded into the fast approaching jeep. But the fucker was still coming. The machine gun was rattling, but the gunner couldn't keep it steady and his shooting was wild and high.

"GET READY TO SWERVE TO THE RIGHT . . . HE EX-PECTS LEFT," Nick shouted to Buchanan. The jeep was about one hundred meters away now. A clicking and silence from the rifle. Nick pulled the other one up . . . no time for careful aiming. He pointed it without aiming and squeezed.

The driver must have been hit because with a sudden lurch the jeep turned onto the right-hand dirt strip and Nick's next shots found the gas tank. A sudden whoosh and twenty foot flames belched out of the jeep in all directions, as the vehicle went bumping off the road into the field.

Nick saw the driver flying up through the air all his clothes aflame as he tumbled over upward then down in a mockery of slow motion.

"Poor bastard," he said aloud, meaning it, and swung the rifle sideways at the flame drenched turning body in the air, firing at it as though he were skeet shooting. He saw the tracers stop at the body and knew that the shots went home. Better to be dead that way than from the agony of burning alive.

The machine gunner had been thrown to the other side of the road by the explosion and miraculously hadn't caught fire. He raised himself as the Peugot approached and Nick saw him pull a grenade from his belt and yank at the pin. Buchanan must have seen it too and sensed what to do because he swerved the car suddenly and down shifted with a burst of speed onto the dirt shoulder.

The jagged metal of the Peugot's left front fender caught the man's middle as he tried to jump back into the grass, and Nick could hear a sickening rip as the car sliced the man with the force of bayonets ripping his guts out. The body was tossed back into the field like a rag doll and seconds later, as Buchanan straightened the car onto the macadam, there was a loud explosion and gobbets of indistinguishable bloody flesh and clothing went flying into the bright air.

A moment later they reached the T-junction of the main road back to the capitol.

Exhausted, Nick fell back onto the back seat. "We're safe now . . . I think," he said to Buchanan, who was stanching the blood on his temple with a handkerchief.

"You okay, Mike?"

"It's superficial, I think."

"Head bleeds a lot."

"I'm all right . . . .. You?"

Nick was drained and he knew that the images of what had just happened would fill his night hours for a long time. Unlike bastards like Volkov, he didn't enjoy bloodshed. Buchanan, he could see, was in a state of wide awake shock.

"Want to change places?" he asked.

"No . . . just to get the hell out of here," answered Buchanan . . . he would be all right.

Nick slumped on the seat, resting his head on the seat back. "Home, James," he said, closing his eyes.

HARARE

"AND YOU SAY THAT BUCHANAN doesn't know?" Nemberton asked Nick again. He had asked the same question four times in his office.

209

Halfway back to Harare, the journalist had suddenly grown weak, continued to lose blood from his head wound and was exhibiting delayed shock, so they had stopped at a service station where Nick shoved him over into the passenger seat, called Nemberton to ask that he have the embassy doctor standing by when they arrived and took over the wheel.

Buchanan was with the doctor now.

"Why would he know?" Nick asked, "unless he was in on the ambush from the beginning, and he's a lot more devious than either of us imagined."

He took another sip of the coffee Nemberton had brought in, and filled the air with the welcome reek of his pipe. Staring reflectively at the wisp of blue smoke rising from the smoldering bowl in his hand, he said, "I don't think so. He was too scared. As I told you, they never fired at us except the tear gas, until the end, and then I think it was to stop the car. Only when they saw that I was popping off at them did they become earnest with that machine gun. Then reflex took over . . . theirs and mine. Phil, I didn't like it!"

"Who does?"

"Some do."

"Those terrorist S-O-Bs, or why else would they be where they are?"

"Who's philosophical now," Nick kidded. "They wanted me," he continued.

"For your body?" Nemberton added wryly.

"Just so," Nick answered with a smile, "but you can damned well believe that I would have ended up in Lubianka laundered clean and waiting for a swap . . . if I was lucky."

"And you're sure it was Volkov?"

"Positive."

"I could understand Volkov being there," Nemberton went on, "but not with White Rabbit . . . their commander, Jean-Luc Moran, is a rabid anti-Red; in fact I had heard that he refused a big contract from Angola a few years ago because he didn't like their politics. It's one of his few principles."

"It's all very peculiar," Nick said. "I see his adjutant, who turns out to be Volkov — one of Moscow's finest — and realize that he's the one who was the mastermind of the Kananga snatch in London."

"How do you know that?"

"I saw a photo of him . . . Goldstein had taken the picture and made himself very obvious doing it and that was why he was killed. He hadn't a chance against a top pro like Volkov . . . or whatever he's calling himself these days . . . once he was spotted."

"But there must have been hundreds of picture snappers in the crowd. Volkov surely would have known that . . . and that eventually one of the security services would have spotted who he was," Nemberton objected.

"Eventually is a long time," Nick answered, pushing his coffee cup across the desk towards Nemberton, who filled it again.

"Meanwhile he would have known that Goldstein's picture would quickly get to OMEGA, and me, and, of course, Goldstein's cover would have been blown."

"By whom?"

"You want the short list or the long one?"

"Short."

"Got a week?"

There was a perfunctory knock on the door, then it opened to admit the journalist, his head was bandaged but he was smiling and cocky.

Buchanan held a copy of the morning's *The Herald*. "I was reading this distinguished rag in the sawbone's office," he said, "since my morning's activities precluded my usual fix and . . .."

"You learned something you didn't know before?" Nemberton asked snidely.

"Haven't had a chance this week," Buchanan said, then laughed and grimaced.

"Hurts when you laugh?" Nemberton inquired.

"Not funny," Buchanan said.

The two men seemed to be on terms of easy camaraderie. Nemberton had said that the social circles were small and overlapping in

Harare . . . "Incestuous," was his word, and the divorce rate among the whites . . . both nationals and the diplomatic corps . . . was the world's highest.

Buchanan had the newspaper folded open to the article which concerned him, "South African Behind Kidnapping" the piece was headlined: "filed from London by Eddington Zumgola."

Zimbabwe's ambassador to London, Herbett Mshbungu revealed today that photographs taken of the persons who kidnapped opposition leader Jeremiah Kananga last week gave clear evidence that at least one of those responsible is a South African mercenary who holds a British passport.

The perpetrator, Ralph Perkins, a former sergeant in the British Commando Unit, once charged with atrocities against Africans during the invasion of Suez in 1956, was identified by sources close to British intelligence services, according to Ambassador Mshbungu.

Mr. Perkins, whose *nom de guerre* is "Wesson" was among the mercenary forces led by Colonel Michael (Mad Mike) Hoare who unsuccessfully besieged the airport in the Seychelles several months ago. Perkins, along with the majority of the attackers was released with a nominal fine after he was found guilty of being accessory to the hijacking of an international airliner.

"The article went on to a shrill rehashing of the 1981 Seychelles episode." Nick stopped reading. "They're attributing that act to London," he said, "and that's questionable."

"Could be a ruse to cover a big leak here," Nemberton said.

"A goddamn flood," Nick said.

"South African villainy is the favorite chestnut," Buchanan said. Nick and Nemberton stared hard at him.

"I didn't know there were pictures . . . honestly," Buchanan protested, suddenly aware that they suspected him of the leak.

Nick looked at the journalist steadily, then lit his pipe with intentional concentration. The the other two sat silent.

"Well who did?" Nemberton asked.

"Whoever benefits from pulling every available fire alarm," Nick said.

"Why me?" the journalist responded. "What's in it for me?"

"Mike . . . are you MI6?" Nick asked bluntly.

"Are you kidding?"

"CIA?"

"No!"

"For Chrissake!" Nemberton objected.

"Who, then?" Nick pressed on.

The journalist averted his eyes. "I dig for random trade offs — source for source. Like any correspondent," he answered in a quiet voice. "Ear to the ground and all that. You know the game, Burns."

"Like Goldstein?" Nemberton asked.

"Yeah, but I never went in for the heroics or the payroll. I've wanted my name in print as the writer, not the subject . . . sorry always the joker."

Nick ignored the attempt to lighten up the conversation. "Well, who *do* you work with?"

"Sorry, wrong number!" Buchanan said flippantly.

"Albert Biggs, at the British Embassy?"

"Good man," Nemberton said.

"Sometimes," Buchanan said. "Sometimes Phil here, others, too, and really none of your business. I'm a reporter, Burns, and take my contacts where I find them. Now lay off! I put my bleeding life on the line today, and ALL YOU CAN THINK IS HOW I MIGHT BE FUCKING YOU OVER, he shouted. "That's gratitude to remember!" He turned towards the door. "Fuck all this African bullshit and intrigue . . . and all you spooks who love to wallow in it."

"Sorry, Mike," Nemberton said, "we're just trying to . . .."

"Shove it!" the journalist interrupted. Then his anger seemed to pass, "I'm going home on accumulated leave from Reuters. I told you true about that. I'm fed up and tired. Sorry I exploded."

"You going to start your search for the girl with the big bum and all?" Nemberton asked, smiling.

"Sure am."

"He's obsessed with that," Nemberton laughed.

"Obscure erotic delights with a suburban Venus," Buchanan said, smacking his lips suggestively.

"Okay, Mike," Nick said, relaxing a bit, "for today. Now I think you should go take it easy."

"Fine by me," the journalist said. "Got any idea about the source?" he asked, "besides me?"

Nemberton thought for a moment. "I do," he said, but . . .."

"But what?"

"She hasn't been around . . .."

"Who?"

"Sir Peter's secretary, Maggie," the CIA man said.

"But she's been away on home leave," Buchanan objected, "and I don't think she's back. She used to be Kananga's little flip-flop . . . until she switched brands, and has been rolling over for your own Ambassador Yogun lately . . . the poor man has had to dine at home for the last few weeks."

Nick looked at Nemberton who affirmed it with a nod.

Then Nemberton handed the journalist a fat wad of American dollars he pulled from his desk drawer.

"What's that for?" Buchanan said.

"Your holiday."

"This is a lot of . . .."

"We bought your car," Nick answered, rising to offer Buchanan his hand.

"Generous indeed," the journalist whistled through his teeth, "but then again, now you know what a great machine it is!"

"Cost of doing business," Nick said, "for everything. I mean it." He squeezed Buchanan's hand firmly. "And thanks."

"I'll call you tomorrow," Nemberton said. "Where will you be?

"At the office . . . tidying up. By the way, do you really want to keep the Peugot?" he asked.

"We don't need it," Nemberton said. "Why don't you use the loot to have it fixed."

Buchanan seemed pleased, "I promised it to someone."

"Enjoy," Nemberton said.

The journalist went into the corridor whistling.

"We've got some tidying up to do ourselves," Nick said after the door had closed behind Buchanan.

Phil Nemberton reached for the telephone, dialed, waited, and then said, "Biggs . . . Nemberton. Can I see you? An hour? Fine."

Nick looked at him with curiosity.

"The first step in tidying . . . Biggs had better babysit for Mike until he's out of the country because he's in the same situation that Goldstein was right now — he's a used up asset for someone to cancel. I don't have enough manpower at the moment."

Nick agreed, "And until Biggs gets around to it?"

Nemberton lifted the telephone again. "What I think," he continued, when he had given orders to Security, "is that White Rabbit is bogus . . . completely . . . just an opposition operation to make us all look bad."

Nick stared at the sunlight on the trees outside and the intense red flowers on a tree that he didn't recognize across the way. After a minute's silence he said, "I don't know, and that doesn't explain Colonel Moran, if he's really in on this. That's who I wanted to see today. Where the hell is he? There are still some other possibilities too. Maybe the whole thing is Umgawe's baby. He takes out Kananga, and discredits the whites and implicates South Africa all with one fell swoop, or . . ." he hurried on before Nemberton could interrupt his train of thought, ". . . it's really an MI6 operation calculated to throw Umgawe's government into disarray and bring back Kananga — the victim as hero — the Brits favored him from the beginning, didn't they?"

Nemberton unwrapped another sour ball, "He was the major force in the Lancaster House agreement and is probably more amenable to their influence than Umgawe, who professes to lean towards China . . . which is why we try to play ball with him. That is as long as

215

we're cozy with the Chinese against the Russians," he said, adding, "until the pendulum swings the other way."

"Then there's us! 'We have met the enemy and he is us!'" Nick said

Nemberton looked puzzled.

"'Pogo,'" Nick left the scholarly citation for the record.

Nemberton looked even more puzzled.

"A 'Commie' comic strip popular when I was in college," Nick teased.

"You really think I'm one of those Bureau clods?" Nemberton asked, offended. "They'd report you as a security risk for reading it. I will ignore your confession magnanimously." He scribbled on a pad.

"Sorry," Nick said, meaning it. "Just age and natural acidity."

There were times like this, when the anarchy of seeming order made him wish for a simple life — a cabin in the woods and a fishing rod — although he knew that within a week he would have the jitters and run from the quiet, but still the image of Edenic simplicity helped.

"If the Company was behind this operation it would mean that we've doubled Volkov, that I'm running him as case officer, and that I sent you out into a trap with full knowledge," Nemberton said. "What do you take me for?"

"A conscientious civil servant doing your job."

"Well we're not running White Rabbit, and certainly not with a turned KGB man in the middle."

"Maybe it's being run around you."

"On my territory? Well, it wouldn't be the first time," Nick said.

"How about the simplest option," Nemberton said, reaching for another hard candy.

Nick lit his pipe again and sat back to listen.

"White Rabbit is really what it says, anti-majority-rule supremacists . . . mercenaries of course, but acting on behalf of some still pretty strong political elements in this country that want them to drain Umgawe's government, make him look like a fool over the Kananga thing, and throw the country into the kind of disarray that proves it can't be done by the blacks."

"In other words," Nick said, "like the newspaper says . . . South Africa behind the dirty work as usual. That's so simple it's scary, but it doesn't explain Volkov."

"Ah, a classic *agent provocateur*."

"But there's still a question with these," Nick said as he pointed at the weapons he had used with such deadly effect a short while ago. "The ZK-383 . . . Czech . . . the choice of right wing mercenaries?"

"The Arabs like the Uzi. It's strictly a question of weapon of choice," Nemberton proffered.

Nick found that hard to believe. "Or gold dust in our eyes," he said.

THERE WAS ONLY one thing for Nick to do, and discretion seemed the better part. He told Nemberton that he would be taking the next flight to London that left on Thursday, so he still had a day for loose ends.

"Are you going back to the New York desk, and sending someone else out here?" Nemberton had asked, as they shook hands at the door of his office.

"And leave show biz?" Nick asked.

Nemberton laughed halfheartedly and raised his hand in a good-bye gesture. But Nick knew he wasn't quits when he got into a taxi at the curb and turned to see two security men in a staff car pull out into traffic behind the cab. He was too tired to object, figuring that Nemberton was taking no chances for further accidents in his bailiwick.

Back at his hotel, he called the British Embassy and made an appointment to see Sir Peter the next morning.

Dozing on the bed, Nick remembered telling Mike Buchanan to break a leg. Maybe he should stick to "good luck" from now on, was his last thought as he drifted into a thankfully dreamless sleep.

13

THE ENGLISH CHANNEL

A LIGHT DRIZZLE WAS FALLING and the helmsman on the flying bridge of the thirty-five foot Chris-Craft was wearing his foul-weather gear.

"What are you going to put on when it really starts to come down," Jean Luc Moran asked him in French, when he reached the top step of the ladder and stood next to the sailor.

"I'll take it off," the man joked, smiling grimly.

Moran looked around, peering into the dense mid-channel gloom.

"Rotten visibility," the sailor said.

"Could have been worse," Moran answered, "fog, maybe, or a bad sea running. Never know with the Channel this time of year."

As far as the helmsman was concerned, it was the English side which was unpredictable. When he and the other crewman had left their sheltered berth in Saint-Malo two days ago, the day had been fair, the sea calm, but when the coast of Brittany dropped out of sight behind them and they were within a few miles of England, the rain and high seas began suddenly, and it was with great relief that they docked at Bright's Marina in Torquay.

Why the boss insisted on making the run back to Saint-Malo at night was beyond the wheelman, but he wasn't paid to ask questions, just to work as professional crew. Monsieur Moran didn't demand too much, but when he did, the sailor complied. It was a good and easy job, looking after the boat and making a run across the Channel or along the coast once in a while to pick up some cargo. Sometimes Moran transported guests or took business associates out for an afternoon of fishing. The sailor didn't ask questions because he wanted to keep the job and M. Moran didn't like questions.

Moran watched the radarscope and listened to the LORAN navigation system for a minute, checked the compass for their heading and studied the chart under its plexiglass cover. The hooded red reading light made an eerie glow on his face. He pointed his finger at a blip on the screen several miles to the northeast of their position.

"Cut your speed to ten knots," he said to the sailor, "and proceed for five minutes on this heading, then return on the complement at the same speed for the same time. Keep repeating that until further notice. We'll rendezvous with this vessel at approximately 23.30 hours. I'll be back shortly."

Without waiting for a response, Moran climbed down from the bridge, stood on the deck peering into the murky night and listened as he heard the twin screw Chrysler 250 throttle back softly and smoothly. The boat purred through the flat sea. He opened the companionway door and stepped into the brightly lit cabin, blinking his eyes for a minute.

"Smith," he said, "coffee!" And as the squat, burly mercenary handed Moran a mug of steaming, black liquid, he added, "and double check that all the curtains are drawn closed across the portholes. I don't want any lights showing."

Ignoring Jeremiah Kananga, who had spread his bulk on a padded cushion in the lounge area and was flicking through a large pile of newspapers and magazines, Moran sat down at the chart table and carefully rechecked the course and distance travelled, measured with dividers, did some dead reckoning with a pencil, proved his results on a small calculator, then looked at the instrumentation duplicated above and watched the blip on the radar screen getting closer to the co-ordinates the motor launch had just crossed. Satisfied, he put the navigational instruments aside, stuck the pencil into a rack and moved across the cabin to where Kananga sat reading a newspaper.

"Are we on schedule?" the African asked, peering at Moran across the top of his reading glasses.

Moran's response was a surly affirmative grunt.

Kananga put down his paper. "M. Moran," he said, "while I do not care if you like me or approve of my methods . . .."

"Colonel Moran, as this is a professional relationship," the mercenary snarled.

". . .Colonel, then," resumed the huge black man taking the interruption in tempo and not letting it alter his own delivery, "I think I have the right to insist upon a courteous response from you, since you are in my employ . . .."

"As a soldier, Mr. Kananga . . . excuse me, General Kananga," he corrected himself, using the old guerrilla leader's rank, without any sarcasm, "I am employed as a soldier, not as a butcher. When we were on opposite sides in the bush a few years ago, I respected you too as a soldier. But not as a murderer. Cutting off heads with machetes is not my idea of soldiering, General Kananga . . . not my idea at all."

Kananga removed his glasses, folded them and put them into his jacket pocket, and asked "How do *you* treat spies, then?"

"Execution after court martial, and a decent burial . . . not some savage mutilation."

Kananga looked angry. "Always the 'savages,' Colonel. Maybe you should throw in 'cannibals' and 'tribal blood feuds' . . . then you'll have the complete picture. Come, Colonel, you've been part of Africa for too long. You know better."

"There was no necessity . . .."

"There was *every* necessity . . .."

The mercenary leaned forward, "If I fight on a foreign battle-field, a hired gun, I am a soldier. If I am accessory to the murder and mutilation of a man in a peacetime situation, I am a criminal, and I choose not to be. Choice! Do you understand? Choice. It's mine. I agreed to work for you, agreed to all this kidnap-ransom hocus pocus. But I did not agree to commit murder in the English countryside. I hold a British passport, General, and strange as it may sound to you, I value it."

"Your patriotism is touching," Kananga said with heavy sarcasm, "but Colonel, tell me — who also holds the same British passport — what did these wonderful English do with traitors up until the last century?"

221

Without waiting for an answer from the mercenary, Kananga continued. "They hanged them, then cut them down while still alive, dragged their bodies through the streets behind horses, and then hacked them up into pieces, and put the heads on spikes outside the bloody Tower for the world to see the fate of traitors. So don't give *me* that rubbish about the rule of law, savagery and the sanctity of the human body in England. Hanged, drawn and quartered. We did far less."

Moran stood up with disgust. "All very clever," he said.

The African smiled.

"And you can be pleased as Punch with yourself," the mercenary continued, "but I don't give a damn about history. All I know is that two days ago, a man was killed, and then he was butchered up like a pig . . . and there you sit, searching all the god damned papers for news of it so you can gloat. That's what I call savagery."

"Your hands are so clean, Colonel?" the fat man asked, still smiling.

"They're plenty bloody, but not like that. And I've taken out a few traitors in my time. But soldierly. And they knew it too."

As he spoke Moran felt the boat turning in a broad circle. He knew that the helmsman would follow the wake he had just made. All the calculations indicated that the two vessels would meet when they both reached the coordinates he had plotted a few minutes ago.

He walked to the below decks control station, checked the course, the radar scope and the other instruments. The blip on the screen and the center that represented the Chris-Craft were coming together as planned.

Moran then returned to the cabin and said to the African, "Okay . . . the philosophy seminar is over. Make sure you are ready and have your gear together for a rendezvous in five minutes."

The fat man stood, steadied himself as the boat rolled slightly in its own backwash and said, "Joseph was like a son to me . . . but he betrayed us . . . all of us. *A member of my own clan working for Umgawe's secret police?* I saw the documents with my own eyes. And he was caught trying to escape, probably to bring the police back with him. Then where would you have been, with all your high and mighty ethics of the soldier of fortune? You'll pardon me, Colonel Moran, but I think that you are the one who is spouting standards that just don't apply. If Volkov hadn't caught Joseph you'd be in custody right now . . . and not only in jail, but also a lot poorer."

"Elegant sophistry," said the mercenary, "but I still don't buy it. Why argue the point? We employ different means, you and I. But while I'm running an operation, mine apply. If you want to take over, get yourself another boy."

He reached into a locker and pulled out some foul weather gear. "Here," he said, tossing Kananga a new package of slicker jacket, trousers and sou'wester hat, sealed in plastic. "Can't have you catching cold on us now, can we? These are larges."

Kananga opened the plastic bag, pulled out the jacket and put it on. It was snug around his belly.

"What's more," the colonel said, "Joseph was the go-between from me to Volkov, when we first started to plan all this. The only African who knew just what we were up to. If Umgawe knows about it, you can forget the whole thing. They will never pay and the whole exercise will have been a waste."

"They'll pay," Moran said, "one way or the other."

He turned off the cabin lights, leaving only the instrumentation on the control center aglow, and stepped up the companionway through the doors onto the deck.

"They'll pay," he repeated ominously as he stepped onto the deck. As long as he had his hands on Kananga, it wouldn't be a waste.

FROM THE FLYING BRIDGE atop the main cabin, Moran watched the radar screen as the boats converged. The General Smuts, a freighter bound from Rotterdam to Capetown would be picking up Kananga and himself, and in about two weeks they'd be landing in South Africa.

The rest of the operation he had sewn up tight. His contacts in the Customs and Immigration Service unions had worked with him before, and responded liberally to the golden handshake. It should be easier to get the fat man on shore than the loads of half-tracks, crates of weapons, and even a helicopter he had taken through the port in other campaigns.

The captain of the General Smuts was a good egg. Moran looked forward to the days at sea. They'd keep Kananga in his cabin and have some good talks.

The helmsman began speaking rapidly in French, and pointing into the darkness. Up ahead, two points off the starboard bow, a large black shape loomed out of the darkness, a half a mile distant, Its red portside light was visible, twinkling through the drizzle.

Any effort to make radio contact was ruled out as the frequencies might be monitored by patrol vessels.

Moran ordered a new heading, and the helmsman, after repeating the compass reading, swung the cruiser to starboard so that its port side was presented to the freighter's port side as the boats now headed in opposite directions. This way the captain on the General Smuts' bridge would be able to see through his binoculars both Moran's red port running light and stern light simultaneously, and could gauge the length of the boat for identification.

Moran moved to the semaphore lamp, and spelled out REQUEST ASSISTANCE. MEDICAL EMERGENCY. EVACUATION. ENGINE FAILURE . . . the message he had worked out with the captain of the General Smuts.

He paused, waited for a response, received none, and repeated it yet again. Halfway through the third repetition, the semaphore aboard the freighter flashed into life.

REPEAT MESSAGE. IDENTIFY VESSEL. REPEAT MESSAGE. IDENTIFY VESSEL flashed the powerful blinkered lamp on the freighter.

Moran repeated the message a fourth time adding AFRICAN KING TORQUAY at the end. Both the name and home port were fabrications, intended for any idly curious crew of the freighter who happened to be on deck.

STANDBY AFRICAN KING from the signal lamp shot across the dark night that had grown blacker as the drizzle became finer.

Patches of fog rolled across both boats now, and the sea underneath the keel of the Chris-Craft lifted it in a groundswell and rolled it from side to side. Underway the boat was fairly stable, but when floating free or at slow speed in heavy seas, its high center of gravity made it a seasick prone landlubber's nightmare.

Just then Kananga burst through the cabin door below and ran to the rail.

Moran could hear him retching and laughed aloud. It would be a medical emergency yet. He hoped Kananga was good and sick.

STANDBY FOR LAUNCH the flashes cut through the fog twice, then END MESSAGE twice more, and blackness.

The freighter was supposed to lower the captain's launch from its davits and come alongside for the passengers, Kananga and Moran plus trusty Smith, of the team Smith and Wesson, who was traveling with them.

The pleasure craft's crew of two would then bring the vessel back to Saint-Malo, their job done.

Kananga continued to vomit over the side after the signaling stopped. Then Moran heard him pulling himself up the ladder.

His head appeared over the top of the ladder like a walrus rising out of the gloom.

"Please stay down on deck," Moran said to him, "there isn't enough room up here for everyone."

Kananga acquiesced to the request — really an order — with a feeble "Aye, aye, sir!"

Moran didn't respond. All he needed was that unwieldy hulk up on the bridge getting in everyone's way, and puking on them all. The man disgusted him. He pressed the intercom to the crew cabin in the cruiser's bow.

"Smith get up on deck, prepare to disembark."

The intercom crackled an "Okay."

"Keep your eye on Kananga," Moran growled when Smith poked his head above the ladder a minute later. "That's precious cargo." Smith dropped down the ladder and Moran could hear him talking to the African on the rear deck below.

MORAN PEERED THROUGH THE GLOOM, steadying himself with one hand on the rail of the bridge. The rolling from port to starboard was worse now and as long as they had to ride broadside to the swell, it would continue, but it felt worse up top at the end of the pendulum than below, near the center of gravity. He had no great love of the sea, but simply accepted its force with respect and tried to use it well.

This escape suited his purposes perfectly, and Volkov had been very clever in making the arrangements. Nobody would pay any but the most perfunctory attention to small craft setting off from the English and French ports that catered to yachtsmen and sport fishermen. Nobody cared, except once in a while a bored or brand new customs official who was looking for something to do or for a bribe to cut through the theoretical red tape, most of which didn't exist for practical purposes. As far as officialdom officially cared, he could have been travelling up and down the coast for several days, never leaving territorial waters. Nothing to explain. The log would be accepted as proof . . . and he kept two, both of which meticulously omitted passenger entries on this run. After all, if a rich man such as Moran wanted his crew to bring his boat across the channel for whatever reason, they did it. The other log recorded a coastal fishing trip. No suspicion of smuggling. Nobody bothered.

In any case, the crew had cleared pratique at Torquay, paid the port fee, and it was all legal, a matter of rubber stamps. A rendez-vous in mid-channel — provided everyone concerned stayed off the wireless — would never be discovered . . . especially at night.

Moran had lost sight of the freighter in the darkness, and the fog had turned to drizzle once again, but the visibility was hardly any better.

He glanced down at the radar scope.

Peculiar.

Where he expected to see a smallish blip detaching itself from the larger mass and heading towards him, there was nothing. Instead, the entire mass of black was closing on the origin of his beam at the center of the screen.

Couldn't be. Must be feedback from a dense cloud at water level.

He pressed the reset and clear buttons. The screen darkened, grew bright again . . . and it was still there.

The large mass was moving rapidly towards the Chris Craft on a collision course.

It had to be a mistake.

Maybe the scope was picking up the launch.

He looked at it again. Pressed the reset once more, lowered the scanning angle. There was no second image. A very large bulk was moving towards them, and closing rapidly.

Moran strained his eyes looking into the murky, grey drizzle. There weren't more than a few boat lengths of real visibility. Somewhere above a plane droned through the night. The moon above the clouds and drizzly murk spread its light in a greenish glow far away in a world of visibility. Moran cursed the darkness.

Then he saw it. The port and starboard navigation lights, red and green cat's eyes widely spaced as on a big ship. You could only see them both at once if you were facing the bow of a boat . . . and he was . . . and the ship was not more than fifty yards away across the dark night.

Funny, he remembered the General Smuts as a smallish tramp. But there was no mistake. The freighter was bearing down upon the cruiser rapidly, and it was no goddamned launch.

Now he saw the prow of the huge ship looming above them like a floating mountain.

The bastards were going to ram him!

God! There'd be nothing left of the Chris-Craft but splinters.

"FULL SPEED AHEAD," Moran screamed at the helmsman.

The startled man turned to look at his boss, who added "What are you waiting for?" and then lunged for the dual throttle controls, knocking the sailor out of the way and slammed them up to the rim of the slide. The twinned Chrysler engines roared out of their quiet nap with the extra fuel suddenly injected into their cylinders and sixteen powerful pistons pounded rapidly, lifting the bow of the Chris-Craft above the water as the boat surged forward.

Ten seconds later the freighter plowing through the dark water at twenty knots crisscrossed the exact spot where the cruiser they knew only as African King had waited for assistance.

There was a tumbling on the deck below as Kananga and Smith, both taken by surprise in the sudden lurch forward, slipped and fell.

"What the hell's going on up there," Smith yelled, bounding up the ladder.

"Tried to ram us, those bastards."

"Must be a mistake."

Moran eased back on the throttle. "We'll see," he said.

At that moment the cruiser was a hundred and fifty yards from the freighter and Moran eased the starboard engine back and then reversed it so that the boat did a quick turn to the right with one engine pushing forward and the other reversing. The cruiser ended up running parallel to the freighter, and matching its speed.

"Let's get closer and see what the hell's going on," he said.

"Should I break out arms, sir," Smith asked.

"Better," Moran answered.

The small arms and rifles kept in the boat's lockers as a precaution couldn't be very effective against the steel mountain which had almost fed them to the fishes, but he knew that Smith would feel less helpless . . . plus the last thing Moran needed was terror and chaos aboard.

Moran steered closer to the freighter, just a hundred yards away. He knew they could see him on their screen, as the radar dish and reflector ball standing on the main mast above the bridge were intended to make the cruiser visible to larger craft.

He kept his speed matched, and edged even closer.

All of a sudden there was a flood of light blinding him as the freighter played a dazzling searchlight as bright as a Klieg light on the small craft.

Moran raised his hand in a wave.

They responded with a stream of tracers fired at him from the steamer's deck. One ripped through the rail two feet from where he stood.

The two crewmen, scared out of their skins, started jabbering in rapid French, .

"Get below," Moran ordered, "and get life vests on everyone, two on the fat man. "MOVE," he screamed in French, and with that he pushed the twin throttles in opposite directions, spun the boat to port and sped at full throttle away from the big ship. The tracers fell to either side as he zig-zagged out of range.

"Turn off all the cabin lights, Smith," he yelled into the intercom, and he switched off all the lights on the control panel with one switch, the running lights, port, starboard and stern, with another. The boat was completely dark except for the faint blue glow of the compass. He slammed the protective hood down over that.

Out of range now, he slowed down. The searchlight on the freighter swept the inky waters, but Moran knew that he was too far away to be picked out as a target.

He dropped down his speed to five knots and turned the boat so that he was facing the ship over his bow.

Smith came tumbling up the ladder clutching some weapons. He laid them on the deck, and thrust something at Moran. "Life jacket for you, Colonel."

Leave it to Smith, Moran thought, the man had been with him for twenty years of different campaigns.

"What the fuck are they doing?"

"I don't know, Smith. The bastards are trying to kill us. Some mistake I assume. Didn't expect this." He slipped the life jacket over his arms and snapped the front.

"What's going on below?" he asked.

"The fat man surprised me. Calm as anything. The sailors are jabbering in frog, sorry, sir . . . you know what I mean, no offense . . . like a couple of babies."

"They're only sailors, Smith. They weren't expecting this . . .!

He didn't finish the sentence because the sky was suddenly filled with the neon blue light of three parachute flares that lit up almost simultaneously. Then there was a flash explosion on the deck of the freighter.

They both heard the report of the big gun after a shell hit the water close by, close enough for the twenty-foot high splash of cold salt to reach them on the bridge in a sudden soaking spray.

"They've still got us on the radar," Moran said as he pushed the boat forward, "and as soon as they get our range . . . .."

"Then let's get out of here. We're outmatched," Smith yelled, as the whistle of another shell made them both duck by instinct. It fell into the water harmlessly fifty yards away. "We're sitting ducks."

"Not as long as I keep this thing moving," Moran shouted into the wind. "I don't understand what's happening."

"Simple," Smith said, "you're being had, fucked over, double crossed. Do I have to spell it out?"

"But by whom? And why?"

"Who the hell cares. Let's get out!"

"Not until I know more."

"You won't know more dead," Smith said, "and then what the hell good will the fat man be to us."

"You're right," Moran shouted, putting the boat into a long arc, "but I can't just cut and run now."

"You're the boss," Smith said, "and not 'Madman Moran' for nothing!"

At another time, he would have knocked the man down who said that to his face . . . but at the moment, it amused him. "You're fucking right, Smitty. Now let's see what this boat has got."

They were about a mile away from the large ship and Moran was working the cruiser on a zigzag course, knowing that he was still on their radar scope, but out of effective range of their cannon, especially if he continued this irregular movement. They'd need some pretty sophisticated equipment to hit him, which Moran was fairly certain they didn't have.

But why the hell should his South African friends . . . this was Captain Voortrecker, an old friend, after all. Maybe it was the Bureau of State Security. If their secret police had gotten onto this and knew that he had Kananga aboard, they could use the opportunity to rid themselves and the whole southern African region of one of its biggest pests and troublemakers. Moran wasn't easy with that explanation, but he had a tidying sort of mind, and needed something, some reason to explain why allies were trying to kill him.

Smith interrupted Moran's ruminations, "We have two Winchester 'thirties, one Mannlicher aught ten, one each of a large bore flare launcher, a flare pistol, a harpoon gun, and a forty five. That's the lot."

Then Moran could hear him checking safeties, opening breeches, fitting magazines.

"All in working order," Smith added.

All legal too, Moran knew. He didn't keep anything on board that wasn't registered or had any other apparent use than fishing, shooting sharks and the like. Trouble was always available, and he didn't need it from Customs or Coast Guard men anywhere.

The other vessel had become invisible in the distance, and as the last of the flares burned out and darkness dropped once again, the only evidence of the big boat was the searchlight still sweeping the night in broad arcs in the direction of the Chris-Craft.

"What's going on?" Kananga shouted from below.

"Don't know yet," Moran yelled back. "Sit tight."

He didn't bother to say anything more. The ship still had the cruiser on the radar, he knew, and he had to keep out of range. He throttled back for a moment, keeping the freighter's light over his bow, centered, to make a smaller target if they tried popping off at him again.

Then the searchlight stopped sweeping. Just blackness, the waters rolling still in a long groundswell, but no wind, no waves. The drizzle had fined down to a mist and hung thick in the air so that you could feel it. A little warmer and it would have been like a Turkish bath. The green glow of the moon had turned grayer and lit the clouds above like a TV screen just switched off.

Moran thought he saw a brighter spot where the clouds opened for an instant, and then, before he could find it again, it wasn't there. Cautiously, he pressed the light switch under the control panel. All the dials brightened, but he ignored them.

He wanted to know what the freighter was doing. On the radar scope, he watched a small blip separating itself from the larger mass of the freighter. He watched as the smaller mass got further from the big boat, but it was not heading towards him. Then he saw it change direction and head his way. A torpedo? No, he wouldn't have picked it up on his screen if it was below the surface, his equipment wasn't so sophisticated. Anyway, it was moving too slowly.

Moran watched as the smaller blip on the screen widened the distance between it and the freighter, then changed direction and headed right for him.

He smiled. Probably the launch they had originally intended. Who knew what the hell kind of error was made. Maybe some crackpot on the freighter's bridge thought that they were being attacked . . . piracy wasn't as rare as the public thought, Moran knew from years along the African coasts. Only the bearded buccaneers with gold earrings and flashing swords were gone. Pirates weren't. But in the English Channel? Why should a freighter suspect that it was being boarded? Besides, the universal code of answering assistance had been used to avoid any confusion, just in case someone other than Captain Voortrecker was on watch. *But they tried to run him down!*

He gave up trying for a reason, which left him more disturbed. He watched the smaller object on the screen close the gap between them.

"Get yourself ready, Smith," he said to the silent man who sat on the locker aft of the helm, and doused the lights on the control panel.

"Small boat approaching, dead ahead," Moran said. "Cover them."

He leaned over the ladder to the deck and ordered the sailors in rapid French to take Kananga below and to lie flat on the cabin floor amidships. He started to repeat the order in English, but he heard Kananga say, "It's all right, Colonel, I understand French."

"Then move yourself," Moran barked, and turned back to the controls. If Kananga would just do as he was told, he'd be out of immediate danger. The cabin sole was below the water line, and were there any weapons fire, it was unlikely he'd be hit. Smith had it right. The African was valued property.

Smith was crouching with one of the Winchesters cradled in a firing position, and the other lying alongside him. Moran shoved the automatic into his belt, and placed the Mannlicher underneath the steering console. He'd stopped charging elephants with that rifle in the old days. Today it seemed like a technological antique with its bolt action and crude elevation sight.

Moran reached for the semaphore. IDENTIFY he flashed when he heard the other boat's high pitched whine approaching across the bleak, eerie silence.

The response was a burst of automatic-weapons fire flashing from the approaching boat. He heard the slugs plunking into the water, but there were no hits. *Cochons.* He wanted a rocket to blast them to hell.

"Okay, Colonel?" Smith asked hoarsely.

"Yeah. You?"

Smith grunted.

"I'll pop a flare," Moran said, "and then start moving quickly to the right. Wait for your range, and then choose your shots."

"With these pop guns?"

"They'll have to do, Smitty. There's no choice."

"Those bleedin' sods have the high tech stuff."

"Sounds like it. Hang on."

Moran waited until he heard the other boat get nearer. Meanwhile he had positioned the cruiser directly in line with the approaching boat but at a forty-five degree angle so he could move out of their path quickly.

When the short flare lit up the sky, Moran was surprised. Instead of a ship's tender, the kind used to run the captain ashore, the boat slipping across the water towards him was a large, working dory with high seaworthy bows and a low flat stern; it was the kind of wooden row boat that large, offshore–fishing trawlers use for going out to tend their nets. In the sudden sharp, blue light from the flare, he saw a very large outboard attached to the squared-off transom. In the boat were four men — one at the tiller, two holding weapons, and one seated forward at some sort of gun mount.

Moran pushed both the cruiser's levers forward to full speed, twisting the wheel hard to port as he did so. It lunged like a porpoise into the air and then as the propellers dug in the boat began to move away quickly. Over the roar of his open throttles, he heard the chugging of automatic rifle fire, but the ground swell and the sudden wake of the cruiser rocked the dory too much and the tracers fell behind the cruiser or whistled over his head.

Moran then heard a whoosh ten feet over his head as a rocket flew over.

"The bastards have a launcher!" he yelled to Smith.

"What the hell can I do?" the burly man shouted over the roar. "We're out of range already for this toy." He threw the Winchester to the deck in disgust.

Moran cut sharply to starboard, then throttled back hard so that the boat would level.

Another rocket pounded into the black water where the cruiser had been only a moment before. Sooner or later one of the rockets would find its way home, and then they'd all feed the fish.

"Take the wheel, Smith!" he shouted, "and keep it steady."

Smith grabbed the steering wheel and Moran reached for the Mannlicher from under the console. "Steady," he shouted, as Smith let the boat yaw. Moran stuffed another flare into the flare pistol and aimed low. No sooner had he fired the pistol than he dropped it to the deck and raised the Mannlicher, and pumped a heavy cartridge into the breach.

The flare exploded twenty feet above the dory with a burst of intense light, made more so for being so low in the air.

Moran took aim quickly and fired, and a second and third time while he knew that the flare above the dory had to blind them momentarily.

An elephant-stopping slug ripped into the man at the gun mount, tearing a hole the size of a saucer in his chest as it flung him sideways over the edge and into the black water.

Further aft another man went down with the second shot. Moran didn't know what happened to the third shot.

"Hit the throttle, Smitty."

"Yessir."

Nothing happened.

"HIT IT, MAN, GO!" Moran screamed.

"It won't move, Colonel," Smith said.

Moran leapt around, pushed him aside and grabbed the controls. He pressed both throttle levers upward, but they wouldn't budge. Nor could they me moved downward. "Shit! Of all the goddamned things."

"What's wrong?"

"The linkage is out somewhere below."

In the last light of the flare Moran saw the dory turning toward them to follow the crippled cruiser. He wanted to squeeze off the remaining cartridges in the Mannlicher, but there was hardly a target now and no time. The throttle had to be fixed or it was all over. He assumed that the dory had a homing device aboard that picked up his engine's vibrations, and if that was the case, they could follow him until daylight, and then, one rocket on target and the game was over. He had to fix the linkage and get the hell out of there. Only distance could do the trick.

"Stay at the wheel, Smitty, just make big eights. I'm going below."

Moran climbed down the ladder to the deck and stepped through the cabin doors.

"Pierre, Francois, where are you?"

The crew men answered him. He heard the fear in their voices. He found a flashlight and aimed it down at the cabin sole. The two crew men lay flat on their faces, arms over their heads paralytic with fear. Kananga lay on his back, his barrel chest and stomach rising and falling in the slow rhythm of sleep. Moran had to hand it to him, the bastard had guts . . . or else he was incredibly stupid. Moran decided it was a combination.

"Help me," he said to Pierre, the senior man, an expert mechanic.

Within a minute they had dismantled the forward panel of the bulk head between the sleeping cabins and the saloon.

The linkage was intact!

"It must be below," the sailor said.

Moran held the flashlight — he didn't dare risk using the cabin lights — while the sailor pulled back the carpeting and then the floor boards that covered the bilges; and then he lowered himself into the dark shallow hollow. They were in front of the engine compartment, and the bulkhead they had just disassembled was right below the steering station on the bridge.

Pierre groped around in the mucky bathtub-sized bilge. "I found it," he said gleefully, then with less enthusiasm, "but I hope it can be fixed."

"It's got to be," Moran said ominously.

Pierre shone the flashlight onto the bottom of the dual throttle linkages, just before an L–bend disappeared through the bulwark into the engine compartment. Two additional rods coming from aft joined the main linkage there. The sailor said they were from the internal control center, which was only used in bad weather or when the boat was on automatic compass in open water. One of the brass rods was sheared off and the other was twisted and bent around the linkage running to the bridge. In the flashlight's glow the brass rod looked like a pretzel, doubled over on itself.

"How the hell . . .?"

The sailor pointed to the steel bulkhead between them and the compartment just aft the housing of the dual engines. Directly behind the spot where the upper and lower linkages meshed was a hole in the steel. It was shallow, more of a sharp dent. He fished his hand in the water and brought up a heavy, brass slug, its point mashed flat.

"One of the bastard's first shots," Moran said ·"when we were headed towards them."

The sailor flashed the light towards the front of the bilge. Water streamed through a three quarter inch hole in the fiberglass. "Nothing the pump can't take care of," he said, and stuffed some brass wool into the hole.

"Okay, okay, enough of this," Moran said impatiently. "Fix the damned thing!"

"I need a hacksaw . . . a blowtorch perhaps," the sailor said.

"There's no fucking time," Moran said, and pulled the sailor out of his way. "Hold the light!" He knelt down in the compartment and wrapped his fingers around the twisted brass. He couldn't budge it.

"Pliers," he yelled, like a frantic surgeon. They'd all die if he didn't fix this.

The sailor handed him the tool.

Moran locked the jaws of the pliers on the linkage and pressed it with all his strength. It moved slightly, but the pressure of keeping the jaws closed with his fingers took away from the force he'd need to exert to budge this bastard.

He heard the rattle of automatic rifles faintly, and then the unmistakable sound of Smith's hated carbine directly above them.

A hatch above them opened and Smith stuck his head down. "They're gaining on us, Colonel . . .."

"Close the goddamned hatch, we're working on it, Smith. Piss on them if you have to!"

The hatch slammed shut.

"Do you have a lock wrench?" he asked the sailor.

The man sloshed forward in the bilge, climbed up and rummaged in a locker, and handed Moran the tool. He tightened the adjusting screw until the wrench grabbed the brass bar and snapped the lock down. Then he began to push with both hands on the end of the tool using it as a lever without a fulcrum. The brass rod moved a little more . . . but not enough. Moran stood up. *What the hell to do?*

Then he put his foot on the tool. The powerful muscles in his leg ached from the sudden strain . . . but the damned thing moved! *Almost there!*

He pushed again . . . and suddenly there was no resistance. "It's free," he shouted.

But it wasn't. The lock wrench had only twisted out of position, and then fell clattering into the bilge.

Moran fished it out and set it again, changing the angle so that the wrench handle was horizontal. One foot on the handle, Moran cautiously balanced his weight on it, placing his hands on the floorboards on either side of him. He lifted his weight by his arms like a gymnast, then the boat rolled suddenly as up above Smith changed direction quickly.

"Open the hatch," he ordered.

The sailor flipped it up.

"Keep it goddamned steady, Smitty."

"They're gaining, Colonel."

"Fuck 'em, Smitty. Steady!"

The sailor dropped the hatch.

Moran lifted his weight with his arms and brought his foot and his entire body down on the lock wrench handle. He prayed that it wouldn't slip. It didn't, but it moved off the horizontal. Elated, he repeated the movement. The wrench handle dropped some more.

He dropped into the bilge and with a strength in his arms that he didn't know he had twisted the now vertical wrench handle into an upright position, tightened the jaw and pressed it as hard as he could. The handle moved a quarter turn back to the horizontal, and with one more superhuman press downward, he had twisted the brass bar free of the rest of the linkage. He pulled on the dual rods with his free hand and felt the motors surge.

WHEN HE THOUGHT ABOUT IT LATER, Moran didn't know what had happened first, because just as he opened the hatch and yelled "Open her up, Smitty!" he heard a splintering crash and a thump that made the deck vibrate. A rocket. He remembered thinking *we're hit*, and waited for the explosion that would end it all. But it didn't come.

He felt the motors surge and the boat leapt ahead, but there was a strain. It didn't sound right. He rushed through the saloon doors, stepping over the supine form of Kananga, still asleep, and the other sailor, curled up like a baby and shivering with terror.

He didn't believe what he saw! A ten foot long steel shaft had splintered through the transom and was buried in the after deck. Heavy link chain attached to the end of the shaft stretched tautly into the darkness behind them.

The bastards had harpooned the boat!

While they had slowed to half-speed and were moping along like some huge lumbering whale, those clever sons of bitches had put a harpoon launcher on the mount in front of their boat and had zipped the barbed steel right into the Chris-Craft's guts.

Moran considered firing another flare and some shots with the Mannlicher, but he knew it was no use. Unless they could rid themselves of the huge steel shaft they'd tow the fucking dory forever, or at least until it was light enough for the bastards to get a clear shot with the rocket launcher. Sitting ducks!

He leapt up the ladder to the bridge and told Smith. "You can't cut it, Smitty," he shouted, exasperated, "you'd need a hacksaw, ten blades, and three hours to do it, and God knows how long the chain is, could be thirty feet until it splices with rope, or it could be all chain. If you try to winch it in they'll be up our ass."

Moran knew that the other boat could winch in the cable any time they wanted, and all he'd be able to do was pop at them with his rifles until the ammunition was gone. Hopeless. Up the creek without a paddle, as the Americans said.

"Can you take the helm, sir, and let me try something?"

Moran took the wheel. The throttle was full out, but he felt the drag of the dory two hundred yards behind them. He was a dead whale making his last run.

"What do you think you can do, Smith?"

The burly man told him.

Moran smiled "Worth a try," he said, and slowed the boat again. No point in wasting petrol now, it might be needed later.

Smith went down to the afterdeck and Moran could hear the clank of metal as Smith rolled a steel drum from its storage locker under the rear bench seat. Then more clanking of metal on metal, pounding . . . like a heavy hammer. A grunt, something heavy rolling, and finally a request. "As slow and steady as you dare, Colonel."

Moran slowed the cruiser to about five knots. The well lubricated twin engines were almost silent in the night and he could hear a splashing gurgle of Smith dumping liquid over the side, then a single splash as he dropped the drum into the wake.

"How long now, Colonel?" Smith asked in a hoarse whisper.

"About three minutes," Moran said.

He watched the illuminated dial of his heavy, steel watch. The sweep second hand crept around once, then twice, and had almost completed its third revolution when Moran called out "NOW SMITTY, NOW!"

The flare ignited just above the surface of the water two hundred yards astern and for a brief second Moran saw the gray prow of the big dory as it was towed along behind his cruiser like a dinghy. He could even see the dark chain where it slanted up from the water to a winch mounted forward.

And then the night was lit up with a blaze and filled with a crackling roar. Gasoline — 100 gallons from the drum that Smitty had hacked open with a fire ax and dropped into the smooth wake — had become a fiery inferno touched off by the flare.

"DOWN, SMITTY, DOWN," Moran shouted, but he knew he couldn't be heard against the deafening noise. He felt a rush of wind as the air all around was drawn in towards the fire.

Whether it was the fire itself or Smith's second flare — shot this time from the rifle-length launcher silhouetted against the orange forty-foot flames — he didn't know, but an instant after the large projectile pierced the wall of flames there was a second, more deafening, explosion from the midst of the inferno. The gas tanks and whatever explosives they had on board blew skyward with the noise of a four-hundred pound bomb and a brilliant flash of light, carrying bits of boat metal and shreds of whatever remained of the roasted carcasses heavenwards.

Moran pushed the throttles to full speed, and felt no more drag. He called down through the hatch for Pierre, and when the sailor scrambled topside, he handed over the wheel and told the man to set a course for home.

It took two hours of work, but only five hacksaw blades, for the other crewman to cut through the harpoon shaft just above where the barbed head had buried itself in the deck. The dragging severed chain was reeled in just as soon as Moran was sure the water had cooled it sufficiently. After the sailor had cut through the shaft he went below and crawled through the under deck space to retrieve the razor sharp head of the primitive weapon that had almost cost them their lives.

MORAN WAS SITTING with his back against the cabin wall — out of the windflow and spray — enjoying a cigar, and tiredly watching the clearing sky, the moon ducking in and out of clouds and the comforting roar of the powerful engines spreading a wide, white wake across the black water. In the east, the sky was getting lighter, and a hint of orange tinted the horizon.

The sailor handed him the harpoon head and went back below.

Moran was a man who liked everything to fall into place. Every phenomenon that touched his life should have an explanation, and he was uneasy if one didn't. What happened this night would trouble him for a long time to come, but it needn't anymore, or, at least, not the bulk of the story . . . only a few details.

In the dim half-light of the early dawn he could just make out the lettering on the harpoon head, and it told him most of what he wanted to know. He dropped the shaft, chain and head overboard followed by the half smoked cigar, and stepped out of the graying air into the cabin.

On the carpeted floor in front of him, Jeremiah Kananga still slept, his bulk heaving up and down with heavy breathes, dreaming perhaps of unusual events during the night.

PART THREE

14

LONDON

NICK PLANNED TO GO directly from Heathrow to meet with Hartsdale-Smythe and settle a detail that had disturbed his ineffectual dozing on the overnight flight from Harare. It wasn't until he groggily watched the brilliant unfiltered dawn over the Algerian Sahara, the smooth ridges of the high dunes passing five miles underneath him waved like an old-fashioned hairdo in a 1930s movie, that he thought of what was nagging at him.

The tall, dark haired stewardess had leaned over his seat with the early coffee he'd requested, and he'd watched her hand as she deftly placed the thick, white china cup and saucer on the lift-up table. When she poured cream from a pitcher he heard jingling and noticed three thick, gold bangles on her wrist.

"Anniversary gift," she smiled.

"Admirer?"

She had Gabrielle's feline smile when she answered, "I hope so," then added, "husband too."

"Lucky man," Nick said, meaning it. Maybe distances and separations could work for some, yet the inclination matured over forty years had leaned him the other way.

Gabrielle probably had it right too . . . nine to five, weekends at home, ten days in the sun midwinter, two weeks with the in-laws in France midsummer and Sunday dinners with his mother and sister in Forest Hills every few weeks.

He remembered the "show biz" remark to Nemberton, and that was when the idea, that had begun to nag at him during his fitful napping, slammed into his brain with such surprising clarity that he couldn't sit still. He drank the rest of the coffee without tasting it, took his toilet kit from the two suiter hung in the locker in front of his first row seat, and went to the head. Shaving was the time for clear thinking.

HARTSDALE-SMYTHE ARRIVED at Randall's London OMEGA office moments after Nick had, and was more than usually rumpled, though freshly shaved and wearing a clean shirt. Forgetful, he dropped ashes on it from the cigarette holder stuck in his teeth, but he had remembered the tape Nick had asked for during his telephone call from Randall's car. A sleepy woman's voice had answered the early call and Nick was sure he'd woken the head of MI6.

"Flurry in Whitehall, old man," Hartsdale-Smythe was saying, "and the backbiting from the other security services is beginning to hurt." Scotland Yard and MI5 had their friends in court, he pointed out, and they were claiming that the lack of results from the joint Anglo-American effort warranted the other services getting into the picture.

"And while you were up in the air last night, there was an attempt to bomb Anthony Trevor-Jones' house in Harare, and the whites are clamoring for us to send a peace-keeping force . . .."

"Sir Peter mentioned that when I saw him the other day," Nick interrupted.

The silver haired aristocrat had been polite, cool and circumspect, a world apart from Hartsdale-Smythe's manner developed during his rise through the ranks. Antithetical in manner and appearance, Sir Peter, with noblesse oblige silently engraved on his brow, had listened to Nick's summation, which omitted some details, thanked him, and ventured nothing. That meeting had had another value, however.

"Set up the tape, Elliot, would you?" Nick asked.

Randall took the cassette copy from the Englishman, who first had to pat the various stuff in pockets of his vested suit and overcoat until he found it.

"And Yogun has cabled State demanding that Company marines land. OMEGA's not up to the job according to him," Randall said.

"Scalzio must love him for that," Nick said.

"Heard that the Secretary sent a two-word reply."

"Wonder what they were?" Nick said.

Hartsdale-Smythe snorted, dropping more ashes on his much abused, old Etonian necktie.

The video screen came to life and film from a shaking camera showed the faces of Kananga and Joseph as the photographer moved closer to them. Then Kananga's face alone filled the screen. The whole tape ran only two minutes and fifteen seconds.

"Run it again, Elliot, please."

Randall rewound the cassette, and started it forward again.

"Now. Can you freeze that?" Nick asked.

Randall stopped the tape.

"No, not his face, back it up a little."

Randall rewound slowly.

The camera shakily moved away from Kananga's face, and showed Joseph still in one piece, then the corner of the room as a hand reached across and turned off the BBC Evening News.

"Right there," Nick said.

"What's right there?" Hartsdale-Smythe asked.

"A woman's hand turning off the set. Elliot, can you bring that in closer?"

"Not on this machine, sir, but there's another downst. . .."

"No time," Nick said. "Magnifying glass?"

Randall rummaged in his desk and handed Nick one with a large round lens.

"Look here, John," Nick said, and pointed to a bracelet on the wrist, silently thanking the stewardess who brought him coffee just a few hours earlier.

"I fail to see. . .," Hartsdale-Smythe said.

Nick explained the "bracelet of privilege" of a royal concubine, everything that Neliwe Goldstein had told him about Kananga's pretensions to ancestral *droit de seigneur*, as briefly as he could.

"And someone else is wearing the identical gold whatsit?" Hartsdale-Smythe said excitedly burning his fingers as he pulled one smoking cigarette from the ivory holder and shoved in another fresh one.

247

"And she's in England?" Randall practically shouted.

"The lad has a firm grasp upon the obvious,"Hartsdale-Smythe said as the wooden match he'd lit scorched his finger.

"When was that news broadcast, John?"

"Last Sunday night."

"It's hard to believe that this has been going on for only a week," Nick said, "seems more like a year"

"I wish it was a year," Hartsdale-Smythe said. "Then the papers would be tired of it all. As it is, they're still on the story and are burning us terribly. My minister is hounding me day and night. I don't even get a decent night in the kip."

Nick remembered the voice of the woman who had answered Hartsdale-Smythe's telephone that morning, and remembered the Englishman saying he was no longer married . . . and thought that there were other things keeping John awake at night.

"It could be a hoax," Randall said.

The senior men looked at him unhappily.

"I mean," he went on, "that the TV program could have been taped here, replayed elsewhere just the way we're doing it now . . . and included on this tape to make it seem simultaneous."

"Oh, shit!" Nick said, annoyed, "why didn't I think of that."

"You're not gadget-minded like young Randall here," Hartsdale-Smythe said, rescuing him mercifully. "Generational, old man. Geezers like us weren't teethed on transistorized rattles."

"I'm not that young," Randall protested.

"'Ah, where ignorance is bliss,'" the Englishman misquoted.

"Listen, there's no time for pleasantries," Nick said, "there's more."

They stared at him questioningly.

He focused the magnifying glass on the gold bracelet and caught a glint of the camera. "I saw the woman who was wearing it!"

"Goldstein's wife, you said," the Englishman reminded him.

"She doesn't have white arms, John."

"Wait, let me back this up a frame or so," Randall said. "It *has* to be in England," he pronounced after examining the few preceding seconds of tape.

The two chiefs waited for a further explanation, hoping that the hypothesis would hold up.

"That set is too old. See the tube model, it's a black and white, and it can't be hooked up to a VCR."

"How do you know that?" Hartsdale-Smythe asked.

"It's the same model we have in our apartment."

"He means flat," Nick said.

"Thank you so much for the translation," the Englishman said.

"Then we can be pretty sure the video was taped last Sunday here in England . . . right?" Nick asked. "Isn't that the point they were trying to make on the tape . . . rubbing our noses in it, and verifying that the tape was made when and where they said?"

"Point?" asked the Englishman.

"The point is that when I went to see Sir Peter Soames in Harare, one of Kananga's most recent extra curricular activities was sitting in his office . . . or just outside."

"But the old lecher distributes his royal favors pretty widely according to what you said a moment ago," Hartsdale-Smythe reminded Nick.

"Yes, including to a lovely young Englishwoman who had just returned from London on the Wednesday night flight, and who, besides being one of Kananga's women, happens to be Sir Peter's secretary, *and* the sometime-mistress of our beloved Ambassador Yogun."

Randall and Hartsdale-Smythe sat with their mouths in the fly-catching position.

Then Hartsdale-Smythe was on his feet and at the door, scattering ashes on everything. Halfway through the door he turned, "Her name, Burns?" he asked looking grim and agitated.

"Maggie Groves . . . Margaret, I suppose." *Was it Nemberton or Buchanan who had told him about Yogun's favorite indoor sport?* "You don't suppose that you could find out where she spent her home-leave, could you, John?" he added.

"I'll damned well try," the Englishman called over his shoulder impatiently, his face darkly flushed with anger. "Sit tight." He stomped off without turning again and Nick saw him duck down the stairs rather than wait for the elevator.

"Did you book me at Claridges?" Nick asked Randall when the door shut itself.

Randall had.

"Call me there . . . the ball's in John's court for a while, and you must have something to keep you busy."

He wrote out several messages, handed them to Randall to have coded and cabled, and then stood and picked up his single piece of luggage.

"I'll run you over," Randall said, also getting up.

"I can walk two blocks, Elliot . . . still," he said.

Nick wanted to get some of the fresh April morning in his lungs and then make a telephone call that was not the business of anyone else.

SAINT-MALO

THE HARBOR OF SAINT-MALO is well protected from the winds that ravage the coast of Brittany from the north and east, howling down the English Channel, raising broad, green waves and smashing the brown sand of the wide, flat beaches and the rocks with blinding spray.

Inside the outer harbor breakwater with its flashing beacon, the local working vessels and fishing boats lie at low tide with their bottoms on the oil blackened mud. Further inside, through a narrow man-made inlet, the dredged inner basin is a cozy refuge for large yachts bearing royal coats-of- arms as well as small runabouts with outboard motors. They all nestle together in the Bassin Vauban either rafted together next to the stone quay or at the several concrete finger piers narrowly dividing the quiet water at the end of the port. The twelfth century ramparts surrounding the old city tower forty feet above the quay. Visitors walking on the ancient wall gape at

250

the forest of masts that reach their eye level and often stare rudely at the pleasure crafts' crews as though they were putting on a show for the amusement of tourists.

Moran had a permanent berth at the end of one of the concrete finger slips, made permanent by regular large tips to the harbormaster and his assistant. Even when the port was mobbed with summer fair-weather sailors, and there was not an inch of space along the quays, the Chris-Craft always had its place. Watchful petty officialdom needed its living supplements too much to allow any other boat to even rest in Moran's berth. And the mercenary, who had spent far more time on his boat than ever before since his "retirement" never ceased to remind the harbor personnel of his own Breton mother, and lapsed into the local dialect whenever they talked about the weather . . . which was all they ever talked about. And the harbormaster, who relished being addressed as "Captain," which he never was despite the gold braid on his blue serge uniform jacket worn shiny at the elbows, always repaid Moran's courtesy and easy dialect by referring to him as "*mon Colonel*". . . which he still was.

The second day after the "heavy weather" — as Moran later referred to the episode in mid-channel — he was sitting on the rear deck of the cruiser, enjoying the bright, cool April day, and admiring the handiwork of the carpenter from a neighboring shipyard who had repaired the damage to the boat. A new plank had been installed in the wooden transom, the hole in the fiberglass deck had been patched and painted, the teak grating overlay replaced, and the hole letting water into the forward bilge had been patched from inside. The fancier cosmetics would be left until the boat was hauled for its mid-season bottom cleaning and repainting.

Throughout the repair work, which had started at eight that morning, Moran had insisted that Kananga remain in his cabin, to emerge only briefly when the workmen broke for lunch and then, only into the saloon. He wanted to take no chances of recognition, and had screwed a heavy hasp and ring bolt to the mahogany door and frame of Kananga's forward cabin and padlocked it shut from the outside.

251

With the workmen gone, Moran had let Kananga into the main saloon again, but forbade that he go to the deck. Tourist season hadn't begun yet, but the ramparts above had sufficient curiosity seekers bristling with binoculars and Brownie cameras to make him extra cautious. He hadn't planned it to be this way and it made him uncomfortable, although he tried not to show it.

Kananga's broad shiny face appeared at the cabin door.

"And what are you doing, Colonel Moran," he asked.

"Watching the paint dry?"

"An admirable pastime."

"It'll do." Moran was generally disinclined to unnecessary conversation. Small talk, particularly now, irritated him.

"I'd be happy to join you and assist you in that task."

"Sit down and get away from the door," Smith growled from inside, then added "please," a little less gruffly. He sat at the dining table studying an arms catalogue from his favorite Austrian dealer, the one who could always supply the Soviet and Czech weapons, for a price.

The mercenaries who worked Africa preferred them. Less temperamental than the American and German stuff, less likely to go on the fritz when you needed them most.

The "D" semi-automatic rifle with a night scope interested him. It was only listed under its initial — a little coy Smith thought — but he knew that it was the one Volkov had told him about, so new it's not known in the west, he had said. The Draganov, a new Soviet issue with high velocity rounds, it could take explosive shells, too. If only he had had that one the other night.

"Sorry, General," Moran said to the dark face he could just see through the slightly ajar door. "Can't take the risk of someone spotting you . . . maybe after dark." He left it vague intentionally. If Jacqure Monnier arrived as planned he'd be able to let the fat man stroll about a bit, on short tether, but he didn't want to make any promises. Monnier was due at six from Paris. Three hours to go.

"I need some exercise," Kananga said.

"Try sleeping," Moran answered, "you're good at that."

"Not very amusing, Colonel. What do you do for exercise?"

"I smoke cigars," Moran answered — a bullfighter had said that once, in a Hemingway novel half a life ago.

"I don't," Kananga said petulantly, and backed away from the door.

A moment later, Moran heard the forward cabin door slam shut. Kananga had taken his advice.

"IT WAS POSSIBLE, but it would be costly," Monnier said sipping his pilsner.

He was a useful man, if you could pay for it, and Moran had no options other than to do so . . . besides, the money for Captain Voortrecker hadn't been paid, so he was still ahead.

Moran sat with his old OAS companion from Algeria and ran through the obligatory "remember when's" from the Battle of Algiers and some of the private contracts they had fulfilled after that.

Monnier, gaunt cheeked and lanky as a string bean had ended his career as a mercenary when he was told he had lung cancer. Eighteen years and one lung removed later, he was still kicking. A supplier now, he could get anything and everything for a price, but only worked for people he had known in the old days, and relived the past as prelude to every new order.

They sat in the dim, oak-paneled gloom of the large cafe in the Place Chateaubriand, just outside the old city wall. Opposite the cafe, the Château Saint-Malo loomed . . . an ominous portcullis lowered halfway in the crenelated entryway as though it would drop on anyone foolish enough to pass underneath.

A crowd of townspeople familiar with each other crowded the room for their evening drinks between the shops and offices and their homes. All the tourists were gone for the day, so no one was sitting in the chill outside.

Monnier pushed a paper-wrapped parcel towards Moran.

"I'll remember it," Moran said.

"Take it now, I don't want to wait too long."

"But we haven't agreed on the price."

"I told you it was 100,000 francs!"

Moran knew that Monnier wanted 50,000 and so had asked double. If Moran had agreed, Monnier would be disappointed that he hadn't asked more. Moran pushed his chair away from the table.

"What do I owe you for this?" He pointed at the twine tied package.

"It's part of the deal."

"And if I don't take the deal?"

Monnier didn't show any emotion. He raised his shoulders in a Gallic shrug.

"Gratis . . . for old times."

"The passport?"

"Included in the *prix fixe* menu."

"A la carte?"

Monnier shrugged again. "Four thousand."

Moran didn't debate. He counted out the wrinkled notes and pushed them across the small, round marble table.

Monnier let the money lie there.

Moran stood. "Fifteen minutes," he said.

"Please," Monnier said. "My wife is at her sister's in Avranches. I said I'd be back for dinner. It's a long drive."

Moran didn't answer. He pushed the parcel under his arm like a rugby ball and turned to walk away.

"Jean Luc!" Monnier called.

Moran turned.

A passing waitress gave him an interested look.

"Thirty minutes," he said to Monnier.

"How much?" Monnier asked.

"Forty thousand," Moran said.

Monnier shook his head sadly. "Sixty . . . minimum!"

"Fifty," Moran said, and saw Monnier smile and nod agreement.

"I like to make you happy, *mon vieux*," he said as Moran returned to the table and picked up the untouched bank notes.

"Twenty-two minutes," Moran said with a grin and off he marched.

The money would buy him the services of a trusted pair of pilots and their Lear jet to take him from the airport at nearby Dinard to Lisbon, with one fuel stop in Bilbao. He didn't want to run any more risks than he had to with French airport officialdom , so he insisted on a refuel in Spain where they didn't give a damn underneath their pomposity, and always welcomed "gifts."

In Lisbon Monnier would arrange for one of his men to meet Moran's plane and facilitate the transfer of the three passengers into first class seats on the TAP Air Portugal flight for Jo'burg. The rest was simple.

Half an hour later, Moran was back in the cafe. The crowd had thinned slightly and Monnier was reading *Paris Match* . . . the pilsner still untouched. He handed the lanky man four passport photographs he had just taken with the Polaroid camera Monnier had included in the bulky parcel.

Monnier let out a short, high-pitched cackle that ended in a one-lunged wheeze. Staring out at them from one of the square photos was a bearded black sheik whose picture would shortly be officially franked into a Sudanese passport.

"You've got to admit, it's a very funny idea," Monnier said, catching his breath.

"I must have missed my vocation," Moran said.

Monnier drained his glass, stood, and offered his hand. "Monday, Dinard airport, 0800 hours," he said.

"You'll have the money?"

"If you're there with the plane and the passports," Moran said.

Moran watched the lanky man's back as he walked out the door and got into a white Citroen illegally parked at the curb. Monnier took the parking ticket off the windshield, stuffed it in his pocket and drove away to his waiting wife in Avranches.

Outside the ramparts, a bearded sheik strolled slowly, enjoying the cool night air, and chuckling to himself at the stares of the few passersby. The grim burly man who walked a few paces behind him with watchful eyes looked like the kind of bodyguard any rich Arab businessman was supposed to have . . . and so he was. Smith didn't seem to enjoy the job, but, thought Jeremiah Kananga, what concern was that of his.

Inside the cafe, Moran signaled to the waitress with the assessing eyes. Her expression, as she approached the table, was unmistakable . . . tonight, he'd be enjoying her company.

15

ENGLAND

THE HERTFORDSHIRE CONSTABULARY hadn't been on red alert since the Great Train Robbery and that was beyond the memory of anyone still working on the force, but that morning Hartsdale-Smythe had to convince his minister, Roger Mattingly of Foreign Affairs, who had to be called out from a high-level meeting at which the past weekend's grouse shoot was being discussed, that the crisis he was dealing with was extremely urgent.

Mattingly was quite annoyed at the interruption. "You know H.S., there *are* priorities," he berated the head of MI6 while thinking *why doesn't the man go to a good tailor instead of wearing those Marks and Spencer numbers off the rack.* He was vaguely embarrassed by Hartsdale-Smythe, his old Eton classmate, and always chose the darkest corner at his club when he had to meet with him.

But Hartsdale-Smythe would not be rebuffed . . . not today. He wanted to remain in charge of the operation and was not going to allow those gumshoes from MI5 to take over the case, whatever the charter said about operations on domestic versus foreign soil.

Fortunately, the minister of Home Affairs was also at the same "high-level" meeting, and was basking in the size of his bag on the shoot that previous weekend, so he was inclined to be generous.

In the end, Hartsdale-Smythe won . . . or at least Mattingly did.

AS THEIR HELICOPTER LIFTED OFF shortly after noon from the RAF pad on the Thames in Chelsea, Hartsdale-Smythe told Nick that he had been "very unsettled" during the time he was with Mattingly. "Inter-departmental rivalries here — as well as across the pond — can be very complicated, as you know," he said.

Nick could hardly hear him over the metallic clatter of the giant rotor overhead as the chopper lifted, followed the river briefly then veered northward.

By the time they set down twenty minutes later in the middle of the village green at Datchworth, a sleepy village they were using as a staging area, Nick heard the rest of the story.

"Maggie Groves had been on home leave and was in England on the very day Kananga was kidnapped. In fact she had stopped in at the Foreign Office the day before to check on the processing of some medical payment vouchers for treatment by a doctor who wasn't on National Health — 'couldn't very well be on our rolls in Zimbabwe, could he now?' — and had said she was staying with her mother in Bramfield — 'farmland . . . an old church where Thomas à Beckett was its first rector . . . a newsagent . . . nothing more.' A local constable said that there were a number of vehicles in the drive recently, but he knew Maggie was around for a home visit, 'saw her in the village buying the papers' and thought nothing of it. RAF reconnaissance fly over an hour ago reported no activity at the house, no cars in the drive. But they might still be there . . . cars in the garage . . . whatnot."

"But, John," Nick said, as they stepped onto the closely cropped grass and ducked under the whirling rotors to walk toward the half-tracks and armored troop carriers of the tactical assault team and a flotilla of police cars completely surrounding the village green, "what makes you think that Kananga's here? And now, at any rate?"

Hartsdale-Smythe stopped in his tracks, his bland face seething, "Look here, Burns, what in hell else do we have to go on . . . some hoods in Zimbabwe shooting at you? Damn it, man, do you think I'm blind? I know the face in Goldstein's picture as well as you do. And I don't want to talk about it now!" he threw in to divert the interruption to protest he saw pending in Nick's expression. "We vetted and trained the damned woman and put her in place. Do you understand what it means for us if she's been turned?"

Without waiting for an answer, the Englishman turned and hurried towards the waiting armada.

Speeders on the motorways, peeping Toms, bank robbers, punk rockers out for a bashing, housebreakers and poachers throughout Hertfordshire could have had a field day that Thursday had they only known that every available man and woman in the Hertfordshire constabulary had been pressed into service. Within minutes of the helicopter's setting down on the Datchworth village green, cars with flashing lights, unmarked detective vehicles, grey vans and blue Paddy wagons were dispersed throughout the back roads, country lanes and secondary highways of the rolling Hertfordshire hills surrounding Bramfield to seal off all access within a half mile radius around the Groves' house, which stood on a slight rise overlooking fertile wheat and barley farms, a stone's throw from the National Parkland Forest Preserve of Bramfield Wood, once the private hunting ground of royalty. Only some drunken brawlers from the legions of the unemployed who filled the football stadiums on weekday afternoons managed to finish their fight at Stevenage with the satisfaction of more broken noses and swollen eyes than they could have boasted another day. For reasons they couldn't and wouldn't know, no police arrived to interrupt them.

For the police, the day was even more unusual because they carried sidearms and rifles that had been issued at each station house. Not used to such baggage, they were excited and somewhat apprehensive, lest they should have to use the weapons, which most of the constables hadn't seen since their rookie days in training.

Every vehicle that exited from the cordoned off area was to be stopped and searched, and no vehicle of any kind was to enter.

Within minutes of the police deployment the more than usually inefficient central telephone switchboard for the entire county at Hertford was jammed with incoming calls.

Once Hartsdale-Smythe's order to close off all electrical service to the area was transmitted, a complete black out was put into effect.

The airport at Luton diverted all flights to London, and no plane was given authorization to leave the ground. RAF interceptors stood by to force down any unidentified plane in the airspace, as if Hertfordshire had gone to war.

A commando unit fanned out through the Bramfield Wood startling hares and deer, while another group crossing a field hidden from the Groves' house by a large hedgerow interrupted a bull's sleep and had to scramble across a stile without soldierly dignity to escape being gored.

Nick and Hartsdale-Smythe accompanied the Special Forces assault team led by the captain who had distinguished himself in the retaking of the Iranian Embassy in London a few months earlier. They remained inside the armored personnel carrier at the end of the long drive leading up to the house while twelve lithe, muscular men in camouflage battle fatigues and black berets tipped rakishly over one eye appeared behind trees and flowering bushes, then near the garage, on the roof, under windows, alongside the front door.

Their commander made an announcement on the bull horn when everyone was in place. Nick and Hartsdale Smythe watched the windows through binoculars, but there was only silence from the house. A second announcement, then the captain signaled with his hands and Nick saw the team move into efficient, concerted action; the trained expertise was a pleasure to watch. Three men on the peaked roof were crouching one minute, the next swinging from the eaves and then crashing through the upper story windows with their heavy boots. Seconds later they were inside. Two others dashed through the cellar door, while the captain rushed the front door, kicked it open with one lunge and disappeared inside; another man followed him. The rest were prone on the ground, weapons aimed and ready.

"If those guys had been at the Embassy in Iran . . .," Nick said to his companion.

"Good, aren't they," Hartsdale-Smythe answered, his eyes not budging from the field glasses.

"Wish they were ours," Nick said.

"Can I quote you?"

"Not for attribution."

The captain in the black beret stood in the doorway, then stepped out onto the lawn and gestured to Hartsdale-Smythe and Nick with his hand. They trotted up from the armored vehicle to where the soldier stood, but the message was clear before they reached him as the assault team one by one exited through the front door.

"Sorry, sir," the craggy captain said. "Nobody home!"

He looked more disappointed than Hartsdale-Smythe.

"Thank you, captain," Hartsdale-Smythe said, offering him a cigarette. The soldier refused. They were all disappointed.

"Great teamwork," Nick said. "Amazing."

The soldier thanked him with a grim smile. "We aim to please," he said, and followed his men to the waiting vehicle.

Nick and Hartsdale-Smythe walked into the house.

It was empty, neat, all the beds made, no disarray of people's normally messy lives anywhere except for the broken glass.

A tall, heavyset man huffed into the room where they stood. "Benjamin Walton, C.I.D.," he said.

"Could you have your team check all those details you're so good at, sir? Prints, hair, debris . . . any and everything?" asked Hartsdale-Smythe. It wasn't really a request.

"It'll take a while."

"I want a report tonight," Hartsdale-Smythe said and turned in dismissal.

The other man lumbered out.

"Can I lift the cordon, sir?" asked the chief of the Hertfordshire Constabulary.

"Yes, yes," said the rumpled MI6 man impatiently. "Call off all the dogs, and, Chief Inspector," he called to the police chief as he backed away, "do you have a maintenance unit?"

"Of course," the other man smiled affably, glad to be of service to history.

"Would you, please send them in tomorrow after C.I.D. finishes and replace the glass, fix up in general and put the place back in order?"

"Done."

"Oh — and I want the place patrolled until further notice."

THEY WERE STANDING in the room where the tape had been made. The television set was against the wall, the couch on which Kananga sat just where it had been. No doubt about it.

"Unusually orderly, John."

"This place? Oh yes . . .."

"No, I mean you . . . requesting repairs and cleanup."

"I know the family."

"They in on this?"

"I strongly doubt it," Hartsdale-Smythe said. He cupped his hand for ashes rather than drop them on the floor with his usual aplomb.

"They travel a lot," he continued, "Far East mostly. He's a consulting engineer. She goes along now that the girl's gone and left home."

"Not in Zimbabwe by any chance?" Nick asked, "like that other house these characters used?"

"Oh no. That, by the way, turned out to be pure happenstance."

"But this isn't!"

"I'm afraid it isn't, Burns, afraid it isn't."

Hartsdale-Smythe turned aside averting his face from Nick, and his shoulders suddenly heaved. A bedraggled handkerchief appeared in his hand and he coughed into it, blew his nose, and quickly wiped his face. When he turned back to face Nick his angry, pained expression had changed to sadness, as extreme as if a loved one had died.

Nick heard the words almost before Hartsdale-Smythe said them:

"Nick, Maggie is my daughter!"

THEY WERE SITTING in a dingy local bar near the house.

Nick was sipping at the miniscule measure of malt whiskey nestling at the bottom of a stem glass . . . the barman had called it a double.

Hartsdale-Smythe was drinking Guinness. "The stuff here is swill," he pronounced, "if you want the real Guinness, you have to go to Dublin. They drink it too fast to export."

For the past two hours conversation between the two master spies had been decorous, seemly, and they'd danced away from the Englishman's evident pain with delicacy.

Events had made it easy. First there was the body. Commandos fanning through Bramfield Wood had discovered it, sort of. Rather, they had come across two lovers, teen-agers from the local grammar school who had eschewed classes that balmy afternoon to embrace each other. Pants half off, they had been scared all the way off by the squad of bayonet-ready assault troops breaking into the clearing where they lay in the tall weeds beneath some ancient copper beeches. It had been the nightmare fulfillment of parental threats that they would look up and see that the army had really been sent out after them.

The sergeant, however, with teen-agers of his own, was sage enough to realize that his men had not seized Kananga's daring kidnapper, and let them off with an admonition, after duly recording their names and addresses in his notebook. He would destroy the page later, he knew, but relished the effect of the lesson. The youngsters were then aimed towards the road with a note for the guard. "I don't want you mucking about in the woods, you two, there's some dangerous criminals loose hereabouts," he had warned them avuncularly, as he watched them hurry off, red-faced and tongue-tied. Then he heard a scream only seconds later, and saw the children come tearing back towards the commandos.

"A man . . . a foot . . . over there . . . some rocks," the girl sobbed. The boy's face was frozen white with speechless terror.

Even the battle-toughened commandos didn't find it a pleasant sight. The corporal stumbled away to retch while the others turned their eyes. A man's leg lay exposed where animals, probably badgers thought the sergeant, had scratched away the dirt from a shallow grave. The shoe was still on the foot, but the trousers were in tatters where the sharp teeth of the night-prowling carnivores had ripped them away to get at the flesh. Congealed blood was caked on the leg and covered with flies and crawling things that had cleaned what the animals had left down to the bone.

The sergeant pushed some more dirt away with the tip of his bayonet. Where the animals hadn't feasted yet, the intact skin was black. He radioed to the command center and asked for the police and medics . . . their job, this. No mortician he, just a soldier, he waited with one other man, while the corporal, pale still but recovered took the rest of the platoon to continue the sweep through the woods. On the ordinance map, there were only several hundred yards more to the open field behind the house, and he doubted that they'd find anything else.

By the time the messenger sent to Hartsdale-Smythe had brought the MI6 chief and Nick back to the woods, the police and medics had the remains dug up and laid out under a plastic tarp.

"It's Kananga's aide," Nick said, looking at the headless trunk with disgust. Worms crawled out of the open cavity of the neck.

"Brutal butchers," said Hartsdale-Smythe, turning aside. "You're sure it's not Kananga?"

"Not unless he's been dieting," Nick said, pushing back his nausea with levity.

"Now who's got the gallows humor?" Hartsdale-Smythe asked.

"Graveyard, pal . . . there's a difference," Nick said. He took one of the Englishman's cigarettes to get the stench out of his nostrils.

"The forensic lab will confirm it all, I suppose," Hartsdale-Smythe said, walking towards the car. His gloom had returned, heavier than before. He gave some orders to the messenger at their heels.

AFTERWARDS NICK AND Hartsdale-Smythe went for drinks at the Plume of Feathers, which was just down the road from the Datchworth village green where the assault on the Groves home had been staged.

"I'm ready," Nick said to Hartsdale-Smythe, draining the rest of his first round of whiskey.

He went to the bar for his second and brought another stout for the Englishman who was staring at the log fire in the pub's stone hearth.

"Not a shining day," Nick ventured.

"By any means," Hartsdale-Smythe agreed. "You know, Burns," he said, livening slightly out of his listless stare at the artificial fire skillfully contrived of logs that didn't burn and were fired from beneath by gas jets in a trompe l'oeil. "I had hoped for a coup of sorts to save the day, you know, 'heroic British assault team under the command of yours truly saves the day, stages daring rescue of Kananga from the jaws of death' and all that. Golden opportunity for HM's government. Save face, no capitulation to terrorists. You know the story."

Nick nodded, sipped, and said nothing, but watched the non-consuming flames.

"Like that, it was," the Englishman continued, opening a fresh box of cigarettes, indicating the fire they stared at. "Light but no heat, no heroic headlines. They might have helped."

"What you'll get from the press will be anything but that," Nick said.

"Oh, no," Hartsdale-Smythe said. "The gag order went out to the press, and we didn't even let them near."

"Official secrets?"

"Convenient."

Nick began to clean his pipe.

The pub was beginning to fill with men and woman on their way home from work. It was getting noisy and the noise seemed to loosen up the Englishman, inspiring confidence by its very anonymity.

"I never kept it a secret," he said, "but never advertised it either . . . I mean the business about Maggie. When she wanted to join the foreign service after university, I even encouraged her. Didn't see much of the girl when she was growing up."

"Why does she have a different name?"

"She wasn't more than a year old when her mother and I parted company, and then after the divorce Edna remarried and I agreed to let her husband adopt the girl. Nice enough chap, that one, and I saw no reason to let biological fact sow confusion in the child's life. She needed and got a secure home without gossipy questions and teasing in school, so why let vanity rule?" He poured the dark ale down his throat leaving only foam in the mug, then got up and went to the men's room.

He came back a few moments later with a refill for himself and for Nick. His shaggy grey hair was damp and the tracks of the comb showed. His Eton 'old boys' tie was spotted with water.

"Vanity did rule, however," he continued, "and when she was recommended by her instructor at our Foreign Service Training Center, I was flattered, let me tell you, Burns, proud as a peacock. Biology is destiny, as the Viennese master said . . .."

"In a different context, I think," Nick said.

"Still holds true here," Hartsdale-Smythe said, smiling sadly. "Universal."

Nick didn't argue. The Englishman's speech sounded slightly slurred to him, and he deserved some reprieve from events turning out cruelly, like a Thomas Hardy universe crushing lives with indifference. Nick guessed his companion was lonely under the bluff, uncompromising facade, and he was willing to lend a rapidly mellowing ear.

"Maybe it's a form of retribution," Hartsdale-Smythe said, "for my abandoning her as a child . . .."

"I don't think you can beat yourself up for that."

"Who then?"

"No one. Circumstances beyond control."

"You don't believe that rubbish, do you, Burns?"

"Sometimes."

"Well not now. I should have stayed around and been a father to the child, whether she was adopted by William or not. Instead I pursued the golden fleece, and now it'll smother her, and me and everything I hoped for myself, and for her, when I bothered to think about her."

"Maybe it's misguided patriotism on her part," Nick said, offering a soporific to complement the alcohol. "Idea of the white man's burden, helping White Rabbit in the cause of empire."

"Wouldn't it be nice to think so, Burns. Thanks." Despite the almost three pints sloshing around in his innards Hartsdale-Smythe wasn't grasping at straws for comfort. "No, Burns, she's been sleeping around out there with a purpose, and it probably isn't ours. I broke my own rule and read the fitness reports her superiors have filed

266

over the past few years. Saw them this morning. Nothing much out of order, but I suspect she'd been turned a few years back, in Lebanon. Too pigheaded she is. Likes causes. I've kept the fatherly eye on her since."

"Any proof?"

"Not until this."

Nick tried a last parry, "White Rabbit . . . Moran, is the most vehement anti-opposition thing going."

"Burns, I'm not the blind fool I look, only when I want to be. Maggie hardly knows Moran. No known contact. It's the Russian who's running her. And why do you think?"

Nick knew already. Maggie Groves could not have had access to information of such sensitivity to be truly important to Moscow. They'd give her busywork, redundant stuff, to set the hook and hold for future use. This must have been the future. They knew who her father was. "To bring you down John, a major discredit to the service."

The Englishman nodded, unable to speak or even to light another cigarette from the already half-consumed box he'd just opened.

They left the pub, followed by a driver who was to take Hartsdale-Smythe back to London, and had been waiting in another section of the bar keeping polite class distance from the men.

"I'll tell you what the worst part is, Burns," Hartsdale-Smythe continued when they were outside in the cool night air. "I could deal with the betrayal, the spitting in the jaundiced face of patriotism. Even the embracing of the opposition cause like some bloody naive schoolgirl idealist. All that I could understand if not condone, but I can't swallow that the fool girl has gotten herself into a criminal position. She's now a damned accessory to murder." He stopped in the dark and stifled a sob. Out came the crumpled handkerchief again. He averted his eyes from the headlights of a car entering the parking area. "They'll put her away to rot for life, you know. She's a bloody fool."

"Maybe you can arrange a trade with the opposition."

Hartsdale-Smythe laughed bitterly. "They don't want her. She's of no importance. A paper doll to be thrown away after use. Completely replaceable commodity. They get her, me and the service. Two birds with one stone is an accomplishment, three, a miracle."

Nick put his hand on the Englishman's shoulder. "Maybe she'll defect. At least, then . . .."

But the rumpled man didn't let Nick finish the sentence. "That would be worse . . . for me, at least. Here, I'd get to see her. Still my flesh and blood, Burns, and I'm no Lear. Not even a third of one."

"You must love her a lot," Nick said, feeling that the words were inane, yet not knowing what he could do or say . . . as at a funeral one has to humbly offer benign words on the altar of another's grief, someone beyond the reach of words. Inadequate stupid sounds grunted into the void of what was lost forever.

"It's what you Yanks call a no-win situation anyway," Harts-dale-Smythe said, suddenly stepping briskly to the car, "the options are gone for Maggie. I ordered her arrest this morning."

16

NORMANDY

THE· GRAY SKY MADE the water look a muddy dark green and a chilly, sharp wind bit in from the east. Nick pulled up the collar of his raincoat, glad for the sweater he'd remembered to put on.

No one had followed him, he was sure.

Half a mile away to his left a fisherman stood on the hard brown sand left by the retreating tide. He held a long fishing pole that was bending over as he reeled in the lure Nick had watched being cast. Off the Normandy beach to the right, some lobstermen tended their traps from a small motorboat. He watched them cranking a double-handled winch in the stern until a box trap was lifted on the boom, then swinging the trap over the deck, freshening the bait and dropping it overboard again. No one else was around.

"Alone," Moran had stipulated.

Nick had quashed Hartsdale-Smythe's objections to the terms.

Hartsdale-Smythe objected to the terms. "You're a bloody maniac! You could wind up like that poor black sod in the woods," he said, but eventually abandoned his argument and made the arrangement for the meet with someone in Paris . . . a trusted quartermaster he knew from his old days in the Middle East.

The plane was the Englishman's detail, although Nick would have gladly forgone it for the boat train to Portsmouth and a ferry to Saint-Malo, but Hartsdale-Smythe insisted "for security."

Nick gave in on that one, but drew the line . . . a rented car, and no surveillance. Nothing to queer the deal. He knew that Moran would take no risks, and also knew that alone he had nothing to fear.

He turned and walked back along the beach toward the path that led up to the parking area. Forty-year-old strands of barbed wire still hung from original wooden pilings at the top of the cliff-like rise, and he imagined seeing the strewn bleeding bodies of the wounded and dying who had piled, wave after wave, onto Omaha beach from the LST's to be sliced into pieces by the machine guns. It had been a bloody slaughter. How many had been lost here when the American, Canadian, English and Free French bodies kept replenishing themselves, more waves brought in from the red stained water?

His father had been one of the lucky ones . . . he'd only had to limp for the rest of his life, and be reminded of his injuries when it rained by the ache from a steel plate where his knee had been.

Nick knew why he never came to the Normandy invasion beaches during all his years in France.

The brown Renault he'd rented was visible now from the path, and when he reached the top there was a black one next to it, also rented, the plates advertised. No one was in it. The only other car was far off to the left, and Nick assumed that it was the lone fisherman's. Empty, bare fields of stubble stretched away behind the hard packed ground where cars and tour buses parked in high season. The nearest houses stood far back on the flat horizon apart from each other, toy models breaking into the dull sky. The entire length of beach was a national monument — battle names frozen in history: Juno, Sword, Omaha . . .. And the French government had made its point well. They left it all bare. Imagination alone peopled the sand with dead and tinted the water with blood. In the little village of Arromanches-les-Bains, through which he had driven earlier this morning, there was a *Musée du débarquement*, the road atlas said. Maybe he'd look at it later, if he had time.

A large round, concrete gun emplacement was nestled in a hollow atop the ridge in front of him. Built for the Reich that would last a thousand years, it looked as if it was put there the day before yesterday. Nick walked toward the moribund grey mass.

THE MERCENARY WAS STANDING inside the emplacement, his back to Nick, looking out to sea over the bunker's edge. He turned at the sound of Nick's shoes on the sandy floor, smiled, and stepped forward with hand outstretched. "You haven't changed much, Burns," he said. His grip was firm and assured.

"Nor you, Jean-Luc."

Moran laughed, "What liars we both are. I'm fatter than ever and am losing my hair, and you are graying fast."

"*Plus ça change.*"

"Your French is still good," the mercenary said. "Did you ever marry the girl?"

"No," Nick said with a shake of his head, "different tracks."

"Big mistake, *mon vieux*," Moran said, "lessons of experience."

"The name we give to our mistakes!"

"Good, very good," Moran said. "Your wit hasn't gone gray."

"Credit Oscar Wilde for the words, Moran."

"We're both getting too old for all this chasing around," the mercenary said. "On a Sunday like this we should be still in bed with warm wives, dreaming."

"Why are you doing it, Jean-Luc? It isn't your style."

Moran's face switched to dead-pan seriousness. The *bonhommie* was gone and his hard, blue eyes glinted. "For the money," he said and added, "and a last fling."

"What the hell is it, a dance, a game?" Nick depended on the mercenary's bluntness to accept his own.

"I wanted Africa again," Moran said, "and not as a tourist."

"Hell of a way you picked to do it," Nick said. His hand dipped into his jacket pocket for his tobacco, and he saw Moran tense, suddenly taut like a steel spring.

"Only this," Nick said, drawing out the rolled up leather pouch.

Moran relaxed, lit a small cigar.

"Want to know why I really hate the communists," Moran asked, "because you can't get good Havanas anymore, that's why!" He laughed at his own joke.

Nick didn't.

"And all this masquerade bullshit, Jean-Luc. White Rabbits, death markers, bullets behind the ear, heads in packages . . . where did you dream that up? I thought you were a soldier."

The mercenary turned and stared out to sea, and changed the subject, "A lot of men died here."

"You want to add me to the list?" Nick asked. *Moran looked genuinely surprised,* Nick thought.

"No . . . of course not, Burns. I thought we were on the same side! Why should I want anything to happen to you?"

"The man you zeroed in London was my man, Jean-Luc, and your boys tried to get me outside Harare the other day."

"I didn't order the first, and didn't know about the second," Moran said, surprised.

"And you think I believe in Santa Claus, too?"

"It's true, Burns, not the Santa Claus, but I didn't know. I thought this was an American assignment, *sub rosa.*"

"Then why would I be here?"

The mercenary shrugged his shoulders. "Change in command? New marching plans? Who knows? Why did you go through Jacqure Monnier, by the way? You knew how to reach me."

"I let my English relatives do it to keep the fucking masquerade you started going for a bit. I didn't want London to get any ideas to confirm their suspicions further."

"Masquerade again, suspicions?" said Moran. "This is your agency's idea. Those clowns sit over there in Washington and dream up comic books. I get paid, so what do I care?"

"How much are they paying you?"

"I'll net about half . . . plus expenses advanced."

"Half of what, Jean-Luc?"

"You really don't know? I don't believe that!"

"Half of what?" Nick repeated.

Moran flicked his cigar into the air through the opening that had hidden the German guns. "Half the ransom," he said.

Nick whistled through his teeth. "That's probably the biggest money you've ever seen."

"Damned right," Moran said bitterly, "more than I've earned in a lifetime. So why should I pass it by."

"Who gets the rest, Jean-Luc?" Nick asked.

"I can't believe you came over here and made me come just to ask me this. Why didn't you read your own files?"

Nick waited, lit his pipe, stalled. He wanted the mercenary to get the idea clear. The red light flashed for silence over the recording room door.

"Don't be coy with me, Burns," Moran said impatiently.

He walked to the rear of the concrete bunker, surveyed the parking area, and turned back, scuffing his shoes in the gritty sand. Outside, clouds thickened and threatened rain.

"I'm not being coy," Nick said finally. "I don't know!"

"Play me for a fool!"

"Who?" Nick asked.

"You," Moran shouted. "Who else?"

"Not me, Jean-Luc, I promise you. It's not my M.O."

"Kananga gets the other half, you bloody asshole," Moran said.

There should have been trumpets, Nick thought, and kettledrums. Someone had advanced that hypothesis before, but he had rejected it out of hand. Now it was his turn to be surprised.

"So Kananga's in on the whole thing?" he said.

"Of course he is. That's why I said it's a masquerade. I'm no body snatcher, Burns . . . it's all theater. I haven't even been over to Africa recently. Only now . . . ." he stopped. "You really didn't know." It wasn't a question.

Nick shook his head.

"So it's his little skit?" Nick asked.

"Chicken or egg question," the mercenary answered. "I think that your guy approached him and then he picked up the ball and ran with it. These black chiefs are shrewd, an untrustworthy bunch of bastards to a man. He couldn't miss an opportunity to fling shit all over Umgawe, could he? . . . and at no risk."

"No risk?"

"If they didn't pay, we were supposed to let him go . . . daring escape story, a few cuts and bruises, maybe a flesh wound. Return of the hero in any case, and I'd get mine anyway."

"According to whom?"

273

"According to your guy, and Kananga. The money was there, just a question of whether it was distributed by an embarrassed Umgawe, or quietly put on deposit in Geneva."

"Ever hear of the London Alliance for World Strategy in London, Jean-Luc?"

"Agency storefront?"

"No. What source?"

Exasperated, the mercenary said, "Who do you think? Your spook, Van Ness."

"You do believe in Santa Claus," Nick said.

"What do you mean?"

"Van Ness is not our guy."

"Then what in hell is going on?" Moran asked. His face was red with rage.

Leaving out the LAWS scenario, Nick told him.

THEY LEFT THE BUNKER and ambled to the edge of the ridge over the beach.

The mercenary fingered a strand of rusty barbed-wire hanging loosely from a weather-beaten wooden post. "What a waste," he said, gesturing towards the beach, "but you know at least there was something to fight for then. A real cause "

"It *was* a waste. You were right the first time," Nick said, thinking of his "lucky" father and all the unlucky ones.

"But there was a cause then," said Moran. "What am I doing now, qualifying to shoot Africans in the bush?"

Nick stopped. "And if you had a cause to choose, how would you make the choice, Jean-Luc? By the size of the pot?"

Moran sneered, "You think I'm a whore, eh? What *you* do is better? Because you work for a government, so you can rationalize selling your body on behalf of an institution? Now who believes in Santa Claus? I work for myself. That's more selfish perhaps, but it's more honest, Burns. For you, they change hats, you go and shoot the other side. The Ministry of Truth changes its message and you all march the other way. Don't tell me you think for yourself!"

274

Nick didn't answer him. *Let the mercenary think what he wanted, feel superior, . . . anything as long as he put the rabbit back in the hat when the time came.* Nick would give the magician the cue.

"I know who I'm for and who I'm against," Moran continued, "and I've never worked against you."

The closest the mercenary got to a real cause, Nick thought; what he said was, "Until now."

Moran lifted both arms in a gesture of futility and walked towards the cars.

A gray Mercedes with two men in the front seat was parked near the dirt track leading back towards the road. The mercenary spoke with quiet fury, "I thought you said you came alone!"

Nick hadn't even told Hartsdale-Smythe or Randall exactly where Moran had set the meeting, and nobody had followed him from the airport . . . he was sure. As for the car, as soon as the attendant had brought it, Nick objected to it and chose another just to be sure there were no wires. The roads had been empty, the villages asleep.

"I meant it, Jean-Luc . . . maybe they followed you!" he said, only half convincingly.

"Goodbye, Burns. Thanks for a lovely morning. We must do it again sometime," Moran said. He didn't offer his hand.

"Damn it, man, we haven't settled anything," Nick said.

"And we won't. It was all nice and simple before. Now it's too convoluted for me, Burns." He twisted and retwisted the barbed-wire on itself. "I'll stick to my plan, you stick to yours. I can tie my own shoelaces without your help."

"You're being crossed, Jean-Luc," Nick said opening the door of his car.

"So it would seem," the mercenary answered, with a glance towards the Mercedes.

Nick was exasperated. "I tell you they're not mine," he said, slamming the door. "And," he continued, as he rolled down the window, "neither is Van Ness!" He started the engine and backed the car away.

"Wait! Whose is he?"

Perturbed, Nick knew the hook was in. "What's the difference," he said, pushing the gear lever into place. The car started to roll. "*En garde*, Jean-Luc!"

"Stop!" Moran said. "Who is he?"

Nick stared at him vacantly.

"Okay," said Moran. "Drive to Caen, it's not far. If it's clear, I'll meet you at the Château, and buy you a coffee."

"And if it's not?"

"It's a nice château," Moran said with a grin.

ARROMANCHES WAS BEGINNING to come to life. Some women and children were entering the church, a few men stood chatting outside a bakery, long baguettes tucked under their arms.

Nick passed the little war museum . . . *that's for another day, another life perhaps,* and continued through the town to the main road.

It was all so familiar, he realized, from the hundreds of war movies shot in those very streets, ideal for house to house patrols, snipers and all the movie stuff that made wars personal and romantic . . . almost Edenic in their simplicity.

The poplar trees dividing fields and lining the main road to Caen were still bare, and Nick drove at a modest fifty, glancing in the rear view mirror. No Mercedes, no Moran. Heavy haunched farm horses chewed at sparse grass, and small groups of Jersey cows clustered near the fences.

Nick could see his destination in the distance. He'd been there years before with Odette on their way to see the tapestries of the Norman conquest in Bayeux.

Thinking of Odette reminded him that it was at least eighteen years ago that she had introduced him to Moran at a party. He was a mercenary in the Congo, and her magazine had sent her to interview him. During the introduction Moran had caught the look in Nick's eyes and pretended that it was a first time the two men had met when actually he had gotten to know Nick as the "press attache" who wore a different hat altogether when he was in Katanga province as a young case officer.

Nick had valued Moran's discretion. It exhibited the Frenchman's respect for lovers' lies when he kept his counsel. After that Nick sent whatever work he could in Moran's direction. From Algiers to Angola, Moran had fulfilled contract after contract for the Western allies, with one exception . . . he wouldn't work for Bonn, and it was rumored that he'd turned down Muammar Gaddafi over Chad. Since the end of the Rhodesian war though, the mercenary had been in retirement, spending his time playing the horses. Even South Africa hadn't been able to lure him with promises, when he'd let it be known he was out of the game . . . until this.

Nick found the Château easily and parked nearby. He might as well see it while he was here. Then he'd call the Paris office and take it from there. But for now, he wanted to plan how he'd crucify Randall if he'd sent those nursemaids.

He crossed the wooden bridge over the moat and was walking towards the entrance when he heard his name called. Nick turned to see the mercenary crossing the street behind him.

"You win the coffee," he said with what did him for a smile, "and so I'll throw in a croissant for good measure." He then led the way down a narrow, cobbled street opposite the Château, to the old quarter of the city.

The area had been recently restored and was now a bit too thick with cutesy little boutique storefronts for the antiquarian in Nick. It was more Gabrielle's taste.

Moran found a window table at a café in the shadow of Eglise St. Pierre and ordered from a crabby little waiter with a frown on his face. "Food first," the mercenary said, "then you can upset my stomach." He then busied himself with the croissants the waiter had brought as though doing them a grand favor.

Meanwhile Nick watched the morning worshipers emerging from the church. Since this whole thing had started a week ago he'd felt the old watchfulness come back into play, a certain way of looking at everything, a heightened sense of detail he had been trained for, and then had acquired from years in the field. Lately he had been focusing on files, and only occasionally was that sensitivity stirred from dormancy when he made a quick trip to coordinate some action, but most of his time out of the office was spent at committee meetings, and he'd become an expert conference table wrangler. It hadn't been his goal in life, and he missed the sense of vibrancy in the face of danger, the awareness of being alive to his fingertips that he'd felt so intensely in the past few days. He envied Moran for being an actor rather than a director, and realized that he always had an envy of people with that kind of gusto . . . the untamed stallions, even the ones who had the mean streak.

The church bell clanged the quarter hour and interrupted his reverie.

"What are you looking for?" the mercenary asked, between dunks of the crisp croissant into the steaming coffee. He'd been watching Nick's eyes darting around, clicking in the details like an automatic camera.

"Ghosts," Nick said, breaking off a piece of a croissant. The taste of France again was like Proust's Madeleine. Memories collided and stumbled over each other.

"I was wondering about that pair in the Mercedes," he said.

"German tourists, father and son from the look of it, loden coats and all," Moran said. "The father had been an artilleryman in that same gun battery. Spoke good French, too. He'll have a long time to bore the kid today with war stories."

"How so?"

"When they went down to the beach I flattened their tires."

"Ah, the schoolboy in you?" Nick laughed.

"Perhaps," the mercenary said. "It was the least I could do. Drop that damned vigilance, Burns, you're making me nervous." He sipped the milky coffee, "Enjoy Sunday in Normandy!" he commanded and ordered another coffee for Nick and two Calvados.

"Hate to spoil yours," Nick said as he put the photographs on the table . . . the ones Goldstein had taken, and two others wired to him the day before.

"Good shots," Moran said.

"Turn the last two over."

The mercenary read, stared, read again and then picked up the pony of apple brandy and dropped all of it down his throat.

"I'll kill the pig. SALAUD, MERDE!"

The little waiter was startled and approached the table, only to be waved away impatiently.

"He thought you were calling him," Nick joked.

He wanted to control Moran's rage; he'd need to channel it later. "Comes from being a greedy bastard, Jean-Luc,"

Moran stood up, dropped some money on the table and strode out of the café.

"What do you want?" he said when Nick caught up with him at the entrance to the church.

Nick told him and Moran, sullen with self pity, agreed, then went into St. Pierre.

Thirty minutes later they were both in Moran's car, Nick's having been left with the rental agency in Caen, and were headed toward Saint-Malo. Only functional monosyllables had been exchanged in the past half hour.

"*Radix malorum est cupiditas,*" Moran said, breaking the silence.

"Very moral suddenly, aren't we?" Nick commented.

"I thought of it in the church," Moran said, "and we have lived by that, *mon ami* . . . both of us. You above all that, all of a sudden?" He glanced over at Nick who was intently cleaning his pipe, like a handy prop. "Hypocrite!"

"As you said, Jean-Luc, we must be getting old for this kind of stuff. I suppose that cupidity depends on whether it's yours or someone else's. Do you use it or are you used."

"It's all the Latin I remember," the mercenary said, "and I forgot it too soon."

Nick was in no mood for breast beating; he assumed the position of case officer, rightly noting that Moran had already accepted the role. The mercenary had revealed his discomfort with the fact that Van Ness had called all the shots and manipulated every detail to suit his plan. He'd thought that Agency twits were out of their heads, but he'd wanted the big payoff.

"A fucking masquerade," Moran repeated. "I've been had, and to think that I almost got killed for that black son of a bitch. I fought him in the bush — you know that — good soldier, by the way, I have to hand him that. And that fuck up on the Channel . . .." He told Nick about the run in with the whaler. "As soon as I saw the Cyrillic letters on that harpoon, I knew what had happened, but now I don't think it was an accident, no fucking accident. It would have been very convenient to find their bodies floating in the Channel and then leak the LAWS documents to the press, no matter that it wouldn't appear in England. It would surface everywhere else and word of mouth would take care of the rest."

"Let's be simple about it, Jean-Luc, you stick to what we agreed because this Van Ness doesn't control any money. I do!"

"What about what he was paid up front?"

"Earnest money, financed the operation to date, Nick replied. "They've got their mileage out of it. But the big dollars come from us and you are not going to get it unless Kananga is released to the proper officials . . . and in Zimbabwe. And then you clear out, rich as Croesus. No more White Rabbit from that minute the exchange is made."

Moran drove silently for a few minutes. They had crossed the border into Brittany, and Nick noticed a perceptible change in the landscape. It was hillier with more trees, and the shape of the hay-stacks was different.

Nick believed that the mercenary would not, finally, respond to points of honor, even among thieves . . . a sobriquet he was willing to share. If Moran was in it for the money, they had to pay. Nick was not ready to pussyfoot around observing the protocol the British demanded, and he felt that it was all a political posture anyway. Their Prime Minister wanted to be re-elected and had to toe the tough line at any cost, as she had done in the Falklands. His own superiors were more pragmatic, although he disliked a lot of their suddenly conveniently-discovered policies, even the ones he carried out. But they had decided to re-decide that Kananga was the man they wanted to see make a lunge for power. They had backed the wrong horse three years ago and were switching bets. Fine by him, but it was going to cost them. As all bureaucrats knew, it was "nobody's money."

Moran slowed the car behind a line of horse drawn carriages and dog carts. All the drivers were dressed in 19th century costumes, like a scene out of an old novel . . . *Madame Bovary's wedding?*

"The towns each have these anniversary celebrations," Moran said, "and they like dressing up. *C'est drole, non?*"

They crawled along waiting for an opportunity to pass.

"*D'accord,*" Moran said, "except for one thing . . .."

Nick, waiting for him to finish his sentence, smiled at a little girl in the carriage just in front of them. The girl waved at him. He waved back.

Finally the mercenary said, "I want to take care of Van Ness myself."

"No deal," Nick answered, waving a goodbye to the little blond girl in her long dress and straw bonnet as Moran edged the Renault into the left lane, raced past the long line of horse carriages, then slowed down.

"Then you've got 'no deal.' I'll stay right here in France and send Kananga back alone. Right to Van Ness. You can play out the rest of the scene for yourself."

"And the money?"

"Fuck the money!" Moran raised his voice, "I want it, but I don't need it. It's enough of this shit. You want Van Ness or whatever his real name is so you can play chess with the 'opposition' as you like to call them. Too bad. Hasn't he taken out enough people, hasn't he made a fool of all of us, almost killed both of us. Enough. Either it's my way on this, or it's off. And *you*, my friend, can walk home . . . or get a ride from one of those horse carts we just passed!"

He slowed the car, as though looking for a place to stop.

"Just drive, Jean-Luc," Nick said. "Enough with the dramatics." He knew he'd have to lose this round, and part of him sympathized with the mercenary, although it went against Nick's professional grain. You didn't take out opposition officers. That was one of the unwritten rules of the intelligence community. You pumped them dry, sweated every drop of information from them and then sent them back, trading off one wreck of a human who would be utterly useless to the game in the future for one of your own that the opposition had taken. That was what they would have done to Nick if they had taken him. It was chess, deadly serious, but with rules and customary bargains. Yet he could never expect the mercenary to understand the game. Reluctantly, he yielded.

17

BRITTANY

KANANGA, WHO WAS well beyond concerns about both money and ideology, was harder to convince. Years of diplomacy, political infighting, soldiering and negotiating with superpowers had left him as tough and wily a horse trader as Nick had ever come up against. There was only one thing Jeremiah Kananga wanted out of the situation, and that was power.

"You must realize, my dear man," he said to Nick "that I myself can pay the ransom money to White Rabbit . . . at a loss of course, but nonetheless fulfilling my expectations. So why should I be inclined to accept your terms. Your own government is perfectly aware that I should be running Zimbabwe, not that mission school zealot and his Oriental friends. Your people have refused to stand up and be counted. Only when the lines between red and white . . . and black, so to speak, have been made clear have they intervened. But when they could have supported me, they didn't. Now they are concerned? Well, that's just too bad, isn't it. Umgawe is a fool, a damned Shona fool. He makes committees and invents slogans and antagonizes the South Africans, who God knows are an abomination, but they have the muscle, don't they? And now that the United States wants to appease them, Uncle Sam will quietly support me. Well, thank you very much, but on my terms, if you please, not yours."

They had been at it for more than three hours, sitting on the afterdeck of Moran's boat riding at anchor in the outer harbor among the fishing boats.

The mercenary had insisted on moving away from the dock "to avoid being overheard," but Nick was sure that Moran also wanted no easy access for anyone's getaway now that the fox and the hound

283

were face to face. Rabbits, white and otherwise could get caught in the middle.

Round and round they went, Kananga ever affable and unruffled "making it clear" . . . an expression he used more and more as the afternoon wore on and his position became less and less clear.

Moran was getting irritable, and asked them several times if they were hungry. Finally he sent the man he called Smith ashore in the dinghy with one of the crew members and shortly after they had returned laden with bottles and bundles.

Kananga, Nick and Moran were called below to be served a feast of fish stew, purchased by the gallon it seemed, from a local restaurant, dozens of steamed mussels, and bottles of crackling cold, local white wine. Captivity hadn't seemed to affect Kananga's appetite based on his size, but he ate the offerings with a surprising delicacy and moderation.

The conversation had changed because Smith and the two crew members joined them at the table. Moran was a democrat by instinct, Nick thought, unlike Kananga, who surprisingly didn't seem too comfortable with the arrangement.

When Smith went up on deck and the crew disappeared forward, Nick drew the ace from his sleeve, "It doesn't bother you, Mr. Kananga, that this Van Ness is a Soviet agent named Oleg Volkov."

"Why should it?" the fat man retorted, sipping some wine, "as long as he has done exactly what I wanted him to do."

"Like murdering your aide-de-camp?"

"Execution for treason," Kananga corrected him, and wouldn't be drawn into a defensive position.

"Do you think," he parried, "that an African really cares where the help to build his nation comes from? Such vanities are for the infants of ideology, Mr. Burns, little moral niceties, which even our scheming, but naive, prime minister can see through. No, sir. A plague on both your houses, and on the Orientals, too. In fact, look at it this way, the Russians and the Chinese have never taken anything away from us, never enslaved us, never made us prisoners of war inside our own land. Why should we not trust them more than we do the Europeans and their American allies? Too ingenuous an argument, sir. Try again."

Nick saw that Moran was getting disgusted, and that Kananga was ready to go on in this way all night. He probably thrived on sophistry and debate, and, having been without it for a week, needed it more than food.

"What good would it do for anyone if you were dead, sir?" Nick asked. He saw the glare in the mercenary's eye as he spoke. This detail Nick had omitted from the earlier talks he and Moran had on the beach in Caen and in the car, and he saw now that he had touched a nerve. He pressed the point, as Kananga hadn't reacted other than with raised eyebrows.

"What you don't understand, Mr. Kananga, is that you aren't running the game, it's running you. You're not a king, as you should be according to you, but a pawn, or if you prefer a different metaphor you're playing Othello to Volkov's Iago. If you go on in your illusion, it will be too late. He is planning to kill you. Moran here will be blamed, and what happens to your country then?"

Nick fell silent. He wanted to let the point sink in. If Kananga wasn't a fool, but only fooled, as Nick thought, he would take what was said and consider it seriously.

Moran got up from the table and paced furiously while muttering to himself.

Kananga didn't say anything, but the look of mountainous indestructibility passed away, along with the affable smile that had played across his features all afternoon, even behind the false whiskers and burnoose he wore while on deck.

"Did you know this?" he asked Moran.

The mercenary denied it vehemently. "I'm a soldier, Kananga, not a fucking murderer. I am a soldier, and you of all people should know it. You fought me for years. Did anyone ever call me a butcher? I shot my own for raping and pillaging . . . you know that, Kananga. Admit it!"

The African lowered his head so that his eyes were not visible. "I know it, Moran, I know it," he said quietly. "Mr. Burns," he went on, "your point about my being a pawn, or an Othello, is very well taken. I would act the martyr on my own, but not be the martyr in someone else's drama, sir!"

Nick thought that it was a pity he was living in such a self-conscious age where everything anyone did or said had a reference point in some action scene or was heard before in a film or on stage or on the ubiquitous television. Because in the dim light of the swinging lamp above the table he wasn't seeing the noble Moor declaring his passion, but rather a composite of Sidney Greenstreet and Charles Laughton, "The Maltese Falcon" and "Henry the Eighth" running simultaneously against a bush Othello. Desdemona was his own archetype. It wasn't until later, when Nick had time to think about what had happened, that he realized why . . . he hadn't taken the fat black man seriously enough. It was the ultimate triumph of cynicism . . . not Kananga's but his own.

Kananga sat with his head in his hands, his ham-like arms leaning on the table. In another life he might have been a tragic actor. "Why should I believe, Mr. Burns," he said after a few silent moments perfectly paced, "that you are not simply arrogating the role of dramaturge to yourself, taking over as puppet master with aims no less sinister than those you ascribe to Volkov? Moreover, how do I know that what you say about him is true?"

"What the fuck are you talking about?" yelled Moran, "why can't you speak simple English! Do you know who Burns is?"

Kananga ignored the first two comments and answered the third, "No, do you?"

"Of course I do!"

Nick showed Kananga his identification card and his diplomatic passport. It was no time for vanity.

"These can be faked easily," he said.

"What do you want," Moran asked, "a letter from his mother?"

That broke the tension with a laugh.

"You've put your life in Moran's hands, sir," Nick said. "And at the moment, I think you don't have any choice but to accept that we are both telling you the truth." His voice remained flat and unemotional, although he really wanted to shake the man hard until he dropped his elaborate defenses.

"Better the devil you know than the one you don't?" Kananga asked with a sly smile.

Nick felt that the point was won or at least taken.

"And how do you know that he plans to kill me?" Kananga continued.

Nick mentioned LAWS.

Kananga smiled. "I know about that," he said.

"How?"

Kananga shook his head. "Suffice it to say that I know. Your walls have been breached, and you don't even know it." There was a triumphant smirk on is face as he continued, "But surely the document you refer to didn't include plans for my assassination . . . I saw it."

"Not the addendum. Volkov worked that in. It included assassination and appears as if we authorized it!"

"It wouldn't be the first time," Kananga said.

Nick didn't answer.

"There are others," Kananga went on.

"You know?"

"Perhaps," said the black man, "when I am freed and alive and ready to take back the reins in Zimbabwe, perhaps then, you'll know too."

"It doesn't seem that I have a choice," Nick said. Again. He held a weak hand dependent on what others discarded.

"You don't," Kananga said. He stood and faced the mercenary and asked, "Did you know Volkov planned to kill me?"

Nick couldn't help but admire the black man's audacity, it even cowed the intrepid Moran.

"He raised that once, I told him to forget it," Moran responded hovering between anger and submission.

"You are an honorable man, Mr. Moran," Kananga said.

Moran didn't reply, snorted, and unwrapped a cigar.

Nick hedged his bets on the assumption that Volkov had a brief to follow and he would. Had Moran been willing to play it Volkov's

287

way? It might simplify things. As it was, Volkov probably had a bullet reserved for Moran.

"I'll handle that," the mercenary said simply, when Nick voiced these fears.

"The exchange?" Nick asked, getting back to the main focus.

"One week from today, at noon," Moran said. He took out some land maps of southern Africa's Four Corners region and placed them on the chart table. The three men leaned over the red lamp's glow as the mercenary plotted co-ordinates.

"Forget it," he said to Nick, folding the maps as an after thought. "I can't chance any funny stuff any more."

"You've trusted me so far."

"It's back in my hands now, Burns. We do it my way. I'll contact you in Salisbury."

"Harare," Kananga corrected.

"Whatever," Moran said. "You be at the Meikles Hotel Friday morning."

Moran turned off the light above the angled mahogany counter, and stepped through the cabin doors onto the deck.

The black man took the move as an opportunity to speak privately with Nick in a conspiratorial manner. He closed the cabin door and said, "If you want your traitor, Mr. Burns, you make sure *everyone* is present at my release, then justice will be done for all to see."

"Who is everyone?"

Kananga spelled out a list of names.

Nick disagreed, "That would be very hard to do."

Kananga smiled, "But it *must* be done!"

"Does Moran know this?" Nick asked.

"Not yet."

"It's a huge security problem."

"You'll work that out, I'm sure." Kananga's face glistened. "Let's say it's insurance for me," he continued, "less risk with more ob-servers, and then you will get your man." He waited, knowing that Nick had no choice. It was a non-negotiable demand.

"Why do you have to orchestrate everything?" Nick asked.

"Because you handed me back the baton, Mr. Burns, and I prefer my own arrangements."

Nick was about to reply when the door opened and Moran stepped in, "I've paged the crew and ordered the boat brought to the Saint-Malo dock. Is everything settled then?"

"All I have to do is move mountains," Nick said.

"And who can do it better than you?" Moran smiled.

The heavy-set hulk called Smith, stepped through the door and padded down the companionway.

Nick turned to see the unexpressive face behind him and then faced the others. "I'll need to arrange some transportation now," he said to Moran.

"You can use that rented car, the contract is inside. Just leave it with Hertz." He tossed Nick the keys.

Nick didn't know whether he saw the startled expression on Kananga's face or caught sight of the swiftly moving hand behind him as he grabbed for the tossed keys, but the next thing Nick remembered was a sharp pain behind his ear and a sudden flash of bright light as the edge of Smith's hardened palm hit him like a hammer. A curtain of darkness dropped.

THE SUN WAS SHINING in his eyes, then blinked off suddenly. *No, it wasn't the sun*, it was too blue, with points like a star. Then it went into eclipse. Soft yellow light diffused through space. He opened his eyes and looked around.

"How do you feel, my friend?" Moran asked. He sat next to the berth where Nick was stretched out. The mercenary was toying with a small flashlight, the kind physicians use when they make you say "aaah!"

Nick shook his head to clear it of fog. It hurt. He tried to rub his eyes. Couldn't. His hands and his feet wouldn't move. He raised his head a bit and saw that he was trussed up like a package, heavy marine rope wound round and round his body from the chest down to his feet.

"Wonderful," he said. "What a great party!"

The mercenary laughed. "I'm glad you still have a sense of humor still."

"I can't wait to return the invitation," Nick said. "Do you always treat your guests so well?"

"Did you really expect that I would let you walk off this boat while we're still here, so that one phone call could have *les flics* all over us?"

"Would I do that to you, Jean Luc?" His head throbbed rhythmically.

"I'm not sure of anything any more, mon ami, so why risk an abortion, 'so-to-speak'." He imitated Kananga perfectly. "Not that I trust him as far as I can throw him, but I don't want to see all of this go down the tube in a gallant rescue effort where he comes up smelling like a fucking rose and I go to prison or the cemetery."

"Might happen anyway," Nick said.

"Well, at least it won't happen tonight." Moran said. He stood up and opened the cabin door. Nick turned his aching head and saw a narrow corridor, realized that he was trussed up in one of the forward cabins of the boat on the side which would be away from the dock.

"Jean Luc," he said.

The mercenary turned, framed by the doorway,

"You let me down . . . or sold out to Volkov."

"And our love affair is over?" Moran interrupted with a hoarse laugh. "Do you really think I would sell out to that fucker, that miserable, soulless Russian prick? Not that I really give a shit about politics, but what's the difference between Andropov and Hitler? Style, that's all, mon ami. Style."

"And us?"

"Also a bunch of whores. But I like free enterprise, Burns. It's better for my business. Besides, you said it before to the big mambo . . . better the devil you know, etcetera, etcetera."

"Go to hell, Moran!" Nick said, turning his face to the wall.

Later Smith came into the room with a glass of water, handed it to Moran and propped Nick up. Moran took two white pills from his pocket and stirred them in the glass until they dissolved.

"You've had a rough day, my friend, and could use a good night's sleep," he said as Smith forced Nick's mouth open. Moran slowly poured the liquid into Nick's throat, holding his nostrils closed to force him to swallow. There was no use fighting, Nick knew, no way out. Smith eased him down and left the cabin.

"What's that?" he asked.

"Sleeping tablets . . . I use them myself. One for insomnia, two for a battlefield, three, you could have surgery, four . . .."

"You're boring me, Jean Luc," Nick said. He stared at the ceiling. It seemed to get brighter and then fade, brighten and fade.

"Think of some nice juicy broad," Moran said, "like that reporter you let walk . . .."

"Get lost!"

"Before it was 'go to hell,'" Moran chuckled.

"I'm getting mellower," Nick slurred. And indeed he was beginning to feel very drowsy, almost high on whatever they had made him swallow.

"Think woman," Moran said.

"Gabrielle . . .," Nick murmured, his eyes closing. A sheet was wrapped around her bare, heavy breasts. She had a sad smile on her face as she looked at him. But it was a hospital room, and she was crying, telling him the baby died. It wasn't Gabrielle; it was Phyllis and she was stiff and cold. He kissed the clammy forehead, shook her. "No, NO!" he screamed.

Moran closed the door and left Nick asleep. Smith was sitting on his berth across the corridor, his door open, on the first watch. Moran looked at the time . . . he had to hurry to where the waitress waited.

AND THEN THERE WAS LIGHT. Nick opened his eyes slowly to the sunlight slanting through the portholes above him, pouring warmth onto his face. There were no ropes on him, he realized, only after he had raised his wrist to look at his watch. "Twelve hours!" he said aloud and sat up on the berth. It was an illusion of adequacy that pushed him up and sudden disillusionment that made him fall back onto the pillow. The back of his head felt inconsolable, as if he'd downed a bottle of whiskey last night. He lay quietly for five minutes and let the world settle itself, then gingerly eased his feet off the berth onto the floor, and opened the cabin door.

No sound from anywhere. He padded into the corridor opening doors as he went. No one home, everything "shipshape and Bristol fashion," even above on deck. All the lines were coiled, the instrument panel in the cockpit covered, the lockers locked. Even the deck looked freshly hosed.

A note was on the table in the main saloon where they had eaten dinner last night, "Sorry, had to leave before you were up," it said. "Razor, aspirin, etc. in head. Shower works. Coffee on stove. Close door behind you. Watchman will lock up." It was as though he was a weekend guest who'd overindulged the night before, and slept it off while everyone else returned to their Monday desks. Very cute.

The keys for the rental car — had he caught them before he was conked or did he drop them? They were resting on the bottom of the note.

His watch read 9:30, and looking at it was an effort, so he decided to take the hint and let the world wait another half hour while he shaved, showered and coffeed up his engine.

By ten o'clock, Nick was on his way, a hangover fading slowly under the caffeine and aspirin assault.

From the post office he telephoned the resident at the Paris embassy, leaving what he called a "regards to the folks" message for transmission to Randall in London, and a priority alert for Washington. The Secretary of State had offered a bail out . . . now Nick wanted the money readied. A code had been pre-arranged, all that was needed was the location for the payment confirmed.

He had missed his scheduled flight to Paris he was told when he called the airport at Dinard, but there was an air taxi he could hire. They switched his call to the charter service and he arranged to be there within the hour.

Then he called the Paris resident again and told him to be at Orly, and gave him the name of the charter company, assuming it had an office in the capital.

292

Nick left the post office just as a policeman was writing a parking ticket for the car . . . he hadn't seen the *interdit* sign in his haste earlier. He saved the man the trouble of sticking the ticket under the windshield wiper and took it from the surprised officer with a polite, "Merci," and drove off.

It was his first good feeling of the morning, knowing that after he destroyed the ticket, the police would trace the license to Hertz and Moran would get a whopping fine in the mail. He chided himself for the childish pleasure and couldn't help laughing anyway.

The second pleasure, a sunburst of memory, occurred as the twin engine Beechcraft overflew Mont Saint-Michel. The fairytale spires of the church and monastery perched on the island rock lunged at the sky celebrating the glory of God.

THE VIEW ALSO BROUGHT back a bygone memory to Nick. On a visit to Mont Saint-Michel, he and Gabrielle had stood outside the high cloister watching the tide sweeping across the basin. She read from a guidebook, and said with a shudder, "And do you know that pilgrims who used to come here would drown in the quicksands out there?"

He remembered putting his arm around her and hugging her. She was a woman with such softness and vulnerability and could imagine such pain . . . and was so different from him . . . and Odette, whose toughness matched his own. For each of them their job was their life.

When he had left Odette, he thought the pain would never heal, and every time he saw her in passing or she cunningly used him as a source, wielding their shared past as a spear to pierce his armor, he would be tempted to start all over again.

But she had had enough and told him so. "I can almost thank you for my success," Odette had said one night when he'd called to ask her to dinner. She turned down the invitation, and when the phone went dead, he was reminded that the doors to her life were closed to him forever.

He'd spent that night with Gabrielle, who asked little but company, and out of guilt, he thought, he'd invited her for the weekend drive down through Normandy to see the great medieval wonder just below him now.

"ONCE I BOMBED A PLACE almost as big as that," the pilot shouted at Nick, who sat next to him. He banked the plane suddenly so his passenger could get a better look at the monument. Man aspiring to God pointed his sword at the sky. Tour buses rolled down the causeway — no more pilgrims in the quicksand — and disgorged what looked like streams of brightly colored ants into the ancient city gate.

"Where?" Nick shouted back when the plane leveled off.

"Indo-China. Also full of tourists. Big Buddhist temple. A feast day," the pilot shouted, as though speech were burst of gun fire. "Direct hit. Right in the center. Escort planes strafed the survivors. Big score."

"Any medals?" Nick shouted. He pointed to his chest, wetting his thumb and touching his jacket.

The pilot adjusted his dark sunglasses and unzipped the cracked leather jacket he wore with the captain's bars still on the epaulets.

"For wounds," he said, and pointed to his shoulder.

"Piece of flak in here. For the bombing, you mean?" He shrugged. "No, just a day's work. You a writer?" the pilot shouted.

"Why do you ask?"

"You look like a writer."

"More or less," Nick answered, and busied himself with a pocket notebook, his best conversation stopper.

HE HAD NEVER WANTED to love Gabrielle; it just happened. What motivated him to avoid and run from commitment to her? He didn't know, but he always raised the "hostages to fortune" shibboleth whenever the idea of settling down arose. There was absolutely no rule in the Agency or OMEGA that demanded celibacy, as there had been for the monks who built the great monument down below. Yet somehow the course he had decided upon became a law unto itself, and he'd talked himself into believing it. Even now, when his work was mostly behind a desk or at a conference table, and he went home at night, he raised the specter of Nick Burns lying dead in an alley. Well, it could have been, couldn't it?

He felt the back of his head behind the ear. It would be sore for days. Four inches lower and his neck would have been broken. That Smith knew exactly what he was doing, and had they wanted Nick dead, he would be.

IN AN HOUR THEY'D BE IN PARIS; in less than a week this damned thing would be over. What are the options then? Struggle to subordinate the kid inside, the one who enjoyed all this, who missed it when he sat in New York and commanded telephones? Who laughed when he thought of the mercenary paying a large traffic fine.

Children's games, played by deadly serious men.

He looked at the pilot next to him. Glory past, he still wore its remnants. Did he tell the same story to every passenger he flew over Mont-Saint-Michel, relive the memory of his moment of greatness? And now what? A taxi driver in the sky.

Nick Burns, too, the youngest director in the history of OMEGA, at the apogee of his profession, becoming a middle-aged bureaucrat dreaming of glorious missions long gone. He knew without vanity that he was legendary in his own profession, but a cryptographic cipher to the rest of the world, even to the woman who would love him were he a garbage collector with no secrets.

They were over land again now, the sea a shimmering grey basin far behind. He looked down at the neat fields of Normandy, the clumps of woods, the lines of plane trees shading the roads. Napoleon planted them, it was said, so his armies could march in the shade . . . mythologies.

"SOMEDAY I WANT to live in the country, Nicholas," Gabrielle always said his full name when she was talking about the future, and pronounced it Neekolaas, "in an old farmhouse with a fireplace, and have a big dog, and some fields to walk in, and gossip with the butcher and the baker." He had asked her what she would do when she wasn't gossiping or chopping wood for the fire. "I'll sit by the window and read books."

"And when it gets too dark to read?"

"I'll feed you supper and take you to bed, you silly man to ask," and she pulled the sheet over their heads and demonstrated how.

"WHERE ARE WE?" he shouted to the pilot pointing down.

A small city was below them, a place where the roads converged from across the wide rolling fields, separated by hedgerows that the Norman conquerers introduced to England.

"Argentan," the bombardier of Buddhists answered, then lit a Gauloises. "Less than an hour to Paris."

"Will we pass over Dreux?" Nick asked.

"Ten, twelve minutes."

The radio crackled with the capital's air control already and the pilot joined the hubbub.

GABRIELLE'S MOTHER LIVED near Dreux in a house near the Eure River.

In the early days of their relationship, before he was transferred to New York, they used to drive down for dinner on a Sunday from time to time. It was only an hour or so from Paris.

When they stayed over, Madame Martin used to put them in separate bedrooms, and Gabrielle would sneak into his room at night and out before dawn. After Gabrielle moved to New York, her mother put them together when they visited.

Every day during their visits Nick and Gabrielle would ride bicycles to town and pick berries along the side of the road. . . the house she'd inherit wasn't much different from the site of her dreams.

"DREUX!" THE PILOT SHOUTED into Nick's reverie and pointed down. Nick saw the central square, followed the river north to the place where he thought the house was.

"You can see Paris from here," the pilot said pointing ahead at a darkish blur on the horizon.

The roads got wider and closer together, the farms smaller, the factories larger, the traffic below and above denser, and soon they had landed at Orly.

Michaelis, the Paris resident, was waiting on the tarmac outside the charter office.

ON THE SECOND FLOOR OF the American Embassy on Avenue Gabriel, Nick went directly to Codes, sent a long cable to the State Department and a shorter one to Randall, and went downstairs to the office — that was once his own — to wait for responses.

He felt strange sitting on the "other side" of the desk, but there was a different desk . . . and different furniture, and a different president adorning the wall.

Michaelis had gone out for lunch, so Nick sat on the couch in the corner, not at the desk, and used the extension.

18

PARIS

HIS FIRST THREE CALLS WERE STRIKES, then, contrary to the rules of the game, he hit a home run . . . although Nick didn't know it at the time.

Gabrielle had left early that afternoon for a doctor's appointment they told him at her office. There was no answer at her apartment either. He worried that she'd gone against their agreement and the temporary embarrassment of fantasy come true was being washed down the drain.

Irritated by this conclusion he phoned Eric and Odette to be told by a maid that they were away on holiday. He was tempted, for a brief moment, by jealous speculation about his former girlfriend in Paris, when his thoughts were interruption by Michaelis's secretary who walked into the room and put some papers on her boss's desk.

After she left, Nick went over to the long French window and watched the thick traffic bottleneck on the road below squeeze into the roundabout at Place de la Concorde and shoot off with centrifugal force onto the roadways branching away from the obelisk, just like the old days when this was his favorite thinking stance.

And then suddenly . . . as though prearranged . . . he called Thad Barnwell, his former chief, whose retirement ten years back and nomination of Nick as successor had pulled the younger man out of this very office, this very life with which he had been so at ease . . . but it was another life no longer his.

He hadn't seen Thad and Katie in three years . . . since they had given up their apartment in New York and moved to Paris "for the duration," as the ex-director liked to say.

There were Christmas cards and an occasional letter full of general

299

goodwill, but little more. Barnwell, who had taken Nick under his wing in the early part of Nick's career, had then pushed him out of the nest to fly on his own and fight his own battles. Barnwell himself had the foresight to retire when he was young enough to enjoy the comfortable pension and the leisure to pursue his own interests; his children were grown and independent, the son a doctor in London, the daughter a musician married to a banker in Paris.

Barnwell insisted on lunch, and shortly thereafter Nick was stepping out of a taxi in a small street of elegant houses behind the Bois de Boulogne.

Thad seemed younger than ever as he ushered Nick into the house, and his pleasure was genuine at the sight of Nick's envy for the collection of master drawings that adorned every wall of the sitting and dining room.

"Decided to specialize, you see," he said over the pâté. "All eighteenth century now, since I've been confining my researches . . .."

Barnwell was something of a scholar and was working on a second volume of a biography of John Wilkes, the eighteenth century English Whig politician and rogue who defied George III and the Tories. Nick had an inscribed copy of Volume I in his study at home.

". . . sold most everything else through Christies before we left New York."

"I would have bought the Daumiers," Nick said.

"Never sell to friends," Katie said as she entered the room, announcing a rule to live by as though it was remembered from a catechism.

"Besides," Thad said, "you couldn't afford them. I know what kind of salaries they pay."

"Oh, there've been a lot of raises since the old days," Nick said as the three of them walked into the dining room for lunch.

"What have you been buying lately?" Thad asked over the fish course.

Nick told them about the young Israeli painter whose work he'd recently acquired.

"Don't go much for moderns," Katie said, smiling sincerely, "too much anarchy for me."

"Tell us about Gabrielle," Thad said over dessert, "what a lovely, charming woman. Still on a separate but equal footing in living arrangements?"

Nick told them that the status quo was still quo.

"Then why don't you marry the girl," Katie said on her way out to read tombstones at Père Lachaise Cemetery with a friend.

"She actually does do that," Branwell said as they got up from the table.

"We're all collectors, I suppose," Nick said.

"You mustn't mind Katie's bluntness, she's rather old-fashioned about, er, ah, living arrangements. We're another generation. Let's go sit in the study," he added.

The maid had brought in coffee.

"Smoke your foul pipe if you like," Barnwell said when they were seated and sipping.

As Nick studiously applied a wooden match to the Caporal tobacco he'd bought for old time's sake, Barnwell said, "What really brought you here today, Nick? Tactical question? You know I'm really out of it . . . really. Last year they asked me to come to Washington for a head session, and I felt like a fossil among those technocrats. It's only through you and a couple of other youngsters I watched grow do I keep in touch. Afraid I only breathe in the twentieth century these days . . . live in the eighteenth."

"Thad . . . I'm thinking of resigning," Nick began, and the words flooded out like pus from a lanced carbuncle that had festered too long. He hadn't allowed himself to think of it, let alone say it before. The idea had been hiding in ambush for a sympathetic ear to victimize, and Nick felt the relief of having the old man to talk to, probably the one person in the world to whom he could open up to.

Barnwell understood the countervailing forces of Nick's career, his personality, the demands of the job, and the pressures of trying to find an accommodation between work that wanted one's life and a life that wanted one's work.

Nick didn't stop talking for a half-an-hour, shamelessly using

Thad as a father confessor.

One of the classic problems of the trade was that the men at the top had no one to talk to. Confidence wasn't possible when there was no one above you but a political appointee who cared only for results, or probable with a subordinate whose conditioned awe for the director excluded the possibility. Every agent on a mission had a case officer to listen, coax, cajole, advise, order, and demand . . . except the director.

Nick had quite simply just handed the role of confidant to his former director, who listened as only he knew how. Thad still had the habit of making a cathedral of his fingers as he listened, of keeping his eyes on the confider without staring, of punctuating the words the confider spoke with brief questions for clarity, and of knowing the point when to stop the confider when he returned to where he began.

That point for Nick was when he explained his reaction to his present mission, "Saving a melodramatic clown from an invented villain while trying to uncover who wrote the farce that might become serious and deadly. And all of it wrapped up in 'the national interest.'"

"Brandy?" Barnwell asked, standing and walking over to a cabinet in the corner. He returned with two snifters.

"You finished?" he asked rhetorically, and went on, "The point I'll start with is the one Katie ended with, in her inimitable fashion. Women have an intuition we lack — oh yes, I'm afraid I'm a sexist, hateful stupid term for understanding differences, isn't it."

Nick looked at him and shook his head when he realized what Barnwell was saying.

"Marry the girl," Barnwell said, and sipped his brandy approvingly, still the elegant connoisseur. He put the snifter down on the low table next to his chair, put his finger-tips together again and then blew his breath through the vaulted arch.

"What made you think I was talking about my personal life?" Nick asked indignantly.

"I've seen this before," Barnwell went on, avoiding Nick's question. "Oh yes, I experienced something like it myself. Of course I didn't expect you to know . . . about it . . . the time you first came into OMEGA."

"You recruited me, Thad, and there was a cause."

"Yes," Barnwell said. "For you. There was Kennedy and Camelot, the best and the brightest . . . you were part of it, not me. Simplistic metaphors hanging on from World War II, and a bullet through the brain in Dallas was the result of starry eyes."

The beach at Normandy, the gun emplacement, the rusted barbed-wire flashed before Nick's eyes.

"If I had believed then for one moment," Barnwell went on, "that you were a zealot, Nick, you wouldn't be sitting here talking to me. I don't trust them, not because I don't admire passion, but because the rush to die on the barricades depends on whichever definition of the cause is most appealing. And idealists are too easily flipped like a coin to the brighter, the more shimmering, side."

"Forget zealots and idealists, Thad. That doesn't apply, because you know I'm not either. I don't want the lecture for occasions when a protégé becomes disgruntled. The stars were out of my eyes years ago, and I never looked for ultimate moral justifications. It has been enough for me that the end results of the way we deal with problems are better than the opposition's. Better in the long — and short — run for more people. You taught me that lesson early and for good. Now you're telling me to build my own nest, hunt well outside, but make sure that my goal is the nesting not the hunting."

"What's wrong with that?" asked the older man.

"It's too cynical, too stripped of any faith . . .."

"There goes the lapsed Catholic," Barnwell scoffed. "Better a sound atheist in battle."

"I thought there weren't any in foxholes," Nick said with half a smile.

"Work that one out when you're in a foxhole," Barnwell answered sharply. "Because you aren't, unless you put yourself there. But since you have a misplaced affection for metaphor, Nick, let's just say that there's no cause except to protect whatever it is we think is a better way to live and let live . . . or make live, if you want. And as long as the opposition works to tear down our bastions, we'll have to blast away at theirs. It's always been that way, and probably always will be, whatever you and I do or say. Am I consistent with my former self?"

"You are. But it's all a bit disheartening, because then there's no end to the battle."

"The only end is to stay alive," Barnwell said. "I suppose you could say that what we were doing was only an elaborated political extension of the so-called 'state of nature.'"

"Turned into an industry," Nick said, "a self-sustaining and self-consuming industry that we keep going if the opposition doesn't . . . just to stay in business. Give the troops something to do so they don't get soft."

"Wrong!" Barnwell said, his voice even lower.

Nick could tell that his former chief was getting really annoyed, and he felt sorry for laying all this on him, but he didn't know where else to turn.

"The trouble with talking in metaphors, Nick, is that after a while the argument comes down to the skill in making up analogies while the substance of what's said remains untouched. Your so-called staying-in-business is the nature of bureaucracy . . . anywhere.

"Neither of us can change that. You can always opt out, conduct your life differently, or, since you are passionate for metaphor, march to a different drummer."

"Like my own Thoreau, go live in a shack by a pond?" Nick said as he thought of living with Gabrielle in the farmhouse in Dreux.

Barnwell laughed, "It's every pressured man's dream. It was mine too, and I suppose I've made my retirement my Walden. But you, Nick, are becoming fanatical in your self denial on an everyday basis, and that would be fine if you really enjoyed the renunciation. Yet all I hear you saying is that you don't, and have begun to doubt whether the cause you serve is worth what you've given up for it."

"Am I?" Nick asked. He was surprised that such a message had gotten through.

"Yes," Barnwell said. "That's what I hear, and all I'm telling you is that you've created a false issue, an artificial set of ideals, and you are living by them in place of anything else because you want to . . . not because you have to.

"The world will go on being exactly the same as it is now and always has been regardless of what you do, or do not. And if the hard work of making things happen more to our satisfaction than theirs has lost its meaning for you, and you have nothing of your own to replace that, and have nothing to bolster yourself up, then you're in a bad way.

"But *you* have the power to choose your way out, and your refusal is a willful act of sabotage and self destruction. I never saw you becoming a full time masochist — thought it was only a bit of a quirk — Nick, but now you have me worried."

Barnwell poured more brandy for both of them,

"This didn't begin yesterday for you, it began way back when you started that monkish denial and flagellation after Phyllis died along with your son."

"Monkish? That's a joke. I didn't deny myself a blessed thing," Nick objected. Cars, women, fancy clothes?"

Barnwell brushed aside Nick's objections, saying, "it was when you bypassed your second chance . . . along the Seine embankment, allowing Odette to walk away from you, square her shoulders, and walk faster . . . that was when I began to worry about fanaticism . . . and I thought long and hard before I decided that you were the next director, but it was half selfish. I wanted to get out too, do what I'd planned."

Barnwell didn't elaborate the rest, it was all around them.

"I assumed," he continued, "that when you settled in New York, and Gabrielle followed, you were taking up a life, a real life . . . the only damned thing that can give you a perspective for the job, son, the only damned thing."

"A family life, with me lying dead in an alley some where, with a sign 'hostage to fortune' hanging around my neck?" Nick had blurted out his creed to his confessor, a reason he thought Barnwell could understand.

But instead Barnwell grew angry . . . in his own style.

First the fingers made the nave, then he whistled wind through it and his voice grew so soft Nick had to strain to hear, "*That* is the worst vanity, the epitome of a messianic fantasy! The world and everyone in it, including your so called hostages would get along without you very well, or me, or anyone for that matter. What you've told me just now isn't noble renunciation, it's a secret pride that puts you and your imagined power at the center of things. Pride is a sin, however. Remember?

"Even when you disguise it with the claptrap of 'moral man' in an immoral universe, savior to all who follow. Indeed! What an arrogant piety! It leads to martyrdom. And what you've done, Nick, is prime yourself, condition yourself for that noble moment. That's what you're telling me. Saint Nicholas, living in the desert on locusts, waiting for the moment when the wicked king will serve up your head on a platter."

"Wrong saint," Nick said.

"Petty carping," Barnwell answered, "but I'll switch the metaphor to please your pedantry, so you'll listen to what I'm saying rather than take issue with the words I use."

Nick didn't answer and Barnwell went on after taking another sip of brandy. Still in a quiet voice. "If you don't find your own center, Nick, you're washed up as a professional, and if you keep that mental image of the alley and your corpse in front of you like some blasted medieval monk kept his death's head, the skull on his desk and slept in his coffin, you're on your way to the looney bin, or worse, you'll start another war."

There was no reason, the old man went on, that Nick should be going out on field missions, no justification for that kind of risk except his desire to fulfill his own prophecy.

"The Secretary handed it to me as a personal responsibility."

"You bloody fool, you were standing with your hands out," Barnwell said. "Moreover, I'm sure he didn't actually send you into the arena."

"Blood and sand, dance of death, grace under pressure," Nick said, smiling. It was what he admired in Moran, wanted for himself.

"Another code for fanatics," Barnwell said. "You keep bringing them up in one form or another. Forget the Hemingway bit or you'll wind up like him, a victim of your own burned out imagination which your life can't copy any longer, and you'll fulfill your own prophecy. What's the difference between your valley somewhere, filthy with vermin, and the leopard on top of Kilimanjaro?"

Nick relit his cold pipe, "Hard to shake the image, Thad."

"Then quit," Barnwell said. "You'll do yourself and OMEGA *and* your country a better service. Maybe you were right to think of it."

"I won't do that, Thad, and you know it. It's my only profession."

"Nonsense," Barnwell said. "You know damned well you could parley your part time teaching into a full time job or, with all your connections, become a consultant to some high-end spy tech manufacturer."

Nick shook his head. "This is my profession."

"Then do it like a professional, do the best damned job you can, and then go home and live your life."

"And the risks, Thad, the risks? Who else gets hurt?"

Barnwell stood and walked to the window of his study and looked through the curtains at the front garden.

Nick thought of Gabrielle standing by their front window looking out at the park, worried that the special telephone would ring, that her peace was at risk, that the life inside her was at risk; then he thought of Hartsdale-Smythe weeping for his daughter.

"Everyone gets hurt," Barnwell said. "We all do, and if you think you can avoid it, you're only part of a person, and you'll accumulate things, even people to fill the gap. No risk disposable junk. Easy come, easy go. Money back guarantee."

He knew that Barnwell was right . . . about most of it, at least. Yet he wondered was it fair to involve Gabrielle beyond the casual, comfortable relationship they had, make her a part of him so that the distinction between their separate lives blurred. And what about that alley?

Barnwell turned from the window, let the net curtain fall back into place obscuring the garden. He must have read Nick's mind. "Commit yourself to Gabrielle, take that chance of becoming human, and I'll bet the alley disappears too."

"Is that fair to her?"

"Why don't you ask her?"

Barnwell turned back to the window, parted the curtain. "There's Katie," he said, and he smiled, stepped over to Nick briskly, and offered his hand, "Think it over. Connect."

"Collect what?" Katie said walking through the study door.

Barnwell's eyes twinkled, "Not tombstones," he said.

"Well, at least I don't bring them home and fill up the walls. You watch out, Nick, he'll have you spending all your money on something he wants for himself," she said laughing, and put her arm through Barnwell's.

"He already has," Nick said. *The woman was blunt and real. Lucky for the old man that he'd chosen a 'secret' life rather than the diplomatic corps.* Nick moved towards the door.

"You won't stay for tea?" Katie asked. She seemed genuinely disappointed.

"Next time," Nick answered. "I have a lot of work to do yet."

"Work, work, work," Katie said. "You know I couldn't get him," she pointed her thumb at her husband, "to take more than a long weekend off when he was director?"

Barnwell looked embarrassed by the revelation . . . caught on the edge of his own advice.

Nick laughed knowingly as Barnwell blushed at Katie's frontal assault.

"Well I'm making up for it now, aren't I?" he pleaded.

"Too much, sometimes," she teased. There was no way of getting past her convictions.

"As soon as I've finished this mission," Nick said, "I'm going to take a long holiday, maybe right here in France."

"And the earth will manage to stay in orbit?" Barnwell asked teasingly.

After another handshake, Barnwell went back into the study,

Katie walked him to the door.

"Well, you'll come for tea then," she said, "and if you let me know a day in advance, I'll cancel any appointments so we can talk. I know Thad loves to see you . . . although he'll never admit it. I hope you guys solved the world's problems while I was out reading about dead people."

He stood on the step, holding her hand, "One of them, at least."

Katie's bright blue eyes widened like a schoolgirl's. "Which one, or is it Top Secret?" she whispered mischievously.

"Better to marry than Burns," he punned.

"Which saint said that?" she asked.

"Nick," he answered, walking down the garden path towards the low iron gate.

Two nannies deep in conversation pushed prams side by side past the house

"But I told you that before!" Katie called out,

"What a pity, to waste the afternoon rehashing it. We all could have gone to the cemetery."

The nannies stared in disapproval at the Americans talking loudly in the street.

"Next time!" Nick said over his shoulder.

"Bring Gabrielle. She can translate."

He waved and closed the gate, catching a glimpse of Thad at the study window.

The nannies stopped talking when he strode past and then started more animated than ever. *"Tout le monde connaît les Americans . . ."* was all he heard.

WHISTLING HAPPILY, Nick bought himself a new shirt at a haberdasher near the hotel. Then remembering that he had nothing with him, he threw in a tie, some socks and briefs. In the pharmacy next door he purchased a razor and toothbrush, and everything that went with them, filling a new leather toilet kit.

From OMEGA's private suite at the Georges Cinq, he placed a call to Gabrielle. No answer. Room service came with the dry martini he had ordered. He tried Gabrielle again. Nothing.

For Nick it was the ultimate irony, he kicked himself that he had finally been pushed into a corner and made a decision that made him feel suddenly unburdened, and at the same time she might have gone and put an end to her pregnancy just to please him and continue things the way he had wanted them.

Barnwell was right — he was a selfish bastard and had taken advantage of her for years. He remembered her again, sleepless, staring out of the window . . . soft, vulnerable, hurt. She had been tortured by the thought of another abortion and he hadn't even known about the other time, or had there been more than one? He shuddered. It would serve him right if she got fed up and quit.

He tried her number again. Still no answer. On a long shot he gave the operator his own number. Gabrielle answered on the second ring with a happy voice. "NEEK!" she shouted, "NEEK!" and she let out a string of words in French so rapidly that he couldn't understand half of them.

"Slow down, slow down," he said laughing. He told her he'd tried to reach her several times, at home, at work they told him she had gone to the doctor, he was worried, what was she doing at his place, how did she feel, he loved her.

"You thought I . . .."

He choked on the word, then completed the sentence, ". . . had the abortion."

"Foolish man. I'm furious with you, but I wouldn't do that when you said to wait. I went to the doctor for some medicine . . I don't feel so well in the mornings, that's all."

He could see her face, her loose hair hanging down, the soft, round, warm, full figure in the nightgown.

"And I came here afterward because the doctor's office is so close by, and I wanted to water your stupid plants. Why didn't you remember to ask me to water them? They were almost dead. Do you really love me?"

Then he told her what he wanted her to do.

Silence, then, "But it's so expensive!"

"Call! I'll ring back in five minutes."

"Neekolaas!"

"Call!" he said, and hung up the phone.

Five minutes later he rang her again.

"It's so expensive!" Gabrielle said.

"Did you do it?" *Not the famous French thrift getting in the way, not now.*

"It's done!" she said, still concerned.

"I'll pay you back," he said.

"You will do no such theeng," she said.

They then argued for five minutes more about whether or not he would or would not be allowed to pay her back.

"What about the plants?" Gabrielle asked in the middle of saying goodbye after he had promised three more times that he really, really, REALLY loved her.

"Leave a note for the cleaning woman, she can water them," he said.

It was five more minutes before he could get off the phone.

The next thing he wanted to do was call Thad and Katie and ask what the hell they had gotten him into. The second was cry with relief. The second came first; the first was forgotten.

BEFORE HE WENT TO MICHAELIS' house for dinner, Nick called Randall at home. The line was unshielded, consequently the conversation was intentionally vague.

"John's hopping mad," Randall said. "Mostly about the hardware order."

"He'll get over it. Can they fulfill?"

"He called me before I left the office to say it was arranged," Randall answered, "but his company doesn't like the price."

"They had a week more. This one's ours. Besides, it's not their money."

"It's the principle, John says."

"Damn the principle, Eliot . . . it's slush to our masters."

"As you say, sir," Randall said.

"And my transport?"

"You're with John out of Heathrow at five on Wednesday as you asked; the hotel is also confirmed on the telex."

"You'll send on my luggage?" Nick asked.

"Aren't you coming through here first?"

Nick hesitated . . . the need to know won out, "I don't think so, Eliot. It's your show there, really, and I think I'll tidy things up here, and get a little rest. Just send the stuff out to the plane with John, I'll take the airbus from here and meet him at the gate . . . oh, and would you call him, please, tonight, my apologies etcetera, etcetera and bring him up to date?"

He thanked Randall and rang off.

Nick thought that Elliot was almost too deferential, but there was no point in thinking about that now, he'd bring it up with him another time. Also Hartsdale-Smythe, unsolicited, had broken a habit of reticence to praise Randall, so Nick supposed that he must have come on as rather prejudiced against him. He'd try to be more sympathetic.

Now for the Michaelis' — he always told funny jokes and she was very pretty — and then tomorrow. Well, after a pit stop at the embassy, he would have it all to himself . . . mostly.

"Congratulations," he said to himself in the mirror of the bathroom. Then he stripped and jumped into the shower.

Only later, when he thought about everything that had happened that day did he realize that he had begun, unwittingly, to search for a successor.

TUESDAY WAS ONE of those early spring days in Paris which move songwriters to compose ageless melodies, lyricists immortal lines, most of which are soon forgotten. Nick kept humming a Piaf tune that hadn't been.

After duty calls at the embassy, he wandered through the Tuileries, as he used to do during the years he'd lived in Paris, took out the bread he'd saved from his breakfast tray, an old habit from the past when a stroll in this park was a daily ritual, and sat on a bench feeding the pigeons. To his own surprise, he was enjoying himself in the midst of a ticklish political situation, and on the threshold of a decision that couldn't but change his life. Where then was the edge of tension he had come to expect as normal, which his quiet demeanor, and relaxed, phlegmatic tinkering with a pipe served to disguise? Gone, hiding? He thought of looking under the bench, searching his pockets.

He filled the air with the cloudy reek of Caporal, and like the croissants in the cafe with the mercenary, the aroma was the key to reflective consciousness, memory.

Ten years ago I sat here after flying overnight from New York. It was a grey morning, and I had just been kicked upstairs. I fed the birds with bread I'd saved from the flight and thought of just being made — at thirty-five — the youngest director in the history of OMEGA. My pride was tinged with regret; my own mistake had cost an agent's life, and I had been a catalyst in the lives of Eric and Odette, changing them forever. Have I only been marking time all these years, building up the facade of a life, insulated with small comforts to keep out the cold?

He brushed the last crumbs from his hands, stood and turned his jacket pocket inside out to get rid of the bits inside. Enough of memory . . . it didn't serve now, but would command, if he let it, and self pity would creep in. No, he thought as he walked purposefully, but not fast, toward Place Vendôme. The quotation — was it Hegel? — Eric had once saddled himself with . . . "Everything is figured out, except how he himself is to live a life," — *no*, he thought walking more briskly, *it didn't apply to Nick Burns, or at least not any more.*

Still humming Piaf's battle standard "*Non, je ne regrette rien,*" he dodged traffic on the Rue de Rivoli, and opened his useless raincoat to the heat of the day. There was enough time to find what he was looking for.

THE AIR FRANCE CONCORDE swooped into Charles de Gaulle airport like a sharp-beaked hawk and had hardly stopped taxiing to the gate when Gabrielle was out of her seat, and ready to get off the plane with her hand luggage over one shoulder. Some of the other passengers, who thought the world of themselves for being able to afford the dubious privilege of crossing the ocean in three hours, stared at her as though she had committed some unpardonable social gaffe.

She returned the looks with a smile, feeling invulnerable for the first time in her life, although that day had been one of the most hectic in her life — arranging a leave of absence on short notice, packing and repacking until she decided that she'd buy some clothes in Paris and packed only the barest necessities, remembering to telephone her surprised mother to announce her sudden visit and surviving a last minute scare when she couldn't find her passport. Then — as could be expected — traffic en route to Kennedy was heavy, and during the flight she felt nothing but her pounding heart.

When the door of the plane finally opened, Gabrielle was first to go down the steel steps. Walking as rapidly as she could in her tight Chanel skirt she knew Nick liked so much, with the matching open jacket swinging like wings, she passed the bored immigration man, was waved through customs without even a glance from the officer and arrived in the terminal lobby in record time.

Nick was waiting, just as she had seen him a thousand times before, leaning back against a counter, standing on one foot, the other crossed casually behind with only the toe touching the ground, his raincoat folded over one arm, the other elbow on the deserted ticket counter and, as usual, a pipe jutted from his face and clouded the air above his head with smoke. He was reading something through those half-lens glasses he'd begun to use more and more lately. And she thought that with his graying temples, he was *trés distingué*, especially with that gesture of his when he took the glasses off to talk — although she didn't know why since you were meant to look over the top — and he looked at you with those piercing green eyes, and she thought he was the handsomest man in the world, and hoped that the baby would look like him, even with green eyes.

Then she began to run, and he saw her and started towards her and they were kissing and embracing in the middle of the bare cav-

314

ern of a lobby, unashamed tears making their faces salty and wet.

Because France runs on *l'amour*, at least in its most cherished mythologies, the passersby who had first noticed the attractive woman in the smart suit running with her hair bouncing over her face and her admirable well-endowed body jiggling and wiggling rhythmically, stopped looking when she ran into the arms of the tall American, and with a shrug and a knowing smile, passed on.

MUCH, MUCH LATER, when they were finishing the last of the champagne, and all the ice in the bucket was only water, Gabrielle looked for the hundredth time at the Tiffany solitaire in the antique setting. She had put the plain gold wedding band on the wrong hand "because it's bad luck to wear it properly before the wedding," she'd said.

Then she remembered something in her handbag and dug it out: the gold medallion engraved with the profile of Emperor Ferdinand I she had given him. A jump ring was placed through a small hole drilled in the rim above the head and the medallion now hung from a long chain.

Gabrielle draped the chain over Nick's head and gently arranged it to nestle on his chest. "This is why I was at your apartment last night when you called. . . to leave this for your return . . . not just to water your ugly plants."

"They'll be your ugly plants, too, soon enough," he said.

"That depends on where we live," she said, with one eye closed in warning.

"I thought we had agreed, and the plants will be at home," Nick said, surrounding her with his arms, "in the middle of Central Park," and kissed her again before she could answer.

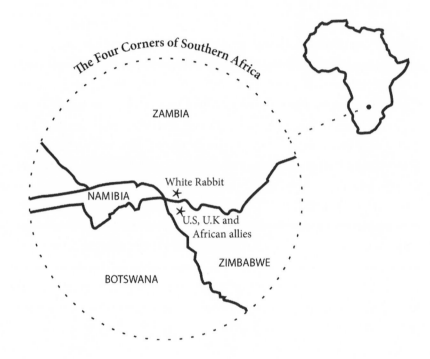
The Four Corners of Southern Africa

ZAMBIA

White Rabbit

NAMIBIA

U.S, U.K and
African allies

ZIMBABWE

BOTSWANA

19

ZAMBIA

NEAR THE FOUR CORNERS

A TWO ENGINE BEECHCRAFT carried the first White Rabbit crew from Johannesburg across Botswana and touched down in Zambia a week before the agreed exchange. Piloted by Wesson, the plane dropped through the tree canopy to land easily alongside a quiet stretch of the Zambezi and taxied to a large stand of tall reeds.

All hands cut enough reeds to conceal the aircraft, and then put up two camouflage tents hidden from each other. Volkov and his henchmen, Alexi and Vigo, shared one tent with Wesson and Smith, while Kananga went to the other as befit his chief status. Moran stayed with him because he didn't trust the old warrior as far as he could throw him . . . and the more Kananga smiled the less Moran trusted him.

When Smith suggested that the Russians accompany him to the other tent, they seemed pleased, but that didn't last long as he drew a pistol and aimed it at Volkov. His henchmen were ready to jump in until they heard Wesson say "don't be stupid" behind them. He held a very large Purdy shotgun, cocked at their backs. A moment later they were handcuffed behind their backs, put in leg irons and chained to a large shade tree.

Wesson then cuffed Volkov behind his back and marched him away from the others.

Attached to a post in a thicket, Volkov was beaten professionally by Smith and Wesson until he hurt in every part of his body. "Why me?" he screamed. More accustomed to giving than receiving beatings Volkov understood that they weren't trying to kill him. "Moran will tell you," was all the response he got.

Finally, the blows stopped, and he heard Moran say his name.

317

Volkov opened his blood laced eyes to see the Frenchman standing in front of him. Smith and Wesson were gone.

"Not another punch if you tell me what I need to hear" said Moran.

Volkov was tough — a man without a conscience — a cool professional tied to a tree in the middle of a jungle. How could he calculate the odds if there were none?

"What is that?" he asked Moran

"Who else was involved in this murderous drama?"

Volkov raised his battered face to look at Moran and murmured, "There is no one else involved in the plan, nobody but Kananga and me and the functionaries, working for hire with no knowledge past their tasks. The big shots are clean . . .." His head dropped to his badly bruised chest.

Moran snapped Volkov's face up and pressed his head against the tree: " Who else," he demanded, "the girl?"

The Russian opened one glazed eye. A short lived smile flitted across his torn mouth: "She thought I was CIA." His eye closed, the lid snapped down like a window shade.

Moran wouldn't let go of his head: "WHO?" he shouted. "You had someone!"

Volkov opened the eye again: "Someone . . . a nobody. Leave him . . .." He lost consciousness.

During this interrogation one of Volkov's hires was so scared he ran off that night. Smith and Wesson waited until the rubber raft was in midstream to open fire. A first scream when he was hit and in the water; a final scream ended with a splash and gurgle when the ever-ready crocs got him. Then silence.

Moran was sorry to lose the expensive raft. Then he ordered his men to dig a grave. The sounds of the spades scraping the dry dirt could be heard on the other side of the camp.

HARARE

TWO DAYS LATER MORAN KNOCKED on Nick's hotel room door. He had casually walked into the hotel, used the stairs for precaution to get to the room, and went unnoticed.

He sat on the sofa while Nick dressed, and outlined the details of how the exchange was to unfold.

Nick didn't flatter himself that he was being trusted. White Rabbit still had Kananga, and the mercenary kept contracts, even the unilateral ones.

"Kananga will finger the traitor," Moran said, "and then I'm to off him personally."

"THE HELL YOU ARE," Nick bellowed, "WE WILL.

"You won't," Moran said, casually buttering one of the rolls on Nick's breakfast tray, "or the contract is off." He bit into the roll and took a sip of Nick's coffee.

"Help yourself," Nick said.

Moran grinned, "I do."

"And Volkov?" Nick asked.

"Still among us," Moran said, finishing Nick's coffee and then reaching for an orange, "but one of his goons, Alexi, met with a big, bad crocodile on patrol the other night, it ate his transmitter, too," he said, peeling the orange.

"I want Volkov," Nick said . . . it was worth a try.

"He doesn't look so pretty any more. Forget it, Burns, he's only on ice until the Kananga exchange. If everything goes well, then we'll see about Volkov, unless the SOB tries to escape . . . which is not likely.

"I dug a grave just to make a point about following the orders, but I won't kill Volkov in cold blood, Nick. I'm a soldier not a murderer. When this is over I'll trade him and his other bodyguard, Vigo, for someone the Russians are holding.

Nick grabbed the coffee jug before Moran could finish that too, and drank a cup in two gulps.

"And what about the money?" Nick asked.

"Professionals always get paid, my friend. Kananga's half can go back to your little treasury if he's unable to use it."

"No worries here, he's a survivor."

"Let's hope," Nick answered, "and no knock-out pills on your way out."

"Sorry, *mon ami*, but I had to keep the big man safe. Now he's seasoned and ready."

"Let's toast the 'seasoned and ready'," and Nick handed a hip flask to Moran. "You know this one: 'Here's to us . . .'?"

Moran nodded and they continued together,

> "Here's to us,
> Who's like us?
> Damn few . . .
> And they're all dead!"

Both drank.

Moran clasped Nick's hand. "By the way, is Nick Burns related to the poet Robert Burns?"

"According to my mother." Nick answered.

20

ZIMBABWE
NEAR THE FOUR CORNERS

THE TOPS OF THE TREES bent over, then lashed up and bent again in the ferocious wind from the rotors of the big helicopter.

Monkeys and baboons swung rapidly from branch to branch to get away from the giant steel monster descending on them from the air. Then finally finding that there were no trees safe enough, they ran along the ground — hundreds of them jabbering in terror.

A herd of elephants led by an old bull broke through the bush and lumbered off into the opposite direction, the cows pushing their bleating babies with their trunks.

A pride of lions in the tall grass a quarter of a mile away was too glutted and sleepy to move far. Slowly they walked toward a clump of trees, growling their annoyance, and laid down in the shade. The large buck sable antelope they had just finished gorging on was left to the flies and later the hyenas, while the lions blinked and watched the noisy man-bird settle beyond the stand of white-thorned acacia trees down near the river where they drank.

MI6'S HARTSDALE-SMYTHE STOOD next to the chopper's open door and watched as the ground came up to meet the machine. He then waited as ten battle-ready Special Forces "advisors" leapt to the ground running, and fanned out in a line parallel with the helicopter body.

Earlier another forty men had arrived in two troop-carriers and were somewhere in the bush by now, deployed in the classic pincer formation their captain had recommended when he studied the map before first light that morning.

Hartsdale-Smythe was standing with the professionals, intentionally keeping his back to the bloody diplomats and politicians who were accompanying them including former PM Anthony Trevor-Jones, President Matthias Umgawe, U.S. Ambassador Warden Yogun and G.B. Ambassador Peter Soames, and Reuters journalist Mike Buchanan. He had a deep aversion to these types, that was intensified by the need to be polite to them. He turned to Nick Burns, who looked cool . . . even dapper . . . in a borrowed camouflage jumpsuit, "You're sure this is the clearing? They all look alike to me," he said.

Nick replied, "The pilot knows what he is doing," and pointed across the clearing. Two hundred yards away to the north a pennant was being hauled up on a halyard attached to a branch of a tree at the edge of the forest. It furled out slightly in the still air, long enough for them to see the White Rabbit insignia through their binoculars, then it went limp as a rag. "Right on the nose."

Burns seems too confident Hartsdale-Smythe thought, *almost cocky, as though he is enjoying all this . . . and well he might be. Once again the United States has bought its way out of a problem.* If the MI6 man had had his way, he would have stuck with Sir Peter, and insisted that the commandos do what they were trained to do . . . wipe out those blasted parasites as soon as the exchange was made. Whitehall wanted that too, and it was made clear to Randall at OMEGA while Burns was off cavorting around France. But the younger man was only a cup bearer and Washington had put Burns in charge.

"Why are you sticking to some abstract idea of Honour, with a capital 'aitche'?" Hartsdale-Smythe had asked Burns several times, in several different ways, on the long flight from London to Harare, and Nick replied something about contracts, and finally was too flippant for the Englishman, with an "*honi soit qui mal y pense*" thrown in, as though he were Sir Gawain, or some such nonsense. Hartsdale-Smythe thought it a fine opportunity to rid this part of the world of one of its scourges, but Burns wouldn't hear of it.

The Englishman thought he could detect an admiration for the blasted mercenary on the part of Nick, and suspected, frankly, that the whole thing *really was* a CIA operation after all, and that *they* had duped the Russian, Volkov, not the other way around. But then there was Maggie . . . back in England in custody, and away from these fools.

The rotors were stopping.

"What now?" asked Trevor-Jones, the white minority leader, whose presence had been a condition of the contract Burns stipulated. The lanky politician was sitting by himself and had also been very quiet on the special jet that had brought them to Victoria Falls earlier that morning. Then he hardly said a word to anyone even in the crush of soldiers on the big whirlybird, but when offered a cigarette by Hartsdale -Smythe he accepted it with aplomb.

In spite of his prejudices, the Englishman rather liked the old Rhodesian whose all-white government suffered under the sanctions of their sixteen-year shunning by their mother country, Great Britain. He had actually maintained liaison with Britain through the secret services, and Hartsdale-Smythe had gotten to know him quite well. *This*, to the Englishman, was what it meant to be a patriot, not all that mouthing off that passed for it . . . malarkey sauce on a plate of anarchy. Trevor-Jones had done what he could for Rhodesia, and paid the price . . . and not with cheap-shot buy-outs.

"Burns will carry the filthy lucre across the clearing, and if the bastards don't kill him, he'll come back here," Hartsdale-Smythe said.

"The battle's over, John," Burns said. "Stop fighting it. The rest is just a big ceremony."

Cheeky bastard, he wouldn't even give me the satisfaction of seeing a needle prick him Hartsdale-Smythe thought.

Trevor-Jones spoke quietly as the rotors stopped and the noise of the bush took over. Like any number of the old Rhodesians, he combined the manners of an Englishman with the bluffness of an American, and he was a man used to the authority he no longer commanded, "I want it for the record, Mr. Burns, that these mercenaries are in no way connected with me or my party . . . not this time."

Trevor-Jones *had* used Moran in the past and it was common knowledge.

"I can't afford to have them hung on me now, and your ambassador seems deaf to all voices but his own."

"I know that, and you don't need to worry about him," Nick answered, as he motioned with his eyes toward Ambassador Yogun who sat glaring on a bench a distance from the door. Only Nick knew that the American ambassador had received a cable earlier that day ordering him back to Washington with the underlying message being "mothballs."

How did Burns' know that about Yogun for sure? Hartsdale-Smythe wondered. *This situation is so far out of my hands and it shouldn't be . . . and this damned heat.* He mopped his brow and lit another cigarette.

"But they'll contrive to put it on me," Trevor-Jones said, "either our fearless leader or his nemesis."

Nick made use of his recently re-acquired French shrug. "Be the first to tell the press," he said, indicating Buchanan, who stood behind them, his head still bandaged. He was the only "outside" witness permitted on the mission, which Nick said was White Rabbit's decree, but actually it was Kananga's demand delivered by the mercenary, Moran. The fat man insisted that there should be one objective eyewitness representing the press.

Trevor-Jones turned to the newsman and conferred in low tones as Nick hopped down onto the ground.

The pilot came into the back bay, opened a storage locker and lifted out two heavy canvas sacks. He then dragged them across the ribbed metal floor of the aircraft and dropped them to the ground at Nick's feet.

"But you would just as soon be rid of Kananga?" he heard Buchanan ask Trevor-Jones.

"Not this way," Trevor-Jones was insisting, "and remember, this is all deep background, Buchanan . . . not for attribution."

Nick looked up to see Buchanan nod in agreement.

"Umgawe's easier to deal with if Kananga isn't around. Otherwise the white minority will get caught between them, and their rivalry works against us."

Nick tuned them out, and concentrated on removing the jump-suit and shirt that he was wearing, leaving on only khaki shorts and *veldtschoen*.

"Why are you undressing?" Yogun asked, coming forward to the open doorway and looking down at Nick.

"To flex my muscles for the photographs," Nick answered, not looking up, and adding "Mr. Ambassador," although he would have liked to add, "but not for long" . . . but didn't.

"Better take off the sunglasses, then," Yogun said.

"He's doing it to show he isn't armed, sir," Hartsdale-Smythe replied.

"Thank you," Yogun said sarcastically.

Buchanan looked over from his conversation with Trevor-Jones, and fantasized one good punch. *Maybe I'll do it later. What the hell, his plane leaves tonight anyway. I'll kick him in the groin on the way back — an accident — "Oh I'm so sorry, I hope I didn't hurt you."*

Burns hoisted a canvas sack on to each shoulder, then turned and started to walk across the clearing.

As the American twisted round, Hartsdale-Smythe saw a gold medallion swinging out from the sweat-matted hair of his chest. He hadn't known that Burns was a religious man. *Renegade Catholic*, he thought. *Gets rid of the church, keeps the idols.*

The sun blazed directly overhead filling the pale sky with its glare. Here, where the plateau of Zimbabwe's central highlands slopes off towards the Zambezi river valley, the air lost the crisp cleanness of the capital district and was heavy and cloying. Cicadas rasped in great waves of sound from the jacaranda trees, and the birds, returning from the helicopter's scare, vocally reclaimed their territory. Some baboons, looking suspiciously behind them, jabbered among themselves and watched Nick as he sweated his way across the elephant trampled grass.

Nick knew that he was covered from behind . . . and most likely from in front . . . so he wasn't worried about a charging lion, but his eyes darted constantly over the ground before him as he *was* concerned about snakes . . . the deadly mamba most of all.

The weight of the money in the bags began to cut into his shoulders. He stopped, put down the bags, and with intentional slowness drew a large, red-printed neckerchief from his pocket, wiped his face, cleaned the steamy moisture from his sunglasses, and tied the cloth around his forehead to keep the sweat out of his eyes.

"What's he doing? Signaling?" Ambassador Yogun asked no one in particular.

"I imagine that he's resting for a moment. It seems such an onerous chore," British Ambassador Sir Peter responded.

"Absurd!" Yogun snapped. "Posturing, playing soldiers. It's all so childish."

"It's their game, I'm afraid, Warden," Sir Peter said, "and either we have to play it their way or not at all. Have you ever dealt with terrorists?"

Sir Peter thought that his question would shut the American ambassador's mouth . . . as they both knew the answer. God help him, but he couldn't stand Yogun, and now that Yogun's tumbling with Maggie Groves was over, he would have no source close enough to the American to bring him tidbits of information. *The fool can't keep his fly buttoned or his boastful mouth closed. He sure doesn't speak too well for the American Foreign Service.* He hadn't known the girl was MI6 when he pushed her under Kananga's nose, and Secret Service hadn't breathed a word . . . now that was useful. Sir Peter wondered who they'd send him . . . *another looker I hope to flatter their vanity.*

Burns stopped, put down the sacks and seemed to be trying to swat at some flies, lifted them again and continued walking.

"Why did they bring us all the way out here," Yogun asked, again addressing the air. "We couldn't get much further from anything."

"It's Kananga's territory," Prime Minister Umgawe said, with a broad toothy smile. "His troops controlled this entire area during the war." Then he stopped. It was enough of an implication, and the attorney in him counseled no more allegations without proof . . . he'd find that later. *Blasted Kananga, he would get a hero's welcome.*

326

Then Umgawe adjusted his glasses while attempting to watch Burns' progress earnestly.

Trevor-Jones held up a map. "Explanation's simpler, begging your pardon, Prime Minister." Trevor-Jones knew what Umgawe was trying to do, and he privately agreed with him, but he would be damned if he'd let the sly son of a bitch air the country's dirty linen in public.

"He needs to take just a few more steps," Trevor-Jones said, pointing at the ordinance map like the schoolmaster he once had been,

"White Rabbit is across the border into Botswana or into South West Africa's handle." *I won't use the ridiculous name Namibia until every one else does.* Even his own country's new name, Zimbabwe, he used for public consumption only. In his mind it would always be Rhodesia, and one day these bastards would pass a law and arrest him for even thinking it.

"He's across the river," he continued, "in Zambia."

"Quickest way out," Buchanan added. "Presto! Gone!"

"With Kananga, and the money too," Hartsdale-Smythe said angrily.

"Or Kananga dead," said Yogun, a prophet of gloom.

"Honor among thieves," Trevor-Jones said. "It's just that nobody will chase them . . . least of all British commandos."

Buchanan shook his head in grudging agreement.

"I wanted our own men," Umgawe said.

He had wanted his handpicked, loyal Tenth Brigade, all from the Shona tribe and Chinese trained, but he was overruled by the Americans and the English, so he decided not to fight the battle. *I'll find another one I can win and get those racist killers . . . someday.* He was sure that Trevor-Jones had some connection with all this, but Umgawe would wait for the appropriate time, gather evidence, and then . . . .

Nick didn't know which was worse, the load on his shoulders or the damned flies that seemed to alert all their brethren to his dripping-wet body. Even his shorts were soaked through. *Twenty yards to go.* He thought he saw movement in the bush in front of him, a body wearing camouflage moving between the trees. *If one of the sharpshooters behind me is trigger happy . . ..* He tried not to think of the possibilities. *Ten yards. Bingo.*

He dropped the money bags off his aching shoulders next to a large stone Moran had said to look for, and, after a brief orgy of fly-swatting, Nick turned and walked slowly back toward the helicopter.

The weight of the canvas knapsacks was replaced by the weight of eyes behind and around him. A giraffe wandered out of the bush to his left and walked obliviously across the clearing towards the other side. Nick stopped. He didn't want to scare the animal into sudden movement that might coax a bullet from the perimeter. The giraffe peered haughtily at him, turned its head away, and walked on.

He thought about Moran's parting words, "Professionals always get paid, my friend." *That explained the* two *knapsacks. The sly bastard was smarter than he looked.*

He took the big handkerchief off his head and wiped his chest, swatted away some flies, touched the medallion and stuffed the useless soaked rag into his pocket.

Halfway to the helicopter and curious about the knapsacks, Nick glanced over his shoulder at the rock and saw two men in beige and green bush fatigues dragging the bags into the bush. *That's a good sign. Moran had kept his word . . . both bags meant that Kananga was still alive.* There hadn't been any funny business. Nick turned and continued walking.

Now came the hard part.

When Nick was fifty yards from the helicopter, he quickened his pace.

The sun was as strong, the cicadas loud, and the monkeys, having come back in full strength, were louder. *The joys of nature indeed, bucolic dreams of poets in cities.*

He swatted at the cousins of the flies he'd already killed, then could see the row of faces in the open bay of the chopper . . . Hartsdale-Smythe, Umgawe, Yogun, Soames, Trevor-Jones and Buchanan

— the whole lot. With binoculars glued to their eyes, they looked like so many huge insects . . . color one Red.

Strangely enough he really didn't have it in for Van Ness . . .he corrected himself . . . Volkov. He was just another pro doing what his government paid him for. He probably wasn't even an ideologue. *Probably could have turned him.*

Moran wouldn't understand that. Dictatorship of the proletariat indeed. That was exactly what the mercenary was doing by calling the shots. And they all knuckled under.

Power came out of the barrel of a gun. *Kkkpeeeyooh!*

Nick heard the single shot echo from the trees and bounce on the empty hills, and he dropped flat to the ground as instinct and training took over.

He wasn't the target, he was sure, but he took no chances. Easing his head up a couple of inches he saw only Hartsdale-Smythe at the door of the chopper, the others had pulled back.

"Their pennant's down," Hartsdale-Smythe yelled between cupped hands, and then held them, palms out, in a gesture of resignation. Nick looked behind him and saw it was so.

"Better stay down, sir," one of the commandos shouted from the bush behind the chopper, his voice suddenly very loud in the ominous silence.

The cicadas and the monkeys had stopped their noise at the sound of the shot and now were slowly beginning again, an antiphonal chorus on opposite sides of the clearing.

Crouching, Nick ran towards the plane.

"Sorry, John," was the first thing he said.

Hartsdale-Smythe managed a brief smile and muttered a hoarse "thanks."

"It's a betrayal!" Warden Yogun shouted in Nick's face. "An outrage, with taxpayers' . . .."

"Hold on, man," Trevor-Jones said, grabbing the American's arm, "have you no sense for what Burns has just done, you damned fool. A fool's a fool, and I couldn't give two farthings about who in hell you are."

Umgawe beamed with secret satisfaction, whether at Trevor-Jones' saying the words everyone thought, or at the possibility that the hated Kananga was dead, it wasn't clear.

Sir Peter averted his eyes, and studied the bush behind the helicopter. *Yogun could be right*, he thought, *but probably wasn't*.

Nick felt sure that Moran would keep his word . . . he was no thief. Kananga would walk into the clearing a few minutes later and then someone . . . all of them . . . would find out what betrayal really was.

He looked at Hartsdale-Smythe, who managed to look more rumpled and ash-strewn than usual . . . even in brand new fatigues . . . and thought of what the Englishman must be feeling having been betrayed by his own daughter. If they had gotten the Russian they might have sweated out of him something, anything to ameliorate the charges against Maggie. But both he and John knew what the dropped pennant meant.

"I don't care what Burns has done," Yogun said, somewhat less shrilly, "because it was unnecessary. Anyone could have carried those bags, or we could have dropped them from the helicopter. Why insist upon these theatrics?"

"They wrote the script, Warden, not us," Sir Peter said.

"Well I don't like it, it should have been different . . ."

"Next time," Hartsdale-Smythe said bitterly, adding, "Mr. Ambassador. Besides, they trust Burns."

Nick had caught his breath meanwhile and now said, "And I think you'll all have to trust me for the next step."

"When do they deliver Kananga, these trustworthy thieves of yours, Mr. Burns?" Yogun asked.

It required Nick's utmost control over his fraying temper to speak calmly to Yogun. *Don't win the battle and lose the war*, he thought. "The two ambassadors and the Prime Minister and the former Prime Minster are to cross the clearing, meet Mr. Kananga and accompany him back to the aircraft," he said flatly.

Silence, the dry rasp of insects and the chattering monkeys took over for a moment.

"What about me?" Buchanan broke in. "I want photos, tapes . . . .."

"The officials only, Mike," Nick said.

"It's *my* story!" he objected.

"Shut up, Buchanan," Hartsdale-Smythe ordered.

Umgawe and Trevor-Jones were first on the ground followed by Sir Peter and lastly Yogun, who hissed at Nick, "I'll have your head for this, breaching every last vestige of security . . . .."

"Just walk calmly to the rock and wait for Kananga," Nick instructed the four dignitaries who stood tensely in front of him, Umgawe smiling, Sir Peter and Trevor-Jones affecting indifference, and Yogun being Yogun.

"And if there should be any firing . . . any, even a single shot, you hit the ground and stay there. You are covered every step of the way and the troops will move in and pull you out. Just lie there and wait."

"And die," Yogun said.

Nick ignored him and handed each of them a flak jacket, and nodded to Hartsdale-Smythe in the helicopter bay. The MI6 man spoke into the two-way radio and then called aloud, "Ready Captain Woolcott?"

"Yes, sir," came the reply from the bush, as the commandos began to work their way forward on both flanks and the helicopter gunner swung the long perforated barrel of the automatic cannon out of the gun bay, high above the heads of the quartet now slowly stepping out of the shadow of protection that had been their cherished illusion. Two more commandos appeared from nowhere and set up a mortar at the perimeter of the field not far from the helicopter.

Nick climbed back aboard and watched the stiffened backs of the four men as they moved away cautiously and tensely into the full blaze of sunlight. The rock reflected diamond-like glitters into the thick air.

He took the automatic rifle Hartsdale-Smythe handed him, and waited, his body keyed up, eyes alert for any suspicious movement in the bush across the field. Sitting ducks, he knew, and there would be a tragedy on his head . . . end of career. There'd be no choice but to resign.

Squawks from the radio.

Hartsdale-Smythe plugged in earphones and listened. "Right," he said into the microphone. "Over and out."

"The two flank teams have the White Rabbit camp in range," he said to Nick.

Burns looked at him briefly in acknowledgment and the Englishman saw the vacant hardness of his eyes, the involuntary twitching of his jaw. He turned to Buchanan who sat listlessly on the bench behind them, out of view of the four men who were halfway across the matted grass.

"I thought you wanted pictures," Hartsdale-Smythe growled at the reporter.

"Of backs?" Buchanan said snidely. He then fiddled with the telescopic lens on his Nikon, stood, aimed the camera at the four departing men, snapped the shutter twice and returned to his seat on the bench. "I'll get them when they return with the bacon," he said to Burns and Hartsdale-Smythe — neither of whom were expecting to answer. Their minds were elsewhere.

Nick was taking every nervous step across the field with the four diplomats and politicians — one of whom would probably be dead within a few minutes. And if it happened as it was likely to, Nick would keep his own promise to Moran, come hell or high water.

The commandos were ready, and despite all the talk about not crossing nearby borders, they would go in at the signal from John, and so would Nick. He checked the safety on the weapon he held; he'd kill the bastard himself if he had to.

Hartsdale-Smythe watched the four backs nearing the rock, but wasn't seeing them at all. He was hearing his daughter's voice in the interrogation room, hearing her anguished sobs. The others had been sent out of the room, the microphone was turned off at his command, and the plug pulled on the voice activated tapes. Only the tapes in his head recorded the twisted tale.

Moran had lined up the telescopic sight of his rifle on the faces of the four men standing near the rock waiting. He could almost reach out and touch them, it seemed. Without the scope they appeared farther away than he'd thought, but it didn't matter . . . from an elevated clump ten feet behind the tree line he had a clear vision of the entire field, and, had he wanted to, he could put a hole into the head of a gunner in the chopper before he would be able to fire a round.

Then Moran raised his arm and signaled to Smith, who stood in the bush with a pistol to Kananga's head. He then saw Smith cut the ropes that bound Kananga's hands, who then began to slowly shuffle through the bush toward the edge of the clearing.

Moran fixed a bead on Kananga's neck as he stepped out of the shadows, and checked the faces of the four other turds in the clearing, enjoying their fear. For once in their lives of sending people to die they'd now know how it felt to be under the gun. He could see each drop of sweat through the sight, and loved it.

Kananga stepped into the sunlight, stopped and blinked for a second, then walked slowly . . . almost hesitantly . . . towards the others sweating in those stupid flak jackets. But Moran wasn't taking chances . . . his bead was drawn . . . and he had never missed.

He sighted the rifle again, ranging across the backs of the five men, with Kananga in the middle, who had begun walking toward the helicopter. Kananga's signal was to be a raised hand behind one of them. Moran hoped he wouldn't give it for Burns' sake; he wanted the traitor for his own. He refocused the sight on the one head that counted. Yet again he adjusted the sight, calculating the fall rate on the line of fire. His aim was steady on target.

The group walked on.

Kananga hadn't seen Van Ness since they got there, and didn't know what he had said. How much did Moran know? Could Kananga take the chance — hand himself the country?

What Kananga didn't know was that if he raised a hand as pre-arranged, but falsely to indicate the "collaborator," the "betrayer," the one whose death would hand him the reins of power or create a great international commotion, then and only then, Jeremiah Kananga, a leader of his people, would be mourned with great public spectacle, after the mercenary's ready bullet blew his head apart.

"Thank God!" Nick had said when he saw Kananga emerge from the shade and walk towards the others.

Buchanan came forward and took some pictures.

Nick watched the five faces through the binoculars as they turned near the glinting stone and slowly walked towards the helicopter. Kananga didn't have his perpetual smile in place, but rather a stern, thoughtful expression.

Sir Peter on his left and Trevor-Jones on his right were moving their heads as they talked, Sir Peter, in most uncharacteristic fashion for the British aristocrat, gesturing fluently with his hands. Kananga held his hands behind his back.

Nick felt the skin bristle on his neck, expecting to see a face disintegrate in front of him as a high powered slug tore through, and to watch a body pitching forward before he heard a sound. But whose?

The cicadas rasped their melodies, suddenly full of menace for Nick, like a moaning chorus at an ancient Greek play, filling the air with premonitions of doom.

"They're turning now, Buchanan, if you want a better picture," he said just to hear words spoken, just to interrupt the horrible sounds of nature screaming death from the trees.

The journalist started down the ladder.

"Stay here," Hartsdale-Smythe snapped at Buchanan. "You're in the line of fire."

Buchanan mumbled and pulled himself back into the open bay.

Umgawe's face was covered with perspiration now and he had removed his glasses, as he usually did when he knew he was to be photographed.

Nick watched as the Prime Minister walked slightly faster as though he wasn't so anxious to talk to Kananga or be seen doing so in a photo. He stepped in front of the other three, and then Yogun was up with him.

Sir Peter, Trevor-Jones, and Kananaga provided natural cover from the line of the mercenary's fire.

Hartsdale-Smythe must have thought the same thing because he knew what Moran had told Nick, or most of it.

"I can't believe this," he said to Nick in an undertone, "do you think . . .?"

"I can't think . . .," Nick snapped, cutting of his sentence.

"Second time we've stood like this in ten days, getting to be a habit, what, Montgomery and Patton?" Hartsdale-Smythe remarked with unusual levity feeling some relief with the end in view.

Nick nodded "yes," glad for the patter, but unable to join in. He had to concentrate. He raised the field glasses to view the vultures in the trees on the other side of the clearing. *Waiting for Volkov probably.* He shuddered.

They were about halfway across the field when Kananga stopped briefly as though to catch his breath, then continued on.

"Hurry up, you ass," Hartsdale-Smythe whispered hoarsely.

Trevor-Jones and Sir Peter were walking ahead chatting with each other as though they were on a Sunday stroll in the park. *The Brits had style, even the old Rhodesian*, Nick had to hand them that.

"Where the hell do they think they are? Hartsdale-Smythe grumbled. "Hurry up, you sods."

Buchanan, who had been fiddling with his camera, moved towards the doorway for a better shot.

Kananga, meanwhile, had gotten his body between Umgawe and Yogun, his two blood brothers . . . one by chance, the other by choice.

Two down, two to go, Nick thought, feeling his palms sweating on the rifle stock while the rest of his body felt cold as winter though perspiration beaded all over him. He slipped the binoculars off his neck, feeling them suddenly very heavy. He didn't need them any more to see the faces.

The five men were now past the halfway mark and getting closer. The two white men were farther ahead, maybe just forty yards away, but Kananga, his face still a somber mask, walked more slowly, his large arms now hanging limply at his sides.

He knew, Nick said to himself, *he knew just what he was going to do, the wily bastard.* "Oh God," he muttered aloud, "let it not be!"

The Englishman looked over and stared at Nick a moment, and then raised his binoculars to look toward the five men.

Could it be Umgawe? Nick wondered. *Would that self-contained little man go to such trouble just to get back at Kananga, whom he had beaten hands down? Not possible. But what if Kananga raised his right hand and with that move voted himself back into office? It was too chancy.*

They were closer now, and Sir Peter and Trevor-Jones were already in the shadow of the trees and walking behind the helicopter.

Nick was no longer hearing the cicadas or the monkeys chatter, only his blood thundering like timpani in his ears.

Kananga plodded on, his face a sullen mask, not talking to the men on either side of him.

Nick thought he saw the Kananga's left arm move towards Yogun. *Shit! Who else could it be? damned power freak putting himself into the middle of history, of all the. . ..* But his arm dropped back into place and he continued to amble toward them.

And then it hit Nick like an exploding shell between the eyes . . . *Kananga's mask! It was no one, nobody else but the fat man himself provoked by Volkov's clever ploy. The son of a bitch was afraid because of Moran. He knew the mercenary would kill him if he fingered any of the others! HE KNEW, or had uncanny intuitions.*

The walk across the field must have been a passage through hell for Kananga as he thought of his finely tuned instrument coming unstrung, too afraid that Moran had gotten it all out of the KGB man. It had to be! That's what the expression on his face was — the fear of acting and the fear of not acting. Paralysis.

Nick felt a surge of relief course through his body as the three men stepped into the shadow the trees had thrown as the sun slid into afternoon.

"Whooopee!" he shouted, not giving a care what anyone thought anymore, and put his weapon down.

"Well done," said Hartsdale-Smythe to Nick and turned towards Buchanan who was clambering down the ladder. But the journalist was already running towards Kananga.

"WHERE IN HELL ARE YOU GOING?" Hartsdale-Smythe shouted . . . but it was too late.

Buchanan had almost reached Kananga covering the ground at a sprint when Kananga screamed hysterically, "IT'S HIM!" pointing at Buchanan.

There was a blur of movement then as the journalist threw his camera bag away, stopped short, and leveled a short-barreled pistol at Kananga.

For a second or two that engraved eternity, everything stopped and then sped up fourfold to make up the time.

Nick leaped from the open helicopter bay to the ground, stumbled, rolled and came up running. The fall probably saved him, as Buchanan saw him coming, turned and fired. Two shots dug into the dirt behind him sending up puffs of dust.

By that time Kananga was down flat with incredible speed for a man of his size, crushing the Prime Minister underneath him, and Yogun was lunging for Buchanan's gun.

The short muzzle spat fire twice and Yogun went down in a screaming heap. Buchanan saw Nick closing on him, swung the weapon towards the prostrate Kananga, hesitated a split second and then suddenly bolted into the open field, running fast for the other side with Nick ten yards behind him.

"HOLD YOUR FIRE," Hartsdale-Smythe yelled, jumped out of the bay — his weapon in hand, and lumbered after them.

Nick felt the adrenalin pounding his heart faster and faster as his bare legs pumped beneath him . . . and then suddenly the runner's "free break" that he hadn't experienced in the many years. . . since he was on his school track team, caught him and he was flying through the air, not conscious of the ground beneath his feet, soaring in great leaping strides with nothing holding him back. He had heard John yell, and hoped that Moran would see what was happening too, but he hadn't time to worry about it. Buchanan was making a last ditch break for his own freedom, and Nick had to stop him. Had to.

The distance closed between them . . . closer, closer . . . maybe five yards now and he thought that Buchanan was slowing.

In the middle of the field the journalist suddenly swerved to the right, whirled around and fired twice. The first shot was wild, but the second caught Nick on the side of his thigh and he felt a hot searing as the bullet cut soft flesh like a knife.

Nick threw himself into the startled Buchanan, diving with head low in a flying tackle. They rolled in the grass in a blur of flying fists and kicking feet.

Buchanan pounded on Nick's ribs with the pistol butt as they rolled, and a sharp pain spread through his body when Buchanan caught a kidney.

Gasping, Nick released his hold and the journalist scrambled to his feet. Nick rolled and was up quickly, facing Buchanan in a crouch while the other leveled his pistol at him.

"You know it's empty," Nick hissed through his teeth, grimacing at the pain.

"Fuck you, Burns . . . let me go, you got what you wanted."

Nick thought of Moran . . . probably grinning down a gun barrel that very second . . . waiting. If Moran thought Nick was in danger he'd kill the journalist . . . and Nick couldn't let that happen.

He moved around rapidly to place himself in Moran's line of fire, and the two men stood prancing like wary beasts looking for an opening . . . an unprotected throat to tear.

"You saved my life once, you slimy bastard," Nick panted heavily, "whether you wanted to or not . . . and I'm returning the favor."

"Who needs . . .?" Buchanan shouted, but Nick was already moving, charging at him, shoulder down like a linebacker. Buchanan brought the pistol butt down as hard as he could at Nick's head, but the blow glanced from Nick's shoulder as he drove his bent left elbow, held rigid by a two-fisted grip, into Buchanan's stomach, slamming the bone forward with the strength of a piston-thrust.

Buchanan staggered, doubled over, the wind driven out of him by steam-hammer force. Then Nick hit him again, on the side of his head with his two fists still locked together. Buchanan went down in a doubled-up heap.

Nick was panting and catching his breath when Hartsdale-Smythe reached him, his rifle leveled at Buchanan unnecessarily while two commandos loaded the groaning journalist onto a stretcher.

338

"I should have had him under my thumb earlier, Burns. I'm sorry." The Englishman's face was drained of blood and his hands shook. He found a cigarette for relief.

"You knew?" Nick straightened up, wincing from the pain in his leg. The thigh was seared with a deep gash where the bullet had grazed it, but it wasn't serious. He waved the approaching medics away. "Why didn't you tell me, John," he asked with a tone of outrage, which he knew he hadn't a right to, considering all that he'd kept from the Englishman. He then took a step, stumbled slightly and grabbed Hartsdale-Smythe's arm for support.

"I wasn't sure. I had no proof until five minutes ago, but then I thought Kananga's insistence on Buchanan's presence was strange. There are more important journalists here if he wants coverage."

"I didn't give it a second thought," Nick said. "Did one of your team blow the whistle?"

"They didn't know," Hartsdale-Smythe said. "Our entire network in East Africa may be compromised. But at least we'll get a chance to sift it out. Buchanan was the outside man here, and must have been doubled, maybe has been for years. But we'll sort all that out soon enough, thanks to you." He squeezed Nick's arm in a gesture of affection and gratitude.

Nick realized what it must have cost him to be so un-English. They walked slowly towards the helicopter, Nick limping painfully. He had already sorted out one part — Buchanan had set him up for the taking when they had been together their trip east, but the guy had finessed a tight situation beautifully, helping Nick escape, even offing his own men. Probably Volkov acted as the cut-out and the mercenaries didn't even know the journalist. Moran hadn't indicated a thing.

"It's odd how he let me out of that ambush," Nick said. He stopped walking for a minute to rest the leg that was throbbing now.

"It was a clever move," Hartsdale-Smythe said, "whether a quick judgment on the spot or planned, because it served to deepen his cover. In any event, Buchanan and Volkov must have counted on the business with the boats in the Channel to cancel out everything else."

339

Nick's spotting of Volkov would never have surfaced then, only as a chalk mark on the secret community's scoreboard.

"They almost succeeded," Nick said.

"If not for the Russian's arrogance and your persistence," Hartsdale-Smythe said, smiling dourly. They had begun to walk again through the trampled grass.

"Sheer luck of the draw," Nick answered. "Moran really did it."

"Pity we couldn't get Volkov in the bargain, but I assumed that pistol shot was White Rabbit's final decree," Hartsdale-Smythe said.

"Why do you think Buchanan tried that last bit?" Nick asked.

"Desperation perhaps, when he saw that Volkov had failed. Or he thought Volkov had killed Moran, and Buchanan could get away with it. If he had killed Kananga, which is what the Russians wanted . . . I think you were right about that . . . by the time the mess had been sorted out the damage would be done. Kananga's people would have gone on a rampage, Umgawe would have had the army out . . . then chaos."

Nick stopped walking and looked into the Englishman's eyes, "All this doesn't bode well for you, John. Especially Maggie's involvement. I'm really sorry."

"Actually that's one bright spot," the Englishman said, averting his eyes and staring into the middle distance, "or, at least not as dim as I had thought it was. It would seem that Buchanan and Volkov suckered her, along with everyone else. She thought it was out-of-channels co-operation with Central Intelligence. A bad rap on the knuckles for her, probably a re-assignment to London for a good long time. But that has its advantages from my point of view."

He smiled to himself and Nick purposely looked away.

"And I suppose I'll weather the storm well enough," Hartsdale-Smythe added.

"I'm glad for you, John," Nick said. At this point his leg was throbbing even more . . . he needed a pain killer. He laid his arm across the Englishman's shoulder for support and hobbled slowly towards the waiting aircraft.

"BURNS!"

Nick and Hartsdale-Smythe heard the shout from behind them and both dropped into a crouch, and separated themselves instinctively. The Englishman dropped into a firing position, his weapon leveled at the woods.

A lone figure emerged from the bush fifty yards away. He was holding a short pole flying a White Rabbit pennant in one hand, and in the other, a stick with a white rag tied to it. It was Moran, unarmed.

"WAIT!" the mercenary shouted as he waved the flag of truce.

Nick heard Hartsdale-Smythe grunt as he aimed his rifle at Moran's squat form.

"Don't, John. For God's sake, DON'T!" Nick hissed between his teeth at the Englishman and stood up, fully exposed.

"It would be good riddance," Hartsdale-Smythe said.

"There's a contract, John. You hear? Lower it!"

The Englishman dropped his rifle into an upright position and rose, reluctantly.

Moran watched them for a moment. then turned and called into the screen of shrub.

Smith and Wesson pushed through the undergrowth carrying Volkov on a stretcher. His bodyguard Vigo shuffled alongside in shackles. As they passed the mercenary, he dropped the White Rabbit pennant and the flag of truce onto the body, then turned and disappeared into the forest.

His face a bloody mess, the Russian opened his eyes slightly, wincing at the sunlight, and saw Nick staring down. The mercenary's pennant draped across his chest was too small for a shroud and not intended as one.

"This round is yours again *tovarich*, eh?" Volkov asked, and fainted with the hint of a smile curling his purple lips.

This was Moran's gift to Nick. Respect had won the decision.

Nick looked at the Englishman who was sweating furiously.

"Bonus on the contract?" Hartsdale-Smythe asked.

"Moran's a soldier, not a murderer," Nick replied.

"That's one way to look at it," the Englishman answered.

341

THE ROAR OF THE ROTORS increased forcing everyone into an unwanted silence. Warden Yogun and Volkov both sleeping in a morphine haze stirred restlessly as the splatting sound increased, the diplomat vaguely aware that the two slugs in his shoulder had touched nothing vital. He was an unplanned hero to his people . . . Volkov wasn't. Two soldiers guarded the Russians in the aft compartment, along with a bound and silent Buchanan.

Next to the pilot, Kananga found relief for once as he stopped trying to talk over the competing noise . . . the better to rehearse his rhetoric. He turned and smiled broadly at Burns, certain that the American was a man of great discretion.

Nick stood by the open bay of the big chopper as it rose above the trees into the torpid air. The sun caught the aircraft in a searing blaze of heat as they cleared the shadow of the trees and rose, slowly gaining altitude. The large craft gently spun on its axis and languidly crossed the clearing . . . the bush amphitheater where competing dramas had played themselves to uncertain endings. Nick looked down at the shimmering rock and saw the lone figure of the mercenary standing there.

Moran stared at Nick for a moment and then snapped his right hand to his forehead in a military salute, his body drawn to a stiff attention.

With one hand gripping the handle above the door jamb, Nick raised the other to his brow and returned the compliment, and running through his mind was: "Here's to us, who's like us? damn few . . ., and they're all dead!

Moran also kept his salute in place as the chopper pulled away, until it turned high above the Zambezi and headed home.

Hartsdale-Smythe watched Nick, then stepped up next to him and tapped him on the shoulder.

"What will the help think?" the Englishman shouted in his ear.

Nick smiled. "Justice?"

Hartsdale-Smythe shook his head, looking baffled. "You a religious man, Burns?" he asked above the din of the engines.

"Why?"

The Englishman pointed to the medallion: "Saint's medal, isn't that?"

"Nope! Strictly secular, from a very earthy lady," Nick yelled into the rushing wind. He held it up for Hartsdale-Smythe to see, "Read it!"

The Englishman examined the emperor's head then turned the shining gold piece over. "'*Fiat Justitia, Pereat Mundus,*'" he read aloud, thought a moment and dropped the gold piece back on Nick's chest. "Fanatical rubbish!" he said finally, and turned away.

Here's Tae Us;
Wha's Like Us?
Damn few . . .
and they're a' deid !!
— *Robert Burns*

Photograph of author: Joan Brandt

New York born and bred, novelist-journalist-editor
Alan Schwartz works in the Americas, Europe and Africa.